The Indian Scout
A Story Of The Aztec City

By

Gustave Aimard

The Indian Scout
A Story Of The Aztec City
by Gustave Aimard

Copyright © 2024

ISBN: 978-93-62207-36-4

Published by

DOUBLE 9 BOOKS

2/13-B, Ansari Road
Daryaganj, New Delhi – 110002
info@double9books.com
www.double9books.com
Tel. 011-40042856

This book is under public domain

ABOUT THE AUTHOR

Gustave Aimard wrote multiple volumes about Latin America and the American frontier. Oliver Aimard was born in Paris. As he previously stated, he was the offspring of two married individuals, "but not to each other". His father, François Sébastiani de la Porta (1775-1851), was a commander in Napoleon's army and a representative of the Louis Philippe government. Sebastiani was married to the Duchess of Coigny. In 1806, the couple had a daughter, Alatrice-Rosalba Fanny. The mother died shortly after she was born. Fanny was reared by her grandmother, Duchess of Coigny. Aimard was placed as a baby with a family that were paid to raise him. By the age of nine or twelve, he was sent off on a herring boat. Later, about 1838, he served briefly with the French Navy. After one more trip to America (when he claims he was adopted into a Comanche tribe), Aimard returned to Paris in 1847, the same year his half-sister, Duchess de Choiseul-Pralin, was cruelly killed by her noble husband. Reconciliation or acknowledgement by his biological family did not occur. After serving briefly in the Garde Mobil, Aimard returned to the Americas.

CONTENTS

PREFACE

The following work has been the most successful of all Gustave Aimard has published in Paris, and it has run through an unparalleled number of Editions. This is not surprising, however, when we bear in mind that he describes in it his personal experiences in the Indian Aztec city, from which no European ever returned prior to him, to tell the tale of his adventures. From this volume we learn to regard the Indians from a very different side than the one hitherto taken; for it is evident that they are something more than savages, and possess their traditions just as much as any nation of the Old World. At the present moment, when the Redskins appear destined to play an important part in the American struggle, I think that such knowledge as our Author is enabled alone to give us about their manners and customs, will be read with interest.

L. W.

CHAPTER I
THE SURPRISE

It was towards the end of May, 1855, in one of the least visited parts of the immense prairies of the Far West, and at a short distance from the Rio Colorado del Norte, which the Indian tribes of those districts call, in their language so full of imagery, "The endless river with the golden waves."

The night was profoundly dark. The moon, which had proceeded two-thirds of its course, displayed between the lofty branches of the trees her pallid face; and the scanty rays of vacillating light scarce brought out the outlines of the abrupt and stern scenery. There was not a breath in the air, not a star in the sky. A silence of death brooded over the desert—a silence only interrupted, at long intervals, by the sharp barking of the coyotes in search of prey, or the savage miaulings of the panthers and jaguars at the watering place.

During the darkness, the great American savannahs, on which no human sound troubles the majesty of night, assume, beneath the eye of heaven, an imposing splendour, which unconsciously affects the heart of the strongest man, and imbues him involuntarily with a feeling of religious respect.

All at once the closely growing branches of a floripondio were cautiously parted, and in the space thus left appeared the anxious head of a man, whose eyes, flashing like those of a wild beast, darted restless glances in every direction. After a few seconds of perfect immobility, the man of whom we speak left the clump of trees in the midst of which he was concealed, and leaped out on the plain.

Although his bronzed complexion had assumed almost a brick colour, still, from his hunting garb, and, above all, the light colour of his long hair, and his bold, frank, and sharply-marked features, it was easy to recognise in this man one of those daring Canadian wood rangers, whose bold race is daily expiring, and will probably disappear ere long.

He walked a few paces, with the barrel of his rifle thrust forward, and his finger on the trigger, minutely inspecting the thickets and numberless bushes that surrounded him; then, probably reassured by the silence and solitude that—continued to prevail around, he stopped, rested the butt of his rifle on the ground, bent forward, and imitated, with rare perfection, the song of the centzontle, the American nightingale.

Scarce had the last modulation of this song, which was gentle as a love sigh, died away in the air, when a second person bounded forward from the same shrub which had already offered passage to the hunter. It was an Indian; he stationed himself by the Canadian's side, and, after a few seconds' silence, said, affecting a tranquillity probably not responded to by his heart,—"Well?"

"All is calm," the hunter answered. "The *Cihuatl* can come."

The Indian shook his head.

"Since the rising of the moon, Mahchsi Karehde has been separated from Eglantine; he knows not where she is at this moment."

A kindly smile played round the hunter's lips.

"Eglantine loves my brother," he said, gently. "The little bird that sings in her heart will have led her on the trail of the Chief. Has Mahchsi Karehde forgotten the song with which he called her to his love meetings in the tribe?"

"The Chief has forgotten nothing."

"Let him call her then."

The Indian did not let the invitation be repeated. The cry of the walkon rose in the silence.

At the same moment a rustling was heard in the branches, and a young woman, bounding like a startled fawn, fell panting into the warrior's arms, which were opened to receive her. This pressure was no longer than a flash of lightning; the Chief, doubtlessly ashamed of the tender emotion he had yielded to in the presence of a white man, even though that white man was a friend, coldly repulsed the young female, saying to her, in a voice in which no trace of feeling was visible, "My sister is fatigued, without doubt; no danger menaces her at this moment; she can sleep; the warriors will watch over her."

"Eglantine is a Comanche maid," she answered in a timid voice. "Her heart is strong; she will obey Mahchsi Karehde (the Flying Eagle). Under the protection of so terrible a chief she knows herself in safety."

The Indian bent on her a glance full of indescribable tenderness; but regaining, almost immediately, that apparent apathy which the Redskins never depart from, "The warriors wish to hold a council; my sister can sleep," he said.

The young woman made no reply; she bowed respectfully to the two men, and withdrawing a few paces, she lay down in the grass, and slept, or feigned to sleep. The Canadian had contented himself with smiling, on seeing the result obtained by the advice he had given the warrior, and listened, with an approving nod of the head, to the few words exchanged between the Redskins. The Chief, buried in thought, stood for a few minutes with his eyes fixed, with a strange expression, on the young, sleeping woman; then he passed his hand several times over his brow, as if to dissipate the clouds that oppressed his mind, and turned to the hunter.

"My brother, the Paleface, has need of rest. The Chief will watch," he said.

"The coyotes have ceased barking, the moon has disappeared, a white streak is rising on the horizon," the Canadian replied. "Day will speedily appear; sleep has fled my eyelids; the men must hold a council."

The Indian bowed, without further remark, and, laying his gun on the ground, collected a few armfuls of dry wood, which he carried near the sleeper. The Canadian struck a light; the wood soon caught, and the flame coloured the trees with its blood red hue. The two men then squatted by each other's side, filled their calumets with *manachie*, the sacred tobacco, and commenced smoking silently, with that imposing gravity which the Indians, under all circumstances, bring to this symbolic operation.

We will profit by this moment of rest, which accident offers us, to draw a portrait of these three persons, who are destined to play an important part in the course of our story.

The Canadian was a man of about forty-five years of age, six feet in height, long, thin, and dry; his was a nervous nature, composed of muscle and sinews, perfectly adapted to the rude profession of wood ranger, which demands a vigour and boldness beyond all expression. Like all his countrymen, the Canadian offered, in his features, the Norman type in its thorough purity. His wide forehead; his grey eyes, full of intelligence; his slightly aquiline nose; his large mouth, full of magnificent teeth; the long light hair, mingled with a few silvery threads which escaped from under his otter skin cap, and fell in enormous ringlets on his shoulders,—all these details gave this man an open, frank, and honest appearance, which attracted sympathy, and pleased at the first glance. This worthy, giant, whose real name was Bonnaire, but who was only known on the prairies by the sobriquet of Marksman, a sobriquet which he fully justified by the correctness of his aim, and his skill in detecting the lurking places of wild beasts, was born in the vicinity of Montreal; but having been taken, while very young, into the forests of Upper Canada, desert life possessed such charms for him, that he had given up civilized society, and for nearly thirty years had traversed the vast solitudes of North America, only consenting to visit the towns and villages when he wanted to dispose of the skins of the animals he had killed, or renew his provision of powder and bullets.

Marksman's companion, Flying Eagle, was one of the most renowned chiefs of the tribe of the White Buffaloes, the most powerful of all forming the warlike Comanche race, that untameable and ferocious nation, which, in its immeasurable pride, haughtily terms itself the Queen of the Prairies, a title which no other tribe dares to challenge. Flying Eagle, though still very young, for he was scarcely four-and-twenty, had already distinguished himself, on several occasions, by deeds of such unheard-of boldness and temerity, that his mere name inspired the countless Indian hordes that constantly traverse the desert in every direction, with invincible terror.

He was tall, well built, and perfectly proportioned; his features were elegant, and his black eyes acquired, beneath the influence of any powerful emotion, that strange rigidity which commands respect; his gestures were noble, and his carriage graceful, and stamped with that majesty inborn in Indians. The Chief was attired in his war dress, and that was so singular, as to deserve a detailed description.

Flying Eagle wore the cap which only distinguished warriors, who have killed many warriors, have the right to assume; it is made of strips of white ermine, with a large piece of red cloth fastened at the back, and falling to the thigh, to which is fastened an upright crest of black and white eagle plumes, which begins at the head, and continues in close order to the extremity. Above his right ear he had passed through his hair a wooden knife, painted red, and about the length of a hand; this knife was the model of one with which he had killed a Dacotah chief; he wore, in addition, eight small wooden skewers, painted blue, and adorned at the upper extremity with a gilt nail, to indicate the number of bullets that had wounded him; over his left ear he wore a large tuft of yellow owl feathers, with the ends painted red, as the totem of the Band of Dogs; one half his face was red, and his body reddish brown, with stripes from which the colour had been removed by a moistened finger. His arms, starting from the shoulder, were adorned with twenty-seven yellow stripes, indicating the number of his exploits, while on his chest he had painted a blue hand, to announce that he had frequently made prisoners. Round his neck he wore a magnificent collar of grizzly bear's claws, three inches in length, and white at the point. His shoulders were covered by a large buffalo robe, falling almost to the ground, and painted of various colours. His breeches, composed of two separate parts, one for each leg, were tightly fastened to his waist belt, and fell almost to his ankles, embroidered externally with coloured porcupine quills, terminating in a long tuft that trailed on the ground. Wide stripes of black and white cloth were rolled round his hips, and fell before and behind in heavy folds. His slippers, of buffalo hide, were but slightly decorated; but wolf tails, trailing on the ground behind him, and equalling in number the enemies he had conquered, were fastened above his ankles. From his waist belt hung, on one side, his powder flask, ball pouch, and scalping knife: on the other, a quiver of panther skin filled with long, sharp arrows, and his tomahawk; his gun was laid on the ground, within reach of his hand.

This warrior, dressed in such a strange costume, had something imposing and sinister about him which inspired terror.

For the present we will confine ourselves to saying that Eglantine was not more than fifteen years of age; that she was very beautiful for an Indian girl; and wore, in all its elegant simplicity, the sweet costume adopted by the women of her nation. Ending here this description, which was perhaps too detailed, but which was necessary in order to know the men we have introduced in the scene, we will return to our narrative.

For a long time the two men smoked side by side without exchanging a syllable; at length, the Canadian shook out the ashes of his pipe on his thumb nail, and addressed his companion.

"Is my brother satisfied?" he said.

"Wah!" the Indian answered, and bowing assent; "my brother has a friend."

"Good!" the hunter continued; "and what will the Chief do now?"

"Flying Eagle will rejoin his tribe with Eglantine, and then return to seek the Apache trail."

"For what purpose?"

"Flying Eagle will avenge himself."

"As you please, Chief. I will certainly not try to dissuade you from projects against enemies who are also mine; still, I do not believe you look at the matter in the right light."

"What would my brother the Paleface warrior say?"

"I mean that we are far from the lodges of the Comanches, and before reaching them we shall have doubtlessly more than one turn-up with the enemies from whom the Chief considers himself freed, perhaps, too prematurely."

The Indian shrugged his shoulders disdainfully.

"The Apaches are old women, chattering, and cowardly," he said. "Flying Eagle despises them."

"That is possible," the hunter replied, with a toss of his head; "still, in my opinion, we should have done better in continuing our journey till sunrise, in order to put a greater distance between them and us, instead of halting so imprudently; we are still very near the camp of our enemies."

"The fire water has stopped the ears and closed the eyes of the Apache dogs; they are stretched on the ground and sleeping."

"Hum! that is not my opinion; I am, on the contrary, persuaded that they are watching and looking for us."

At the same instant, as if chance wished to justify the apprehensions of the prudent hunter, some dozen shots were fired; a horrible war cry, to which the Canadian and the Comanche responded, with a yell of defiance, was heard in the forest, and nearly thirty Indians rushed howling toward the fire, at which our three characters were seated; but the latter had disappeared, as if by enchantment.

The Apaches stopped with an outburst of passion, not knowing in what direction to turn, in order to find their crafty foes again. Suddenly three shots were fired from the interior of the forest, and three Apaches rolled on the ground, with holes in their chests. The Indians uttered a yell of fury, and rushed in the direction of the shots. At the moment they reached the edge of the forest, a man stepped forward, waving in his right hand a buffalo robe, as a signal of peace. It was Marksman, the Canadian.

The Apaches stopped with an ill-omened hesitation, but the Canadian, without seeming to notice the movement, walked resolutely toward them with the slow and careless step habitual to him; on recognizing him, the Indians brandished their weapons wrathfully, and wished to rush upon him, for they had many reasons for hating the hunter; but their Chief arrested them with a peremptory gesture.

"Let my brothers be patient," he said, with a sinister smile, "they will lose nothing by waiting."

CHAPTER II
THE GUEST

On the same day that our story begins, and about three miles from where the events narrated in our preceding chapter occurred, a numerous caravan had halted at sunset, in a vast clearing situated on the skirt of an immense virgin forest, the last species of which ended on the banks of the Rio Colorado.

This caravan came from the south-east, that is, from Mexico. It appeared to have been on the march for a long time, as far as possible to judge by the state in which the clothes of the men were, as well as the harness of the horses and mules. In fact, the poor beasts themselves were reduced to a state of leanness and weakness, which amply testified to the rude fatigue they must have endured. The caravan was composed of some thirty-five persons, all attired in the picturesque and characteristic costume of the half-bred hunters and Gambusinos, who alone, or in small bands, at the most of four, incessantly traverse the Far West, which they explore in its most mysterious depths, for the purpose of hunting, trapping, or discovering the numberless gold veins it contains in its bosom.

The adventurers halted, dismounted, fastened their horses to picket ropes, and began immediately, with that skill and quickness only attained by long habit, making their preparations to bivouac. The grass was pulled up over a considerable extent of ground; the baggage, piled up in a circle, formed a breastwork, behind which a sudden attack of the desert marauders might be resisted; and then fires were lighted in the shape of a St. Andrew's cross in the interior of the camp.

When all this had been attended to, some of the adventurers put up a large tent above a palanquin hermetically closed, which was carried by two mules, one before and one behind. When the tent was pitched, the mules were taken out of the palanquin, and the curtains, in falling, covered it so completely, that it was entirely concealed.

This palanquin was a riddle to the adventurers. No one knew what it contained, though the general curiosity was singularly aroused on the subject of a mystery so specially incomprehensible in this deserted country; each kept carefully to himself the opinions he had formed about it—above all, since the day when, in the midst of a difficult piece of country, and during the momentary absence of the chief of the Cuadrilla, who usually never left the palanquin, which he guarded like a miser does his treasure, a hunter leaned over and slightly opened one of the curtains; but the man had scarce time to take a furtive peep through the opening, ere the chief, suddenly coming up, split his skull open with a blow of his machete, and laid him dead at his feet. Then he turned to the terrified witnesses, and said calmly,—"Is there another among you who would like to discover what I think proper to keep secret?"

These words were uttered in such a tone of implacable raillery and furious cruelty, that these villains, for the most part without faith or law, and accustomed to brave, with a laugh, the greatest perils, felt an internal shudder, and their blood stagnated in their veins. This lesson had been sufficient. No one tried afterwards to discover the captain's secret.

The final arrangements had been scarcely made for the encampment, ere the sound of horses was heard, and two horsemen arrived at a gallop.

"Here is the Captain," the adventurers said to each other.

The newcomers gave their reins to men who ran up to receive them, and walked hastily toward the tent. On arriving there, the first stopped and addressed his companion:—"Caballero," he said to him, "you are welcome among us; although very poor ourselves, we will gladly share the little we possess with you."

"Thanks," the second said, with a bow, "I will not abuse your gracious hospitality; tomorrow, at sunrise, I think I shall be sufficiently rested to continue my journey."

"You will act as you think proper: seat yourself by this fire prepared for us, while I go for a few moments into that tent. I will soon rejoin you, and have the honour of keeping you company."

The stranger bowed, and took his place by the fire, lighted a short distance from the tent, while the captain let the curtain he had lifted fail behind him, and disappeared from his guest's sight.

The latter was a man of marked features, his stalwart limbs denoting a far from ordinary strength; the few wrinkles that furrowed his energetic face served to indicate that he had already passed midlife, though no trace of decrepitude was visible on his solidly-built body, and not a white hair silvered his long and thick locks, which were black as a raven's wing. He wore the costume of the rich Mexican hacenderos, that is to say, the mança; the zarapé, of many colours; the velvet calzoneras, open at the knee, and botas vaqueras; his hat, of vicuna skin, gallooned with gold, was drawn in by a rich toquilla, fastened with a costly diamond; a sheathless machete hung from his right hip, merely passed through an iron ring: the barrels of two six-chambered revolvers shone in his waist belt, and he had thrown on the grass by his side an American rifle, beautifully damascened with silver.

When the Captain left him alone, this man, while installing himself before the fire in the most comfortable way possible, that is to say, arranging his zarapé and water bottles to serve as a bed, if necessary, had cast a furtive glance around, whose expression would, doubtless, have supplied the adventurers with serious matter of thought had they been able to notice it; but all were busied in getting the bivouac snug, and preparations for supper; and trusting entirely in the loyalty of prairie hospitality, they did not at all dream of watching what the stranger seated at their fire was about.

The unknown, after a few moments' reflection, rose and walked up to a party of trappers, whose conversation seemed very animated, and who were gesticulating with that fire natural to southern races.

"Eh!" one of them said, on noticing the stranger, "this señor will set us right with a word."

The latter, thus directly appealed to, turned toward the speaker.

"What is the matter, caballeros?" he asked.

"Oh, a very simple matter," the adventurer made answer; "your horse, a noble and handsome animal, I must allow, señor, will not associate with others; it stamps its feet and bites at the companions we have given it."

"Oh, that is, indeed, simple enough," a second adventurer remarked, with a grin; "that horse is a *costeño*, and too proud to associate with poor *tierras interiores* like our horses."

At this singular reason, all burst into an Homeric laugh. The stranger smiled cunningly.

"It may be the reason you state, or perhaps some other," he said gently; "at any rate, there is a very simple way of settling the dispute, which I will employ."

"Ah!" the second speaker said, "what is it?"

"This," the stranger replied, with the same air of placidity.

Then, walking up to the horse, which two men had a difficulty in holding, he said,—"Let go!"

"But if we let go, nobody knows what will happen."

"Let go! I answer for all then," addressing his horse,—"Lillo!" he said.

At this name, the horse raised its noble head, and fixing its sparkling eye on the man who had called it, with a sharp and irresistible movement, it threw off the two men who tried to check it, sent them rolling on the grass, to the shouts of their comrades, and rubbed its head against its master's chest with a neigh of pleasure.

"You see," the stranger said, as he patted the noble animal, "it is not difficult."

"Hum!" the first adventurer who picked himself up said, in an angry tone, and rubbing his shoulder; "that is a *demonio* to which I would not entrust my skin, old and wrinkled as it is at present."

"Do not trouble yourself any further about the horse, I will attend to it."

"On the faith of Domingo, I have had enough, for my part; 'tis a noble brute, but it has a fiend inside it."

The stranger shrugged his shoulders without replying, and returned to the fire, followed by his horse, which paced step by step behind him, not evincing the slightest wish to indulge further in those eccentricities which had so greatly astonished the adventurers, who are, however, all men well versed in the equine art. This horse was a pure barb of Arab stock, and had probably cost its present owner an enormous sum, and its pace seemed strange to men accustomed to American horses. Its master gave it provender, hobbled it near him, and then sat down again by the fire: at the same instant the Captain appeared in the entrance of the tent.

"I beg your pardon," he said, with that charming courtesy natural to the Hispano-Americans; "I beg your pardon, Señor Caballero, for having neglected you so long, but an imperative duty claimed my presence. Now, I am quite at your service."

The stranger bowed. "On the contrary," he replied, "I must ask you to accept my apologies for the cool manner in which I avail myself of your hospitality."

"Not a word more on this head, if you wish not to annoy me."

The Captain seated himself by his guest's side.

"We will dine," he said. "I can only offer you scanty fare; but one must put up with it, and I am reduced to tasajo and red beans with pimento."

"That is delicious, and I should assuredly do honour to it if I felt the slightest appetite; but, at the present moment, it would be impossible for me to swallow the smallest mouthful."

"Ah!" the Captain said, looking distrustfully at the stranger.

But he met a face so simply calm, a smile so frank, that he felt ashamed of his suspicions, and his face, which had grown gloomy, at once regained all its serenity.

"I am vexed. Still, I will ask permission to dine at once; for, differently from you, Caballero, I must confess to you that I am literally dying of hunger."

"I should be in despair at causing you the slightest delay."

"Domingo," the Captain shouted, "my dinner."

The adventurer, whom the stranger's horse had treated so roughly, soon came up limping, and carrying his chief's supper in a wooden tray; a few tortillas he held in his hand completed the meal, which was worthy of an anchorite.

Domingo was an Indian half-bred, with a knowing look, angular features, and crafty face: he appeared to be about fifty years of age, so far as it is possible to judge an Indian's age by his looks. Since his misadventure with the horse, Domingo felt a malice for the stranger.

"*Con su permiso,*" the Captain said, as he broke a tortilla.

"I will smoke a cigarette, if that can be called keeping you company," the stranger said, with his stereotyped smile.

The other bowed politely, and fell to on his meagre repast with that eagerness which denotes a lengthened abstinence. We will take advantage of the opportunity to draw for the reader a portrait of the chief of the caravan.

Don Miguel Ortega, for such was the name by which he was known to his comrades, was an elegant and handsome young man, not more than six and twenty years of age, with a bronzed complexion, delicate features, haughty and flashing eyes; while his tall stature, well-shaped limbs, and wide and arched chest, denoted rare vigour. Assuredly, through the whole extent of the old Spanish colonies, it would have been difficult—if not impossible—to meet a more seductive cavalier, whom the picturesque Mexican costume became so well, or combining to the same extent as he did, those external advantages which charm women and captivate the populace. Still, for the observer, Don Miguel had too great a depth in his eye, too rude a frown, and a smile too false and perfidious, not to conceal, beneath his pleasing exterior, an ulcerated soul and evil instincts.

A hunter's meal, seasoned by appetite, is never long. The present one was promptly disposed of.

"There," the Captain said, as he wiped his fingers with a tuft of grass; "now for a cigarette to help digestion, and then I shall have the honour to wish you good night. Of course, you do not intend to leave us before daybreak."

"I can hardly tell you. That will depend, to some extent, on the weather tonight. I am in a considerable hurry, and you know, Caballero, that—as our neighbours, the Gringos, so justly remark—time is money."

"You know better than I do, Caballero, what you have to do. Act as you please; but, before I retire, accept my wishes for a pleasant night's rest, and the success of your plans."

"I thank you, Caballero."

"One last word, or rather, one last question before separating?"

"Ask it."

"Of course, if this question appears to you indiscreet, you are at perfect liberty not to answer it."

"It would surprise me, on the part of so accomplished a Caballero. Hence, be kind enough to explain yourself."

"My name is Don Miguel Ortega."

"And mine, Don Stefano Cohecho."

The Captain bowed.

"Will you allow me, in my turn," the stranger said, "to ask you a question?"

"I beg you to do so."

"Why this exchange of names?"

"Because, on the prairie it is good to be able to distinguish friends from foes."

"That is true. And now?"

"Now I am certain that I do not count you among the latter."

"*¿Quién sabe?*" Don Stefano retorted, with a laugh. "There are such strange accidents."

The two men, after exchanging a few more words in the most friendly manner, cordially shook hands. Don Miguel went into the tent, and Don Stefano, after turning his feet towards the fire, slept, or pretended to do so.

An hour later, the deepest silence reigned in the camp. The fires only produced a doubtful gleam; and the sentinels, leaning on their rifles, were themselves yielding to that species of vague somnolency, which is not quite sleep, but is no longer watching. All at once, an owl, probably hidden in a neighbouring tree, twice uttered its melancholy hu-hu.

Don Stefano suddenly opened his eyes, without changing his position; he assured himself, by an investigating glance, that all was quiet around him; then, after convincing himself that his machete and revolvers had not left him, he took up his rifle, and in his turn imitated the cry of the owl, which was answered by a similar whoop.

The stranger, after arranging his zarapé, so as to imitate a human body, whispered a few words to his horse while patting it, in order to calm it; and laying himself at full length on the ground, he crawled towards one of the outlets from the camp, stopping at intervals to look around him.

All continued to be tranquil. On reaching the foot of the breastwork formed by the baggage, he jumped up, leapt over the obstacles with a tiger's bound, and disappeared in the prairie. At the same instant a man rose, sprang over the entrenchment, and rushed in pursuit of him.

That man was Domingo.

CHAPTER III
A NIGHT CONFERENCE

Don Stefano Cohecho seemed to be thoroughly acquainted with the desert. So soon as he was on the prairie, and fancied himself safe from any curious eye, he raised his head haughtily, his step grew more confident, his eye sparkled with a gloomy fire, and he walked with long steps towards a clump of palm trees, whose small fans formed but a scanty protection by day against the burning sunbeams.

Still he neglected no precaution; at times he stopped hurriedly, to listen to the slightest suspicious sound, or interrogate with searching glance the gloomy depths of the forest. But after a few seconds, re-assured by the calm that prevailed around him, he jogged onwards with that deliberate step he had adopted on leaving the camp.

Domingo walked literally in his steps; spying and watching each of his movements with that sagacity peculiar to the half-breeds, while carefully keeping on his guard against any surprise on the part of the man he was following. Domingo was one of those men of whom only too many are met with on the frontiers. Gifted with great qualities and great vices, equally fit for good and evil, capable of accomplishing extraordinary things in either sense; but who, for the most part, are only guided by their evil instincts.

He was at this moment following the stranger, without exactly knowing the motive that made him do so; not, even having decided whether to be for or against him; awaiting, to make up his mind, a little better knowledge of the state of affairs, and the chance of weighing the advantage he should derive from treachery or the performance of his duty. Hence, he carefully avoided letting his presence be suspected, for he guessed that the mystery he wished to detect would, if he succeeded, offer him great advantages, especially if he knew how to work it.

The two men marched thus for nearly an hour, one behind the other, Don Stefano not suspecting for a moment that he was so cleverly watched, and that one of the most knowing scoundrels on the prairie was at his heels.

After numberless turnings in the tall grass, Don Stefano at length arrived at the bank of the Rio Colorado, which at this spot was as wide and placid as a lake, running over a bed of sand, bordered by thick clumps of cottonwood trees, and tall poplars, whose roots were bathed in the water. On reaching the river, the stranger stopped, listened for a moment, and, raising his fingers to his mouth, imitated the bark of a coyote. Almost immediately, the same signal rose in the midst of the mangrove trees, and a little birchbark canoe, pulled by two men, appeared on the bank.

"Eh!" Don Stefano said, in a suppressed voice, "I had given up all hopes of meeting you."

"Did you not hear our signal?" one of the men in the canoe answered.

"Should I have come without that? Still, it seems to me you could have come nearer to me."

"It was not possible."

The canoe ran on to the sand; the two men leaped on lightly, and in a second joined Don Stefano. Both were dressed and armed like prairie hunters.

"Hum!" Don Stefano continued; "it is a long journey from the camp here, and I am afraid that my absence may be noticed."

"That is a risk you must run," the first speaker remarked—a man of tall stature, with a grave and stern face, whose hair, white as snow, fell in long curls on his shoulders.

"Well, as you are here at last, let us come to an understanding; and make haste about it, for time is precious. What have you done since we parted?"

"Not much; we followed you at a distance, that is all, ready to come to your assistance if needed."

"Thanks; no news?"

"None. Who could have given us any?"

"That is true; and have you not met your friend Marksman?"

"No."

"¡Cuerpo de Cristo! That is annoying; for, if my presentiment do not deceive me, we shall soon have to play at knives."

"We will do so."

"I know it, Brighteye. I have long been acquainted with your courage; but you, Ruperto your comrade, and myself, are only three men, after all."

"What matter?"

"What matter? you say, when we shall have to fight thirty or forty hardened hunters! On my word, Brighteye, you will drive me mad with your notions. You doubt about nothing; but remember, that this time we have not to contend against badly-armed Indians, but white men, thorough game for the galleys, who will die without yielding an inch, and to whom we must inevitably succumb."

"That is true; I did not think of that; they are numerous."

"If we fall, what will become of her?"

"Good, good," the hunter said, with a shake of his head. "I repeat to you that I did not think of that."

"You see, then, that it is indispensable for us to come to an understanding with Marksman and the men he may have at his disposal."

"Yes; but where are you going to find in the desert the trail of a man like Marksman? Who knows where he is at this moment? He may be within gunshot of us, or five hundred miles off."

"It is enough to drive me mad."

"The fact is, that the position is grave. Are you, at least, sure this time that you are not mistaken, but are in the right trail?"

"I cannot say with certainty, though everything leads me to suppose that I am not mistaken. However, I shall soon know what I have to depend on."

"Besides, it is the same trail we have followed ever since leaving Monterey; the chances are it is they."

"What do we resolve on?"

"Hang it! I do not know what to say!"

"On my word, you are a most heart breaking fellow! What! cannot you suggest any way?"

"I must have a certainty, and then, as you said yourself, it would be madness for us thus to try a sudden attack."

"You are right. I will return to the camp; tomorrow night we will meet again, and I shall be very unlucky if this time I do not discover what it is so important for us all to know. Do you, in the meanwhile, ransack the prairie in every direction, and, if possible, bring me news of Marksman."

"The recommendation is unnecessary. I shall not be idle."

Don Stefano seized the old hunter's hand, and pressed it between his own.

"Brighteye," he said to him, with considerable emotion,

"I will not speak of our old friendship, nor of the services which I have been several times so fortunate as to render you; I will only repeat, and I know it will be sufficient for you, that the happiness of my whole life depends on the success of our expedition."

"Good, good; have confidence in me, Don José. I am too old to change my friends; I do not know who is right or wrong in this business; I wish that justice may be on your side; but that does not affect me. Whatever may happen, I will be a good and faithful companion to you."

"Thanks, my old friend. Tomorrow night, then."

After uttering these few words, Don Stefano, or, at least, the man who called himself so, made a move as if to withdraw; but Brighteye stopped him, with a sudden gesture.

"What is the matter?" the stranger asked.

The hunter laid a forefinger on his mouth, to recommend silence, and turned to Ruperto, who had remained silent and apathetic during the interview.

"*Coyote,*" he said to him, in a low voice.

Without replying, Ruperto bounded like a jaguar, and disappeared in a clump of cottonwood trees, which was a short distance off. After a few moments, the two men who had remained, with their bodies bent forward in the attitude of listeners, without uttering a syllable, heard a rustling of leaves, a noise of broken branches, followed by the fall of a heavy body on the ground, and after that nothing. Almost immediately the cry of the owl rose in the night air.

"Ruperto calls us," Brighteye then said, "all is over

"What has happened?" Don Stefano asked anxiously.

"Less than nothing," the hunter replied, making him a sign to follow. "You had a spy at your heels; that is all."

"A spy?"

"By Jove! you shall see."

"Oh, oh! that is serious."

"Less than you suppose, as we have him."

"In that case, though, we must kill the man."

"Who knows? That will probably depend on the explanation we may have with him. At any rate, there is no great harm in crushing such vipers."

While speaking thus, Brighteye and his companion had entered the thicket. Domingo, thrown down, and tightly garotted by means of Ruperto's reata, was vainly struggling to break the bonds that cut into, his flesh. Ruperto, with his hands resting on the muzzle of his rifle, was listening with a grin, but no other reply, to the flood of insults and recriminations which rage drew from the half-breed.

"¡Dios me ampare!" the latter shouted, writhing like a viper. "¡Verdugo del Demonio! Is this the way to behave between gente de razón? Am I a Redskin, to be tied like a plug of tobacco, and have my limbs fettered like a calf that is being taken to the shambles? If ever you fall into my hands, accursed dog! you shall pay for the trick you have played me."

"Instead of threatening, my good man," Brighteye interposed, "it seems to me you would do better by frankly allowing that you are in our power, and acting in accordance."

The bandit sharply turned his head, the only part of his person at liberty, toward the hunter.

"What right have you to call me good man, and give me advice, old trapper of muskrats?" he said to him, irritably. "Are you white men or Indians, to treat a hunter thus?"

"If, instead of hearing what did not concern you, Señor Domingo, for I believe that is your name," Don Stefano said, with a cunning look, "you had remained quietly asleep in your camp, the little annoyance of which you complain would not have occurred."

"I am bound to recognize the justice of your reasoning," the bandit replied ironically; "but, hang it! what would you have? I have ever suffered from a mania of trying to find out what people sought to hide from me."

The stranger looked at him suspiciously.

"And have you had the mania long, my good friend?" he asked him.

"Since my earliest youth," he answered, with effrontery.

"Only think of that! Then you must have learned a good many things?"

"An enormous quantity, worthy sir."

Don Stefano turned to Brighteye.

"My friend," he said to him, "just unloosen this man's bonds a little. There is much to be gained in his company; I wish to enjoy his conversation for a little while."

The hunter silently executed the orders he received. The bandit uttered a sigh of satisfaction at finding himself more at his ease, and sat up.

"*¡Cuerpo de Cristo!*" he exclaimed, with a mocking accent. "The position is now, at any rate, bearable. We can talk."

"I think so."

"My faith! yes. I am quite at your service, for anything you please, Excellency."

"I will profit by your complaisance."

"Profit by it! profit by it, Excellency? I can only gain in talking with you."

"Do you believe so?"

"I am convinced of it."

"Indeed, you may be right; but tell me, beside that noble curiosity, which you so frankly confessed, have you not, by accident, a few other defects?"

The bandit appeared to reflect conscientiously for two or three minutes, and then answered, with an affable grin, —

"My faith! no, Excellency. I cannot find any."

"Are you sure of that?"

"Hum! it may be so, yet I do not believe it."

"Come, you see, you are not sure."

"That is indeed true!" the bandit exclaimed, with pretended candour. "As you know, Excellency, human nature is so imperfect."

Don Stefano gave a nod of assent.

"If I were to help you," he said, "perhaps—"

"We might find it out, Excellency," Domingo quickly interrupted him. "Well, help me, help me, I ask for nothing better."

"Hum! for instance—but notice that I affirm nothing; I suppose, that is all."

"*¡Caray!* I am well aware of it. Go on, Excellency, do not trouble yourself."

"Then, I say—have you not a certain weakness for money?"

"For gold, especially."

"That is what I meant to say."

"The fact is, gold is very tempting, Excellency."

"I do not wish to regard it as a crime, my friend. I only mention it; besides, that passion is so natural—"

"Is it not?"

"That you must be affected by it."

"Well, I confess, Excellency, that you have guessed it."

"Look you! I was sure of it."

"Yes, money gained honestly."

"Of course! Thus, for instance, suppose anyone offered you a thousand piastres to discover the secret of Don Miguel Ortega's palanquin?"

"Hang it!" the bandit said, fixing a sharp glance on the stranger, who, for his part, examined him attentively.

"And if that somebody," Don Stefano went on, "gave you in addition, as earnest penny, a ring like this?" While saying this, he made a magnificent diamond ring flash in the bandit's eyes.

"I would accept," the latter said, with a greedy accent, "even if I were compelled, in order to discover that secret, to imperil the share I hope for in Paradise."

Don Stefano turned to Brighteye. "Unfasten this man," he said, coldly, "we understand each other."

On feeling himself free, the half-breed gave a bound of joy. "The ring!" he said.

"There it is," Don Stefano said, as he handed it to him; "all is arranged."

Domingo laid his right-hand thumb across the left, and raised his head proudly. "On the Holy Cross of the Redeemer," he said, in a clear and impressive voice, "I swear to employ all my efforts in discovering the secret Don Miguel hides so jealously; I swear never to betray the Caballero with whom I am treating at this moment: this oath I take in the presence of these three Caballeros, pledging myself, if I break it, to endure any punishment, even death, which it may please these three Caballeros to inflict on me."

The oath taken by Domingo is the most terrible a Spanish American can offer; there is not a single instance of it ever having been broken. Don Stefano bowed, convinced of the bandit's sincerity.

At this moment, several shots, followed by horrible yells, were heard at a short distance off. Brighteye started. "Don José," he said to the stranger, as he laid his hands on his shoulder, "Heaven favours us. Return to the camp; tomorrow night I shall probably have some news for you."

"But those shots?"

"Do not trouble yourself about them, but return to the camp, I tell you, and let me act."

"Well, as you wish it, I will retire."

"Till tomorrow?"

"Tomorrow."

"And I?" Domingo said. "Caramba, comrades, if you are going to play at knives, can you not take me with you?"

The old hunter looked at him attentively. "Eh!" he said, at the expiration of a moment, "your idea is not a bad one; you can come if you desire it."

"That is capital, for it is a pretext ready made to explain my absence."

Don Stefano smiled, and after reminding Brighteye once again of their meeting for the following night, he left the thicket, and proceeded toward the camp. The two hunters and the half-breed were left alone.

CHAPTER IV
INDIANS AND HUNTERS

As we have already said, at the spot where the three hunters were standing, the Rio Colorado formed a wide sheet, whose silvery waters wound through a superb and picturesque country. At times, on either bank, the ground rose almost suddenly into bold mountains of grand appearance; at other places, the river ran through fresh and laughing prairies, covered with luxuriant vegetation, or graceful and undulating valleys, in which grew trees of every description.

It was in one of these valleys that Brighteye's canoe had been pulled in. Sheltered on all sides by lofty forests, which begirt them with a dense curtain of verdure, the hunters would have escaped, even during the day, from the investigations of curious or indiscreet persons, who might have attempted to surprise them at this advanced hour of the night, by the flickering rays of the moon which only reached them after being followed through the leafy dome that covered them: they could consider themselves as being perfectly secure.

Reassured by the strength of his position, Brighteye, so soon as Don Stefano had left him, formed his plan of action with that lucidity which can only be obtained from a lengthened knowledge of the desert.

"Comrade," he said to the half-breed, "do you know the desert?"

"Not so well as you, certainly, old hunter," the latter answered, modestly, "but well enough to be of good service to you in the expedition you wish to attempt."

"I like that way of answering, for it shows a desire of doing well. Listen to me attentively; the colour of my hair, and the wrinkles that furrow my forehead, tell you sufficiently that I must possess a certain amount of experience; my whole life has been spent in the woods; there is not a blade of grass I do not know, a sound which I cannot explain, a footstep which I cannot discover. A few moments back, several shots were fired not far from us, followed by the Indian war yell; among those shots I am certain I recognized the rifle of a man for whom I feel the warmest friendship; that man is in danger at this moment—he is fighting the Apaches, who have surprised and attacked him during sleep. The number of shots leads me to suppose that my friend has only two companions with him; if we do not go to his help, he is lost, for his adversaries are numerous; the thing I am about to attempt is almost desperate; we have every chance against us, so reflect before replying. Are you still resolved to accompany Ruperto and myself; in a word, risk your scalp in our company?"

"Bah!" the bandit said, carelessly, "a man can only die once; perhaps I shall never again have so fine an opportunity of dying honestly. Dispose of me, old trapper—I am yours, body and soul."

"Good; I expected that answer; still, it was my duty to warn you of the danger that threatened you: now, no more talking, but let us act, for time presses, and every minute we waste is an age for the man we wish to save. Walk in my moccasins; keep your eye and ear on the watch; above all, be prudent, and do nothing without orders."

After having carefully inspected the cap on his rifle, a precaution imitated by his two companions, Brighteye looked round him for a few seconds, then, with that hunter's instinct which in them is almost second sight, he advanced with a rapid though silent step in the direction of the fighting, while making the men a sign to follow him.

It is impossible to form an idea, even a distant one, of what a night march is on the prairie, on foot, through the shrubs, the trees which have grown together, the creepers that twine in every direction. Walking on a shifting soil, composed of detritus of every nature accumulated during centuries, at one place forming mounds several feet high, surrounded by deep ditches, not only is it difficult to find a path through this inextricable confusion, when walking quietly onward, with no fear of betraying one's presence, but this becomes almost impossible when you have to open a passage silently, not letting a branch spring back, or a leaf rustle; for that sound, though almost imperceptible, would be enough to place the enemy you wish to surprise on his guard.

A long residence in the desert can alone enable a man to acquire the necessary skill to carry out this rude task successfully. This skill Brighteye possessed in the highest degree; he seemed to guess the obstacles which rose at each step before him—obstacles the slightest of which, under such circumstances, would have made the most resolute man recoil, through his conviction of it being an impossibility to surmount them.

The two other hunters had only to follow the track so cleverly and laboriously made by their guide. Fortunately, the adventurers were only a short distance from the men they were going to help; had it been otherwise, they would have needed nearly the whole night to join them. Had Brighteye wished it, he could have skirted the forest and walked in the long grass—a road incomparably more easy, and especially less fatiguing; but, with his usual correctness of conception, the hunter understood that the direction he took was the only one which would permit him to go straight to the scene of action without being discovered by the Indians, who, in spite of all their sagacity, would never suspect that a man would dare to attempt such a route.

After a walk of about twenty minutes, Brighteye stopped—the hunters had arrived. On lightly moving the branches and brambles aside, they witnessed the following scene.

Before them, and scarce ten paces off, was a clearing. In the centre of that clearing three fires were burning, and were surrounded by Apache warriors, smoking gravely, while their horses, fastened to pickets, were nibbling the young tree shoots.

Marksman was standing motionless near the chiefs, leaning on his rifle, and exchanging a few words with them at intervals. Brighteye understood nothing of what he saw; all these men seemed on the best terms with the hunter, who, for his part, did not display the slightest uneasiness, either by his gestures or his face.

We have said that, after the Indians' sudden attack, Marksman advanced towards them, waving a buffalo robe in sign of peace. The Indians stopped, with that courteous deference which they display in all their relations, in order to listen to the hunter's explanations. A chief even stepped towards him, politely inviting him to say what he wanted.

"My red brother does not know me! Then, is it necessary that I should tell him my name, that he may know with whom he is speaking?" Marksman said, angrily.

"That is useless. I know that my brother is a great white warrior. My ears are open; I await the explanation he will be good enough to give me."

The hunter shrugged his shoulders disdainfully.

"Have the Apaches become cowardly or plundering coyotes, setting out in flocks to hunt on the prairies? Why have they attacked me?"

"My brother knows it."

"No, as I ask it. The Antelope Apaches had a chief—a great warrior—named Red Wolf. That chief was my friend. I had made a treaty with him. But Red Wolf is, doubtlessly, dead; his scalp adorns the lodge of a Comanche, as the young men of his tribe have come to attack me, treacherously, and against the sworn peace, during my sleep."

The Chief frowned, and drew himself up.

"The Paleface, like all his countrymen, has a viper's tongue," he said, rudely; "a skin covers his heart, and the words his chest exhales are so many perfidies. Red Wolf is not dead; his scalp does not adorn the lodge of a Comanche dog; he is still the first chief of the Antelope Apaches. The hunter knows it well, since he is speaking to him at this moment."

"I am glad that my brother has made himself known," the hunter replied, "for I should not have recognized him from his way of acting."

"Yes, there is a traitor between us," the Chief said, drily; "but that traitor is a Paleface, and not an Indian!"

"I wait till my brother explains himself. I do not understand him; a mist has spread over my eyes—my mind is veiled. The words of the Chief, I have no doubt, will dissipate this cloud."

"I hope so! Let the hunter answer with an honest tongue, and no deceit. His voice is a music which for a long time sounded pleasantly in my ears, and rejoiced my heart. I should be glad if his explanation restored me the friend whom I fancied I had lost."

"Let my brother speak. I will answer his questions."

At a sign from Red Wolf, the Apaches had kindled several fires, and formed a temporary camp. In spite of all his cleverness, doubt had entered the heart of the Apache chief, and he wished to prove to the white hunter, whom he feared, that he was acting frankly, and entertained no ill design against him. The Apaches, seeing the good understanding that apparently prevailed between their sachem and the hunter, had hastened to execute the order they received. All traces of the contest disappeared in a moment, and the clearing offered the appearance of a bivouac of peaceful hunters receiving the visit of a friend.

Marksman smiled internally at the success of his plan, and the way in which he managed, by a few words, to give quite a different turn to the position of affairs. Still he was not without anxiety about the explanation the Chief was going to ask of him. He felt he was in a wasps' nest, from which he did not know how he should contrive to emerge, without some providential accident. Redskin invited the hunter to take a seat by his side at the fire, which he declined, however, not being at all certain how matters would end, and wishing to retain a chance of escape in the event of the explanation becoming stormy.

"Is the pale hunter ready to reply?" Red Wolf asked him.

"I am awaiting my brother's good pleasure."

"Good! Let my brother open his ears, then. A Chief is about to speak."

"I am listening."

"Red Wolf is a renowned Chief. His name is cared by the Comanches, who fly before him like timid squaws. One day, at the head of his young men, Red Wolf entered an altopelt (village) of the Comanches. The Buffalo Comanches were hunting on the prairies; their warriors and young men were absent. Red Wolf burned the cabins, and carried off the women prisoners. Is that true?"

"It is true."

"Among the women was one for whom the heart of the Apache chief spoke. That woman was the Cihuatl of the sachem of the Buffalo Comanches. Red Wolf led her to his hut and treated her not as a prisoner, but as a well-beloved sister."

"What did the pale hunter?"

The Chief broke off and looked steadily at Marksman; but the latter did not move a feature.

"I wait till my brother answers me, in order to know with what he reproaches me," he said.

Red Wolf continued, with a certain degree of animation in his voice,—

"The pale hunter, abusing the friendship of the Chief, introduced himself into his village, under the pretext of visiting his red brother. As he was known and beloved by all, he traversed the village as he pleased, sauntered about everywhere, and when he had discovered Eglantine, he carried her off during a dark night, like a traitor and a coward."

At this insult, the hunter pressed the barrel of his rifle with a convulsive movement; but he immediately recovered his coolness.

"The Chief is a great warrior," he said, "he speaks well. The words reach his lips with an abundance that is charming. Unfortunately, he lets himself be led astray by passion, and does not describe matters as they occurred."

"Wah!" the Chief exclaimed, "Red Wolf is an impostor, and his lying tongue ought to be thrown to the dogs."

"I have listened patiently to the Chief's words, it is his turn to hear mine."

"Good! Let my brother speak."

At this moment, a whistle, no louder than a sigh, was audible. The Indians paid no attention to it, but the hunter quivered, his eye flashed, and a smile played round the corner of his lips.

"I will be brief," he said. "It is true that I introduced myself into my brother's village, but frankly and loyally to ask of him, in the name of Mahchsi-Karehde, the great sachem of the Buffalo Comanches, his wife, whom Red Wolf had carried off. I offered for her a rich ransom, composed of four guns, six hides of she-buffalos, and two necklaces of grizzly bears' claws. I acted thus, in the intention of preventing a war between the Buffalo Comanches and the Antelope Apaches. My brother, Red Wolf, instead of accepting my friendly proposals, despised them. I then warned him, that, by will or force, Flying Eagle would recover his wife, treacherously carried off from his village while he was absent. Then I withdrew. What reproach can my brother address to me? Under what circumstances did I behave badly to him? Flying Eagle has got back his wife; he has acted well—he was in the right. Red Wolf has nothing to say to that. Under similar circumstances, he would have done the same. I have spoken. Let my brother answer if his heart proves to him that I was wrong."

"Good!" the Chief answered. "My brother was here with Eglantine a few minutes ago; he will tell me where she is hidden, Red Wolf will capture her again, and there will no longer be a cloud between Red Wolf and his friend."

"The Chief will forget that woman who does not love him and who cannot be his. That will be better, especially as Flying Eagle will never consent to give her up."

"Red Wolf has warriors to support his words," the Indian said, proudly, "Flying Eagle is alone; how will he oppose the will of the sachem?"

Marksman smiled.

"Flying Eagle has numerous friends," he said, "he is at this moment sheltered in the camp of the Palefaces, whose fires Red Wolf can see from here, glistening in the darkness. Let my brother listen. I believe I hear the sound of footsteps in the forest."

The Indian rose with agitation.

At this moment three men entered the clearing. They were Brighteye, Ruperto, and Domingo.

At the sight of them, the Apaches, who were thoroughly acquainted with them, rose tumultuously and uttered a cry of astonishment, almost of terror, while seizing their weapons. The three hunters continued to advance calmly, not caring to trouble themselves about these almost hostile demonstrations.

We will explain in a few words the appearance of the hunters and their interference, which was probably about to change the aspect of affairs.

CHAPTER V
MUTUAL EXPLANATIONS

Brighteye and his two companions, owing to the position they occupied, not only saw all that occurred in the clearing, but also heard, without losing a word, the conversation between Marksman and Red Wolf.

For many long years the two Canadian hunters had been on intimate terms. Many times had they undertaken together some of those daring expeditions which the wood rangers frequently carry out against the Indians. These two men had no secrets from each other; all was in common between them—hatred as well as friendship.

Brighteye was thoroughly acquainted with the events to which Marksman alluded, and, had not certain reasons, we shall learn presently, prevented him, he would have probably aided his friend in rescuing Eglantine from Red Wolf. Still, one point remained obscure on his mind; that was the presence of Marksman in the middle of the Indians, the quarrel which had begun in shouts and yells, and had now apparently terminated with an amicable conversation.

By what strange concourse of events was it that Marksman, the man best acquainted with Indian tricks, whose reputation for skill and courage was universal among the hunters and trappers of the Western Prairies, now found himself in an equivocal position, in the midst of thirty or forty Apaches, the most scoundrelly treacherous and ferocious of all the Indians who wander about the desert? This it was that the worthy hunter could not explain, and which rendered him so thoughtful. At the risk of whatever might happen, he resolved to reveal his presence to his friend by means of a signal arranged between them long ago, in order to warn him that, in case of need, a friend was watching over him. It was then that he gave the whistle, at the sound of which we saw the hunter start. But this signal had a result which Brighteye was far from expecting. The branches of the tree, against the trunk of which the Canadian was leaning, parted, and a man, hanging by his arms, fell suddenly to the ground a couple of yards from him, but so lightly, that his fall did not produce the slightest sound.

At the first glance, Brighteye recognized the man who seemed thus to fall from the sky. Owing to his self-command, he displayed none of the amazement this unforeseen appearance produced in him. The hunter rested the butt of his rifle on the ground, and addressed the Indian politely.

"That is a strange idea of yours, Chief," he said, with a smile, "to go promenading on the trees at this hour of the night."

"Flying Eagle is watching the Apaches," the Indian answered, with a guttural accent. "Did not my brother expect to see me?"

"In the prairie we must expect everything, Chief. Still, I confess that few meetings would be so agreeable to me as yours, especially at this moment."

"My brother is on the trail of the Antelopes?"

"I declare to you, Chief, that an hour ago I did not expect I was so near them. Had I not heard your shots, it is probable that at this moment I should be quietly asleep in my bivouac."

"Yes, my brother heard the rifle of a friend sing, and he has come."

"You have guessed rightly, Chief. But now tell me all about it, for I know nothing."

"Has not my pale brother heard Red Wolf?"

"Of course; but is there nothing else?"

"Nothing. Flying Eagle rescued his wife; the Apaches pursued him, like cowardly coyotes, and this night surprised him at his fire."

"Very good. Is Eglantine in safety?"

"Eglantine is a Comanche woman; she knows not fear."

"I am aware of that—she is a good creature; but that is not the question at this moment. What do you purpose doing?"

"Wait for a favourable moment, then utter my war yell, and fall on these dogs."

"Hum! your project is rather quick. If you will allow me, I will make a slight change."

"Wisdom speaks by the mouth of the pale hunter. Flying Eagle is young: he will obey."

"Good; the more so, because I shall only act for your welfare. But now let me listen, for the conversation seems to me to be taking a turn extremely interesting for us."

The Indian bowed, but made no reply, while Brighteye bent forward, better to hear what was said. After a few minutes the hunter probably considered that it was time for him to interfere, for he turned to the Chief and whispered in his ear, as he had done during the whole of the previous conversation—"Let my brother leave this affair to me; his presence would be more injurious than useful to us. We cannot attempt to fight so large a number of enemies, so prudence demands that we should have recourse to stratagem."

"The Apaches are dogs," the Comanche muttered, angrily.

"I am of your opinion; but, for the present, let us feign not to consider them such. Believe me, we shall soon take our revenge; besides, the advantage will be on our side, as we are cheating them."

Flying Eagle let his head drop.

"Will the Chief promise me not to make a move without a signal from me?" the hunter said, earnestly.

"Flying Eagle is a sachem. He has said that he will obey Greyhead."

"Good. Now look, you will not have long to wait."

After muttering these words, with that mocking accent peculiar to him, the old hunter resolutely thrust the brambles on one side, and walked firmly into the clearing, followed by his two companions. We have already described the emotion produced by this unforeseen arrival.

Flying Eagle returned to his ambush up the tree, from which he had only come down to speak with the hunter, and give him the information he required. Brighteye stopped by Markham's side.

"Friend," he then said, in Spanish, a language which most of the Indians understand, "your order is executed. Flying Eagle and his wife are at this moment in the camp of the Gambusinos."

"Good," Marksman answered, catching his meaning at once; "who are the two men who accompany you?"

"Two hunters the Chief of the Gachupinos sent to accompany me, in spite of my assurances that you were among friends. He will soon arrive himself at the head of thirty horsemen."

"Return to him, and tell him that he has no longer any occasion to trouble himself; or, stay, I will go myself, to prevent any misunderstanding."

These words, spoken without any emphasis, and naturally, by a man whom each of the Indians present had been frequently in a position to appreciate, produced on them an effect impossible to describe.

We have already mentioned several times, in our different works, that the Redskins unite the greatest prudence with the maddest temerity, and never attempt any enterprise without calculating beforehand all the chances of success it may offer. So soon as those chances disappear, to make room for probable ill results, they are not ashamed to recoil, for the very simple reason that with them honour, as we understand it in Europe, only holds a secondary place, and success alone is regarded.

Red Wolf was assuredly a brave man; he had given innumerable proofs of that in many a combat; still, he did not hesitate, in behalf of the general welfare, to sacrifice his secret desires, and in doing so, as we believe, he gave a grand proof of that family feeling, and almost instinctive patriotism, which is one of the strongest points in the Indian character. Clever as he was, the Apache Chief was completely deluded by Brighteye, whose imperturbable coolness and unexpected arrival would have sufficed to lead astray an individual even more intelligent than the man with whom he had to deal. Red Wolf made up his mind at once, without any thought of self.

"Greyhead, my brother, is welcome at my fire," he said; "my heart rejoices at greeting a friend; his companions and himself can take their places round the council fire; the calumet of a Chief is ready to be offered them."

"Red Wolf is a great Chief," Brighteye replied; "I am pleased at the kindly feeling he experiences towards me. I would accept his offer with the greatest pleasure, did not urgent reasons oblige me to rejoin, as soon as possible, my brothers the Palefaces, who are waiting for me at a short distance from the spot where the Antelope Apaches are encamped."

"I hope that no cloud has arisen between Greyhead and his brother, Red Wolf," the Chief remarked, in a cautious tone: "two warriors must esteem each other."

"That is my opinion too, Chief, and that is why I have presented myself so frankly in your camp, when it would have been easy to have had several warriors of my nation to accompany me."

Brighteye knew perfectly well that the Apaches understood Spanish, and consequently nothing he had said to Markham escaped them; but it was to his interest, as well as that of his comrade, to pretend to be ignorant of the fact, and accept as current coin the insidious propositions of the Chief.

"His friends, the Palefaces, are encamped not far from here?" the Chief remarked.

"Yes," Brighteye replied, "at the most from four to five bowshots in a westerly direction."

"Wah! I am vexed at it," the Indian said, "for I would have accompanied my brother to their camp."

"And what prevents your coming with us?" the old hunter said, distinctly. "Would you fear an ill reception by chance?"

"Och! who would dare not to receive Red Wolf with the respect due to him?" the Apache said, haughtily.

"No one, assuredly."

Red Wolf leaned over to a subaltern chief, and whispered a few words in his ear; the man rose, and left the clearing. The hunters saw this movement with anxiety, and exchanged a glance, which said, "Let us keep on our guard." They also fell back a few paces, as if accidentally, and drew nearer together, in order to be ready at the first suspicious sign; for they knew the perfidy of the men among whom they were, and expected anything from them. The Indian sent off by the Chief re-entered the clearing at this moment. He had been absent hardly ten minutes.

"Well?" Red Wolf asked him.

"It is true," the Indian answered, laconically.

The sachem's face was overclouded; he felt certain then that Brighteye had not deceived him; for the man he had sent out of the camp had been ordered by him to assure himself whether the fires of a party of white men could be really seen a short distance off; his emissary's reply proved to him that no treachery could be possible, that he must continue to feign kindly feelings, and separate on proper terms from the troublesome guests, whom he would have liked so much to be rid of in a very different manner. At his order the horses were unhobbled, and the warriors mounted.

"Day is approaching," he said; "the moon has again entered the great mountain. I am about to start with my young men. May the Wacondah protect my pale brothers!"

"Thank you, Chief," Marksman answered. "But will you not come with us?"

"We are not following the same path," the Chief replied drily, as he let his horse go.

"That is probable, accursed dog!" Brighteye growled between his teeth.

The whole band started at full speed, and disappeared in the gloom. Soon the sound of their horses' hoofs could no longer be heard, as they became mingled in the distance with those thousand sounds, coming from no apparent cause, which incessantly trouble the majestic silence of the desert.

The hunters were alone. Like the Augurs of ancient Rome, who could not look at each other without laughing, little was needed for the hunters to burst into a loud burst of delight after the hurried departure of the Apaches. At a signal from Marksman, Flying Eagle and Eglantine came to join the wood rangers, who had already seated themselves unceremoniously at the fire of which they had so cleverly dispossessed their enemies.

"Hum!" Brighteye said, as he charged his pipe, "I shall laugh for a long time at this trick; it is almost as good as the one I played the Pawnees in 1827, on the Upper Arkansas. I was very young at that time; I had been traversing the prairie for only a few years, and was not, as I now am, accustomed to Indian devilries; I remember that—"

"By what accident did I meet you here, Brighteye?" his friend asked, hastily interrupting him.

Marksman knew that so soon as Brighteye began a story, no power on earth would stop him. The worthy man, during the course of a long and varied career, had seen and done so many extraordinary things, that the slightest event which occurred to him, or of which he was merely a witness, immediately became an excuse for one of his interminable stories. His friends, who knew his weakness, felt no hesitation about interrupting him; still we must do Brighteye the justice of saying that he was never angry with his disturbers; for ten minutes later he would begin another story, which they as mercilessly interrupted in a similar way.

To Marksman's question, he replied,—"We will talk, and I will tell you that." Then, turning to Domingo, he said,—"My friend, I thank you for the assistance you have given us. Return to the camp, and do not forget your promise. Above all, do not omit to narrate all you have seen, to—you know who!"

"That is agreed, old hunter. Don't be uneasy. Good-bye."

"Here's luck."

Domingo threw his rifle over his shoulder, lit his pipe, and walked in the direction of the camp, where he arrived an hour later.

"There," Marksman said, "now I believe nothing will prevent your going ahead."

"Yes; one thing, my friend."

"What is it?"

"The night is nearly spent; it has been fatiguing to everybody. I presume that two or three hours' sleep are necessary, if not indispensable, especially as we are in no hurry."

"Tell me only one thing first, and then I will let you sleep as long as you please."

"What is it?"

"How you happened so fortunately to come to my aid."

"Confound it! That is exactly what I was afraid of. Your question obliges me to enter into details far too long for me to be able to satisfy you at this moment."

"The truth is, my friend, that, in spite of the lively desire I feel to spend a few days with you, I am compelled to leave you at sunrise."

"Nonsense! It is not possible."

"It is, indeed."

"But what is your hurry?"

"I have engaged myself as scout with a caravan, which I have given the meeting at two o'clock tomorrow afternoon, at the Del Rubio ford. That appointment has been made for the last two months. You know that an engagement is sacred with us hunters, and you would not like to make me break my word!"

"Not for the hides of all the buffalos killed every year on the prairie. Towards what part of the Far West will you guide these men?"

"I shall know that tomorrow."

"And with what sort of people have you to do? Are they Spaniards, or Gringos?"

"On my word, I fancy they are Mexicans. Their chief's name, I think, is Don Miguel Ortega, or something like it."

"Hallo!" Brighteye exclaimed, with a start of surprise; "what's that you said?"

"Don Miguel Ortega. I may be mistaken, but I hardly think so."

"That is strange," the old hunter said, as if speaking to himself.

"I do not see anything strange in it; the name appears to me common enough."

"To you, possibly. And you have made an agreement with him?"

"Signed and sealed."

"As scout?"

"Yes, I say, a thousand times."

"Well, comfort yourself, Marksman; we have many a long day to spend together."

"Do you belong to his party?"

"Heaven forbid!"

"Then, I don't understand anything."

Brighteye seemed to be reflecting seriously for a few moments; then he turned to his friend, and said,—

"Listen to me, Marksman! So surely as you are my oldest friend, I do not wish to see you going to the deuce your own road. I must give you certain information, which will be indispensable to you in doing your duty properly. I see that we shall not sleep this night, so listen to me attentively. What you are about to hear is worth the trouble."

Marksman, startled by the old hunter's solemn accent, looked at him anxiously. "Speak!" he said to him.

Brighteye collected his thoughts for a moment, and then took the word, beginning a long history, to which his audience listened with a degree of interest and attention which increased with every moment; for never, till that day, had they heard the narrative of events so strange and extraordinary.

The sun had risen for a long time, but the hunter was still talking.

CHAPTER VI
A DARK HISTORY

Freed from all the observations, more or less pertinent, with which it pleased the prolix hunter to embellish it, the following is the remarkable story the Canadian told his hearers. This narrative is so closely connected with our story, that we are compelled to repeat it in all its details:—

"Few cities offer a more enchanting appearance than Mexico. The ancient capital of the Aztecs lies stretched out, slothful and idle as a Creole maid, half veiled by the thick curtain of lofty willows which border at a distance the canals and roads. Built at exactly equal distance from two oceans, at about 7,500 feet above their level, or at the same height as the hospice of St. Bernard, this city, however, enjoys a delicious tempered climate, between two magnificent mountains—Popocatepetl, or the burning mountain, and Intaczehuatl, or the white woman—whose rugged peaks, covered with eternal snows, are lost in the clouds. The stranger who arrives before Mexico at sunset, by the eastern road—one of the four great ways that lead to the City of the Aztecs, and the only one now remaining isolated in the middle of the waters of Lake Tezcuco, on which it is built— experiences, at the first sight of this city, a strange emotion, for which he cannot account. The Moorish architecture of the edifices; the houses painted of bright colours; the numberless domes of churches and convents which rise above the azoteas, and cover—if we may use the expression—the entire capital with their vast yellow, blue, and red parasols, gilded by the parching rays of the declining sun; the warm and perfumed evening breeze which comes sporting through the leaf-laden branches; all this combines to give Mexico a perfectly Eastern air, which astonishes and seduces at the same time. Mexico, entirely burnt down by Fernando Cortez, was rebuilt by that conqueror after the original plan; all the streets intersect at right angles, and lead to the Plaza Mayor by five principal arteries."

"All Spanish towns in the New World have this in common—that, in all, the Plaza Mayor is built after the same plan. Thus, at Mexico, on one side are the Cathedral and the Sagrario; on the second, the Palace of the President of the Republic, containing the ministerial offices—four in number, barracks, a prison, &c.; on the third side is the Ayuntamiento; while the fourth is occupied by two bazaars—the Parián, and the Portal de los Flores."

"On July 10, 1854, at ten of the night, after a torrid heat, which compelled the inhabitants to shut themselves up in their houses the whole day through, the breeze rose and refreshed the air, and everybody, mounted on the flower-covered azoteas, which make them resemble hanging gardens, hastened to enjoy that serene placidity of American evenings, which seems to rain stars from the azure sky. The streets and square were thronged with promenaders; there was an inextricable throng of foot passengers, horsemen, men, women, Indians and their squaws, where the rags, silk and gold were arranged in the quaintest manner, in the midst of cries, jests, and merry bursts of laughter. In a word, Mexico, like the enchanted city of the Arabian Nights, seemed to have been aroused by the bell of Oración from a centennial sleep—such joy did all faces display, and so happy did all seem to inhale the fresh air."

"At this moment, a non-commissioned officer, who could be easily recognised as such by the vine stick he held in his hand, turned out of the Calle San Francisco, and mingled with the crowd that thronged the Plaza Mayor, giving himself all the airs peculiar to soldiers in all parts of the world. He was a young man, of elegant features, haughty glance, and his slight moustache was coquettishly turned up. After walking round the square two or three times, ogling maidens and elbowing the men, he approached, with the same careless air he had displayed from the beginning, a shop built against one of the portales, in which an old man with a ferret-face and cunning look was shutting up in the drawers of a poor table, stained with a countless number of ink spots, paper, pens, sand, and envelopes—in a word, all the articles requisite for the profession of a public writer—the trade which the little old man really carried on, as could be seen from a board hung over the door of his shop, on which was written, in white letters on a black ground,—*Juan Battista Leporello, Evangelista.* The sergeant looked for a few seconds through the panes, which were covered with specimens of calligraphy, and then, doubtless satisfied with what he saw, he tapped thrice with his stick on the door."

"A chain was moved in the interior; the soldier heard a key turned in the lock, then the door opened slightly, and the evangelista thrust his head out timidly."

"'Ah, 'tis you, Don Annibal! *Dios me ampare.* I did not expect you so soon,' he said, in that cringing tone which some men employ when they feel themselves in the hands of a man stronger than themselves."

"'¡*Cuerpo de Cristo!* play the innocent, old coyote,' the sergeant replied roughly, 'who but I would dare to set foot in your accursed den?'"

"The evangelista shrugged his shoulders with a grin, and pushed his silver spectacles with their round glasses up on his forehead."

"'Eh, eh,' he said, coughing mysteriously, 'many people have recourse to my good offices, my young Springold.'"

"'It is possible,' the soldier answered, thrusting him rudely back, and entering the shop. 'I pity them for falling into the hands of an old bird of prey like you; but it is not that which brings me here.'"

"'Perhaps it would be better for both you and me, if your visits had another motive from the one that brings you here!' the evangelista remarked, timidly."

"'Truce to your sermons; shut the door, fasten the shutters, so that no one can see us from the street, and let us talk, for we have no time to lose.'"

"The old man made no reply; he at once set about closing the shutters, which at night protected his shop from the assaults of the rateros, with a celerity for which no one would have given him credit; then he sat down by his visitor's side, after carefully bolting the door."

"These two men, seen thus by the light of a smoky candle, offered a striking contrast; one young, handsome, strong, and daring; the other old, broken, and hypocritical: both taking side glances at each other, full of a strange expression, and with an apparent cordiality, which probably hid a deep hatred, talking in a low voice ear to ear, they resembled two demons conspiring the ruin of an angel."

"The soldier was the first to speak, in a tone hardly above his breath, so much did he seem to fear being overheard."

"'Look you, Tío Leporello,' he said, 'let us come to an understanding; the half hour has just struck at the Sagrario, so speak; what have you learnt new?'"

"'Hum!' the other said, 'not much that is interesting.'"

"The soldier flashed a suspicious glance at him, and appeared to be reflecting."

"'That is true,' he said, at the end of a moment, 'I did not think of that; where could my head be?'"

"He drew from the breast pocket of his uniform a purse tolerably well filled, through the meshes of which glistened sundry ounces, and then a long navaja, which he opened and placed on the table near him. The old man trembled at the sight of the sharpened blade, whose blue steel sent forth sinister rays; the soldier opened the purse, and poured forth the pieces in a joyous cascade before him. The evangelista immediately forgot the knife, only to attend to the gold, attracted involuntarily by the trinkling of the metal, as by an irresistible magnet."

"The soldier had done all we have just described with the coolness of a man who knows that he has unfailing arguments in his possession."

"'Then,' he said, 'rake up your memory, old demon, if you do not wish my navaja to teach you with whom you have to deal, in case you have forgotten.'"

"The evangelista smiled pleasantly, while looking covetously at the ounces. 'I know too well what I owe you, Don Annibal,' he said, 'not to try to satisfy you by all the means in my power.'"

"'A truce to your unnecessary and hypocritical compliments, old ape, and come to facts. Take this first, it will encourage you to be sincere.'"

"He placed several ounces in his hand, which the evangelista disposed of with such sleight of hand, that it was impossible for the soldier to know where they had gone."

"'You are generous, Don Annibal—that will bring you good fortune.'"

"'Go on; I want facts.'"

"'I am coming to them.'"

"'I am listening.'"

"And the sergeant leaned his elbows on the table, in the position of a man preparing to listen, while the evangelista coughed, spat, and by an old habit of prudence, though alone with the sergeant in his shop, looked round him suspiciously."

"The sounds on the Plaza Mayor had died out one after the other; the crowd had dispersed in every direction, and returned to their houses, and the greatest silence prevailed outside; at this moment eleven o'clock struck slowly from the Cathedral, and the two men started involuntarily at the mournful sounds of the clock; the serenos chanted the hour in their drawling, drunken voice; then all was quiet."

"'Will you speak, yes or no?' the soldier suddenly said, with a menacing accent."

"The evangelista bounded on his butaca, as if aroused from sleep, and passed his hand several times over his forehead. 'I am beginning,' he said in a humble voice."

"'That is lucky,' the other remarked, coarsely."

"'You must know, then——but,' he observed, suddenly interrupting himself, 'must I enter into all the details?'"

"'*Demonios!*' the soldier exclaimed, passionately, 'let us have an end of this once for all; you know I want to have the most complete information; *Canarios!* do not play with me like a cat with a mouse; old man, I warn you, that game will be dangerous for you.'"

"'Well, this morning, I had just settled myself in my office; I was arranging my papers and mending my pens, when I heard a discreet tap at the door; I rose and went to open it; it was a young and lovely lady, as far as I could judge, for she was *embossed* in her black mantilla, so as not to be seen.'"

"'Then it was not the woman who has come to you every day for a month?' the soldier interrupted."

"'Yes; but as you have doubtlessly remarked, on each of her visits, she is careful to change her dress, in order to prevent my recognizing her; but, in spite of these precautions, I have been too long accustomed to ladies' tricks to allow myself to be deceived, and I recognized her by the first glance that shot from her black eye.'"

"'Very good: go on.'"

"'She stood for a moment before me in silence, playing with her fan, with an air of embarrassment. I offered her a chair politely, pretending not to recognize her, and asking her how I could be of service to her.' 'Oh,' she answered me, with a petulant voice, 'I want a very simple matter.' 'Speak, señorita; if it is connected with my profession, believe me, I shall make a point of obeying you.' 'Should I have come, had it not been so?' she replied; 'but are you a man who can be trusted?' and while saying this, she fixed on me a searching glance. I drew myself up, and replied in my most serious tone, as I laid my hand on my heart—'An evangelista is a confessor; all secrets die in his breast.' She then drew a paper from the pocket of her saga, and turned it about in her fingers, but suddenly began laughing, as she said, 'How foolish I am, I make a mystery of a trifle; besides, at this moment you are only a machine, as you will not understand what you write.' I bowed at all hazards, expecting some diabolical combination, like those she has brought to me every day for a month.'"

"'A truce to reflections,' the sergeant interrupted."

"'She gave me the paper,' the evangelista continued, 'and, as was arranged between you and me, I took a sheet of paper, which I laid upon another prepared beforehand, and blackened on one side, so that the words I wrote on my papers were reproduced by the black page on another—the poor Niña not in the least suspecting it. After all, the letter was not long, only two or three lines; but, may I be sent to purgatory,' he added, crossing himself piously, 'if I understood a syllable of the horrible gibberish I copied: it was doubtlessly Morisco.'"

"'Afterwards?'"

"'I folded up the paper in the shape of a letter, and addressed it.'"

"'Ah, ah!' the soldier said, with interest, 'that is the first time.'"

"'Yes, but the information will not be of much use to you.'"

"'Perhaps:—what was the address?'"

"'Z. p. v. 2, calle S. P. Z.'"

"'Hum!' the soldier said, thoughtfully; 'that is certainly rather vague. What next?'"

"'Then she went away, after giving me a gold ounce.'"

"'She is generous.'"

"'Pore Niña!' the evangelista said, laying his hooked fingers over his dry eyes, with an air of tenderness."

"'Enough of that mummery, which I do not believe. Is that all she said to you?'"

"'Nearly so,' the other said, with hesitation."

"The sergeant looked at him. 'Is there anything else?' he remarked, as he threw him several gold coins, which the evangelista disposed of at once."

"'Almost nothing.'"

"'You had better tell me, Tío Leporello, for, as an evangelista, you know that the reason why letters are written, is generally found in the postscript.'"

"'On leaving my office, the señorita made a sign to a *providencia* which was passing. The carriage stopped, and though the niña spoke in a very low voice, I heard her say to the driver, 'To the convent of the Bernardines.''"

"The sergeant gave an almost imperceptible start."

"'Hum!' he said, with an indifferent air, perfectly well assumed; 'that address does not mean much. Now give me the paper.'"

"The evangelista fumbled in his drawer, and drew from it a sheet of white paper, on which a few almost illegible words were written. So soon as the soldier had the paper in his hands he eagerly perused it; it appeared to have a great interest for him, for he turned visibly pale, and a convulsive tremor passed over his limbs; but he recovered himself almost immediately."

"'It is well,' he said, as he tore up the paper into imperceptible fragments; 'here's for you.'"

"And he threw a fresh handful of ounces on the table."

"'Thanks, caballero,' Tío Leporello exclaimed, as he bounded greedily on the precious metal."

"An ironical smile played round the soldier's lips, and, taking advantage of the old man's position, as he leant over the table to collect the gold, he raised his knife, and buried it to the hilt between the evangelista's shoulders. The blow was dealt so truly, and with such a firm hand, that the old man fell like a log, without uttering a sigh or giving a cry. The soldier regarded him for a moment coldly and apathetically, then, reassured by the immobility of his victim, whom he believed dead,—"

"'Come,' he muttered, 'that is all the better; at any rate, he will not speak in that way.'"

"After this philosophical funeral oration, the assassin tranquilly wiped his knife, picked up the gold, put out the candle, opened the door, closed it carefully after him, and walked off with the steady, though somewhat hasty step of a belated traveller hurrying to his home."

"The Plaza Mayor was deserted."

CHAPTER VII
A DARK HISIORY CONTINUED

"Ancient Mexico was traversed by canals, like Venice, or, to speak more correctly, like Dutch towns, for generally in all the streets there was a path between the canal and the houses. At the present day, when all the streets are paved, and the canals have disappeared save in one quarter of the city, it is difficult to understand how Cervantes, in one of his novels, could compare Venice with Mexico; but if the canals are no longer visible, they still exist underground; and in certain low quarters, where they have been converted into drains, they manifest their presence by the foetid odours which they exhale, or by the heaps of filth and stagnant water."

"The sergeant, after so skilfully settling accounts with the hapless evangelista, crossed the Plaza, and entered the Calle de la Monterilla."

"He walked for a long time along the streets with the same quiet step he had adopted on leaving the evangelista's stall. At length, after about twenty minutes' walk through deserted streets and gloomy lanes, whose miserable appearance became with every step more menacing, he stopped before a house of more than suspicious aspect, above the door of which a flaring candle burned behind *un retablo de las animas veneritas;* the windows of the house were lit up, and on the azotea the watchdogs were mournfully baying the moon. The sergeant tapped twice on the door of this sinister abode with his vine stick."

"It was a long time ere he was answered. The shouts and singing suddenly ceased in the inside: at length the soldier heard a heavy step approaching; the door was partly opened—for everywhere in Mexico an iron chain is put up at night—and a drunken voice said harshly,—"

"'*¿Quién es?* (Who's there?)'"

"'Gente de paz,' the sergeant answered."

"'Hum! it is very late to run about the *tuna* and enter the vilaio,' the other remarked, apparently reflecting."

"'I do not wish to enter.'"

"'Then what the deuce do you want?'"

"'*Pan y sal por los Caballeros errantes,*' [1] the sergeant answered, in a tone of authority, and placing himself so that the moonbeams should fall on his face."

"The man fell back, uttering an exclamation of surprise."

"'*¡Valga me Dios!* señor Don Torribio!' he exclaimed, with an accent of profound respect; 'who could have recognized your Excellency under that wretched dress? Come in! come in! they are waiting impatiently for you.'"

"And the man, who had become as obsequious as he had been insolent a few moments previously, hastened to undo the chain, and threw the door wide open."

"'It is unnecessary, Pepito,' the soldier continued, 'I repeat to you that I shall not come in. How many are there?'"

"'Twenty, Excellency.'"

"'Armed?'"

"'Completely.'"

"'Let them come down directly. I will wait for them here. Go, my son, time presses.'"

"'And you? Excellency,'"

"'You will bring me a hat, an esclavina, my sword and pistols. Come, make haste!'"

"Pepito did not let the order be repeated. Leaving the door open, he ran off. A few minutes after, some twenty bandits, armed to the teeth, rushed into the street, jostling one another. On coming up to the soldier, they saluted respectfully, and, at a sign from him, remained motionless and silent."

"Pepito had brought the articles demanded by the man whom the evangelista called Don Annibal, himself Don Torribio, and who, probably, had several other names, although we will keep temporarily to the latter."

"'Are the horses ready?' Don Torribio asked, as he concealed his uniform under the esclavina, and placed in his girdle a long rapier and a pair of double-barrelled pistols."

"'Yes, Excellency,' Pepito answered, hat in hand."

"'Good, my son. You will bring them to the spot I told you; but as it is forbidden to go about the streets on horseback by night, you will pay attention to the celadores and serenos.'"

"All the bandits burst into a laugh at this singular recommendation."

"'There,' Don Torribio continued, as he put on a broad brimmed hat, which Pepito had brought him with the other things, 'that is all right; we can now start. Listen to me attentively, Caballeros!'"

"The leperos and other scoundrels who composed the audience, flattered by being treated as caballeros, drew nearer to Don Torribio, in order to hear his instructions. The latter continued, — "

"'Twenty men, marching, in a troop, through the streets of the city would, doubtless, arouse the susceptibility and suspicions of the police agents; we must employ the greatest prudence, and, above all, the utmost secrecy in order to succeed in the expedition for which I have collected you. You will, therefore, separate, and go one by one under the walls of the convent of the Bernardines; on arriving there, you will conceal yourselves as well as you can, and not stir without my orders. Above all, no disputes, no quarrelling. You have understood me clearly?'"

"'Yes, Excellency,' the bandits answered, unanimously."

"'Very good. Be off, then, for you must reach the convent in a quarter of an hour.'"

"The bandits dispersed in every direction with the rapidity of a flock of buzzards. Two minutes later they had disappeared round the corners of the nearest streets. Pepito alone remained."

"'And I?' he respectfully asked Don Torribio. 'Do you not wish, Excellency, for me to accompany you? I should be very bored if I remained here alone.'"

"'I should be glad enough to take you with me; but who would get the horses ready if you went with me?'"

"'That is true. I did not think of it.'"

"'But do not be alarmed, Muchacho, if I succeed as I hope, you shall soon come with me.'"

"Pepito, completely reassured by this promise, bowed respectfully to the mysterious man, who seemed to be his chief, and re-entered his house, carefully closing the door after him."

"Don Torribio, when left alone, remained for several seconds plunged in deep thought. At length he raised his head, drew his hat over his eyes, carefully wrapped himself in his esclavina, and walked off hurriedly, muttering, 'Shall I succeed?'"

"A question which no one, not even himself, could have answered."

"The convent of the Bernardines stands in one of the handsomest quarters of Mexico, not far from the Paseo de Bernardo, the fashionable promenade. It is a vast edifice, built entirely of hewn stone, which dates from the rebuilding of the city after the conquest, and was founded by Fernando Cortez himself. Its general appearance is imposing and majestic, like all Spanish convents; it is almost a small city within a large one, for it contains all that can be agreeable and useful for life—a church, a hospital, a laundry, a large kitchen garden, and a well-laid out flower garden, which offers pleasant shade, reserved for the exercise of the nuns. There are wide cloisters, decorated with grand pictures by good masters, representing scenes in the life of the Virgin, and of St. Bernard, to whom the convent is dedicated; these cloisters, bordered by circular galleries, out of which the cells of the nuns open, enclose sandy courts, adorned with pieces of water, in which fountains refresh the air at the burning midday hour. The cells are charming retreats, in which nothing that can promote comfort is wanting: a bed; two butacas covered with prepared Cordovan leather, a *prie Dieu*, a small toilet table, in the drawer of which you are sure to find a looking-glass, and several holy pictures, occupy the principal space. In a corner of the room may be seen, between a guitar and a scourge, a statue of the Virgin, of wood or alabaster, wearing a coronal of white roses, before which a lamp is continually burning. Such is the furniture which, with but few exceptions, you are certain to find in the nuns' cells."

"The convent of the Bernardines contained, at the period when our story is laid, one hundred and fifty nuns, and about sixty novices. In this country of toleration, it is rare to see nuns cloistered. The sisters can go into town, pay and receive visits; the regulations are extremely mild, and, with the exception of the offices, at which they are bound to be present with great punctuality, the nuns, when they have entered their cells, are almost at liberty to do as they please, nobody taking the trouble, or seeming to do so, of watching them."

"We have described the convent cells, which are all alike; but that of the Mother Superior merits a particular description. Nothing could be more luxurious, more religious, and yet more worldly, than its general appearance. It was an immense square room, with large Gothic windows, with small panes set in lead, upon which sacred subjects were painted with admirable finish and admirable touch. The walls were covered with long, stamped, and gilded hangings of Cordovan leather, while valuable pictures, representing the principal events in the life of the patron saint of the convent, were arranged with that symmetry and taste only to be met with in people belonging to the Church. Between the pictures hung a magnificent Virgin, by Raphael, before which was an altar. A silver lamp, full of perfumed oil, hung from the ceiling, and burnt night and day before the altar, which thick damask curtains hid, when thought proper. The furniture consisted of a large Chinese screen, concealing the couch of the abbess, — a simple frame of carved oak, surrounded by white gauze mosquito curtains. A square table, also of oak, on which were a few books and a desk, occupied the centre of the room; in a corner a vast library, containing books on religious subjects, and displaying the rich bindings of rare and precious works through the glass doors, a few butacas and chairs, with twisted feet, were arranged against the wall. Lastly, a silver brazier, filled with olive kernels, stood opposite a superb coffer, the chasing of which was a masterpiece of the Renaissance."

"During the day, the light, filtered through the coloured glass, spread but a gentle and mystic radiance around, which caused the visitor to experience a feeling of respect and devotion, by giving this vast apartment a stern and almost mournful aspect."

"At the moment when we introduce the reader into this cell, that is to say, a few moments prior to the scene we have just described, the abbess was seated in a large straight-backed easy chair, which was surmounted by an abbatical crown, while the cushion of gilt leather was adorned with a double fringe of silk and gold."

"The abbess was a little, plump woman, of about sixty years of age, whose features would have appeared unmeaning, had it not been for the bright and piercing glance that shot, like a jet of lava, from her grey eyes, when a violent emotion agitated her. She held in her hand an open book, and seemed plunged in profound meditation."

"The door of the cell opened gently, and a girl, dressed in the novice's robe, advanced timidly, scarce grazing the floor with her light and hesitating foot. She stopped in front of the easy chair, and waited silently till the abbess raised her eyes to her."

"'Ah! it is you, my child,' the Mother Superior at length said, noticing the novice's presence; 'come hither.'"

"The latter advanced a few paces nearer."

"'Why did you go out this morning without asking my permission?'"

"On hearing these words, which the maiden, however, must have expected, she turned pale, and stammered a few unintelligible words."

"The abbess continued, in a stern voice: — "

"'Take care, Niña! although you are still a novice, and will not take the veil for several months, like all your companions, you are under my authority—mine alone.'"

"These words were spoken with an intonation which made the maiden tremble."

"'I Holy mother!' she murmured."

"'You were the intimate friend, almost the sister, of that young fool whom her resistance to our sovereign will snapped asunder like a reed, and who died this morning.'"

"'Do you really believe that she is dead, mother?' the girl answered timidly, and in a voice interrupted by grief."

"'Who doubts it?' the abbess exclaimed, violently, as she half rose in her chair, and fixed a viper's glance on the poor child."

"'No one, madam, no one,' she said, falling back with terror."

"'Were you not, like the other members of the community,' the abbess continued, with a terrible accent, 'present at her funeral? Did you not hear the prayers uttered over her coffin?'"

"'It is true, my mother!'"

"'Did you not see her body lowered into the convent vaults, and the tombstone laid over it, which the angel of divine justice can alone raise at the day of judgment? Say, were you not present at this sad and terrible ceremony? Would you dare to assert that this did not take place, and that the wretched creature still lives, whom God suddenly smote in his wrath, that she might serve as a warning to those whom Satan impels to revolt?'"

"'Pardon, holy mother, pardon! I saw what you say. I was present at Doña Laura's interment. Alas! doubt is no longer possible; she is really dead!'"

"While uttering the last words, the maiden could not restrain her tears, which flowed copiously. The abbess surveyed her with a suspicious air."

"'It is well,' she said; 'you can retire: but I repeat to you, take care; I know that a spirit of revolt has seized on your heart as well, and I shall watch you.'"

"The maiden bowed humbly to the Mother Superior, and moved as if to obey the order she had received."

"At this moment a terrible disturbance was heard. Cries of terror and threats reechoed in the corridor, and the hurried steps of a tumultuous crowd could be heard rapidly approaching."

"'What is the meaning of this?' the abbess asked with terror; 'What is this noise?'"

"She rose in agitation, and walked with tottering step toward the door of the cell, on which repeated blows were being struck."

"'Oh, heavens!' the novice murmured, as she turned a suppliant glance toward the statue of the Virgin, which seemed to smile on her; 'Have our liberators at length arrived?'"

"We will return to Don Torribio, whom we left walking with his companions toward the convent."

"As tad been arranged between himself and his accomplices, the young man found all the band collected under the convent walls. Along the streets the bandits, not to be disturbed by the serenos, had tied and gagged them and carried them off, as they met them, separately. Thanks to this skilful manoeuvre, they reached their destination without hindrance. Twelve serenos were captured in this way: and, on reaching the convent, Don Torribio gave orders for them to be laid one atop of the other at the foot of the wall."

"Then, drawing from his pocket a velvet mask, he covered his face with it (a precaution imitated by his comrades), and, approaching a wretched hut which stood a short distance off, he stove in the door with his shoulder. The owner rose up, frightened and half dressed, to inquire the meaning of this unusual mode of rapping at his door; but the poor fellow fell back with a cry of terror on perceiving the masked men assembled before his door. Don Torribio, being in a hurry, commenced the conversation by going straight to the subject matter:—'Buenas noches Tío Salado. I am delighted to see you in good health,' he said to him."

"The other answered, not knowing exactly what he said,—"

"'I thank you, Caballero. You are too kind.'"

"'Make haste! get your cloak, and come with us.'"

"'I?' Salado said, with a start of terror."

"'Yourself.'"

"'But how can I be of service to you?'"

"'I will tell you. I know that you are highly respected at the convent of the Bernardines—in the first place as a pulquero; and, secondly, as hombre de bien y religioso.'"

"'Oh! oh! to a certain extent,' the pulquero answered, evasively."

"'No false modesty. I know you have the power to get the gates of that house opened when you please; it is for that reason I invite you to accompany us.'"

"'*¡Maria Purísima!* What are you thinking of, Caballero' the poor fellow exclaimed, with terror."

"'No remarks! Make haste! or, by Nuestra señora del Carmen, I will burn your rookery.'"

"'A hollow groan issued from Salado's chest; but, after taking one despairing glance at the black masks that surrounded him, he prepared to obey. From the pulquería to the convent was only a few paces—they were soon passed, and Don Torribio turned to his prisoner, who was more dead than alive."

"'There, *compadre*,' he said, distinctly, 'we have arrived. It is now your place to get the door opened for us.'"

"'In heaven's name,' the pulquero exclaimed, making one last effort at resistance, 'how do you expect me to set about it? You forget that I have no means—'"

"'Listen,' Don Torribio said, imperiously; 'you understand that I have no time for discussion. You will either introduce us into the convent, and this purse, which contains fifty ounces, is yours; or you refuse, and in that case,' he added, coldly, as he drew a pistol from his girdle, 'I blow out your brains with this.'"

"A cold perspiration bedewed the pulquero's temples. He was too well acquainted with the bandits of his country to insult them for a moment by doubting their words."

"'Well!' the other asked, as he cocked the pistol, 'have you reflected?'"

"'*Cáspita*, Caballero! Do not play with that thing. I will try.'"

"'Here is the purse to sharpen your wits,' Don Torribio said."

"The pulquero clutched it with a movement of joy, any idea of which it is impossible to give; then he walked slowly towards the convent gate, while cudgelling his brains for some way in which to earn the sum he had received, without running any risk—a problem, we confess, of which it was not easy to find the solution."

[1] Literally "Bread and salt for the knight-errants."

CHAPTER VIII
A DARK HISTORY CONCLUDED

"The pulquero at length decided on obedience. Suddenly a luminous thought crossed his brain, and it was with a smile on his lips that he lifted the knocker. At the moment he was going to let it fall, Don Torribio caught his arm."

"'What is the matter?' Salado asked."

"'Eleven o'clock struck long ago; everybody must be asleep in the convent, so perhaps it would be better to try another plan.'"

"'You are mistaken, Caballero,' the pulquero answered; 'the portress is awake.'"

"'Are you sure of it?'"

"'Caramba!' the other answered, who had formed his plan, and was afraid he would be obliged to return the money, if his employé changed his mind. 'The convent of the Bernardines is open day and night to persons who come for medicines. Leave me to manage it.'"

"'Go on, then,' the chief of the band said, letting loose his arm."

"Salado did not allow the permission to be repeated, through fear of a fresh objection, and he hastened to let go the knocker, which resounded on a copper bolt. Don Torribio and his companions were crouching under the wall."

"In a moment the trapdoor was pushed back, and the wrinkled face of the portress appeared."

"'Who are you, my brother?' she asked, in a peevish, sleepy voice. 'Why do you come at this late hour to tap at the gates of the convent?'"

"'*Ave Maria purísima!*' Salado said, in his most nasal tone."

"'*Sin pecado concebida*, my brother,—are you ill?'"

"'I am a poor sinner, you know, sister; my soul is plunged in affliction.'"

"'Who are you, brother? I really believe that I can recognise your voice; but the night is so dark, that I am unable to distinguish your features.'"

"'And I sincerely trust you will not see them,' Salado said, mentally; then added, in a louder voice, 'I am Señor Templado, and keep a locanda in the Calle Plateros.'"

"'Ah! I remember you now, brother.'"

"'I fancy that is biting,' the pulquero muttered."

"'What do you desire, brother? Make haste to tell me, in the most holy name of your Saviour!' she said, crossing herself devotedly, a movement imitated by Salado; 'for the air is very cold, and I must continue my orisons, which you have interrupted.'"

"'Vulgo mi Dios! sister; my wife and two children are ill; the Reverend Pater Guardian, of the Franciscans, urged me to come and ask you for three bottles of your miraculous water.'"

"We will observe, parenthetically, that every convent manufactures in Mexico a so-called miraculous water, the receipt of which is carefully kept secret; this water, we were told, cures all maladies—a miracle which we were never in a position to test, for our part. We need hardly say, that this universal panacea is sold at a very high rate, and produces the best part of the community's revenue."

"'Maria!' the old woman exclaimed, her eyes sparkling with joy at the pulquero's large order. 'Three bottles!'"

"'Yes, sister. I will also ask your permission to rest myself a little; for I have come so quick, and the emotion produced by the illness of my wife and children has so crushed me, that I find it difficult to keep on my legs.'"

"'Poor man!' the portress said, with pity."

"'Oh! it would really be an act of charity, my sister.'"

"'Señor Templado, please look around you, to make sure there is no one in the street. We live in such wicked times, that a body cannot take enough precautions.'"

"'There is no one, my sister,' the pulquero answered, making the bandits a sign to get ready."

"'Then I will open.'"

"'Heaven will reward you, my sister.'"

"'Amen,' she said, piously."

"The noise of a key turned in a lock could be heard, then the rumbling of bolts, and the door opened."

"'Come in quickly, brother,' the nun said."

"But Salado had prudently withdrawn, and yielded his place to Don Torribio. The latter rushed at the portress, not giving her time to look round, seized her by the throat, and squeezed her windpipe as if his hand were a vice."

"'One word, sorceress,' he said to her, 'and I will kill you!'"

"Terrified by this sudden attack from a man whose face was covered by a black mask, the old woman fell back senseless."

"'Devil take the old witch!' Don Torribio exclaimed, passionately; 'Who will guide us now?'"

"He tried to restore the portress to her senses, but soon perceiving that he should not succeed, he made a sign to two of his men to tie and gag her securely; then, after recommending them to stand sentry at the door, he seized the bunch of keys entrusted to the nun, and began, followed by his comrades, to find his way into the building inhabited by the sisters. It was not an easy thing to discover, in this immense Thebaïd, the cell occupied by the abbess, for it was that lady alone whom Don Torribio wanted."

"Now, to converse with the abbess, she must first be found, and it was this that embarrassed the bandits, though masters of the place they had seized by stratagem. At the moment, however, when they began to lose all hopes, an incident, produced by their inopportune presence, came to their aid."

"The bandits had spread, like a torrent that had burst its dykes, through the courts and cloisters, not troubling themselves in the least as to the consequences their invasion might have for the convent; and, shouting and cursing like demons, they appeared to wish to leave no nook, however secret it might be, unvisited; but it is true that, in acting thus, they only obeyed the orders of their chief."

"The nuns, accustomed to calmness and silence, were soon aroused by this disturbance, which they, for a moment, believed occasioned by an earthquake; they rushed hurriedly from their beds, and, only half dressed, went, like a flock of frightened doves, to seek shelter in the cell of the abbess."

"The Mother Superior, sharing the error of her nuns, had succeeded in opening her door; and, collecting her flock around her, she walked toward the spot whence the noise came, leaning majestically on her abbatical cross."

"Suddenly she perceived a band of masked demons, yelling, howling, and brandishing weapons of every description. But, before she could utter a cry, Don Torribio rushed toward her. 'No noise!' he said. 'We do not wish to do you any harm; we have come, on the contrary, to repair that which you have done.'"

"Dumb with terror at the sight of so many masked men, the women stood as if petrified."

"'What do you want of me?' the Mother Superior stammered, in a trembling voice."

"'You shall know,' the Chief answered; and, turning to one of his men, he said, 'the sulphur matches.'"

"A bandit silently gave him what he asked for."

"'Now listen to me attentively, Señora. Yesterday, a novice belonging to your convent, who some days back refused to take the veil, died suddenly.'"

"The abbess looked around her with a commanding air, and then addressed the man who was speaking to her."

"'I do not know what you mean,' she replied boldly."

"'Very good! I expected that answer. I will go on; this novice, scarcely sixteen years of age, was Doña Laura de Acevedo del Real del Monte; she belonged to one of the first families in the Republic. This morning, her obsequies were performed, with all the ceremony employed on such occasions, in the church of this convent; her body was then lowered, with great pomp, into the vaults reserved for the burial of the nuns.'"

"He stopped, and fixed on the Mother Superior eyes that flashed through his mask like lightning."

"'I repeat to you that I do not know what you mean,' she replied coldly."

"'Ah, very good! Then listen to this, señora, and profit by it; for you have fallen, I swear it, into the hands of men who will show you no mercy, and will be moved neither by your tears nor your airs of grace, if you compel them to proceed to extremities.'"

"'You can do as you please,' the Mother Superior answered, still perfectly collected. 'I am in your hands. I know that for the moment, at least, I have no help to expect from any one; but Heaven will give me strength to suffer martyrdom.'"

"'Madam,' Don Torribio said with a grin, 'you are blaspheming, you are wittingly committing a deadly sin; but no matter, that is your business: this is mine. You will at once point out to me the entrance of the vault, and the spot where Doña Laura is reposing. I have sworn to carry off her body from here, no matter at what cost. I will fulfil my oath, whatever may happen. If you consent to what I ask, my companions and myself will retire, taking with us the body of the poor deceased, but not touching a pin of the immense riches the convent contains.'"

"'And if I refuse?' she said, angrily."

"'If you refuse,' he replied, laying a stress on each word, as if he wished the lady addressed fully to understand them, 'the convent will be sacked, these timid doves will become the prey of the demon.' He added, with a gesture which made the nuns quiver with terror. 'And I will apply to you a certain torture, which I do not doubt will loosen your tongue.'"

"The abbess smiled contemptuously."

"'Begin with me,' she said."

"'That is my intention. Come,' he added, in a rough voice, 'to work.'"

"Two men stepped forward, and seized the Mother Superior; but she made no attempt to defend herself. She remained motionless, seemingly apathetic; still an almost imperceptible contraction of her eyebrows evidenced the internal emotion she endured."

"'Is that your last word, señora?' Don Torribio inquired."

"'Do your duty, villains!' she replied, with disdain. 'Try to conquer the will of an old woman.'"

"'We are going to do so. Begin!' he ordered."

"The two bandits prepared to obey their chief."

"'Stay, in Heaven's name!' a maiden exclaimed, as she rushed bravely before the Mother Superior, and repulsed the bandits."

"It was the novice with whom the abbess was speaking at the moment the convent was invaded. There was a moment of breathless hesitation."

"'Be silent, I command you!' the abbess shrieked. 'Let me suffer. God sees us!'"

"'It is because He sees us that I will speak,' the maiden answered, peremptorily; 'it is He who has sent these men I do not know, to prevent a great crime. Follow me, Caballeros; you have not a moment to lose; I will lead you to the vaults.'"

"'Wretch!' the abbess cried, writhing furiously in the hands of the men who held her. 'Wretch! my wrath will fall on you.'"

"'I know it,' the maiden responded, sadly; 'but no personal consideration will prevent my accomplishing a sacred duty.'"

"'Gag that old wretch. We must finish our work,' the Chief commanded."

"The order was immediately executed. In spite of her desperate resistance, the Mother Superior was reduced to a state of impotence in a few moments."

"'One of you will guard her,' Don Torribio continued, 'and at the least suspicious sign blow out her brains,' Then, changing his tone, he addressed the novice, 'A thousand thanks, señorita! complete what you have so well begun, and guide us to these terrible vaults.'"

"'Come, Caballeros,' she answered, placing herself at their head."

"The bandits, who had suddenly become quiet, followed her in silence, with marks of the most profound respect. At a peremptory order from Don Torribio, the nuns, now reassured, had dispersed and returned to their cells."

"While crossing the corridor, Don Torribio went up to the girl, and whispered in her ear two or three words, which made her start."

"'Fear nothing,' he added. 'I but wished to prove to you that I knew all. I only desire, señorita, to be your most respectful and devoted friend.'"

"The maiden sighed, but made no reply."

"'What will become of you afterwards? Alone in this convent, exposed defencelessly to the hatred of this fury, who regards nothing as sacred, you will soon take the place of her we are about to deliver. Is it not better to follow her?'"

"'Alas, poor Laura!' she muttered, hoarsely."

"'Will you, who have done so much for her up to the present, abandon her at this supreme moment, when your assistance and support will become more than ever necessary to her? Are you not her foster sister? her dearest friend? What prevents? You! an orphan from your earliest youth, all your affections are concentrated on Laura. Answer me, Doña Luisa, I conjure you!'"

"The maiden gave a start of surprise, almost of terror."

"'You know me!' she said."

"'Have I not already said that I knew all? Come, my child, if not for your own sake, then for hers, accompany her. Do not compel me to leave you here in the hands of terrible enemies, who will inflict frightful tortures on you.'"

"'You wish it?' she stammered sadly."

"'She begs you by my lips.'"

"'Well, be it so; the sacrifice shall be complete. I will follow you, though I know not whether, in doing so, I am acting rightly or wrongly; but, although I do not know you, although a mask conceals your features, I have faith in your words. You seem to have a noble heart, and may heaven grant that I am not committing an error.'"

"'It is the God of goodness and mercy who inspires you with this resolution, poor child.'"

"Doña Luisa let her head sink on her breast as she breathed a sigh that resembled a sob."

"'They went onwards, side by side, without exchanging another word. The party had left the cloisters, and were now crossing some unfinished buildings, which did not seem to have been inhabited for many a long year."

"'Where are you leading us, then, Niña?' Don Torribio asked. 'I fancied that in this convent, as in others, the vaults were under the chapel.'"

"The maiden smiled sadly. 'I am not leading you to the vaults,' she answered, in a trembling voice."

"'Where to, then?'"

"'To the *in pace!*'"

"Don Torribio stifled an angry oath."

"'Oh!' he muttered."

"'The coffin that was lowered into the vaults this morning in the sight of all,' Doña Luisa continued, 'really contained the body of my poor Laura; it was impossible to do otherwise, owing to the custom which demands that the dead should be buried in their clothes, and with uncovered faces; but so soon as the crowd had departed, and the doors of the chapel were closed on the congregation, the Mother Superior had the tombstone removed again, the body brought up, and transferred to the deepest *in pace* of the convent. But here we are,' she said, as she stopped and pointed to a large stone in the paved floor of the apartment in which they were."

"The scene had something mournful and striking about it. In the deserted apartment the masked men were grouped around the maiden dressed in white, and only illumined by the ruddy glare of the torches they waved, bore a strange likeness to those mysterious judges who in old times met in ruins to try kings and emperors."

"'Raise the stone,' Don Torribio said, in a hollow voice."

"After a few efforts the stone was raised, leaving open a dark gulf, from which poured a blast of hot and foetid air. Don Torribio took a torch, and bent over the orifice."

"'Why,' he said, at the expiration of a moment, 'this vault is deserted.'"

"'Yes,' Doña Luisa answered, simply, 'she, whom you seek, is lower.'"

"'What! lower?' he cried, with a movement of terror, which he could not control."

"'That vault is not deep enough; an accident might cause a discovery; shrieks could be heard from outside. There are two other vaults like this, built above each other. When, through any reason, the abbess has resolved on the disappearance of a nun, and that she shall be cut off for ever from the number of the living, the victim is let down into the last cave, called *Hell!* There all noise dies away; every sob remains unechoed; every complaint is vain. Oh! the Inquisition managed matters well; and it is so short a time since its rule ended in Mexico, that some of its customs have been maintained in the convents. Seek lower, Caballero, seek lower!'"

"Don Torribio, at these words, felt a cold perspiration beading at the roots of his hair. He believed himself a prey to a horrible nightmare. Making a supreme effort to subdue the emotion that overpowered him, he went down into the vault by means of a light ladder leaning against one of the walls, and several of his comrades followed him. After some searching, they discovered a stone like the first. Don Torribio plunged a torch into the gulf."

"'Empty!' he exclaimed, in horror."

"'Lower, I tell you! Look lower,' Doña Luisa cried, in a gloomy voice, who had remained on the edge of the topmost vault."

"'What had this adorable creature done to them to endure such martyrdom?' Don Torribio exclaimed, in his despair."

"'Avarice and hatred are two terrible counsellors,' the maiden answered; 'but make haste! make haste! every moment that passes is an age for her who is waiting.'"

"Don Torribio, a prey to incredible fury, began seeking the last vault. After a few moments, his exertions were crowned with success. The stone was scarce lifted, ere, paying no attention to the mephitic air which rushed from the opening and almost extinguished his torch, he bent over."

"'I see her! I see her!' he said, with a cry more resembling a howl than a human voice."

"And, waiting no longer, without even calculating the height, he leaped into the vault. A few moments later he returned to the hall, bearing in his arms Doña Laura's inanimate body."

"'Away, friends, away!' he exclaimed, addressing his companions; 'let us not stay an instant longer in this den of wild beasts with human faces!'"

"At a sign from him, Doña Luisa was lifted in the arms of a sturdy lepero, and all ran off in the direction of the cloisters. They soon reached the cell of the Mother Superior. On seeing them, the abbess made a violent effort to break her bonds, and writhed impotently like a tiger, while flashing, at the men who had foiled her hideous projects, glances full of hatred and rage."

"'Wretch!' Don Torribio shouted, as he passed near her, and disdainfully spurned her with his foot; 'be accursed! your chastisement commences, for your victim escapes you.'"

"By one of those efforts which only hatred which has reached its paroxysm can render possible, the abbess succeeded in removing her gag slightly."

"Perhaps!' she yelled, in a voice which sounded like a knell in Don Torribio's ears."

"Overcome by this great effort, she fainted."

"Five minutes after, there was no one in the convent beyond its usual inmates."

CHAPTER IX
BRIGHTEYE AND MARKSMAN

At this point in his narrative Brighteye stopped, and began, with a thoughtful air, filling his Indian pipe with tobacco.

There was a lengthened silence. His auditors, still under the influence of this extraordinary influence, dared not venture any reflections. At length Marksman raised his head. "That story is very dramatic and very gloomy," he said, "but pardon my rude frankness, old and dear comrade, it seems to me to have no reference to what is going on around us, and the events in which we shall, probably, be called upon to be interested spectators, if not actors."

"In truth," Ruperto observed, "what do we wood rangers care for adventures that happen in Mexico, or any other city of the *Tierras Adentro*? We are here in the desert to hunt, trap, and thrash the Redskins. Any other question can affect us but slightly."

Brighteye tossed his head in a significant manner, and laid his pipe mechanically by his side.

"You are mistaken, comrades," he continued; "do you believe, then, that I should have made you waste your time in listening to this long story, if it did not possess an important reality for us?"

"Explain yourself, then, my friend," Marksman observed, "for I honestly confess that, for my part, I have understood nothing of what you have been good enough to tell us."

The old Canadian raised his head, and seemed, for a few moments, to be calculating the sun's height. "It is half past six," he said; "you have still more than sufficient time to reach the ford of the Rubio, where the man is to wait, to whom you have engaged yourself as guide. Listen to me, therefore, for I have not quite finished. Now that I have told you the mystery, you must learn what has come out to clear it up."

"Speak!" Marksman replied, in the tone of a man who is resolved to listen through politeness to a story which he knows cannot interest him.

Brighteye, not seeming to remark his friend's apathetic condescension, went on in the following terms:—"You have remarked that Don Torribio provided for everything with a degree of prudence which must keep off any suspicion, and cover this adventure with an impenetrable veil. Unfortunately for him, the evangelista was not killed. He could not only speak, but show a copy of each of the letters he daily handed to the young man—letters which the latter paid so dearly for, and which, with that prudence innate in the Mexican race, he had previously guarded, to employ, if needed, as a weapon against Don Torribio; or, as was more probable, to avenge himself if he fell a victim to any treachery. This was what happened:—The evangelista, found in a dying state by an early customer, had strength enough to make a regular declaration to the Juez de Lettras, and hand him the letters ere he died. This assassination, taken in connection with the attack on the serenos by a numerous band, and the invasion of the Convent of the Bernardines, furnished a clue which the police begun following with extreme tenacity; especially as the young lady whose body had been so audaciously carried off had powerful relations, who, for certain reasons known to themselves, would not let this crime pass unpunished, and spent their gold profusely. It was soon learned that the bandits, on leaving the convent, mounted horses brought by their confidants, and started at full speed in the direction of the Presidios. The police even succeeded in discovering one of the men who supplied the horses. This individual, Pepito by name, bought over by the money offered him, rather than frightened by threats, stated that he had sold to Don Torribio Carvajal twenty-five post horses, to be delivered at the Convent of the Bernardines at two o'clock in the morning. As these horses were paid for in advance, he, Pepito, did not trouble himself at all about the singularity of the spot, or of the hour. Don Torribio and his companions had arrived, bearing with them two women, one of whom appeared to have fainted, and immediately galloped off. The trail of the ravishers was then followed to the Presidio de Tubar, where Don Torribio allowed his party to rest for several days. There he purchased a close palanquin, a field tent, and all the provisions necessary for a lengthened journey in the desert, and one night suddenly disappeared, with all his band, which was augmented by all the adventurers he could pick up at the Presidio, no one being able to say in what direction he had gone. This information, though vague, was sufficient up to a certain point, and the relations of the young lady were continuing their search."

"I fancy I am beginning to see what you want to arrive at," Marksman interrupted him; "but conclude your story; when you have finished, I will make sundry observations, whose justice you will recognize, I am sure."

"I shall be delighted to hear them," Brighteye said, and went on:—"A man who, twenty years ago, did me a rather important service, whom I had not seen since, and whom I should assuredly not have recognized, had he not told me his name — the only thing I had not forgotten — came to me and my partner Ruperto, while we were at the Presidio de Tubar, selling a few panther and tiger skins. This man told me what I have just repeated to you: he added that he was a near relation of the young lady, reminded me of the service he had rendered me — in a word, he affected me so greatly, that I agreed to take vengeance on his enemy. Two days later we took up the trail. For a man like myself, accustomed to follow Indians' signs, it was child's play and I soon led him almost into the Spanish caravan commanded by Don Miguel Ortega."

"The other was called Don Torribio Carvajal."

"Could he not have changed his name?"

"For what good in the desert?"

"In the consciousness that he would be pursued."

"Then the relatives had a great interest in this pursuit?"

"Don José told me he was the young lady's uncle, and felt a paternal tenderness for her."

"But I fancy she is dead, or at least you told me so, if I am not mistaken."

Brighteye scratched his ear. "That is the awkward part of the affair," he said; "it seems she is not dead at all; on the contrary."

"What!" Marksman exclaimed; "she is not dead! That uncle knows it, then; it was by his consent that the poor creature was buried alive! But, if that is the case, there must be some odious machination in the business."

"On my word, if I must confess it, I fear so too," the Canadian said, in a hesitating voice. "Still, this man rendered me a great service. I have no proof in support of my suspicions, and— —"

Marksman rose, and stood in front of the old hunter. "Brighteye," he said to him, sternly; "we are fellow countrymen; we love each other like brothers; for many long years we have slept side by side on the prairie, sharing good fortune and ill between us, saving each other's lives a hundred times, either in our struggles with wild beasts, or our fights with the Indians — is it so?"

"It is true, Marksman, it is true, and anyone who said the contrary would lie," the hunter replied with emotion.

"My friend, my brother, a great crime has been committed, or is on the point of being committed. Let us watch — watch carefully; who knows if we may not be the instruments chosen by Providence to unmask the guilty, and cause the innocent to triumph? This Don José, you say, wishes me to join you; well, I accept. Yourself, Ruperto, and I, will go to the ford of the Rubio, and, believe me, my friend, now that I am warned, I will discover the guilty party, whoever he may be."

"I prefer things to be so," the hunter answered, simply. "I confess that the strange position in which I found myself weighed heavily upon me. I am only a poor hunter, and do not at all understand these infamies of the cities."

"You are an honest man, whose heart is just and mind upright. But time is slipping away. Now that we are agreed as to our parts, and understand one another, I believe we shall do well by starting."

"I will go whenever you please."

"One moment. Can you do without Ruperto for a little while?"

"Yes."

"What's the matter?" the latter asked.

"You can do me a service."

"Speak, Marksman, I am waiting."

"No man can foresee the future. Perhaps, in a few days we shall need allies on whom we may be able to count. These allies the Chief here present will give us whenever we ask for them. Accompany him to his village, Ruperto: and, so soon as he has arrived there, leave him, and take up our trail—not positively joining us, but managing so that, if necessary, we should know where to find you."

"I have understood," the hunter said, laconically, as he rose. "All right."

Marksman turned to Flying Eagle, and explained what he wanted of him.

"My brother saved Eglantine," the Chief answered, nobly; "Flying Eagle is a sachem of his tribe. Two hundred warriors will follow the warpath at the first signal from my father. The Comanches are men; the words they utter come from the heart."

"Thanks, Chief," Marksman answered, warmly pressing the hand the Redskin extended to him; "may the Wacondah watch over you during your journey!"

After hastily eating a slice of venison cooked on the ashes, and drinking a draught of pulque—from which, after the custom of his nation, the only one which does not drink strong liquors, the Comanche declined to take a share—the four men separated; Ruperto, Flying Eagle, and Eglantine going into the prairie in a western direction; while Brighteye and Marksman, bending slightly to the left, proceeded in an easterly course, in order to reach the ford of the Rubio, where the latter was expected.

"Hum!" Brighteye observed, as he threw his rifle on to his left arm, and starting with that elastic step peculiar to the wood rangers; "we have some tough work cut out for us."

"Who knows, my friend?" Marksman answered, anxiously. "At any rate, we must discover the truth."

"That is my opinion, too."

"There is one thing I want to know, above all."

"What is it?"

"What Don Miguel's carefully-closed palanquin contains."

"Why, hang it! a woman, of course."

"Who told you so?"

"Nobody; but I presume so."

"Prejudge nothing, my friend; with time, all will be cleared up."

"God grant it!"

"He sees everything, and knows everything, my friend. Believe me, that if it hath pleased Him to set those suspicions growing in our hearts that trouble us now, it is because, as I told you a moment ago, He wishes to make us the instruments of His justice."

"May His will be done!" Brighteye answered, raising his cap piously. "I am ready to obey Him in all that He may order me."

After this mutual exchange of thoughts, the hunters, who till this moment had walked side by side, proceeded in Indian file, in consequence of the difficult nature of the ground. On reaching the tall grass, after emerging from the forest, they stopped a moment to look around.

"It is late," Marksman observed.

"Yes, it is nearly midday. Follow me, we shall soon catch up lost time."

"How so?"

"Instead of walking, would you not be inclined to ride?"

"Yes, if we had horses."

"That is just what I am going to procure."

"You have horses?"

"Last night Ruperto and I left our horses close by here, while going to the meeting Don José had made with us, and in which I was obliged to employ a canoe."

"Eh! eh! those brave beasts turn up at a lucky moment. For my part, I am worn out. I have been walking for many a long day over the prairie, and my legs are beginning to refuse to carry me."

"Come this way, we shall soon see them."

In fact, the hunters had not walked one hundred yards in the direction indicated by Brighteye, ere they found the horses quietly engaged in nibbling the pea vines and young tree shoots. The noble animals, on hearing a whistle, raised their intelligent heads, and hastened toward the hunters with a neigh of pleasure. According to the usual fashion in the prairies, they were saddled, but their *bozal* was hung round their necks. The hunters bridled them, leapt on their backs, and started again.

"Now that we have each a good horse between our legs we are certain of arriving in time," Marksman observed; "hence, it is useless to hurry on, and we can talk at our ease. Tell me, Brighteye, have you seen Don Miguel Ortega yet?"

"Never, I allow."

"Then you do not know him?"

"If I may believe Don José, he is a villain. For my own part, never having had any relations with him, I should be considerably troubled to form any opinion, bad or good, about him."

"With me it is different. I know him."

"Ah!"

"Very well indeed."

"For any length of time?"

"Long enough, I believe, at any rate to enable me to form an opinion about him."

"Ah! Well, what do you think of him?"

"Much good and much bad."

"Hang it? ah!"

"Why are you surprised? Are not all men in the same case?"

"Nearly so, I grant."

"This man is no worse or no better than the rest. This morning, as I foresaw that you were about to speak to me about him, I wished to leave you liberty of action by telling you that I was only slightly acquainted with him; but it is possible that your opinion will soon be greatly modified, and, perhaps, you will regret the support you have hitherto given Don José, as you call him."

"Would you like me to speak candidly, Marksman, now that no one, but He above, can hear us?"

"Do so, my friend. I should not be sorry to know your whole thoughts."

"I am certain that you know a great deal more about the story I told you last night than you pretend to do."

"Perhaps you are right; but what makes you think so?"

"Many things; and in the first place this."

"Go on."

"You are too sensible a man. You have acquired too great an experience of the things of this world, to undertake, without serious cause, the defence of a man who, according to the principles we profess on the prairie, you ought to regard, if not as an enemy, still as one of those men whom it is often disagreeable to come in contact, or have any relations with."

Marksman burst into a laugh. "There is truth in what you say, Brighteye," he at length remarked.

"Is there not?"

"I will not attempt to play at cunning with you; but I have powerful reasons for undertaking the defence of this man, but I cannot tell you them at this moment. It is a secret which does not belong to me, and of which I am only the depositary. I trust you will soon know all; but, till then, rely on my old friendship, and leave me to act in any way."

"Very good! At any rate, I am now beginning to see clearly, and, whatever may happen, you can reckon upon me."

"By Jove! I felt certain we should end by understanding one another; but, silence, and let nothing be seen. We are at the meeting place. Hang it! the Mexicans have not kept us waiting. They have already pitched their camp on the other side of the river."

In fact, a hunter's camp could be seen a short distance off, one side resting on the river, the other on the forest, and presenting perfectly fortified outworks, with the front turned to the prairies, and composed of bales and trees stoutly interlaced.

The two hunters made themselves known to the sentries, and entered without any difficulty. Don Miguel was absent; but the Gambusinos expected him at any moment. The hunters dismounted, hobbled their horses, and sat down quietly by the fire.

Don Stefano Cohecho had left the Gambusinos at daybreak, as he had announced on the previous evening.

CHAPTER X
FRESH CHARACTERS

In order to a right comprehension of ensuing facts, we will take advantage of our privilege as story tellers, to go back a fortnight, and allow the reader to be witness of a scene intimately connected with the most important events of this history, and which took place a few hundred miles from the spot where accident had collected our principal characters.

The Cordillera of the Andes, that immense spine of the American continent, the whole length of which it traverses under different names from north to south, forms, at various elevations, immense *llanos*, on which entire people live at a height at which all vegetation ceases in Europe.

After crossing the Presidio de Tubar, the advanced post of civilization on the extreme limit of the desert, and advancing into the mediano region of the *tierra caliente* for about one hundred and twenty miles, the traveller finds himself suddenly, and without any transition, in front of a virgin forest, which is no less than three hundred and twenty miles deep, by eighty odd miles wide.

The most practised pen is powerless to describe the marvels innumerable inclosed in that inexhaustible network of vegetation called a virgin forest, and the sight, at once strange and peculiar, majestic and imposing, which it offers to the dazzled sight. The most powerful imagination recoils before this prodigious fecundity of elementary nature, continually springing up again from its own destruction with a strength and vigour ever new. The creepers, which run from tree to tree, from branch to branch, plunge, at one moment, into the earth, and then rise once more to the sky, and form, by their interlacing and crossing, an almost insurmountable barrier, as if jealous nature wished to hide from profane eyes the mysterious secrets of these forests, beneath whose shade man's footsteps have only reached at long intervals, and never unpunished. Trees of every age and species grow without order or symmetry, as if sown by chance, like wheat in the furrows. Some, tall and slight, count only a few years; the extremities of their branches are covered by the tall and wide boughs of those whose haughty heads have seen centuries pass over them. Beneath their foliage softly murmur pure and limpid streams, which escape from the fissures of the rocks, and, after a thousand meanderings, are lost in some lake or unknown river, whose bright waters had never reflected aught in their clear mirror save the sublime secrets of the solitude. There may be found, pell-mell and in picturesque confusion, all the magnificent productions of tropical regions:—The acajou, the ebony, the palisander; the stunted mahogany; the black oak; the cork; the maple; the mimosa, with its silvery foliage; and the tamarind, thrusting in every direction their branches, laden with, flowers, fruits, and leaves, which form a dome impenetrable to the sunbeams. From the vast and unexplored depths of these forests emerge, from time to time, inexplicable noises—furious howls, feline miauls, mocking yells, mingled with shrill whistling or the joyous and harmonious song of the birds.

After plunging boldly into the centre of this chaos, and struggling hand to hand with this uncultivated and wild nature, the traveller succeeds, with axe in one hand and torch in the other, in gaining, inch by inch, step by step, a road impossible to describe. At one moment, by crawling like a reptile over the decaying leaves, dead wood, or guano, piled up for centuries; or by leaping from branch to branch, at the tops of the trees, standing, as it were, in the air. But woe to the man who neglects to have his eye constantly open to all that surrounds him, and his ear on the watch: for, in addition to the obstacles caused by nature, he has to fear the venomous stings of the serpents startled in their lairs, and the furious attacks of the wild beasts. He must also carefully watch the course of the rivers and streams he meets with, determine the position of the sun during the day, or guide himself at night by the Southern Cross; for, once astray in a virgin forest, it is impossible to get out of it—it is a maze, from which no Ariadne's web would help to find the issue.

At last the traveller, after he has succeeded in surmounting the dangers we have describe, and a thousand others no less terrible, which we have passed over in silence, emerges on an immense plain, in the centre of which stands an Indian city. That is to say, he finds himself before one of those mysterious cities into which no European has yet penetrated, whose exact position even is unknown, and which, since the conquest, have served as an asylum for the last relics of Aztec civilization.

The fabulous accounts given by some travellers about the incalculable wealth buried in these cities, has inflamed the covetousness and avarice of a great number of adventurers, who, at various periods, have attempted to find the lost road to these queens of the Mexican prairies and savannahs. Others again, only impelled by the irresistible attraction extraordinary enterprises offer to vagabond imaginations, have also, especially during the last fifty years, set out in search of these Indian cities, though up to the present time success has never crowned these various expeditions.

Some have returned disenchanted, and half killed by this journey toward the unknown; a considerable number have left their bodies at the foot of precipices or in the quebradas, to serve as food for birds of prey; while others, more unfortunate still, have disappeared without leaving a trace, and no one has ever heard what has become of them.

Owing to events, too long to narrate here, but which we shall describe some day, we have lived, against our will, in one of these impenetrable cities, though, more fortunate than our predecessors, whose whitened bones we saw scattered along the road, we succeeded in escaping from it, through dangers innumerable, all miraculously avoided. The description we are about to give, then, is scrupulously exact, and cannot be doubted, for we write from personal observation.

Quiepaa Tani, the city which presents itself to the traveller's sight after leaving the virgin forest, of which we have given a sketch, extends from east to west, and forms a parallelogram. A wide stream, over which several bridges of incredible lightness and elegance are thrown, runs through its entire length. At each corner of the square an enormous block of rock cut perpendicularly on the side that faces the plains, serves as an almost impregnable fortress; these four citadels are also connected by a wall twenty feet thick, and forty feet high, which, inside the city, forms a slope sixty feet wide at the base. This wall is built of native bricks, made of sandy earth and chopped straw; they are called *adobes*, and are about a yard long. A wide and deep fosse almost doubles the height of the walls. Two gates alone give access to the city. These gates are flanked by towers and pepper boxes, exactly like a mediaeval fortress; and, what adds to the correctness of our comparison, a small bridge, made of planks, extremely narrow and light, and so arranged as to be carried away on the slightest alarm, is the only communication between these gates and the exterior.

The houses are low, and terminate in terraces, connected with each other; they are slight, and built of wicker and canaverales covered with cement, in consequence of the earthquakes so frequent in these regions; but they are large, airy, and pierced with numerous windows. None of them are more than one story in height, and the fronts are covered with a varnish of dazzling whiteness.

This strange city, seen from a distance, as it rises in the midst of the tall prairie grass, offers the most singular and seductive sight.

On a fine evening in the month of October, five travellers, whose features or dress it would have been impossible to distinguish, owing to the obscurity, came out of the forest we have described above, stopped for a moment, with marked indecision, on the extreme edge of the wood, and began examining the ground. Before them rose a hillock, which, if no great height, yet cut the horizon at right angles.

After exchanging a few words, two of these persons remained where they were; the other three lay down on their faces, and, crawling on their hands and feet, advanced through the rank grass, which they caused to undulate, and which completely concealed their bodies. On reaching the top of the mound, which they had found such difficulty in scaling, they looked out into the country, and remained struck with astonishment and admiration.

The eminence, at the top of which they were, was perpendicular on the other side, like all the rest of the ground which extended on either side. A magnificent plain lay expanded a hundred feet below them, and in the centre of the plain, at a distance of about a thousand yards from them, stood, proud and imposing, Quiepaa Tani,[1] the mysterious city, defended by its massive towers and thick walls. The sight of this vast city in the midst of the desert produced on the minds of the three men a feeling of stupor, which they could not explain, and which for a few moments rendered them dumb with surprise. At length one of them rose on his elbow, and addressed his comrades.

"Are my brothers satisfied?" he said, with a guttural accent, which, though he expressed himself in Spanish, proved him to be an Indian. "Has Addick (the Stag) kept his promise?"

"Addick is one of the first warriors of his tribe; his tongue is straight, and the blood flows clearly in his veins," one of the men he addressed, answered.

The Indian smiled silently, without replying;—this smile would have given his companions much matter for thought, had they seen it.

"It seems to me," the one who had not yet spoken said, "that it is very late to enter the city."

"Tomorrow, at sunrise, Addick will lead the two Paleface maidens to Quiepaa Tani," the Indian answered; "the night is too dark."

"The warrior is right," the second speaker remarked, "we must put off the affair till tomorrow."

"Yes, let us return to our friends, whom a longer absence may alarm."

Joining deeds to words, the first speaker turned round, and, exactly following the track his body had left in the grass, he soon found himself, as well as his companions, who imitated all his movements, at the skirt of the forest, into which, after their departure, the two persons they left behind had returned.

The silence which reigns beneath these gloomy roofs of foliage and branches during the day, had been succeeded by the dull sounds of a wild concert, formed by the shrill cries of the night birds, which woke, and prepared to attack the loros, humming birds, and cardinals, belated far from their nests; the roaring of the cougars; the hypocritical miauling of the jaguars and panthers, and the snappish barks of the coyotes, which reechoed, with a mournful sound, from the roofs of the inaccessible caverns and gaping pits which served as lurking places for these dangerous guests.

Returning on the trail they had traced with their axes, the three men soon found themselves near a fire of dead wood, burning in the centre of a small clearing. Two women, or rather girls, were crouching, pensive and sad, by the fire. They counted scarce thirty years between them; they were lovely, and of that creole beauty which the divine pencil of a Raphael has been alone able to reproduce. But at this moment they were pale, seemed fatigued, and their faces reflected a gloomy sorrow; At the sound of the approaching steps they raised their eyes, and a flash of joy illumined their faces like a sunbeam.

The Indian threw some sticks on the fire, which was threatening to go out, while one of the hunters occupied himself with giving their provender to the horses, hobbled a short distance off.

"Well, Don Miguel," one of the ladies said, addressing the hunter who had taken a seat by her side, "shall we soon near the end of our journey?"

"You have arrived, señorita; tomorrow, under the guidance of our friend Addick, you will enter the city, that inviolable asylum, where no one will pursue you."

"Ah!" she continued, looking absently at the Indian's gloomy and apathetic face; "we shall separate tomorrow."

"We must, señorita; the care for your safety demands it."

"Who would dare to seek me in these unknown districts?"

"Hatred dares everything. I implore you, señorita, to put faith in my experience; my devotion to you is unbounded. Though still very young, you have suffered enough, and it is time that a blessed sunbeam should brighten your dreary brow, and dispel the clouds which thought and grief have been so long collecting on it."

"Alas!" she said, as she let her head droop, to hide the tears that ran down her cheeks.

"My sister, my friend, my Laura!" the other maiden said, embracing her tenderly, "be courageous to the end. Shall I not be with you? Oh, fear nothing!" she added, with a charming expression. "I will take half your grief on myself, and your burthen will seem less heavy."

"Poor Luisa!" the maiden murmured, as she returned her caresses. "You are unhappy through me. How shall I ever be able to repay your devotion?"

"By loving me, as I love you, cherished angel, and by regaining hope."

"Before a month, I trust," Don Miguel said, "your persecutors will be prevented from troubling you again. I am playing a terrible game with them, in which my head is the stake; but I care little, so long as I save you. On leaving you, permit me to take with me, in my heart, the hope that you will in no way attempt to leave the refuge I have found for you, and that you will patiently await my return."

"Alas, Caballero! you are aware that I live only by a miracle; my relatives, my friends, indeed, all those I loved, have abandoned me, except my Luisa, my foster sister, whose devotion to me has never swerved; and you, whom I do not know, whom I never saw, and who suddenly revealed yourself to me in my tomb, like the angel of divine justice; since that terrible night, when, thanks to you, I emerged from my sepulchre, like Lazarus, you have shown me the kindest and most delicate attentions; you have taken the place of those who betrayed me; you have been to me more than a father."

"Señorita!" said the young man, at once confused and happy at these words.

"I say this to you, Don Miguel," she continued, with a certain feverish animation, "because I am anxious to prove to you that I am not ungrateful. I know not what God, in His wisdom, may do with me; but I tell you, that my last thought, my last prayer will be for you. You wish me to await you; I will obey you. Believe me, I only dispute my life through a certain feeling of anxiety, like the gambler at his last stake," she added, with a heartbreaking smile; "but I understand how much you need liberty of action for the rude game you have undertaken. Hence, you can go in peace; I have faith in you."

"Thanks, señorita; this promise doubles my strength. Oh, now I am certain of success!"

A rude jacal of branches had been prepared for the maidens by the other hunters and the Indian warrior, and they retired to rest.

Although the young man's mind was so full of restless alarms, after a few moments of deep thought he laid himself down by the side of his companions, and soon fell asleep. In the desert nature never surrenders its claims, and the greatest grief rarely succeeds in gaining the victory over the material claims of the human organization.

Scarce had the first sunbeams begun to tinge the sky of an opal hue, ere the hunters opened their eyes. The preparations for starting were soon completed; the moment of separation arrived, and the parting was a sad one. The two hunters had accompanied the maidens to the edge of the forest, in order to remain longer with them.

Doña Luisa, taking advantage of an instant when the road became so narrow that it became almost impossible for two to walk side by side, drew nearer Don Miguel's hunting companion.

"Do me a service," she whispered, hurriedly.

"Speak," he answered, in the same key.

"That Indian inspires me with but slight confidence."

"You are wrong; I know him."

She shook her head petulantly. "That is possible," she said; "but will you do me the service I want of you?—if not, I will ask Don Miguel, though I should have preferred him not knowing it."

"Speak, I tell you."

"Give me a knife and your pistols."

The hunter looked her in the face. "Good!" he said presently. "You are a brave child. Here is what you ask for." And, without anyone noticing it, he gave the objects she wished to obtain from him, adding to them two little pouches, one of gunpowder, the other of bullets.

"No one knows what may happen," he said.

"Thanks," she answered, with a movement of joy she could not master.

This was all that she said; and the weapons disappeared under her clothes, with a speed and resolution which made the hunter smile. Five minutes after, they reached the skirt of the virgin forest.

"Addick," the hunter said laconically; "remember that you will answer to me for these two women."

"Addick has sworn it," the Indian merely replied. They separated; it was impossible to remain longer at the spot where they were, without running the risk of being discovered by the Indians. The maidens and the warrior proceeded toward the city.

"Let us mount the hill," Don Miguel said, "in order to see them for the last time."

"I was going to propose it," the hunter said, simply.

They went, with similar precautions, to the spot they had occupied for a few moments on the previous evening.

In the brilliant beams of the sun, which had gloriously risen, the verdurous landscape had assumed, a truly enchanting aspect. Nature was aroused from her sleep, and a most varied spectacle had been substituted for the gloomy and solitary view of the previous night. From the gates of the city, which were now widely opened, emerged groups of Indians on horseback and on foot, who dispersed in all directions with shouts of joy and shriller bursts of laughter. Numerous canoes traversed the stream, the fields were populated with flocks of vicunas, and horses led by Indians, armed with long goads, who were proceeding toward the city. Women quaintly attired, and bearing on their heads long wicker baskets filled with meat, fruit, and vegetables, walked along conversing together, and accompanying each phrase with that continual, sharp, and metallic laugh, of which the Indian nation possess the secret, and the noise of which resembles very closely that produced by the full of a quantity of pebbles on a copper dish.

The maidens and their guide were soon mixed up in this motley crowd, in the midst of which they disappeared. Don Miguel sighed.

"Let us go," he said in a deep voice.

They returned to the forest. A few moments later, they set out again.

"We must separate," Don Miguel said when they had crossed the forest; "I shall return to Tubar."

"And I am going to try to render a small service to an Indian chief, a friend of mine."

"You are always thinking of others, and never of yourself, my worthy Marksman; you are ever anxious to be of use to someone."

"What would you have, Don Miguel? It seems to be my mission—you know that every man has one."

"Yes!" the young man answered in a hollow voice. "Good-bye!" he added presently, "do not forget our meeting."

"All right! In a fortnight, at the ford of the Rubio; that is settled."

"Forgive me my chariness of speech during the few days we have spent together; the secret is not mine alone, Marksman; I am not at liberty to divulge it, even to so kind a friend as yourself."

"Keep your secret, my friend; I am in no way curious to know it; still, it is understood that we do not know one another."

"Yes; that is very important."

"Then, good-bye."

"Good-bye!"

The two horsemen shook hands, one turned to the right, the other to the left, and they set off at full speed.

[1] Literally, *Quiepaa*, sky, *tani*, mountain, in the Zapothecan language.

CHAPTER XI
THE FORD OF THE RUBIO

The night was gloomy, not a star shone in the sky; the wind blew violently through the heavy boughs of the virgin forest, with that sad and monotonous soughing which resembles the sound of great waters when the tempest menaces; the clouds were low, black, and charged with electricity; they coursed rapidly through the sky, incessantly veiling the wan disk of the moon, whose cold rays only rendered the gloom denser; the atmosphere was oppressive, and those nameless noises, dashed back by the echoes like the rolling of distant thunder, rose from the quebradas and unknown barrancas of the prairies; the beasts howled sadly all the notes of the human register, and the night birds, troubled in their sleep by this strange uneasiness of nature, uttered hoarse and discordant cries.

In the camp of the Gambusinos all was calm; the sentries were watching, leaning on their rifles, and crouching near the expiring fire. In the centre of the camp two men were smoking their Indian pipes, and talking in a low voice. They were Brighteye and Marksman.

At length, Brighteye knocked the ashes out of his pipe, thrust it into his girdle, stifled a yawn, and rose, throwing out his legs and arms to restore the circulation.

"What are you going to do?" Marksman asked him, turning cautiously round.

"Sleep," the hunter answered.

"Sleep!"

"Why not? the night is advanced; we are the only persons watching, I feel convinced; it is more than probable that we shall not see Don Miguel before sunrise. Hum! the best plan for the moment, at least, is to sleep, at any rate, if you have not decided otherwise."

Marksman laid his finger on his lip, as if to recommend silence to his friend.

"The night is advanced," he said, in a low voice; "a terrible storm is rising. Where can Don Miguel be gone? This prolonged absence alarms me more than I can express: he is not the man to leave his friends thus, without some powerful reason, or perhaps—"

The hunter stopped, and shook his head sorrowfully.

"Go on," Brighteye said; "tell me your whole thought."

"Well, I am afraid lest some misfortune has happened to him."

"Oh, oh, do you think so? Still, this Don Miguel, from what I have heard you say, is a man of well-tried courage and uncommon strength."

"All that is true," Marksman replied, with a preoccupied air.

"Well! do you think that such a man, well armed, and acquainted with prairie life, is not able to draw himself out of a difficulty, whatever the danger which threatens him?"

"Yes, if he has to deal with a loyal foe, who stands resolutely before him, and fights with equal weapons."

"What other danger can he fear?"

"Brighteye, Brighteye!" the hunter continued, sadly, "you have lived too long among the Missouri fur traders."

"Which means—?" the Canadian asked, somewhat piqued.

"Come, my friend, do not feel vexed at my remarks; but it is evident to me, that you have, in a great measure, forgotten prairie habits."

"Hum! that is a serious charge against a hunter, Marksman; and in what, if you please, have I forgotten desert manners?"

"By Jove! in seeming no longer to remember that, in the country where we now are, every weapon is good to get rid of an enemy."

"Eh! I know that as well as you, my friend; I know, too, that the most dangerous weapon is that which is concealed."

"That is to say, treachery."

The Canadian started. "Do you fear treachery, then?" he asked.

"What else can I fear?"

"That is true," the hunter said, with a drooping head; "but," he added, a moment after, "what is to be done?"

"That is the very thing that embarrasses me. Still I cannot remain much longer in this state; the uncertainty is killing me; at all risks I must know what has happened."

"But in what way?"

"I know not, Heaven will inspire me."

"Still, you have an idea?"

"Of course, I have."

"What is it?"

"This—and I count on you to help me in carrying it out."

Brighteye affectionately pressed his friend's hand. "You are right," he said: "now for your idea."

"It is very simple; we will leave the camp directly, and go along the river side."

"Yes,—I would merely draw your attention to the fact, that the storm will soon break out, and the rain is already falling in large drops."

"The greater reason to make haste."

"That is true."

"Then you will accompany me?"

"By Jove! did you doubt it, perchance?"

"I am a goose; forgive me, brother, and thank you."

"Why so? on the contrary, I ought to thank you."

"How so?"

"Why, thanks to you, I am going to take a delightful walk."

Marksman did not answer; the hunters saddled and bridled their horses, and after inspecting their arms with all the care of men who are convinced that they will soon have occasion to use them, they mounted and rode toward the gate of the camp. Two sentries were standing motionless and upright at the gate; they placed themselves before the wood rangers. The latter had no intention of going out unseen, as they had no reason for hiding their departure.

"You are going away?" one of the sentries asked.

"No; we are merely going to make a survey of the country."

"At this hour?"

"Why not?"

"Hang it! I think it pleasanter to sleep in such weather, than ride about the prairie."

"You think wrong, comrade," Marksman answered, in a peremptory tone; "and, in the first place, bear this in mind, I am not accountable for my actions to anyone; if I go out at this hour in the storm which is threatening, I have possibly powerful motives for my conduct; now, will you or no let us pass? Remember, however, that I shall hold you responsible for any delay you occasion in the execution of my plans."

The tone employed by the hunter in addressing them struck the two sentries; they consulted together in a low voice; after which, the man who had hitherto spoken turned to the two hunters, who were quietly awaiting the result of this deliberation. "You can pass," he said; "you are at liberty to go wherever you think proper. I have done my duty in questioning you, and may Heaven grant you are doing yours in going out thus."

"You will soon know. One word more."

"I am listening."

"Our absence will probably be short; if not, we shall return by sunrise; still, pay great attention to this recommendation: should you hear the cry of the jaguar repeated thrice, at equal intervals, mount at full speed, and come, not you alone, but followed by a dozen of your comrades, for, when you hear that cry, a great danger will menace the Cuadrilla. Now, you understand me?"

"Perfectly."

"And will you do what I advise?"

"I will do so, because you are the friends we expected, and treachery could not be feared from you."

"Good."

"I wish you luck."

The hunters went on, and the gate was immediately closed after them.

The wood rangers had scarce entered the prairie, ere the hurricane, which had threatened since sunset, broke out furiously. A brilliant flash of lightning crossed the sky, followed almost instantaneously by a startling clap of thunder. The trees bowed beneath the fury of the blast, and the rain began falling in torrents. The adventurers advanced with extreme difficulty, amid the chaos of the infuriated elements; their horses, startled by the howling of the tempest, reared and shied at every step. The darkness had become so dense, that, although walking side by side, the two men could scarce see each other. The trees, twisted by the omnipotent blast, uttered almost human cries, answered by the mournful howling of the terrified wild beasts, while the stream, swollen by the rain, rose into waves, whose foaming crests broke with a crash against the sandy banks.

Brighteye and Marksman, case-hardened against the desert temporales, shook their heads contemptuously at every effort of the gust, which passed over them like an ardent simoom, and continued to advance, searching with the eye the gloom that enveloped them like a heavy shroud, and listening to the noises which the echoes bandied about.

In this way they reached the ford of the Rubio, without exchanging a syllable. Then they stopped, as if by mutual agreement.

The Rubio, a lost and unknown affluent of the Great Rio Colorado del Norte, into which it falls after a winding course of hardly twenty leagues, is in ordinary times a narrow stream, on which Indian canoes have a difficulty in floating, and which horses can ford almost anywhere, with the water scarce up to their girths; but at this hour the placid stream had suddenly become a mad and impetuous torrent, noisily rolling along, in its deep and muddy waters, uprooted trees, and even masses of rock.

To dream of crossing the Rubio at this moment would have been signal folly; a man so rash as to attempt the enterprise, would have been carried off in a few seconds by its furious waves, whose yellow surface grew wider every moment.

The hunters remained for a moment motionless beneath the torrents of rain that inundated them, regarding with thoughtful eye the water that still rose and rose, and holding in with great difficulty their startled horses, which reared with hoarse snorts of fear.

These men, with their hearts of bronze, stood stoically amid the frightful uproar of the unchained elements, not seeming to notice the awful tempest that howled around them, and as calm and easy minded as if they were comfortably seated in some snug cave, near a merry fire of twigs. They had only one idea, that of assisting the man whom they suspected of running a terrible danger at this moment.

Suddenly they started, and quickly raised their heads, while looking fixedly and eagerly in front of them. But the darkness was too thick; they could distinguish nothing.

In the midst of the thousand sounds of the tempest, a cry had struck their ear. This cry was a last appeal, a harsh and prolonged cry of agony, such as the strong man conquered by fatality utters, when he is forced to confess his impotence, when everything fails him at once, and he has no other resource than Heaven. The two men leaned forward quickly, and placing their hands to their mouth funnel wise, uttered in their turn a shrill and lengthened cry.

Then they listened. At the end of a moment a second cry, more piercing and desperate than the first, reached their ears.

"Oh!" Marksman shouted, as he rose in his stirrups and closed his fists in fury, "that man is in danger of death."

"Whoever he is, we must save him," Brighteye answered, boldly.

They had understood each other. But how to save this man? Where was he? What danger menaced him? Who could answer these questions which they mentally asked themselves?

At the risk of being carried off by the torrent, the hunters forced their horses to enter the river, and lying almost on the necks of the noble animals, they investigated the waters. But, as we have said, the darkness was too thick, they could see nothing.

"The demon interferes," Marksman said, in despair. "Oh, heavens! shall we let this man die without going to his aid?"

At this moment a flash of lightning crossed the sky, with a dazzling zigzag. By its fugitive gleam, the hunters saw a horseman struggling furiously against the efforts of the waves.

"Courage! courage!" they shouted.

"Help!" the stranger replied, in a shaking voice.

There was no time for hesitation, for every second was an age.

The man and horse struggled courageously against the torrent that bore them away, and the hunters' resolution was formed in a second. They silently shook hands, and at the same moment dug their spurs into their horses' flanks; the animals reared with a shriek of pain, but, compelled to obey the iron hands that held them, they bounded in terror into the middle of the stream.

Suddenly two shots were heard; a bullet passed with a whistle between our two friends, and a cry of pain was heard from the water. The man they had come to help was wounded. The storm was still increasing; the flashes succeeded each other with extraordinary rapidity. The hunters noticed the stranger clinging to his saddle, and letting his horse carry him where it liked; then, on the other bank, a man with his body bent forward, and his rifle shouldered, in readiness to fire.

"Each man his own," Marksman said, laconically.

"Good!" Brighteye said, with equal brevity.

The Canadian took the reata hanging at the saddlebow, and swinging it round his head, awaited the gleam of the next flash. It did not last long, but though it was so rapid, Brighteye had taken advantage of the transient gleam to hurl his reata. The leather cord whizzed out, and the running knot at the end fell on the neck of the horse which wrestled so bravely with the torrent.

"Courage! courage!" Brighteye shouted; "help, Marksman, help!" And giving a smart shake to his horse, he made it rise on its hind legs just as it was losing its footing, and forced it toward the river.

"Here I am," Marksman said, who was watching for the opportunity to fire: "patience, I am coming."

Suddenly he pulled the trigger, the bullet went forth, and from the other bank a cry of pain and rage reached the hunters.

"He is hit," Marksman said; "tomorrow I shall know who the scamp is;" and throwing his rifle behind him, he hurried forward to join Brighteye.

The horse the Canadian had lassoed, feeling itself supported and dragged toward the bank, seconded, with that intelligence possessed by these noble animals, the efforts made to save it.

The two hunters held on the reata. The united strength of their steeds, helped by the lassoed horse, succeeded in breasting the current, and after a minute's struggle, they at length reached the bank. So soon as they were comparatively in safety, the Canadians leaped from their saddles, and rushed toward the stranger's horse.

So soon as it felt *terra firma* under its feet, the noble animal had stopped, apparently comprehending that, if it advanced, it would cast its master against the rocks that covered the ground, for, although insensible, he still held the bridle firmly clasped in his clenched hand. The hunters cut the bridle, raised the man they had so miraculously saved in their arms, and carried him a few paces further to the foot of a tree, where they gently laid him; then, both eagerly bending over his body, awaited a flash which would enable them to see him.

"Oh!" Marksman said, as he drew himself up, with an expression of grief, mingled with terror, "Don Miguel Ortega!"

CHAPTER XII
DON STEFANO COHECHO

As we related a short time back, after leaving Brighteye Don Stefano had returned to the camp of the Gambusinos, into which he had managed to enter again unseen.

Once inside the camp, the Mexican had nothing more to fear; he went back to the fire, near which his horse was picketed, patted the noble brute, which turned toward him, and pricked up its ears at his approach, and then lay down calmly, rolled himself in his wraps, and fell asleep with that placidity peculiar to consciences at rest.

Several hours elapsed, and no sound arose to disturb the calmness that brooded over the camp. Suddenly Don Stefano opened his eyes, for a hand had been gently laid on his right shoulder.

The Mexican looked at the man who interrupted his sleep; by the light of the paling stars he recognized Domingo. Don Stefano rose, and silently followed the Gambusino. The latter led him to the entrenchments, probably with the design of speaking without fearing indiscreet ears.

"Well?" Don Stefano asked him, when the Gambusino had made a sign that he could speak.

Domingo, obeying the order he had received from Brighteye, concisely related to him all that had happened in the prairie. On learning that the Canadian had succeeded in meeting Marksman, Don Stefano gave a start of joy, and began listening to the Gambusino's story with increasing interest. When the latter at last finished, or at any rate remained silent, he asked him—"Is that all?"

"All," the other answered.

Don Stefano drew out his purse, and took from it several gold pieces, which he handed to Domingo; the latter took them with a gesture of pleasure.

"Did Brighteye give you no message for me?" the Mexican asked again.

The other seemed to reflect for a moment. "Ah!" he said, "I forgot; the hunter bade me tell you, Excellency, not to leave the camp."

"Do you know the reason of this recommendation?"

"Certainly; he intends to join the Cuadrilla this evening at the ford of the Rubio."

The Mexican's brow grew dark. "You are sure of that?" he said.

"That is what he said to me."

There was a few moments' silence. "Good!" he then continued; "the hunter added nothing further?"

"Nothing."

"Hum!" Don Stefano muttered, "after all, it is of no consequence;" then, leaning heavily on the Gambusino's shoulder, he looked him fiercely in the face. "Now," he added, laying a stress upon every word, "remember this carefully; you do not know me, whatever happens; you will not breathe a syllable of the way in which we met on the prairie."

"You may be assured of it, Excellency."

"I am assured," the Mexican replied, with an accent which made Domingo tremble, brave as he was: "remember the oath you took, and the pledge you gave me."

"I shall remember."

"If you keep your promise, and are faithful to me, it will be mine to keep you from want for life,—if not, look out."

The Gambusino shook his shoulders with disdain, and answered ill-temperedly—"It is unnecessary to threaten me, Excellency; what is said is said; what is promised is promised."

"We shall see."

"If you have nothing else to recommend to me, I believe we had better separate. The day is beginning to break; my comrades will soon awake, and I fancy you are no more anxious than I am to be surprised together."

"You are right." They then parted. Don Stefano returned to his place, while the Gambusino laid himself down where he was, and both slept, or seemed to do so.

With the first beams of the sun, Don Miguel raised the curtain of the tent, and walked toward his guest; the latter was soundly asleep. Don Miguel felt unwilling to trouble this peaceful sleep; he sat down at the fire, brought together the logs, blew them up, rolled one maize cigarette, and smoked philosophically, while awaiting his guest's awakening.

By this time all was movement in the camp; the Gambusinos were attending to their morning duties, some leading the horses to water, others lighting the fires, in order to prepare breakfast for the Cuadrilla; in short, everybody was engaged in his own way on the general behalf.

At length Don Stefano, on whose face a sunbeam had been playing for some minutes, thought it advisable to wake; he turned round, stretched his limbs, and opened his eyes, while yawning several times.

"*Caramba!*" he said, as he drew himself up, "it is day already; how quickly a night is passed; I feel as if I had been hardly an hour asleep."

"I see with pleasure that you have slept soundly, Caballero," Don Miguel said politely to him.

"What! is that you, my host?" Don Stefano exclaimed, with perfectly well-acted surprise; "the day will be a happy one for me, since the first face I notice, on opening my eyes, is that of a friend."

"I accept the compliment as politeness on your part."

"On my word, no: I assure you that what I say to you is the sincere expression of my thought," the Mexican said, simply; "it is impossible to do the honours of the desert better, or comprehend the holy laws of hospitality more thoroughly."

"I thank you for the good opinion you are kind enough to have of me. I trust that you will not leave us yet, but consent to remain several days with us."

"Would I could, Don Miguel—Heaven is my witness, that I should be delighted to enjoy your charming company for a short time; unfortunately, that is utterly impossible."

"Why so?"

"Alas! an imperious duty compels me to leave you this very day; I am really in despair at this vexatious mischance."

"What motive can be so powerful as to force you to leave us so suddenly?"

"A very trivial motive, and which will probably make you smile. I am a merchant of Santa Fé; a few days back, the successive failures of several houses at Monterey, with which I am extensively connected, obliged me to leave my house suddenly, in order to try and save, by my presence, a few waifs from the shipwreck with which I am threatened; I set out without asking anybody's advice, and here I am."

"But," Don Miguel objected, "you are still along way from Monterey."

"I know it; and it is that which drives me to despair. I have a frightful fear of arriving too late; the more so, as I have been warned that the people with whom I have to do are rogues: the sums they owe me are large, and form, I am sorry to say, the largest part of my fortune."

"*Cáspita!* if that is the case, I can understand that you are anxious to get there. I could not suspect that you had so serious a motive for pressing on."

"You see how it is; so pity me, Don Miguel."

All this conversation was carried on by the two men with a charming ease, and a simplicity perfectly well assumed on both sides; still neither was duped: Don Stefano, as so often happens, had committed the enormous fault of being too clever, and advancing beyond the limits of prudence, while trying to persuade this man of the sincerity of his words. This feigned sincerity had aroused Don Miguel's suspicions for two reasons: in the first place, if Don Stefano were going from Santa Fé to Monterey, he was not only off the road he ought to have followed, but was completely turning his back on those two towns—an error which his ignorance of the topography of the country made him commit without suspecting it. The second instance was equally premature: no merchant would have ever attempted, however grave the motive of such a journey, to cross the desert alone, for fear of the Indian bravos, the pirates, the wild beasts, and countless other dangers no less great, to which he would be exposed, without possible hope of escaping them.

Still, Don Miguel pretended to admit, without discussion, the reasons his guest offered him, and it was with an air of the utmost conviction that he answered,—"In spite of the earnest desire I may have of enjoying your agreeable society longer, I will not detain you, friend, for I understand how urgent it must be for you to hurry on."

Don Stefano bowed with an almost imperceptible smile of triumph.

"In short," Don Miguel added, "I wish that you may succeed in saving your fortune from the claws of those rogues; but at any rate, I hope, Caballero, that we shall not separate before breakfasting. I confess that your refusal to accept a share of my scanty supper last night pained me."

"Oh," Don Stefano interrupted him, "believe me, Caballero—"

"You gave me a very admirable excuse," Don Miguel continued, "but," he added, significantly, "we Gambusinos and adventurers are singular fellows—we fancy, rightly or wrongly, that the guest who refuses to eat with us is our enemy, or will become so."

Don Stefano gave a slight start at this unforeseen attack. "How can you imagine such a thing, Caballero?" he said, evasively.

"It is not I who suppose, but all of us; it is a prejudice, a foolish superstition; call it as you like, but so it is," he said, with a smile as sharp as a dagger's point, "and nothing will change our nature; so that is settled, we will breakfast together, then I will wish you a prosperous journey, and we shall part."

Don Stefano's face assumed an expression of despair.

"Really, I am the plaything of ill luck," he said, with a toss of the head.

"How so?"

"Good gracious, I know not how to explain it to you; it is so absurd, that I really dare not—"

"Pray speak, Caballero; although I am only an illiterate adventurer, I may possibly manage to understand you."

"The truth is, I shall hurt your feelings."

"Not the least in the world: are you not my guest? a guest is sent by heaven, that is to say, is sacred."

Don Stefano hesitated.

"Well," Don Miguel said, with a laugh, "I will have breakfast served; perhaps that will undo your tongue."

"That is the embarrassing point!" the Mexican exclaimed, quickly, with an accent of chagrin; "the fact is, that, in spite of my great desire to be agreeable to you, I cannot accept your kind invitation."

The young man frowned. "Ah, ah!" he said, fixing a suspicious glance on the speaker, "why so?"

"That is the very thing I dare not confess to you."

"You can, Caballero; have I not told you that you had the right to say anything?"

"Good heavens, you force me to it," he continued, in a voice that grew even more melancholy; "first imagine, then, that I have made a vow to Nuestra señora de los Ángeles, never to take food before sunset, so long as this accursed journey lasts."

"Ah!" Don Miguel said, with an accent of but slight conversion, "but last evening, when I offered you supper, the sun had set a long time, I fancy."

"Listen; I have not finished."

"Go on."

"And even then," the Mexican continued, "only to eat one of the maize tortillas I carry with me in my alforjas, and which I had blessed by a priest, prior to my departure from Santa Fé; you see, all this must seem to you very ridiculous, but we are fellow countrymen, we have Spanish blood in our veins, and instead of laughing at my foolish superstition, you will pity me."

"*Cáspita!* the more so, because you have a rude penance to undergo. I will not attempt to make you give up your superstition, for I too have mine; I believe that it is best not to return to the subject."

"You are not angry with me, at least?"

"I—why should I be angry?"

"Then we are still good friends?"

"More than ever," Don Miguel remarked, with a laugh. Still, the way in which these words were pronounced, but slightly reassured the Mexican— he took a side glance at the speaker, and then rose.

"Are you going?" the young man asked him.

"If you will permit me, I shall start."

"Do so, my guest."

Don Stefano, without further reply, immediately began saddling his horse.

"You have a noble brute there," Don Miguel observed.

"Yes, he is a purely bred barb."

"That is the first time I ever saw one of that precious race."

"Pray have a good look at him."

"I thank you, but I should be afraid of delaying you;—hola! my horse," he added, addressing Domingo.

The latter brought up a mustang full of fire, on the back of which Don Miguel leaped at a bound, while Don Stefano also mounted.

"If you have no objection, I will have the honour of accompanying you a little way, unless," he added, with a sarcastic smile, "you have made a vow which prevents it."

"Come," Don Stefano said, reproachfully, "you are angry with me."

"On my faith, no; I swear it."

"Very good: we will start when you please."

"I am at your orders."

They spurred their horses, and went out of the camp. They had scarce gone twenty yards, ere Don Miguel pulled up his horse and stopped.

"Are you going to leave me already?" Don Stefano asked him.

"I shall not go a step further," the young man answered, and drawing himself up fiercely and frowning, he said in a haughty tone, "Here you are no longer my guest; we are out of my camp in the desert; I can, therefore, explain myself clearly and plainly, and *voto a brios*, I will do so."

The Mexican regarded him with surprise. "I do not understand you," he said.

"Perhaps so: I hope it is so, but I do not believe it. So long as you were my guest, I pretended to believe the falsehoods you told me; but now that you are to me no more than the first comer, a stranger, I wish to tell you my thoughts frankly. I do not know by what name to address you to your livid face, but I am certain that you are my enemy, or, at any rate, a spy of my enemies."

"Caballero! these words—" Don Stefano exclaimed.

"Do not interrupt me," the young man continued, violently. "I care little who you are; it is sufficient to have asked you: I thank you for having entered my camp, at any rate; if ever I meet you again, I shall recognize you: but let me give you one piece of advice on parting: shake the dust off your boots on leaving me, and do not come across me again, for it might bring you misfortune."

"Threats!" the Mexican interrupted, pale with rage.

"Take my words as you please, but remember them in the interest of your safety; although I am only an adventurer, I give you at this moment a lesson in honesty you will do well to profit by; nothing would be easier for me than to acquire proofs of your treachery; I have with me twenty devoted comrades, who, at a sign, would treat you very scurvily; and who, by searching your clothes and alforjas, would doubtless find among your *blessed tortillas*," he said, with a sardonic smile, "the reasons for the conduct you have employed toward me ever since we met; but you have been my guest, and that title is your safeguard: go in peace, but do not cross my path again."

While uttering the last words, he raised his arm and dealt a vigorous blow with his *chicote* on the rear of Don Stefano's horse. The barb, but little used to such treatment, started off like an arrow from a bow, in spite of all his rider's efforts to hold him in.

Don Miguel looked after him for a moment, and then returned to the camp, laughing heartily at the way in which he had ended the interview.

"Come, lads," he said to the Gambusinos, "let us be off at once; we must reach the ford of the Rubio before sunset, where the guide is awaiting us."

And half an hour later the caravan set out.

CHAPTER XIII
THE AMBUSCADE

No incident worthy of description troubled the journey during the day. The Cuadrilla traversed an undulating country, intersected by streams of slight depth, on the banks of which grew tall bushes, and clumps of cottonwood trees, peopled by an infinity of birds, of every description and variety of plumage: on the horizon a long yellowish line, above which hung a dense cloud which indicated the Rio Colorado Grande del Norte.

As Don Miguel had announced, the ford of the Rubio was reached a few minutes before sunset. We will explain here in a few words the mode in which caravans camp in the desert; this description is indispensable, in order that the reader may understand how it is easy to leave or return to the camp unnoticed.

The Cuadrilla, in addition to the baggage mules, had with it fifteen waggons, loaded with merchandise. When the spot for camping was selected, the waggons were arranged in a square, with a distance of thirty-five feet between each: between the intervals were stationed six or eight men, who lit a fire, round which they assembled to cook, eat, smoke, and sleep. The horses were placed in the middle of the square, not far from the mysterious tent, which occupied exactly the centre. Each horse had the two off legs hobbled with a cord twenty inches long. We may remark that, although a horse thus hobbled feels very awkward at first, it soon accustoms itself to it sufficiently to be able to walk slowly. Besides, this prudential measure is taken in order that the horses may not stray, or be carried off by the Indians. Two horses are also put together, one with its feet tied, and the other only held by a picket rope, so that, in case of an alarm, it may gallop round its companion, which thus serves, as it were, as a pivot.

The space left free between the waggons was filled up with fascines, trees piled up on top of one another, and the mule bales.

Nothing is more singular than the appearance of one of these camps on the prairie. The fires are surrounded by picturesque groups, seated or standing; some cooking, others mending their clothes or their horses' trappings, others furbishing their weapons; at intervals, bursts of laughter rise from the midst of the groups, which announce that merry stories are going the rounds, and that they are trying to forget the fatigues of the day, and preparing for those of the morrow. Then, to complete the picture, from distance to distance behind the entrenchments sentinels, calm and motionless, lean on their rifles.

From the description we have given, it is easy to understand that the waggons form a species of embrasures, by means of which an active man crawling under the carts can easily go out without being noticed by the sentries, and return whenever he pleases, without attracting the attention of his comrades, whose glances, usually directed on the prairie, have no reason to watch what goes on inside the camp.

So soon as all was in order, and each installed as comfortably as circumstances permitted, Don Miguel had a fresh horse brought him, which he mounted, and addressed his comrades collected around him. "Señores," he said, "business of a pressing nature obliges me to go out for a few hours. Watch carefully over the camp during my absence; above all, let no one enter. We are now in regions where the greatest caution is necessary to guard against the treachery which incessantly menaces, and assumes every shape in order to deceive those whom negligence prevents being on their guard. The guide we are expecting so impatiently will, doubtless, arrive in a few moments. All know him by repute; perhaps he may come alone, or he may have somebody with him. This man, in whom we must place the greatest confidence, must, during my absence, be entirely free in his actions—go and come without the slightest obstacle being offered him. You have understood me; so follow my instructions point by point. Besides, I repeat, I shall soon return."

After making a farewell signal to his comrades, Don Miguel left the camp, and proceeded to the Rubio, the ford of which, being nearly dry at the moment, he easily crossed.

What the chief of the adventurers had said to his comrades with reference to Marksman, was an inspiration of Heaven; for, if he had not peremptorily ordered that the hunter should be allowed to act as he pleased, it is probable that the sentinels would have barred his passage; and, in that case, the young man, deprived of the providential aid of the two backwoodsmen, would have been hopelessly lost.

After crossing the ford, Don Miguel urged his horse at full speed straight ahead. This furious race lasted nearly two hours, through thickets, which at every moment grew more closely together, and gradually were metamorphosed into a forest.

After crossing a deep gorge, whose perpendicular sides were covered with impenetrable thickets, the young man arrived at a species of narrow lane, into which the paths of wild beasts opened, and in the centre of which an Indian, dressed in his war costume, and smoking gravely, crouched over a fire of *bois de vache*; while his horse, hobbled a short distance off, was busily browsing on the young tree shoots. So soon as he saw the Indian, Don Miguel pushed on even at greater speed. "Good evening, Chief!" he said, as he leaped lightly to the ground, and amicably pressed the hand the warrior held out to him.

"Wah!" the Chief said to him, "I no longer expected my pale brother."

"Why so, as I had promised to come?"

"Perhaps it would have been better for the Paleface to remain in his camp. Addick is a warrior; he has discovered a trail."

"Good; but trails are not wanting on the prairie."

"Och! this is wide, and incautiously trodden; it is a Paleface trail."

"Bah! what do I care?" the young man remarked, carelessly. "Do you fancy my band the only one crossing the prairie at this moment?"

The Redskin shook his head. "An Indian warrior is not mistaken on the war trail. It is the trail of an enemy of my brother's."

"What makes you suppose that?"

The Indian did not seem willing to explain himself more clearly; he turned his head, and, after a moment, said, "My brother will see."

"I am strong—well-armed. I care very little for those who would try to surprise us."

"One man is not worth ten," the Indian remarked, sententiously.

"Who knows?" the young man answered, lightly. "But," he continued, "that is not the question of the moment. I have come here to seek the news the Chief promised me."

"The promise of Addick is sacred."

"I know it, Chief, and that is why I did not hesitate to come. But time is slipping away. I have a long journey to go, to join my comrades again. A storm is getting up; and I confess that I should like very little to be exposed to it during my return. Be kind enough to be brief."

The Chief bowed in assent, and pointed to a place by his side.

"Good. Now begin, Chief; I am all attention," Don Miguel said, as he threw himself on the ground. "And, in the first place, how comes it that I have not seen you till today?"

"Because," the Indian answered, phlegmatically, "as my brother knows, it is far from here to Queche Pitao (the City of God). A warrior is but a man; Addick has accomplished impossibilities to join his Paleface brother sooner."

"Be it so, Chief; I thank you. Now let us come to facts. What has happened to you since our parting?"

"Quiepaa Tani opened its gates wide before the two young pale virgins. They are in safety, in the Queche, far from the eyes of their enemies."

"And did they give you no message for me?"

The Indian hesitated for a second.

"No," he said at length; "they are happy, and they wait."

Don Miguel sighed. "That's strange," he muttered.

The Chief took a stealthy look at him. "What will my brother do?" he asked.

"I shall soon be near them."

"My brother is wrong. No one knows where they are. For what good reveal their refuge?"

"Soon, I hope, I shall be free to act without fearing indiscreet eyes."

A gloomy flame sparkled in the Indian's eye.

"Wacondah alone is master of tomorrow," he said.

Don Miguel looked at him.

"What does the Chief mean?"

"Nothing but what I say."

"Good. Will my brother accompany me to my camp?"

"Addick will return to Quiepaa Tani, that he may watch over those whom his brother has confided to him."

"Shall I see you again soon?"

"Perhaps so," he answered evasively: "but," he added, "did not my brother say that he expected soon to go to the Queche?"

"Yes."

"When will my brother come?"

"At the latest, on the first day of next month. Why this question?"

"My brother is a Paleface: if Addick himself does not introduce him into the Queche, the white Chief cannot enter it."

"That is true; at the period I stated, I will meet you at the foot of the mound where we parted."

"Addick will be there."

"Good! I count upon you; but now I must leave you: night is rapidly falling; the wind is beginning to blow furiously. I must be off."

"Farewell," the Chief said laconically, making no attempt to stop him.

"Good-bye."

The young man leapt into the saddle, and started at full speed. Addick watched him depart with a pensive air; then, when he had disappeared behind a clump of trees, he leaned slightly forward, and imitated twice the hiss of a cobra capello. At this signal the branches of a thicket a short distance from the fire parted cautiously, and a man appeared. After looking suspiciously around him, he walked toward the Chief, in front of whom he stopped.

The man was Don Stefano Cohecho. "Well?" he said.

"Has my father heard?" the Indian asked, in an equivocal tone.

"All."

"Then I have nothing to tell my father."

"Nothing."

"The storm is beginning: what will my father do?"

"What is agreed on. Are the Chiefs warriors ready?"

"Yes."

"Where are they?"

"At the appointed spot."

"Good; let us start."

"I am ready."

These two men, who had evidently known each other for a long while, came to an understanding in a few words.

"Come!" Don Stefano said in a loud voice.

A dozen Mexican horsemen appeared.

"Here is a reinforcement, in case the warriors are not sufficient," he said, turning to the Chief.

The latter checked a movement of ill temper, and replied, as he shrugged his shoulders disdainfully, —"What need of twenty warriors against a single man?"

"Because the man is worth a hundred," Don Stefano said, with an accent of conviction which caused the Chief to reflect.

They started. In the meantime, Don Miguel had galloped on: still, he was far from suspecting the plot that was at this moment being formed against him; and, if he hurried on, it was not through any apprehension, but because the wind, whose violence increased every minute, and the heavy drops of rain, which began falling, warned him to seek shelter as speedily as possible. While galloping, he reflected on the short interview he had had with the Redskin warrior. While turning over in his mind the words exchanged between them, he felt a vague alarm, a secret fear, invade his heart, though it was impossible to account for the emotion he experienced; he fancied he could read treachery behind the Chief's studied reticence; he now remembered that he at times seemed embarrassed while talking with him. Trembling lest a misfortune had happened to the young ladies, or a peril menaced them, he felt his anxiety heightened; the more so, as he knew not what means he should employ to insure the fidelity of the man whom he suspected of perfidiousness.

Suddenly, a dazzling flash shot across the open, his horse suddenly bounded aside, and two or three bullets whistled past him. The young man sat up in his saddle. He was in the middle of the gorge he had traversed a few hours previously; a profound obscurity enveloped him on all sides, and in the shadow all around him, he fancied he could detect the outlines of human forms. At this moment, other shots were fired at him, his hat was carried off by a bullet, and several arrows passed close to his face.

Don Miguel raised his head boldly. "Ah! traitors!" he shouted in a loud voice. And, lifting his horse with his knees, he rushed forward at headlong speed, holding the bridle between his teeth, half bending over his steed's neck, and with a revolver in each hand.

A frightful war yell was heard, mingled with piercing imprecations uttered in Spanish.

Don Miguel passed like a tornado through the body of men moving round him, and discharged his revolvers in the thickest of his unknown enemies. Cries of pain and rage, bullets and arrows pursued him, but did not check the headlong speed of his horse, which seemed no longer to touch the earth, and rapidly did it course along.

Behind him the young man heard the galloping of several horses, hastening in pursuit. "Treachery, treachery!" he shouted, brandishing his sabre, making his horse rear, and bounding like a jackal in the midst of the throng which incessantly closed in upon him.

Suddenly, at the height of the contest, at the superior moment when he felt his strength was deserting him, three shots came from the darkness, and his assailants, attacked in the rear, were compelled in their turn to defend themselves against invisible foes.

"We are coming!" a stout voice shouted, whose energetic accent made the assailants tremble. "Hold your own! hold your own!"

Don Miguel responded by a terrific yell, and threw himself into the thick of the fight with redoubled efforts: now that he knew himself to be supported, he felt he was saved. The crowd gave way in the shadow, like ripe corn beneath the reaper's scythe; the compact mass of assailants parted asunder, and three men, or three demons, rushed into the hole they had made, and bounded forward to the side of the adventurer.

"Ah, ah!" the latter exclaimed, with a bitter burst of laughter, "the fight is now equal; forward, comrades, forward!" And he threw himself once more into the medley, followed by these intrepid allies.

Who were these men? Whence did they come? he did not know or dream of asking them. Besides, this was not the moment for explanations: they must conquer or die.

"Kill him, kill him!" a man yelled, who rushed upon him every moment with uplifted sabre, and in all the ferocious ardour of an inveterate hatred.

"Ah! it is you, Don Stefano Cohecho!" Don Miguel shouted; "I felt sure we should meet; your voice has denounced you."

"Death to him!" the latter answered.

The two men rushed upon each other, their horses met with a terrible shock, and the man whom the adventurer took for Don Stefano rolled on the ground.

"Victory!" Don Miguel shouted, as he cut down with his machete all within his reach.

His unknown friends, who were still by his side, rushed after him. In spite of all their efforts, the attacking party were unable to keep their position, and began flying in every direction. The gorge was free; no obstacle longer opposed Don Miguel's flight: he pressed his horse, and the noble beast redoubled its ardour. When so far free, the young man looked around him. His unknown defenders had suddenly disappeared, as if by enchantment.

"What is the meaning of this?" he murmured.

At this moment he felt on his left arm something resembling a blow from a whip: a bullet had struck him. This wound recalled him to a sense of his present position.

His enemies had rallied, and recommenced their pursuit. Before him he heard the yellow waters of the Rubio growling; the wrath of heaven and of man seemed leagued together to overwhelm him; it was then that a mad terror seized upon him; he fancied himself lost, and uttered that first cry of agony heard by the hunters.

Still, his pursuers gained rapidly upon him; without hesitation or reflection, he plunged into the Rubio with his horse; some twenty bullets dashed up the water round him; he turned bravely on his steed, and fired the last shots from his revolvers, uttering that cry to which the hunters had replied with the word, —"Courage!"

But human nature has limits which it cannot pass. This last effort exhausted the little strength left him, and, frantically clutching the bridle of his horse, he rolled into the river and fainted, while saying, in a stifled voice, —"Laura, Laura!"

Two shots crossed each other above his head, one fired by the man who was aiming at him from the bank, the other by Marksman. The stranger uttered a yell like a wild beast, turned away staggering like a drunken man, and disappeared.

Who was this man? —was he dead or merely wounded?

CHAPTER XIV
THE TRAVELLERS

The events we have undertaken to narrate are so mingled with incidents intertwined in each other by that fatality of accident which governs human life that we are compelled once more, to our great regret, to interrupt our story, and let the reader be present at a scene which took place not far from the Rubio ford, on the same day that the events occurred which we have described in preceding chapters.

At about one o'clock of the *tarde*, that is to say, at the moment when the beams of the sun, which has reached its zenith, pour down on the prairie such an intense heat, that everything which lives and breathes seeks shelter in the deepest part of the woods, three horsemen passed over the ford, and boldly entered the path Don Miguel Ortega was destined to follow a few hours later.

These horsemen were white men, and what is more, Mexicans; it was easy to perceive, at the first glance, that they had not the slightest connection with any class of the adventurers who, under various names, such as Gambusinos, hunters, trappers, wood rangers, or pirates, swarm on the Western Prairies, which they incessantly cross in every direction.

The dress of these horsemen was that usually worn by the Mexican hacenderos on the frontiers:—The wide brimmed hat, gallooned, and decorated with the toquilla, the manga; the short calzoneras, open at the knee; the zarapé; the *botas vaqueras*, and the *armas de agua*, without which no one ventures on the desert. They were armed with rifles, revolvers, navajas, and machetes. Their horses, at this moment oppressed by the heat, but slightly refreshed by passing the ford, held their heads up proudly, and showed that, if necessary, they could have gone a long journey, in spite of their apparent fatigue.

Of the three horsemen, one seemed to be the master, or at least the superior, of the other two. He was a man of fifty years of age, with hard, energetic features, imprinted, however, with rare frankness, and great resolution; he was tall, well built, and robust; and he sat upright and stiff on his saddle, with that confidence which denotes the old soldier. His companions belonged to the class of Indios Manzos, a bastard race, in which

Spanish blood and Indian blood are so mixed that it is impossible to assign them any characteristic type. Still, the richness of their dress, and the way in which they rode by the first horseman's side, rendered it easy to guess that they were confidential servants, men whose fidelity had been long proved—almost friends, in short, and not domestics, in the vulgar acceptation of the term. As far as it is possible to recognize the age of an Indian, in whose face traces of decrepitude are nearly always invisible, these two men must have reached middle age, that is, from forty to forty-five years.

These three horsemen rode a short distance behind each other, with a thoughtful and sorrowful air: at times they turned a glance of discouragement around, stifled a sigh, and continued their journey with drooping heads, like men convinced they have undertaken a task beyond their strength, but whom their will and, before all, their devotion urge onwards at all risks.

The presence of these strangers on the banks of the Rubio was, indeed, one of those unusual facts which no one would have been able to explain, and which would certainly have greatly surprised the hunters or Indians who might have seen them.

In the country where they now were, animals were rare; hence they were not hunting. These regions, remote from all civilized zones, fatally bordered unexplored countries, the last refuge of the Indians; these men were, therefore, neither traders nor ordinary travellers.

What reason could have been so powerful as to urge them to bury themselves in the desert, so few in number, where every human face must be to them that of an enemy? Where were they going? what were they seeking? This question none but the men themselves could have answered.

The ford had been passed; before them lay extended a barren and sandy plain, opening on the gorge to which we have already alluded. On this plain not a blade of grass glistened: the burning beams of the sun descended perpendicularly on the parched sand, which rendered the heat, if possible, more oppressive and stifling. The eldest of the travellers turned to his companions:—"Courage, Muchachos!" he said, in a gentle voice and a sad smile, as he pointed to the edge of the forest, not more than three miles from them, whose close and thick vegetation promised them a refreshing shade. "Courage! we shall soon rest."

"Your Excellency need not trouble yourself about us," one of the criados answered; "what your Excellency endures without complaining, we can also endure."

"The heat is stifling: hence, like yourselves, I feel the want of a few hours' rest."

"If absolutely necessary, we could go on a long time yet," the man who had already spoken said, "but our horses can hardly drag themselves along. The poor beasts are almost foundered."

"Yes, men and beasts want rest. However strong our will may be, there are limits before which the human organization must yield. Courage! in an hour we shall have arrived."

"Come, come, Excellency, do not think of us any more."

The first traveller made no answer, and they continued their journey in silence.

They soon reached the gorge, which they passed through, and found themselves among thickets, which, gently approaching, began to offer them a scanty shade, but, just as they reached the spot the first traveller had pointed out for their halt, he suddenly stopped and turned to his companions,—"Look there," he said, "Do you not see a slight pillar of smoke rising in the thicket, down there in front of us, a little on the left of the skirt of the forest?"

They looked. "In truth," the elder answered, "there can be no mistake about it, although from here it might be taken for a mist; still, the way in which the spiral rises, and its blue tinge, prove that it is smoke."

"After the ten mortal days we have been wandering about these immense solitudes without meeting a living soul, that fire must be welcome to us, for it indicates man, that is, friends; let us go straight up to them, then; perhaps we shall obtain from them some valuable information about the object of our journey."

"Pardon me, Excellency," the criado answered, quickly, "when we quitted the Presidio, you promised to place yourself in my hands, so excuse my giving you some advice, which, under present circumstances, will be very useful to you."

"Speak, my excellent Bermudez, I place the most perfect confidence in your experience and fidelity; your advice will be well received by me."

"Thanks, Excellency," the man answered, whom he had called Bermudez, "I have been a long time your vaquero, and in that capacity have been frequently mixed up both with hunters and Indians, which has given me certain notions of desert life, by which I have profited, although I never before went so far on to the prairie as today. Hence, in the spot where we are, we must above all avoid a meeting with our fellow men, and only accost them prudently, while employing the greatest precautions; the more so, as we do not know whom we have before us, and if we have to deal with friend or foe."

"It is true; your remark is correct; but, unfortunately, it is a little late."

"Why so?"

"Because, if we have seen the smoke of their fire, it is probable the people down there saw us long ago, and are spying all our movements, especially as we made no attempt at concealment."

"That is certain, Don Mariano, that is certain," Bermudez continued, with a shake of his head. "Hear, then, what, with your permission, Excellency, I propose, in order to avoid any misunderstanding, which is always unpleasant; you will remain here with Juanito, while I go on alone, and push on my reconnoissance up to the fire."

Don Mariano hesitated to reply, for it seemed to him hard to refuse his old servant thus.

"Decide, Excellency," the latter said, quickly; "I know the Redskin way of talking; they will salute me either with a shower of arrows, or a bullet; but, as they are generally very bad shots, they are almost certain not to hit me, and then I will easily enter into negotiations with them. You see that the risk I have to run is not tremendous."

"Bermudez is right, Excellency," Juanito answered, sententiously; being a methodical and silent man, who never took the word save under grave circumstances; "you must let him act as he thinks proper."

"No!" Don Mariano said, resolutely, "I will never consent to that. God is master of our existence; He alone can dispose of it at His will: if any accident happened to you, my poor Bermudez, I should never pardon myself; we will continue to advance together; at any rate, if they are enemies before us, we shall be able to defend ourselves."

Bermudez and Juanito were preparing to answer their master's objections, and the discussion would have probably lasted a long while, but at this moment the galloping of a horse was heard, the grass parted, and a rider appeared about a dozen paces from the group. It was a white man, and dressed in the garb of the prairie hunters. "Hold, Caballeros," he cried, as he made a friendly sign with his hand, and checked his horse; "advance without fear, you are welcome: I noticed your indecision, and am come to put an end to it."

The three men exchanged glances.

"I thank you for your cordial invitation," Don Mariano at length answered, "and accept it gladly."

All suspicion being done away with, the four persons walked together toward the fire, which they reached a few moments later. Near this fire were two Indians, man and wife.

The travellers dismounted, took off saddle and bridle, and after giving their horses food, seated themselves with a sign of satisfaction by their new friends, who did the honour of their provisions and bivouac with all the cordial simplicity of the desert.

The reader has doubtless recognized Ruperto, Flying Eagle, and Eglantine, whom we left proceeding toward the Chief's village, whither Ruperto had received orders from Marksman to accompany the Chief.

Don Mariano and his companions were not only fatigued, but also excessively hungry; the hunter and the Indians left them at full liberty to assuage their appetites, and when they saw them light their papelitos, they imitated them, and the conversation began. Turning at first on the ordinary topics of the desert, the weather, the heat, and the abundance of game, it soon grew more intricate, and assumed even a serious character.

"Now that the meal is ended, Chief," Ruperto said, "put out the fire; it is unnecessary for us to reveal our presence to the vagabonds who are doubtless prowling about the prairie."

Eglantine, at a sign from Flying Eagle, put out the fire.

"It was, indeed, your smoke which betrayed you," Don Mariano remarked.

"Oh!" Ruperto said, with a laugh, "because we wished it; had we not, we should have made our fire so as to remain unseen."

"You wish, then, to be discovered?"

"Yes; it was a throw of the dice."

"I do not understand you."

"What I say to you seems an enigma, but you will soon be able to understand it. Look," the hunter added, stretching out his arm in the direction of the gorge, "do you see that horseman going at full speed? In a quarter of an hour, at the most, he will be up with us; owing to the precaution I have taken, he will pass without noticing us."

"Do you fear anything from that horseman?"

"Nothing; on the contrary, the Chief and myself are here to help him."

"You know him then?"

"Not the least in the world."

"Hum! you are becoming more and more incomprehensible, Caballero."

"Patience," the hunter said, with a laugh, "did I not tell you you should soon have a solution of the enigma?"

"Yes, and I confess that my curiosity is so excited, that I am impatiently waiting it."

In the meanwhile, the horseman Ruperto had pointed out to Don Mariano came up rapidly, and soon passed, as the hunter had foreseen, a few paces from the bivouac, without noticing it. So soon as he had disappeared in the forest, Ruperto began again:—"A few hours ago," he said, "not far from the spot where we now are, the Chief and I, without wishing it, overheard a conversation of which this horseman was the object, a conversation in which the question was simply to make him fall into an odious snare. I do not know who this horseman is, nor do I wish to know it, but I have an instinctive repulsion to all that in the slightest degree resembles treachery. This Indian Chief, like myself, immediately resolved on saving this Caballero, if it were possible; we knew that he must pass by here, as he had an appointment with one of the men whom accident, or rather Providence, had made us so singularly listen to. Two men, however brave they may be, are very weak against some twenty bandits, still we did not lose courage, but resolved, if Heaven sent us no allies, bravely to attempt the adventure by ourselves; the more so, as the persons whose bloodthirsty plans we had surprised seemed to us to be atrocious villains; still, by the Chief's advice, I lit this fire, certain that if any traveller came this way the smoke would serve him as a beacon, and assuredly lead him here; you see, Caballero, that I was not mistaken, as you have come."

"And I am glad I have," Don Mariano warmly replied: "I most readily join in your plan, which appears to be suggested in every respect by an honest and good heart."

"Do not make me out better than I am, Caballero," the hunter made answer; "I am only a poor devil of a wood ranger, very ignorant of city matters; but under all circumstances, I obey the inspirations of my heart."

"And you are right, for they are sound and just."

"Thanks; now we are in force, I assure you that the pícaros, however numerous they may be, will see some fun; but we have still time before us; rest yourselves, sleep a few hours; when the moment arrives, we will arrange what to do."

Don Mariano was too tired to need a repetition of this invitation; a few moments later he and his companions were plunged in a deep and restorative sleep. At sunset Ruperto woke them, "It is time," he said.

They rose; for the few hours' rest had restored them all their strength. The arrangements to be made were simple, and soon decided on.

We have seen what took place; Addick and Don Stefano, themselves surprised, when they expected to surprise Don Miguel, not knowing how many enemies they had to contend with, fled after an obstinate struggle. Don Mariano and Ruperto, satisfied with having saved Don Miguel, retired so soon as the issue of the combat appeared no longer dubious.

Recalled, however, to the banks of the Rubio by the shots fired at the last moment by Don Miguel, they saw a man and rushed toward him, possibly more with the hope of helping him than taking him prisoner. The man had fainted. Don Mariano and Ruperto raised him in their arms, and transported him beneath the covert of the forest, where Eglantine had contrived with great difficulty to light a fire; but when they were enabled to see the wounded man's face by the glare, both uttered a cry of stupefaction.

"Don Stefano Cohecho!" Ruperto exclaimed.

"My brother!" Don Mariano said, with mingled grief and horror.

CHAPTER XV
RECALLED TO LIFE

With the first gleam of day, the terrible hurricane, which had raged so cruelly through nearly the whole night, gradually calmed; the wind had swept the sky, and borne far away the gloomy clouds which studded the blue heavens with black spots; the sun rose majestically in floods of light; the trees, refreshed by the tempests, had reassumed that pale green hue, sullied on the previous day by the dusty sand of the desert; and the birds, hid in countless myriads beneath the dense foliage, poured forth that harmonious concert which they offer every morning at sunrise to the All High—a sublime and grand hymn, a ravishing hymn, whose rhythm, full of simple melodies, causes the man buried in this ocean of verdure to indulge in sweet dreams, and plunges him unconsciously into a melancholy reverie of the hope, whose realization is in heaven.

As we have said, Don Miguel Ortega, saved by the tried courage and presence of mind of the two wood rangers, was carried by them to the foot of a tree, beneath which they laid him.

The young man had fainted. The hunters' first care was to examine his wounds: he had two, one on the right arm, the other on the head, but neither of them was dangerous. The wound in the arm bled profusely, a bullet had torn the flesh, but had produced no fracture of the bone, or any grave accident; as for the wound in the head, evidently produced by a sharp instrument, the hair had already matted over it, and checked the haemorrhage.

Don Miguel's faintness was produced by the loss of blood in the first place, and next by the nervous excitement of a long and obstinate struggle, and the immense amount of strength he had been compelled to expend to resist the numerous enemies who had treacherously attacked him.

The wood rangers, owing to the life they led, and the innumerable accidents to which they are constantly exposed, are obliged to possess some practical knowledge of medicine, and particularly of surgery. Pupils of the Redskins, simples play a great part in their medical system. Brighteye and Marksman were masters of the art of treating wounds summarily, after the Indian fashion. After carefully washing the wounds, and removing the hair from that on the head, they plucked *oregano* leaves, formed them into a species of cataplasm, by slightly moistening them with spirits diluted in water, and applied this primitive remedy to the wounds, fastening it on with leaves of the *abanigo*, cut into strips, round which they wound aloe threads. Then, with the blade of a knife, they slightly opened the wounded man's tightly closed jaws, and poured a few drops of spirits into his mouth. In a few moments Don Miguel half opened his eyes, and a fugitive glow coloured his pallid cheeks.

The hunters, with their hands crossed on the muzzles of their rifles, carefully inspected the wounded man's face, trying to read on his features the probable results of the means they had thought it necessary to employ, in order to relieve him.

The man who recovers from a deep fainting fit is not at the first moment conscious of external objects, nor does he remember what has happened: the equilibrium of his faculties, suddenly interrupted by the successive blows they have experienced, is only re-established slowly and gradually, in proportion as the eye grows brighter, the memory clearer. Don Miguel looked around him with a glance that contained no warmth or expression, and almost immediately closed his eyes again, as if already wearied by the effort he had been forced to make in opening them.

"In a few hours his strength will be restored, and before three days there will not be a trace of it," Brighteye said, tossing his head sententiously. "By Jove! he is one of those sturdy fellows I like."

"Is he not?" Marksman answered,—"so young and so valiant? What a rude attack he sustained."

"Yes, and bravely, we must say; still, for all that, if we had not been there, he would have found it difficult to get out of the scrape."

"He would have perished, there is not the least doubt of it, and that would have been unfortunate."

"Very unfortunate! however, he is well out of it. By the way, what are we going to do with him now? We cannot stay here for ever; on the other hand, he is unable to make a movement; but we must take him back to the camp, his men will feel alarmed at his absence, and who knows what would happen if it were prolonged?"

"That is true; we cannot think of putting him on his horse, so we must hit on some other expedient."

"By Jove! that will not trouble us; the torpor into which he has fallen will last about two hours; in the meantime, he will be hardly capable of uttering a few words, and vaguely recalling what has happened to him; it is not, therefore, necessary for both of us to remain by him, one will be enough—say myself: you will go to the camp, state what has occurred, tell the Gambusinos in what condition their Chief is, ask for help, and bring it here as speedily as possible."

"You are right, Brighteye, on my word; your advice is excellent, and I will set about it at once. I shall not be gone more than two hours, so keep good watch, for we do not know who may be prowling round us, and spying our movements."

"Don't be frightened, Marksman, I am not one of those men who let themselves be surprised;—stay, I remember an adventure that occurred to me in every respect similar to this. It was a long time ago, in 1824, I was very young, and—"

But Marksman, who heard with secret terror his comrade beginning one of his interminable stories, hastily interrupted him without ceremony, saying—"By Jove! I have been acquainted with you for a long time, Brighteye, and know what manner of man you are, so I go perfectly easy in mind."

"No matter," the hunter replied, "if you would let me explain—"

"Useless, useless, my friend; explanations are uncalled for from a man of your stamp and experience," Marksman said, as he leaped into his saddle, and started at full speed.

Brighteye looked after him for a long time. "Hum!" he said, thoughtfully; "the Lord is my witness that that man is one of the most excellent creatures in existence; I love him as a brother, and regret that I can never make him understand how useful and precious it is to keep up a recollection of past events, so as not to feel embarrassed when any of those difficulties so common in desert life suddenly spring up:—well, I cannot help it." And he began once more examining the wounded man, with that intelligent attention he had not once ceased testifying toward him.

Don Miguel had not made a movement; more than an hour had elapsed, and when the effects of the fainting fit wore off, he instantaneously fell into that heavy, agitated sleep, from which nothing could arouse him for a long time. Brighteye, seated by his side, with his rifle betwixt his legs, philosophically smoked his Indian pipe, waiting, with the patience peculiar to hunters, till some symptom told him that the wounded man had succeeded in shaking off that torpor of evil augury which had seized upon him.

The old Canadian would have desired, even at the risk of an intense fever setting in, that a sudden commotion should recall the young man roughly to life; he built on the arrival of the Gambusinos to obtain this result, and he frequently consulted the desert with anxiety to try and perceive them, but he saw and heard nothing: all was silent around him.

"Come," he muttered at times, bending a dissatisfied glance at Don Miguel, who lay stretched at his feet, "the shock has been too rude, and nothing *will* happen to restore him to a consciousness of life; on my soul, I am most unlucky."

At the moment when, perhaps for the hundredth time, he repeated this sentence with ever-increasing annoyance, he heard at a short distance off a rather loud rustling, and the breaking of some dead branches.

"Eh, eh!" the hunter said, "what is the meaning of this?"

He raised his head smartly, and looked carefully around; suddenly he broke into a concentrated burst of laughter, and his eyes sparkled with joy.

"By Jove!" he said, gaily, "this is exactly what I want. Heaven has sent that young gentleman to draw me from my dilemma, and he is right welcome."

At about twenty paces from the hunter, a magnificent jaguar, crouching on the largest branch of an enormous cochineal tree, fixed a glaring look upon him, while at intervals passing one of its fore claws over its ears, with the airs and purring sound peculiar to the feline race. This wild beast, probably terrified by the hurricane of the past night, had not been able to regain its den, toward which it was proceeding, when it found the two men in its path.

The jaguar, or American tiger, far from attacking men, carefully avoids a meeting with them, and only accepts a combat when compelled and driven to bay, but then it becomes terrible, and a contest with it is frequently mortal, unless its opponent is accustomed to the numerous tricks it employs to insure the victory. At the moment the tiger perceived the hunter, the latter saw the tiger, hence the combat was imminent. The two enemies remained for several minutes in an attitude of observation; their glances crossed like sword blades.

"Come, make up your mind, sluggard," Brighteye muttered.

The jaguar uttered a hoarse yell, sharpened its formidable claws for a few seconds on the branch which served it for a pedestal, and then, drawing itself up, bounded on the hunter. The latter did not stir; with his rifle to his shoulder, his feet well apart and firmly fixed, and his body bent slightly forward, he followed with a careful eye all the movements of the wild beast; at the moment the latter made its spring, the hunter pulled the trigger.

The tiger turned a somersault with a ferocious yell, and fell at Brighteye's feet. The Canadian bent down to it, but the jaguar was dead; the hunter's bullet had entered its brain through the right eye, and killed it on the spot. At the howl of the brute, and the sound of Brighteye's rifle, Don Miguel opened his eyes and suddenly raised himself on his elbow, with a terrified look, and features contracted by a strange and terrible emotion, which reddened his face.

"Help! help!" he shouted in a thundering voice.

"Here I am!" Brighteye exclaimed, as he rose up, and forced him to lie down again.

Don Miguel looked at him.

"Who are you?" he said, at the expiration of a minute; "what do you want with me? I do not know you."

"That is true," the hunter said, imperturbably, and addressing him like a child, "but you will soon know me: do not be alarmed; for the moment, it is enough for you to know that I am a friend."

"A friend!" the wounded man repeated, trying to restore order to his ideas, which were still confused, "what friend?"

"By Jove!" the hunter said, "you do not count them by thousands, I suppose; I have been your friend for some hours past. I saved you at the moment when you were dying."

"But all that tells me nothing—teaches me nothing. How am I here? how are you here?"

"Those are a good many questions all at once, and it is impossible for me to answer them: you are wounded, and your state forbids any conversation. Will you drink?"

"Yes," Don Miguel answered, mechanically. Brighteye held his gourd to him.

"Still," he continued, after a moment, "I have not been dreaming."

"Who knows?"

"Those shots, the shouts I heard?"

"Quite a trifle;—a jaguar I killed, and which you can see a few yards off."

There was silence for a few minutes: Don Miguel was thinking deeply; light was beginning to dawn on his mind, his memory was returning. The hunter anxiously followed on the young man's face the incessant progress of returning thought. At length a flash of intelligence lit up the young man's eye, and fixing his feverish glance on the old hunter, he asked him,—"How long is it since you saved me?"

"Scarce three hours."

"Then, since the events that brought me here—there has only passed—?"

"One night."

"Yes!" the young man continued in a deep voice, a terrible voice, "I fancied I was dead."

"You only escaped by a miracle."

"Thanks."

"I was not alone."

"Who else came to my assistance? tell me his name, that I may preserve it preciously in my memory."

"Marksman."

"Marksman!" the wounded man exclaimed, tenderly, "always he. Oh! I ought to have expected that name, for he loves me."

"Yes."

"And what is your name?"

"Brighteye."

The young man trembled, and held out his arm. "Your hand," he said; "you were right just now in saying you were a friend, you have been so for a long time, Marksman has often spoken to me about you."

"We have been connected for thirty years."

"I know it: but where is he, that I do not see him?"

"He went, about two hours back, to the camp of the Cuadrilla to bring help."

"He thinks of everything."

"I remained here to watch over and take care of you during his absence; but he will soon return."

"Do you believe that I shall be long helpless?"

"No; your wounds are not serious. What floors you at this moment is the moral shock you received, and chiefly the blood you lost when you fell in a fainting state into the Rubio."

"Then that river—"

"Is the Rubio."

"I am, then, on the spot where the struggle ended?"

"Yes."

"How many days do you think I shall remain in this state?"

"Four or five at the most."

There was silence for several minutes.

"You told me that it is the weakness of my senses, produced by the moral shock I received, which overpowers me, I think?" Don Miguel began again.

"Yes, I said so."

"Do you believe that a firm and powerful will could produce a favourable reaction?"

"I do."

"Give me your hand."

"There it is."

"Good: now help me."

"What are you going to do?"

"Get up."

"By Jove! I was right in saying you were a man. Come, I consent: have a try."

After a few minutes spent in fruitless efforts, Don Miguel at length succeeded in standing upright.

"At last!" he said, triumphantly.

At the first step he took, he lost his balance, and rolled on the ground. Brighteye rushed toward him.

"Leave me," he shouted to him, "leave me; I wish to get up by myself."

He succeeded: this time he took his precautions better, and succeeded in walking a few steps. Brighteye regarded him with admiration.

"Oh! the will must subdue the matter," Don Miguel continued, with frowning brow and swollen veins, "I will succeed."

"You will kill yourself."

"No, for I must live; give me something to drink."

For the second time Brighteye handed him the gourd; the young man eagerly raised it to his lips. "Now!" he exclaimed, with a feverish accent, as he returned the gourd to the hunter, "to horse."

"What, to horse?" Brighteye said, with stupefaction.

"Yes; I must be moving."

"Why, that is madness."

"Let me alone, I tell you, I will hold on; but as the wound in the left arm prevents my getting into the saddle, I must claim your assistance."

"You wish it."

"I insist on it."

"Be it so; and may God be merciful to us."

"He will protect us, be assured."

Brighteye helped the young man into the saddle; against the hunter's previsions, he kept firm and upright. "Now," he said, "take up your jaguar's skin, and let us be off."

"Where are we going?"

"To the camp; Marksman will be greatly astonished to see me, when he believes me to be half dead."

Brighteye silently followed the young man; he gave up any further attempts to understand this strange character.

CHAPTER XVI
THE SEARCH AFTER TRUTH

In spite of Don Miguel's firm will to overcome the pain, the horse's movement occasioned him a degree of suffering which made his features quiver, and drops of cold perspiration stand on his face, which was pale as that of a corpse; at times his sight troubled him, he found everything turning around him, he tottered in his saddle, and held on convulsively to his horse's mane through fear of falling.

"Stupid matter," he muttered in a hoarse voice, "shall I not succeed in conquering you?"

Then he redoubled his efforts to seem apathetic, smiled on Brighteye, and gaily addressed him.

For the first time in his life, the old hunter felt himself nonplussed: though he ransacked his memory to try and find an analogous circumstance to this in the course of his varied life, to his great regret he was forced to confess to himself that he had never witnessed anything like it. This annoyed him, and he therefore walked with a dissatisfied air by the young man's side.

Still they advanced. Suddenly, however, they heard the sound of horses near them on the trail they were following.

"Here is Marksman," Don Miguel said.

"That is probable."

"He will be greatly astonished to meet me coming toward the help he is bringing."

"That is certain."

"Let us hurry our horses on a little."

Brighteye looked at him. "You have sworn, then, to bring on a congestion of the brain?" he said to him plainly.

"How so?" the young man asked in surprise.

"By Jove! that is easy to see," the hunter went on, hastily; "for an hour you have been committing one act of madness after the other; but do not deceive yourself, Caballero, what you take for strength is only fever. It is that alone which sustains you, so take care, do not obstinately continue an impossible struggle, from which, I warn you, you will not emerge the victor. I let you act as you pleased, because I saw no harm in doing so up to the present; but, believe me, you have done enough. You have measured your strength, and know what you are capable of doing under urgent circumstances. That is all you want; so now let us stop and wait."

"Thank you," Don Miguel said, cordially squeezing his hand; "you are really my friend, your rude words prove it to me. Yes, I am a madman; but what would you? I am in a strange position, when every hour I lose may entail extreme dangers on myself and other persons, and I am afraid of succumbing before I have accomplished the task which misfortune has imposed on me."

"You will succumb much sooner if you will not be reasonable. Four or five days are soon passed; and, besides, what you cannot do, your friends will accomplish."

"That is true. You make me blush for myself. I am not only mad, but also ungrateful."

"Come, do not talk about that any more. The noise is approaching. They are probably your companions; still they might be enemies, for everything must be expected in the desert. Let us enter this thicket, where we shall be perfectly concealed from the eyes of the comers. If it be Marksman, we will show ourselves; if not, we will keep close."

Don Miguel warmly approved of the idea, for he understood that, in case of a fight, he should be but slight help to his companion in his present condition. The two men disappeared in the thicket, which closed on them, and they awaited, pistol in hand, the arrival of the persons.

Brighteye was not mistaken. It was really Marksman, returning with some fifteen Gambusinos. When they were only a few paces off, the two horsemen showed themselves. Marksman could not believe his eyes. He did not understand how the man he had left deprived of consciousness, stretched out on the ground like an inert and almost lifeless body, had possessed the strength to come and meet him, and to sit so upright and firm in his saddle.

Don Miguel enjoyed for a little while his triumph, and the admiration he inspired in these men, with whom the sole supremacy is that of strength, and then bent down with a smile to Marksman.

"You are not the less welcome with the help you bring me," he said in a low voice; "this help has become, at this moment, very necessary, if not indispensable; for my resolution alone keeps me in the saddle."

"You must make haste to return to the camp, and, for fear of accident, lie down on a litter."

"A litter?" Don Miguel objected.

"You must, believe me. It is urgent that you should reassume, as soon as possible, the command of your Cuadrilla, so do not waste your strength in useless bravado."

Don Miguel bowed without replying, for he understood the truth of the hunter's remark. So, after getting off his horse with the aid of the two Canadians, he himself ordered his companions to make the litter in which he should be carried to the camp.

Marksman passed his arm through the young man's, and, making a sign to Brighteye to follow them, led him a few paces from the party, and made him sit down on the grass.

"Now that you are in a condition to answer me, profit by the time during which your litter is being made. You have plenty to tell me."

The young man sighed. "Question me," he said.

"Yes, that will be better. How and by whom were you attacked?"

"I cannot tell you. It is a strange history; so confused that it is impossible for me, in spite of all my efforts, to disentangle it."

"No matter. Tell me what happened to you; perhaps we, who are better accustomed to the prairies than yourself, will find a thread which will guide us through this apparently inextricable labyrinth."

Don Miguel then told all the facts that had occurred, in all their detail. At the name of Addick, Marksman frowned; when the Mexican spoke of Don Stefano, the hunters exchanged an intelligent glance; but when the young man reached that singular turn in the combat when, on the point of succumbing, he had been suddenly surrounded by strangers, who disappeared as if by enchantment, after disengaging him, the hunters displayed marks of the greatest surprise.

"Such," Don Miguel concluded, "was the odious ambush into which I fell; and to which I should have been a victim, if you had not arrived so opportunely to save me. Now that you know all as well as I do, what is your opinion?"

"Hum!" the hunter said; "all that is really very extraordinary. There is at the bottom of the affair a dark machination, carried out with a diabolical skill and perversity which startles me. I have certain suspicions which I wish first to clear up; hence, I cannot give you my opinion at once. Before all, I must investigate certain matters; but trust to me for that. But these men who came so fortunately to your help—did you not see them?—did you not speak to them?"

"You forget," Don Miguel said, with a smile, "that they appeared in the thick of the fight; brought as it were by the hurricane, that raged so furiously. The time would have been badly chosen for conversation."

"That is true; I did not know what I was saying. But," the hunter added, striking the ground with the butt of his rifle, "I will not be beaten. I swear to you that I shall soon have discovered who your enemies are, whatever care they may take, and precautions employ, to conceal themselves."

"Oh! I intend to go in pursuit of them, so soon as I have got back my strength."

"You, Caballero," Marksman remarked drily, "have first to get well. On reaching your camp, you will have to shut yourself up, as in a citadel, and not take a step till you have seen me again."

"What! do you intend to leave me, then?"

"Brighteye and myself are going to start directly. We should be of no use near you, while we may be of service elsewhere."

"What do you intend to do?"

"On our return, you shall know all."

"I cannot remain in such a state of uncertainty. Besides, I do not understand you."

"Yet it is clear enough. I intend, aided by Brighteye, to tear the mask from this Don Stefano—a mask which, in my opinion, hides a very ugly countenance—to know who this man is, and why he is such an obstinate enemy to you."

"Thanks, Marksman; now I am easy in my mind. Go; do all that seems proper to you. I am convinced that you will accomplish everything that can be humanly accomplished. But, before separating, promise me one thing."

"What is it?"

"Promise me, that so soon as you have obtained all the information you are going to seek, you will bring it to me, without undertaking anything against this man, on whom I intend to take personally—you understand me, Marksman, personally—exemplary vengeance."

"That is your affair. I shall not interfere with you. Every man has his task in this world; the man is your enemy, and not mine. So soon as I have succeeded in bringing you face to face, or at least putting you opposite each other in an equal position, you will do as you please. I shall wash my hands of it."

"Good, good!" Don Miguel muttered. "If any day I hold that demon in my clutches, as he held me in his, he shall not escape, I swear!"

"So it is settled, we can start?"

"When you please."

Brighteye had hitherto listened calmly to the conversation; but at this remark he stepped forward, and laid his hand on Marksman's arm. "One moment," he said.

"What, more last words?" the hunter answered.

"Only a word; but one which, I fancy, possesses some value in the present state of affairs."

"Make haste, then!"

"You wish to discover who this Don Stefano is, as he thinks proper to call himself, and I approve it; but there is another matter, I fancy, quite as serious, which we ought to try and make out first."

"What is it?"

Brighteye turned his head to the right, and then to the left, bent his body slightly forward, and lowering his voice so that the persons he addressed could hardly hear him, he continued in a severe tone,—"Desert life in no way resembles that in the towns. Down there people know each other slightly or intimately, either by name or through personal relations; they are frequently connected by interests more or less direct; in a word, socialities exist between all the inhabitants of towns, attaching them one to the other, and forming them, as it were, into one family. In the desert this is no longer the case; egotism and personality are the masters; the 'I' is the supreme law; each man only thinks of himself, only acts for himself, and I will say, further, only loves himself."

"Cut it short, for goodness sake, Brighteye; cut it short!" Marksman said impatiently. "What the deuce are you driving at?"

"Patience!" the imperturbable Canadian said; "patience! and you shall know. In short, then, in the desert, unless a man has lived for years side by side with another—sharing pain and pleasure, good fortune and ill, with him—he lives alone, without friends, only counting indifferent persons as enemies. In the trap to which Don Miguel almost fell a victim last night, two sorts of people revealed themselves spontaneously to him. These were, first, inveterate enemies, and then equally staunch friends. Do not fancy," the hunter continued, growing warm, "that I have not calculated the range of the words I have just made use of; you would be greatly mistaken. Does it not seem strange to you, as it does to me, now that you are cool, and reason in all the plenitude of your faculties,—does it not seem strange to you, I repeat, that, at a given moment, without it being possible to know how or why—these men suddenly emerged, as it were, from the ground, to lend you a hand; then, when the danger was past, or nearly so, they disappeared as suddenly as they came, leaving no trace of their passage, and not breaking the incognito which covered them,—is not this strange?—answer!"

"In truth," Marksman muttered, "I did not think of that till now; the conduct of those men is inexplicable."

"That is exactly what must be explained!" Brighteye exclaimed violently. "The prairie is not so densely populated that, at a given moment, and amid a frightful hurricane, there should be men ready to defend you for the mere satisfaction of doing so; those people must have had secret motives for doing so, and that object it is urgent for us to discover. Who tells us that they did not form part of the band which attacked you? that it was not a trick to seize you more easily—a part of the game, the execution of which our unforeseen presence destroyed? I repeat to you, we must, before all, find these men, know who they are, and what they want; in a word, whether they are friends or enemies."

"It is very late now to undertake such a search," Don Miguel observed.

The two hunters smiled, as they exchanged a significant glance. "Very late for you, certainly, who do not possess the key of the desert," Brighteye replied; "but with us it is different."

"Yes," Marksman supported him: "let us only find a trace of their passage, however light it may be—a footstep on the damp sand, so as to hold one end of their trail—that will be enough to reach the other, and we shall give a good account of these strangers, whose conduct, as Brighteye observed very truly, is too strange and too fine to be honest."

"Oh! why cannot I follow you?" Don Miguel exclaimed, regretfully.

"Get well first; then, I am certain, your part will begin; for, before three days, we shall bring you all the information you want today, and without which you can effect nothing."

"So you promise me that in three days—"

"Yes, in three days we shall return from our expedition. Trust to our promise, and nurse yourself, so as to be able to begin the campaign at once."

"I shall be ready."

"So, now, good-bye! the sun is already high in the heavens; we have not a moment to lose."

"Good-bye, and good luck!"

The hunters cordially pressed Don Miguel's hand, remounted their horses, and went off rapidly in the direction of the Rubio ford. The chief of the Gambusinos, laid on a litter, went quickly back to his camp, which he reached a little before sunset.

CHAPTER XVII
DON MARIANO

We will now return to Don Stefano Cohecho, whom we left in a fainting state between Ruperto and Don Mariano.

The double exclamation drawn from the hunter and the Mexican traveller, on recognizing the man they had picked up on the river bank, had plunged all three of them into a profound state of stupefaction. Bermudez was the first to recover his coolness, and he walked up to his master. "Come, Don Mariano," he said to him, "do not stay here. Perhaps it will be as well that, when your brother opens his eyes, he should not see you."

Don Mariano fixed a burning glance on the wounded man. "How is it that I find him here?" he said, as if speaking to himself. "What is he doing in these savage regions? It was false, then, what he wrote about important business calling him to the United States, and that he had started for New Orleans?"

"Señor Don Estevan, your brother," Bermudez replied gravely, "is one of those darkly-intriguing men with whom it is impossible to know their thoughts, or guess their motives or action. You see the hunter gives him a name which does not belong to him. For what purpose does he conceal himself, then? Believe me, Don Mariano, there is a mystery beneath this which we will clear up, with the aid of Heaven; but let us be prudent; let us not reveal our presence to Don Estevan; there will always be time to do so when we discover that we have been deceived."

"That is true, Bermudez; your advice is good, and I will follow it; but, before retiring, let me assure myself as to his present condition. That man is my brother; and, however great the injuries he has done me may be, I should not like to see him die without assistance."

"Perhaps it would be better," Bermudez muttered.

Don Mariano looked at him angrily, and bent over the wounded man. The latter was still in a fainting state. Eglantine lavished on him those delicate and intelligent attentions, of which women of all nations and every colour possess the secret, but yet could not recall him to life.

"Pray, Excellency, take my advice," Bermudez urged, "and retire."

Don Mariano took a last look at his brother, and seemed to hesitate; then turning away, with an effort, he said—"Let us go." The old servant's face brightened.

"I recommend this man to you," Don Mariano added, addressing Ruperto. "Pay him all the attention his condition demands and humanity orders."

The hunter bowed. The Mexican gentleman walked a few steps toward his horse, which, with those of his companions, was fastened to a young ebony tree. Don Mariano retired with regret: a secret voice seemed to warn him to remain. At the moment he placed his foot in the stirrup, a hand was laid on his arm, and he turned sharply. A man was standing by his side. It was Flying Eagle.

The chief had left to the whites the care of transporting the wounded. With the instinct peculiar to his race, he had examined with the utmost attention the scene of the ambush and all the spots whither the accidents of the combat had led the fighters. His object in thus acting had been to discover some trace, some sign, which, in case of need, might be useful to those who had an interest in discovering the causes of the snare laid for Don Miguel. Accident had aided him admirably, by supplying him with a proof whose value must be immense, and which, doubtlessly, Don Stefano would have bought back with his best blood, in order to destroy it. Unfortunately, this proof, interesting as it was, was a sealed letter for the Indian, and in his hands possessed no value.

Flying Eagle immediately thought of Don Mariano, who would probably explain to him the importance of the mysterious find he had made. After turning it over several times, he hid it in his bosom, and with the characteristic decision of his race, walked rapidly back to the camp, where he was certain of finding the Mexican.

"Is my father going away?" the Redskin asked.

"Yes," Don Mariano answered; "but I am glad to see you, Chief, before my departure, that I may thank you for your cordial hospitality."

The Indian bowed. "My father can decipher the 'collars' of the Palefaces. I think," he continued, "the whites have great knowledge. My father must be a chief of his nation."

Don Mariano looked at the Comanche in surprise.

"What do you mean?" he asked him.

"Our Indian fathers taught us to preserve, on the skins of animals, prepared for the purpose, the interesting events that happened in our tribe in the old ages of the world. The Palefaces know all; they possess the great medicine; they also have collars."

"Certainly, we have books, in which, by means of recognized signs, the history of nations, and even the thoughts of men, can be traced."

The Indian made a gesture of joy.

"Good!" he said; "my father must know these signs, for his head is grey."

"I do know them. Can the simple knowledge I possess be of any service to you?"

Flying Eagle shook his head negatively.

"No," he said; "not to me, but perhaps to others."

"I do not understand you, Chief; be good enough, therefore, to explain yourself more clearly, for I wish to go away before that man regains his consciousness."

The Indian took a side glance at the injured man.

"He will not open his eyes for an hour," he said. "Flying Eagle can talk to his father."

In spite of himself, Don Mariano felt interested in knowing what the Indian wished to tell him; so he resolved to wait, and made him a sign to speak. The chief continued in a low voice,—"Let my father listen," he said. "Flying Eagle is not an old gossiping woman; he is a renowned chief. The words his breast breathes are all inspired by the Wacondah. Flying Eagle loves the Palefaces, because they have been good to him, and have, in certain circumstances, rendered him great services. After the fight, the Chief went over the field of battle; near the spot where the man fell whom my father brought here, Flying Eagle found a medicine bag, containing several collars. The Indian looked at them on all sides, but could not understand them, because the Wacondah had spread over his eyes the thick bandage which prevents the Redskins equalling the Whites. Still the Chief, suspecting that perhaps this mysterious bag, useless to him, might be important for my father, or some of his friends, previously concealed it in his breast, and ran in all haste to hand it to my father. Here it is," he added, drawing a portfolio from his bosom, and handing it to Don Mariano; "let my father take it; perhaps he will be able to discover what it contains."

Though the Redskin's action was perfectly natural on his part, and the portfolio and its contents might be matters of indifference to the gentleman, he only took it from the Chief's hands with reluctance. The Indian folded his arms and waited, perfectly satisfied with what he had done.

Don Mariano absently examined the portfolio he held in his hand. It was made of very ordinary shagreen, with no ornaments or gilding; it could be seen that it was more for use than luxury; and it was crammed with papers, and fastened with a small silver clasp. The examination, begun absently, suddenly assumed a great importance for Don Mariano, for his eyes had fallen on these words, half effaced, engraved in letters of gold on one of the sides of the portfolio,—"Don Estevan de Real del Monte."

At the sight of these words, which revealed to him the name of the owner of the object he held, he gave a start of surprise. While turning and speaking, he came on his brother, who still lay unconscious, and by a movement independent of his will, his hand squeezed it forcibly. This pressure opened the hasp, and several papers fell out.

Bermudez stooped quickly, and handed them to his master. The latter mechanically held out his hand to receive them, and return them to the portfolio; but Bermudez checked him resolutely.

"Heaven gives you the means to know the truth at last," he said; "do not neglect the opportunity it affords you, or you may repent it when too late."

"Violate my brother's secrets!" Don Mariano muttered, with a movement of repulsion.

"No," Bermudez retorted drily, "but learn how he became master of yours. Excellency, remember the object of our journey."

"But if I were discovered—if he were not guilty?"

"All the better. In that way you will acquire certainty."

"What you urge me to do is wrong. I have no right to act so."

"Well, I, who am only a wretched Criado, Excellency, whose actions have no serious import, will assume that right for your sake, Excellency." And by a gesture swift as thought, he seized the portfolio.

"Wretch!" Don Mariano shouted. "Stay, what are you going to do?"

"Save, perhaps, her you love, as you dare not do it yourself."

"My father will leave his slave free," the Indian interposed, "the Wacondah inspires him."

Don Mariano had not the courage to resist longer, for involuntarily an unknown feeling he could not explain, told him that he was wrong, and Bermudez did well to act so. The half-caste had, with the greatest coolness, opened the papers, not appearing to care for any seeming impropriety in his conduct.

"Oh!" he suddenly exclaimed, "did I not tell you, Excellency, that Heaven placed in your hands the proofs you had so long been seeking in vain? Read! read! and if it be possible, still doubt the testimony of your eyes, and refuse longer to believe in your brother's perfidy, and odious treason."

Don Mariano seized the papers with a feverish gesture, and hurriedly read them. After reading them two or three times, he stopped, raised his eyes to heaven, and then let his head fall in his hands with an expression of the utmost pain. "Oh, oh!" he muttered, in despair, "my brother! my brother!"

"Courage!" Bermudez said, softly.

"I will have it," he answered; "the hour of justice has arrived."

A strange change had suddenly taken place in him. This man, a few moments previously so timid, and whose hesitation was extreme, was metamorphosed. He seemed to have grown; his features had assumed an imposing rigidity, and his eyes flashed fire.

"No more childish fears," he said; "no further tergiversation. We must act."

Then turning to Flying Eagle, he asked him, —

"Is that man seriously wounded?"

The Indian carefully examined Don Stefano.

During the whole period of the examination, no one uttered a word. Everyone understood that Don Mariano had at length formed an energetic resolution, and that he would accomplish it remorselessly, and without hesitation, no matter what the consequences might be to him hereafter.

Flying Eagle returned in a few minutes.

"Well?" the gentleman asked him.

"That man is not really wounded," the Indian answered; "he has only received a serious contusion on the head, which has plunged him into a sort of lethargic faint, from which he will not recover for an hour."

"Very well; and on waking, in what state will he be?"

"Very weak; but that weakness will soon wear off, and tomorrow he will be as right as before he received the blow."

A bitter smile played round Don Mariano's lips. "Tell that hunter, your friend, to come here; I must speak to you both," he said. "I have a service to ask of you."

The Chief obeyed.

"I am at your service, Excellency," Ruperto remarked.

"We will hold a council," Don Mariano then said. "Is not that the term you employ in the desert when you have to discuss important business?"

The hunter and the Indian made a sign of assent.

"Listen to me attentively," the gentleman continued, in a firm and impressive voice. "The man there is my brother, and he must die. I do not wish to kill him, but to try him. All you now present will be his judges; I his accuser. Will you aid me to accomplish an act of vengeance, but a deed of the most rigorous justice? I repeat to you, I will accuse him before you all, and documents in hand. He will be at liberty to defend himself; your conscience will be clear; he will have entire freedom to do so; and, moreover, you will condemn or acquit him, according to the opinion you form on the evidence. You have heard me; reflect; I await your reply."

There was a supreme silence. After a few moments, Ruperto took the word. "In the desert, where human justice does not penetrate," he said, "the law of God must prevail. If we have a right to kill the noxious and malevolent brutes, why should we not the right to punish a villain? I accept the office you offer me, because in my heart I am persuaded that in doing so I am doing my duty, and am useful to society, of which I make myself the avenger."

"Good!" Don Mariano answered. "I thank you. And you, Chief?"

"I accept," the Comanche said distinctly. "Traitors must be punished, no matter to what race they belong. Flying Eagle is a chief; he has the right to sit at the council fire, in the first rank of the Sachems, and condemn or acquit."

"It is now your turn," Don Mariano continued, addressing his servant; "answer."

Bermudez stepped forward a pace, and bowed respectfully to Don Mariano. "Excellency," he said, "we knew this man when he was a child; we dandled him on our knees. At a later date he became our master; our hearts would not be free in his presence. We cannot judge him; we ought not to condemn him. We are only fit to execute the sentence, whatever it may be, which is dealt out to him, if we receive the order. Old slaves, liberated by the kindness of their master, are never equal to him."

"Those feelings are what I expected from you. I thank you for your frankness, my children. In truth, you should not interfere in this matter. Heaven, I hope, will send us two men with loyal hearts and firm will to take your places, and fulfil the duty of judges impartially."

"Heaven has heard you, Caballero," a rough voice said; "we are here at your disposal."

The branches of the thicket near which our characters were, were then torn boldly asunder, and two men appeared. They walked a few steps forward, rested their rifles on the ground, and waited.

"Who are you?" Don Mariano asked.

"Hunters."

"Your name?"

"Marksman."

"And yours?"

"Brighteye. For about half an hour we have been hidden behind this bush. We heard all you said, and hence it is useless to repeat your statement. But there is another man who must be present at the trial."

"Another man! Who?"

"The one he attacked so traitorously, whom you drew from his hand, and whom we saved."

"Ha! who knows where to find that man at present?"

"We do," Marksman said, "as we only left him an hour ago, to take up your trail."

"Oh, if that is the case, you are right; that man must come."

"Unfortunately, he is seriously wounded; but if he cannot come of himself, he can be carried: and I know not why, but his presence seems to me not only necessary, but even indispensable, in order to clear up certain facts which it is our duty to fathom."

"What do you mean?"

"Patience, Caballero! you will soon understand. This man's camp is not far off, and he can be here before sunset."

"But who will warn him?"

"Myself," Brighteye answered.

"I thank you for the hearty offer."

"We are possibly more interested than yourself in clearing up this mysterious machination," Marksman answered.

At a sign from his friend, Brighteye remounted his horse, which he had left in the thicket, and rode off at full speed, while Don Mariano followed him with a glance at once curious and puzzled. "You speak to me in riddles," he said to Marksman, who was still leaning on his rifle.

The latter shook his head.

"The history, whose odious incidents will be unrolled before you, is a sad one, Excellency, and you have not the key, in spite of the proofs you believe you possess."

Don Mariano sighed, and two burning tears ran down his cheeks, which were furrowed by grief.

"Courage, *mi amo!*" Bermudez said. "Heaven is at length on your side."

The gentleman pressed the hand of his faithful servant, and turned his head away to conceal the emotion he felt.

CHAPTER XVIII
BEFORE THE TRIAL

When Brighteye went off, Marksman, the Indian, and Ruperto approached the wounded man, who was still plunged in the same state of lethargy, and collected around him, in order to await his recovery.

Don Mariano, whose scruples were now extinguished, and who was anxious to know all the windings of his brother's dark machinations, in order to have solid arguments for the accusations he was about to bring against him before that supreme tribunal he had so unexpectedly found, withdrew from his servants into a dense coppice, where, free from all glances, he opened the portfolio with feverish impatience, and began reading the papers it contained, with a horror that increased with every fresh letter he unfolded.

Don Mariano did not wish his brother to be aware of his presence before being confronted with his judges, for he counted on his unexpected apparition to foil his perspicacity and presence of mind, by making him lose his coolness. Hence he concealed himself in a spot invisible to the most searching glance, reserving the right of appearing at the decisive moment.

More than an hour elapsed, ere Don Stefano, in spite of Eglantine's incessant care, made a movement indicating his return to life. Still the three men, crouched silently round him, did not for a moment relax in their watchfulness; they understood the full extent of the act they were about to accomplish, and desired, with that intuitive mistrusting possessed by loyal souls, that the man they were about to try should be sufficiently collected, and so far in possession of his faculties, as to defend his life bravely.

At the moment when the sun, rapidly declining on the horizon, lengthened the shadows of the trees, and only appeared through the lower branches like a huge ball of fire, the evening breeze passed like a fresh breath over the pale brow of the wounded man, who uttered a deep sigh at the feeling of comfort this beneficial freshness caused him to experience, after the stifling heat of the day.

"He is going to open his eyes," Marksman muttered.

Flying Eagle laid his finger on his lips as he pointed to the wounded man.

Low as the hunter had spoken, Don Stefano had heard him; though not, perhaps, understanding the meaning of the words that had struck his ears, but sufficiently so to recall him to a sense of existence.

Don Stefano was no common man, and a worthy son of the bastard race of Mexico. Cunning was the most prominent point in his eminently dissimulating character; accustomed ever to judge men and things badly, distrust seemed innate in his heart. Marksman's words warned him to keep on his guard, without stirring, without opening his eyes, lest he should reveal his return to life; he made a supreme effort to recall the events that preceded his accident, so as to arrive, from deduction to deduction, at the position in which he now was, and guess, if that were possible, into whose hands chance, or his ill fortune, had made him fall.

The task Don Stefano imposed on himself was not easy, for, by the force of circumstances, he was deprived of his most potent auxiliary, sight, which would have enabled him to recognize the persons who surrounded him, or, at any rate, perceive were they friends or enemies. Thus, though he listened with the utmost attention, in order to catch a word or a phrase to guide him in his suppositions, and show him how to base his calculations on probable, if not positive, data, as the hunters, warned by the Chief, and suspecting a trick, abstained for their part from making a gesture or uttering a word, all his previsions were foiled, and he remained in the most utter ignorance.

This prolonged silence further heightened Don Stefano's anxiety, and presently threw him into such a state of alarm that he resolved, at all risks, on removing his doubts. Putting his plans almost at once into execution, he made a movement as if to rise, and suddenly opened his eyes, and took an inquiring and searching glance around.

"How do you feel?" Marksman asked, as he bent over him.

"Very weak," Don Stefano answered, in a suffering voice. "I feel a general heaviness, and frightful buzzing in my ears."

"Good," the hunter continued, "that is not dangerous. It is always so after a fall."

"I have had a fall, then?" the wounded man continued, whom the sight of Ruperto, an old acquaintance, began to reassure.

"Hang it! it is probable, as we found you lying on the banks of the Rubio."

"Ah, you found me, then?"

"Yes, about three hours back."

"Thanks for the aid you gave me; had it not been for that, I should probably be dead."

"Very possibly; but do not be in a hurry to thank us."

"Why not?" Don Stefano suddenly said, as he cocked his ears at this ambiguous answer, which seemed to him a disguised threat.

"Eh, who knows?" Marksman retorted, simply; "No one can answer for the future."

Don Stefano, whose strength was rapidly returning, and who had already regained all his lucidity of mind, rose quickly, and fixed on the Canadian a glance which seemed meant to read his most intricate thoughts. "I am not your prisoner, though?"

"Hum!" was all the hunter replied.

This interjection made the wounded man thoughtful, and disturbed him more than a long phrase. "Let us speak frankly," he said, after a few moments' reflection.

"I wish for nothing better."

"Of you, then, there is one I know," he continued, pointing to Ruperto, who gave a silent nod of assent. "I never, to my knowledge, injured that man; on the contrary—"

"That is true," Ruperto answered.

"I never saw you, so you can have no feelings of animosity against me."

"That is correct. This is the first time Providence has brought us face to face."

"There remains this Indian warrior, who, like yourself, is a perfect stranger to me."

"All that is correct."

"For what reason, then, can I be your prisoner? Unless, as I cannot believe, you belong to those birds of prey, called pirates, who swarm in the desert?"

"We are not pirates, but frank and honest hunters."

"A further reason why I should address my question to you again, and ask you if I am your prisoner or no?"

"The question is not so simple as you suppose, although we have no reproaches to bring against you personally. Have you not insulted or offended other persons since you have been on the prairie?"

"I?"

"Who else but you? Did you not try, no later than last night, to assassinate a man in an ambuscade you laid for him?"

"Yes; but that man is my enemy."

"Well! Suppose, for a moment, we are friends of that man!"

"But it is not so. It cannot be."

"Why not? What makes you suppose so?"

Don Stefano shrugged his shoulders contemptuously.

"You must think me very foolish," he said, "if you would try to make me believe that quibble."

"It is not so much one as you imagine."

"Nonsense! If I had fallen into the hands of that man, he would have had me conveyed to his camp, in order to revenge himself on me in the presence of the bandits he commands, and to whom the sight of my punishment would, doubtlessly, have been too agreeable for him to have tried to deprive them of the delightful sight."

The old hunter, whose language had hitherto been ironical and face malicious, suddenly changed his tone, and became as serious and stern as he had previously been sarcastic. "Listen," he said, "and profit by what you are going to hear. We are not the dupes of your feigned weakness. We know very well that your strength has nearly returned. The advice I give you is frank, and intended to guard you against yourself; you are not our prisoner, it is true, and yet you are not free."

"I do not understand you," Don Stefano interrupted him, the last words clouding over his face, which had suddenly grown brighter.

"Not one of the persons present," Marksman continued, "has any charge to bring against you. We do not know who you are; and before today, I, at least, was entirely ignorant of your existence; but there is a man who asserts that he has against you—not feelings of hatred, for that would be a matter to settle between yourselves in a fair fight—but motives of complaint sufficiently great to justify your immediate trial."

"My trial!" Don Stefano repeated, in the utmost astonishment; "but before what tribunal does that man intend to try me? We are here in the desert."

"Yes; and you seem to forget it. In the desert, where the laws of cities are powerless to punish the guilty, there is a terrible, summary, implacable legislature, to which, in the common welfare, every aggrieved person has a right to appeal, when suspicious circumstances demand it."

"And what is this law?" Don Stefano asked, whose pale face had already assumed a cadaverous hue. —

"It is Lynch law."

"Lynch law?"

"Yes; and in the name of that law we, who, as you say, you do not know, have been assembled to try you."

"Try me! But that is impossible. What crime have I committed? Who is the man that accuses me?"

"I cannot answer these questions. I do not know the crime of which you are accused, nor the name of your accuser; but believe me, we have no hatred or prejudice against you, and we shall, therefore, be impartial. Prepare your defence during the few moments left you, and when the moment arrives, try to prove your innocence, by confounding your accuser — a thing which I ardently desire."

Don Stefano let his head fall in his hands with an expression of despair. "But how would you have me prepare my defence, when I am ignorant of the nature of the crimes imputed to me? Give me a light through the darkness, a flash, however slight, that I may be able to guide myself, and know where I am."

"In speaking as I did, Caballero, I obeyed my conscience, which ordered me to warn you of the danger that threatened you. It would be impossible for me to tell you more, for I am as ignorant as yourself."

"Oh! it is enough to drive a man mad," Don Stefano exclaimed.

At a sign from Marksman, Ruperto and Flying Eagle rose. The hunter nodded to Eglantine to imitate their example. All four withdrew, and Don Stefano was left alone.

The Mexican rolled on the ground with the insensate fury of a man before whom an insurmountable obstacle suddenly rises, and who, driven into a desperate position, is forced to confess himself vanquished. A prey to the deepest anxiety, ignorant whither to turn in order to dispel the tempest growling over his head, he sought in vain in his mind for the means to escape from the hands that held him. His inventive genius, so fertile in schemes of every description, furnished him with no subterfuge, no stratagem, that would aid him advantageously in supporting this supreme contest with the unknown. In vain he racked his brains: he found nothing. Suddenly he drew himself up, and by a movement rapid as thought, thrust his hand into his chest. "Ah!" he exclaimed, sorrowfully, and let his hand fall again by his side, "what has become of my portfolio?" He searched eagerly around him, but found nothing. "I am lost," he added, "if those men have found it. What shall I do? What will become of me?"

A sound of horses was heard in the distance, gradually approaching the spot where the hunters were encamped. The sound soon became more distinct, and it was easy to recognize the advent of a numerous party of horsemen. In fact, within a quarter of an hour, some thirty mounted men, led by Brighteye, entered the clearing. "Brighteye among these bandits!" Don Stefano muttered. "What can be the meaning of it?"

His uncertainty did not last long. The new arrivals escorted a man whom Don Stefano recognized at once. "Don Miguel Ortega! oh, oh!" Then he added, with one of those cunning smiles habitual to him, "Now I know my accuser. Come, come," he said to himself, "the position is not so desperate as I supposed. It is evident these men know nothing, and my precious papers have not fallen into their hands. Hum! I fancy that this terrible Lynch law will be wrong this time, and I shall escape from this peril, as I have done from so many others."

Don Miguel had passed without seeing Don Stefano, or perhaps, as was more likely, without appearing to notice him. As for the prisoner, interested as he was in observing everything, and not allowing the slightest detail to escape his notice, he followed with watchful eye, while feigning the most indifferent behaviour, all the movements of the hunters. After gently depositing the litter at the side of the clearing opposite to that where Don Stefano lay, the Gambusinos, instead of dismounting, formed a large circle, and remained motionless, rifle on thigh, thus rendering any attempt at flight impossible.

Buffalo skulls, intended to act as seats, were arranged in a semicircle round a fire of dry branches. On these skulls, five in number, five men immediately took their seats, arranged in the following order:—Don Miguel Ortega, performing the duties of president, in the centre, having on his right Marksman, on his left Brighteye, and then the Indian Chief and a Gambusino. This tribunal in the open air, in the heart of the virgin forest, surrounded by these horsemen, in their strange costume, motionless as bronze statues, produced an effect at once imposing and striking. These five men, with stern looks and frowning eyebrows, calm and apathetic, bore a marvellous resemblance to that Holy Vehm, which in old times, on the banks of the Rhine, took the place of legal justice, no longer able to repress crime, and gave its judgments in the open air, to the hoarse growling of the winds, and the mysterious murmurs of the waters.

In spite of his daring, Don Stefano felt a shudder of terror all over him, as he looked round the clearing, and saw all eyes fatally fixed upon him, with the implacable rigidity of desert force and justice. "Hum!" he muttered to himself, "I believe I shall have a difficulty to get out of the scrape, and was too hasty in claiming victory."

At this moment, two hunters, at a sign from Don Miguel, quitted the ranks, dismounted, and approached the wounded man. The latter made an effort, and succeeded in gaining his feet. The hunters took him by the arms, and led him before the tribunal. Don Stefano drew himself up, crossed his arms on his chest, and bent a sardonic glance on the men before whom he was led. "Oh, oh!" he said, with a mocking accent, addressing Don Miguel, "it is you, then, Caballero, who are my accuser?"

The captain shrugged his shoulders slightly. "No," he replied; "I am not your accuser, but your judge."

CHAPTER XIX
FACE TO FACE

After these words, there was a moment of expectation—almost of hesitation. A leaden silence seemed to brood over the forest.

Don Stefano was the first to overcome the feeling of terror which involuntarily pervaded him. "Well!" he said, with a contemptuous tone, and a clear, cutting voice; "if it be not you, where is this accuser? Will he hide himself, now that the hour has arrived? Will he recoil before the responsibility he has assumed? Let him appear—I am ready for him!"

Don Miguel shook his head. "When he does appear, you may, perhaps, find that he has come too soon," he answered.

"What do you want with me, then?"

"You shall hear."

Don Miguel was pale and sombre; a sad smile played round his discoloured lips; it was evident that he was making extraordinary exertions to overcome his weakness and keep his seat. After a few moments' consideration, he raised his head. "What is your name?" he asked.

"Don Stefano Cohecho," the accused answered without hesitation.

The judges exchanged a glance.

"Where were you born?"

"At Mazatlán, in 1808."

"What is your profession?"

"Merchant, at Santa Fé."

"What motive brought you into the desert?"

"I have told you already."

"Repeat it!" Don Miguel said, with perfect coldness.

"I would remark that these questions, perfectly unnecessary for you, are beginning to grow tiresome."

"I ask you what motive brought you into the desert?"

"The failure of several of my correspondents compelled me to take a journey, in the hope of saving some fragments of my endangered fortune. I am in the desert, because there is no other road to the town I wish to reach."

"Where are you going?"

"To Monterey. You see the docility with which I answer all your questions," he said, with the impertinent tone he had assumed ever since he was led before his judges.

"Yes," Don Miguel replied, slowly, and laying a stress on each word, "you display great docility. I wish, for your own sake, you were equally truthful."

"What do you mean by that remark?" Don Stefano asked, haughtily.

"I mean that you have answered each of my questions with a falsehood," Don Miguel said, coolly and drily.

Don Stefano frowned, and his tawny eye emitted a flash. "Caballero!" he said, violently, "such an insult—"

"It is no insult," the adventurer answered, in his old tone; "it is the truth, and you know it as well as I."

"I should be curious to know the meaning of this," the Mexican tried to say.

Don Miguel looked at him fixedly; and, in spite of his impudence, Don Stefano could not endure the glance.

"I will satisfy you," the adventurer said.

"I am listening."

"To my first question you answered that your name was Don Stefano Cohecho?"

"Well?"

"That is false; for your name is Don Estevan de Real del Monte."

The accused gave a slight start. Don Miguel continued:—"To my second question, you replied that you were born at Mazatlán, in 1808. That is false; you were born at Guanajuato, in 1805."

The adventurer waited a moment, to give the man he addressed time to reply. But Don Estevan, whose right name we will in future adhere to, did not think it advisable to do so. He remained cold and gloomy. Don Miguel smiled contemptuously, and continued:—

"To my third question, you answered that you carried on the business of a merchant, and were established at Santa Fé. That is all false. You never were a merchant. You are a senator, and reside in Mexico. Lastly—You said you were only crossing the desert on your road to Monterey, where the interests of your pretended business called you. As for the latter assertion, I need hardly, I believe, prove its falsehood to you, for that is palpable from the other answers you made. Now I await your reply, if you have one to make—which I doubt."

Don Estevan had had time enough to recover from the rude blow he had received; hence he did not feel alarmed, as he believed he could guess whence the attack came, and by what means those in whose presence he now was had obtained this information about him. Hence he replied in a sarcastic tone, and drawing in his lips spitefully,—"Why do you fancy I cannot answer you, Caballero? Nothing is more easy; on the contrary, *cáspita!* because, during my fainting fit, you—shall I say robbed me? No, I am polite; I will therefore say—adroitly carried off my portfolio; and because, after opening it, you obtained certain information, you throw it in my face, convinced that I shall feel disarmed by your being so conversant with my affairs. Nonsense! You are mad, on my soul. All these things are absurdities, which will not bear analysis. Yes, it is true that my name is Don Estevan. I was born at Guanajuato, in 1805, and am a senator—what next? Those are strong motives on which to base an accusation against a Caballero! *Cuerpo de Cristo!* Am I the only man in the desert who assumes a name other than his own? By what right do you, who only call each other by your surnames, wish to prevent me from following your example? It is the height of absurdity; and if you have no better reason to allege, I must ask you to let me go and attend to my affairs in peace."

"We have others," Don Miguel answered, in an icy tone.

"I know your reasons. You, Don Miguel, who are also called Don Torribio, and sometimes Don José, accuse me of having laid a trap for you, from which you were only saved by a miracle. But that is a matter between ourselves, in which Heaven alone must be the arbiter."

"Do not bring that name forward. I have already told you that I was not your accuser, but your judge."

"Very good. Restore me my portfolio, and let us stop here, believe me, for in all this there is no advantage for you, unless you have resolved to assassinate me, which is very possible; and in that case I am at your service. I do not pretend to contend against the thirty or forty bandits who surround me. So kill me if you think proper, and let us have an end of it."

Don Stefano uttered these words with a tone of sovereign contempt, which his judges, like men whose mind is made up beforehand, did not appear to notice.

"We have not stolen your portfolio," Don Miguel answered; "not one of us has seen it, much less opened it. We are not bandits, and have no design to assassinate you. We are assembled to try you according to the regulations of Lynch Law; and we perform this duty with all the impartiality of which we are capable."

"If that be the case, let my accuser appear, and I will confound him. Why does he hide himself so obstinately? Justice must be done in the sight of all. Let this man come, who asserts that he has such heavy crimes to bring against me—let him come, and I will prove him a vile calumniator."

Don Estevan had scarcely uttered these words, ere the branches of a neighbouring bush were drawn back, and a man appeared. He walked hastily toward the Mexican, and laid his hand boldly on his shoulder.

"Prove to me, then, that I am a vile calumniator, Don Estevan," he said, in a low and concentrated voice, as he regarded him with an expression of implacable hatred.

"Oh," Don Estevan exclaimed, "my brother!" and lolling like a drunken man, he recoiled a few paces, his face covered with a deadly pallor, his eyes suffused with blood, and immeasurably dilated. Don Mariano held him with a firm hand, to prevent him falling on the ground, and placed his face almost close to his.

"I am your accuser, Estevan," he said. "Accursed one, what have you done with my daughter?"

The other made no reply. Don Mariano regarded him for a moment with an expression impossible to describe, and disdainfully threw him off with a gesture of sovereign contempt. The wretch tottered, and stretched out his arms, trying instinctively to keep up; but his strength failed him; he fell on his knees, and buried his face in his hand, with an expression of despair and baffled rage, the hideousness of which no pencil could render.

The spectators remained calm and stoical. They had not uttered a word or made a sign; but a secret terror had seized upon them, and they exchanged looks which, if the accused had seen them, would have revealed to him the fate which in their minds they reserved for him.

Don Mariano gave his two servants a signal to follow him, and, with one on either side, he took his place in the centre of the clearing, in front of the improvised tribunal, and began speaking in a powerful, clear, and accented voice. "Listen to me, Caballeros, and when I have told you all I have to say about the man you see there crushed and confounded, before I had even uttered a word, you will judge him according to your conscience, without hatred or anger. That man is my brother. When young, for a reason it is unnecessary to explain here, my father wished to drive him from his presence. I interceded for him, and though I did not obtain his entire pardon, still he was tolerated beneath the paternal roof. Days passed, years slipped away; the boy became a man; my father, at his death, gave me his whole fortune, to the prejudice of his other son, whom he had cursed. I tore up the will, summoned that man to my side, and restored him, a beggar and a wretch, that share of the wealth and comfort of which his father, in my opinion, had not the right to deprive him."

Don Mariano stopped, and turned to his servants. The two men stretched out their right hands together, took off their hats, and said, in one voice, as if replying to their master's dumb questioning, — "We affirm that all this is strictly true."

"Hence this man owed me everything — fortune, position, future; for, owing to my influence, I succeeded in having him elected a senator. Let us now see how he rewarded me for so many kindnesses, and the extent of his gratitude. He had succeeded in making me forget what I regarded as errors of youth, and persuade myself that he was entirely reformed: his conduct was ostensibly irreproachable; under certain circumstances, he had even displayed a rigour of principle, for which I was obliged to reprove him; in a word, he had succeeded in making me his dupe. Married, and father of two children, he brought them up with a strictness which, in my eyes, was a proof of his reformation; and he carefully repeated to me often — 'I do not wish my children to become what I have been.' Owing to one of those numberless *pronunciamientos* which undermine and dismember our fine country, I was an object of suspicion to the new government, through some dark machination, and compelled to fly at once to save my threatened life, I knew not to whom to confide my wife and daughter, who, in spite of their desire, could not follow me. My brother offered to watch over them. A secret presentiment, a voice from heaven, which I did wrong to despise, warned my heart not to put faith in this man, nor accept his proposition. Time pressed; I must depart; the soldiers sent to arrest me were thundering at the door of my house; I confided what was dearest to me in the world to that coward there, and fled. During the two years my absence lasted, I wrote letter after letter to my brother, and received no reply. I was suffering from mortal alarm, and was almost resolved, at all risks, to return to Mexico, when, thanks to certain friends who were indefatigable in my behalf, my name was erased from the list of postscripts, and I was permitted to return to my country. Scarcely two hours after receiving the news, I set out. I arrived at Veracruz four days later. Without taking time to rest, I mounted a horse, and galloped off, only leaving my wearied steed to take another, along the seventy leagues of road separating the capital from the port, and dismounted at my brother's door. He was away, but a letter from him informed me that, compelled by urgent business to proceed to New Orleans, he would return in a month, and begged me to await him. But not a word about my wife and daughter; not a syllable about the fortune I had entrusted to him. My alarm was changed into terror, and I presaged a misfortune. I left my brother's house, half mad, remounted the almost foundered horse that had brought me there, and proceeded as rapidly as possible to my own house. Windows and doors were closed; the house I had left so gay and animated was silent and gloomy as a tomb. I stood for a moment, not daring to rap at the door. At length I made up my mind, preferring the reality, however horrible it might be, to the uncertainty which drove me mad."

At this point in his story Don Mariano stopped. His voice was broken by the internal emotion he experienced, and which it was impossible for him to master any longer.

There was a solemn silence. Don Estevan had not changed his position. Since the beginning of his brother's narrative, he appeared to be plunged in profound grief, and crushed by remorse.

Presently, Bermudez, seeing that his master was incapable of continuing his narrative, took the word in his turn, —"It was I who opened the door. Heaven is my witness that I love my master, and unhesitatingly would lay down my life for him. Alas! I was fated to cause him the greatest grief it is possible for a man to suffer—forced to answer the questions he pressed on me. I told him of the decease of his wife and daughter, who had died a few weeks after each other in the convent of the Bernardines. The blow was terrible; Don Mariano fell as if struck by lightning. One evening, when, as was his custom since his return, Don Mariano was alone in his bedroom, with his face buried in his hands, giving way to sorrowful reflections, while regarding, with eyes full of tears, the portrait of the dear beings he was never to see again, a man wrapped up in a large cloak, and with a sombrero pulled down over his eyes, demanded speech of señor de Real del Monte. On my remarking that his Excellency saw nobody, this man insisted with strange tenacity, declaring he had to hand to my master a letter, the contents of which were of the utmost importance. I know not how it was, but the man's tone appeared to me so sincere, that, in spite of myself, I infringed the positive orders I had received, and led him to Don Mariano."

That gentleman at this moment raised his head, and laid his hand on the old servant's arm. "Let me continue now, Bermudez," he said. "What I have to add is not much."

Then, turning to the hunters, who still appeared cold and apathetic, he went on, —"When this man was in my presence, he said, without any introductory remarks, 'Excellency, you weep for two persons who were very dear to you, and whose fate is unknown to you.' 'They are dead,' I replied. 'Perhaps so,' he said. 'What will you give the man who brings you, I will not say good news, but a slight hope?'"

"Without replying, I rose, and went to a cabinet, in which I kept my gold and jewels. 'Hold out your hat,' I said to him. In a second the hat was full of gold and diamonds. The stranger put them all out of sight, and said, with a low bow,—'My name is Pepito; I am a little of all trades. A man, whose name you need not know, gave me this strip of paper, with orders to hand it to you immediately on your arrival in Mexico. I only learned your return this morning, and have now come to carry out the order I received.'"

"I tore the paper from his hands, and read it, while Pepito deluged me with thanks, to which I did not listen, and then retired. This was what the paper contained."

Don Miguel stretched out his arm toward Don Mariano.

"'A friend of the Real del Monte family,'" the Gambusino said, in a loud voice, "'warns Don Mariano that he has been shamelessly deceived by the man in whom he placed entire confidence, and who owed everything to him. That man poisoned Doña Serafina de Real del Monte. Don Mariano's daughter was buried alive in the *In pace* of the Bernardine convent. If señor del Monte desires to examine thoroughly the frightful machinations of which he has been the victim, and perchance see again one of the two persons whom the man who deceived fancied had disappeared for ever, let Don Mariano keep the contents of this letter the most profound secret, feign the same ignorance, but quietly make preparations for a long journey, which no one must suspect. On the next 5th November, at sunset, a man will be at the Teocali do Quinametzin (the Giant). This man will accost Don Mariano by pronouncing two names, those of his wife and daughter. Then he will tell him all that he is ignorant of, and perhaps be able to restore him a little of the happiness he has lost.' The note ended here, and was not signed."

"That is true," Don Mariano said, utterly astounded; "but how did you learn these details? It was doubtlessly yourself who—"

"When the time arrives, I will answer you," Don Miguel said, in a peremptory tone. "Go on."

"What more shall I say? I started for the strange meeting promised me, nourishing in my heart I know not what mad hopes. Alas! man is so constituted that he clings to everything which can aid him in doubting a misfortune. This day, God, who has probably taken pity on me, made me meet the man who is my brother; the sight of him caused me an astonishment

I cannot express. How could it be him, when he had written me he was gone to New Orleans? A vague suspicion, which I had hitherto repulsed, gnawed at my heart with such force, that I began to believe, though it appeared to me very horrible, that my brother was the traitor to whom I owed all my misfortunes. Still I doubted, I was undecided, when this portfolio, lost by the wretch and found by the Indian Chief, Flying Eagle, suddenly tore off the thick bandage that covered my eyes, by giving me all the proofs of the odious machinations and crimes committed by this wretch, this cruel fratricide, for the ignoble object of robbing me of my fortune to enrich his children. Here is the portfolio. Read the papers it contains, and decide between my villainous brother and myself."

While saying this, Don Mariano offered the portfolio to Don Miguel, who, however, declined it.

"Those proofs are unnecessary for us, Don Mariano," he said; "we possess others more convincing still."

"What do you mean?"

"You shall understand." And Don Miguel rose.

Without being able to explain why it was so, Don Estevan felt a shiver all over his body, for he guessed, by a species of intuition, that his brother's accusation contained nothing so terrible as the facts Don Miguel was preparing to reveal. He threw up his head slightly, bent forward, and with panting chest and dilated nostrils, fascinated, as it were, by the chief of the adventurers, he awaited, with constantly increasing anxiety, what Don Miguel was going to say.

CHAPTER XX
THE JUDGMENT

The sun had disappeared on the horizon; shadows had assumed the place of light; the darkness falling from the sky had covered the forest with an impenetrable brown shroud. The Gambusinos lighted branches of *ocote*, and then the clearing, in which the events we are describing took place, was fantastically lighted by torches, whose flickering, ensanguined glare played on the trees and the persons collected under their dense foliage, and gave the whole scene a strange and sinister stamp.

Don Miguel, after looking around to demand attention, began speaking:—"As you have found that portfolio," he said, "I have nothing more to tell you. It was really your brother who committed the fearful crime with which you charge him. Fortunately, his object could not be completely attained. Your wife is dead, it is true, Don Mariano; but your daughter still lives. She is in safety, and it was I who was fortunate enough to tear her from her tortures, and from that *In pace* in which she was thrust alive. I will restore your daughter to you, Don Mariano, pure and uncontaminated as when I took her from her tomb."

Don Mariano, so fierce in grief, was unable to bear joy. The commotion the news produced was so violent, that he rolled unconsciously on the ground; clasping his hands fervently with a last effort to thank Heaven for having granted him so much joy, after visiting him with so much suffering. The gentleman's servants, aided by several Gambusinos, hastened round him, and paid him all the attention his condition demanded.

Don Miguel allowed time for the emotion produced by Don Mariano's fall to calm, and then made a sign for silence. "It is now our turn, Don Estevan," he said. "Furious at seeing one of your victims escape you, you did not fear to pursue her even to this spot. Knowing that it was I who saved her, you laid a snare for me, in which you hoped I should perish. The hour has arrived to settle our accounts."

On seeing that he no longer had his brother as his adversary, Don Estevan regained all his boldness and impudence. At this address he drew himself up coldly, and fixed a sarcastic glance on the young man. "Oh! oh!" he said ironically; "my good gentleman, you would not be sorry to assassinate me, eh? so as to make me hold my tongue. Do you fancy me the dupe of the fine sentiments you utter so complacently? Yes, you saved my niece, that is true; and I should thank you for it, did I not know you so thoroughly."

At these singular words, his hearers made a movement of surprise, which did not escape Don Estevan's notice. Satisfied with the effect he found he had produced, he went on.

The scoundrel had judged the question at the first glance. Unable completely to exonerate himself, he resolved to turn the difficulty, which he expected to do the more easily, because the only person capable of contradicting him was unable to hear him and put matters in the right light. He assumed a placid countenance, and said, with affected honesty:—"Good heavens! not one of us is infallible. Who does not commit an error, at least once in his life? Far from me be the thought of lessening the opprobrium of the deed I am accused of. Yes, I broke my pledged faith; I deceived my brother, the man to whom I owed all. You see, Caballeros, that I do not attempt to exculpate myself; but between that fault and the committal of a crime, there is a vast difference, and, thanks to Heaven, I cannot be accused of an assassination; and I throw back the responsibility of this shameful deed on the right person."

"Who is that man?" Don Miguel asked, involuntarily astonished and terrified by the fellow's cunning.

"Oh," he said, with imperturbable coolness, "I will throw the responsibility on those too zealous people who ever understand much more than they should understand, and who, either through covetousness or some other motive, always go further than they ought. I confess that I certainly desired to get hold of my brother's fortune; but I intended to do so legally."

The Gambusinos, all scoundrels gifted with a marvellously elastic conscience, which naturally rendered them very unscrupulous as to deeds more or less reprehensible, were, however, terrified on hearing such a theory. They asked each other, in a low voice, with the simple credulity of semi-savages, if the man before them, who spoke thus, were really their fellow being, or whether the Evil Spirit had not assumed this shape in order to deceive them?

"Understand me clearly, Caballeros," Don Estevan continued, in a voice growing, every moment firmer, "the Mother Superior of the Bernardines is my relative, and has an unbounded affection for me. When I let her see through my plans, she urged me to persevere, assuring me that she knew an infallible means to make my projects succeed. I believed her words the more easily, because these means were very simple, and consisted in compelling my niece to take the veil. I looked no further, I swear to you. Poor child, I loved her too dearly to desire her death! All went on as I desired, though I in no way interfered; my sister-in-law died; that death seemed to me perfectly natural, after the numberless sorrows that had overpowered her. I am accused of having poisoned her. It is false! Perhaps she was so; I will not affirm the contrary; but in that case my relative must be accused of the crime, whose object it was, evidently, to bring the fortune I coveted nearer to my grasp. I wrote at once to my brother, telling him of this death, which really grieved me; but he did not receive the letter. I see nothing astonishing in that, because he was continually going from town to town, as his fancy led him. I frequently went to the convent to visit my niece; she seemed to me determined to take the veil. The Mother Superior, for her part, incessantly told me not to trouble myself about anything; hence I let matters go on without any interference on my part. On the day my niece was to take the veil, I went to the convent; then, something unusual and scandalous occurred. At the moment of professing, the girl refused distinctly to become a nun, and I retired in despair at this misadventure. In the evening, a nun came to my house and told me that my niece, after a very violent scene with the Mother Superior, had been attacked by congestion of the brain, and died suddenly. This news caused me considerable grief. All night I walked about my room, deploring the irreparable misfortune which overwhelmed my unhappy brother. On reflection, a suspicion sprung up in my mind. This death appeared to me peculiar, and I dreaded a crime. In order to clear up my doubts, I hurried to the convent at daybreak; there a fresh surprise awaited me. The community were upset—terror was visible on every face. During the night a band of armed men entered the convent; my niece was torn from her tomb and carried off by these men, who at the same time took away a young novice. Then, convinced that I was not deceived, and that a crime had been committed, I shut myself up with the Mother Superior in her cell, and, by menaces and entreaties, succeeded in dragging the truth from her. My horror was extreme on learning that my unfortunate niece had really been interred alive. One thing was left me to do; one duty to fulfil. I must discover traces of her, rescue her, and restore her to her father's arms. I did not hesitate, but set out two days later. That is the entire truth; my conduct has been reprehensible, even culpable; but, I swear it, it has not been criminal."

The audience had listened to this daring justification with icy silence. When Don Estevan stopped speaking, not a sign of approval gave him a hope of having convinced his hearers.

"Supposing—though I do not admit it, for there are too many proofs to the contrary—that what you assert be true," Don Miguel answered him, "for what reason did you wish to assassinate me, when I had saved her whom you had wished to restore to her father's arms?"

"Do you not understand that?" Don Estevan exclaimed, in feigned surprise. "Must I tell you everything?"

"Yes, everything," the young man answered, coldly.

"Well, yes, I did wish to assassinate you, because at the Presidio de Tubar I was assured that you had only carried off my niece for the purpose of dishonouring her. I wished to avenge on you the outrage I believed you had done her."

Don Miguel turned pale at this insult. "Villain!" he shouted, in a voice of thunder, "do you dare to utter such an atrocious calumny?"

The auditors had started in horror at Don Estevan's words, and, feeling himself conquered, in spite of all his audacity, he was compelled to bow his head beneath the weight of the general reprobation.

Marksman then rose. "Caballeros," he said, "you have heard the accusation brought against this man by his brother. During the whole time that accusation lasted, you remarked his countenance; now you have heard his defence. We have allowed him to say what he pleased, without trying to interrupt or intimidate him: the hour has now arrived to pronounce judgment. It is always a serious thing to condemn a man, even the worst of malefactors. Lynch law, you know as well as I, admits no compromises; it kills or it acquits. Although chosen to try this man, we will not alone assume the responsibility of the act. Reflect, then, seriously before answering the questions I shall address to you, and, before all, remember that on your answer depends the life or death of this wretched man. Caballeros, on your soul and conscience, is this man guilty?"

There was a moment of supreme silence; all the faces were grave, all hearts beat forcibly. Don Estevan, with frowning brow, pale face, but firm look—for he was brave—waited, a prey to an anxiety which he could only conceal by the firmness of his will.

Marksman, after waiting several minutes, went on in a slow and solemn voice,—"Caballeros, is this man guilty?"

"Yes!" all exclaimed, unanimously.

At this moment, Don Mariano, through the care of his servants, was beginning to give signs of life, precursors of his return to consciousness.

Brighteye bent over to Marksman. "Is it right," he whispered, "that Don Mariano should be present at his brother's condemnation?"

"Certainly not," the old hunter said, quickly; "the more so, as now that the first outbreak of wrath has passed, he would probably intercede in his favour. But how shall we get him away?"

"I'll manage that, and take him to the Gambusinos' camp."

"Make haste!"

Brighteye rose, and walked to Bermudez, in whose ear he whispered a few words; then the two servants, taking their master under the arms, disappeared with him in the thickets, followed by the hunter and Eglantine, to whom the Canadian had made a sign to come. In the state of agitation and excitement the Gambusinos were in, no one noticed this departure, and not even the sound of several horses going away was heard.

Don Estevan alone noticed this removal, the purpose of which he understood. "I am lost," he muttered.

Marksman made a sign, and silence was restored, as if by enchantment. "What penalty does the culprit deserve?" he asked.

"Death!" the audience replied, like a funeral echo.

Then, turning to the condemned man, Marksman continued—"Don Estevan de Real del Monte, you, who came into the desert with criminal intentions, have fallen beneath the stroke of Lynch law; it is the law of God; eye for eye, tooth for tooth; it admits of only one punishment, that of retaliation; it is the primitive law of old times restored to humanity. You condemned a hapless maiden to be buried alive, and perish of hunger. You will also be buried alive, to die of hunger; but as you might long call on death ere it came to your aid, we will give you the means to put an end to your sufferings when the courage to endure them longer fails you. We are more merciful than you were to your unhappy victim; for you will be only interred up to the armpits, your left arm will remain at liberty, and we will place within your reach a pistol, with which you can blow out your brains when you have suffered sufficiently. I have spoken. Is this sentence just?" he added, addressing his audience.

"Yes," they said, in a low and concentrated voice. "Eye for eye, tooth for tooth!"

Don Estevan had listened with horror to the old hunter's words; the fearful punishment to which he was condemned had struck him with stupor; for though he expected death, that prepared for him seemed so frightful, that at first he could not believe it; still, when he saw, at a sign from Marksman, two Gambusinos set to work digging a hole, his hair stood upright with terror, an icy perspiration beaded on his temples, and he cried, in a hoarse voice, as he clasped his hands,—"Oh, not that atrocious death, I implore you; kill me at once!"

"You are condemned, and must endure your punishment, such as it was pronounced," the old hunter answered.

"Oh, give me the pistol you promised me, that I may blow out my brains on the spot. You will be avenged."

"We are not taking vengeance; the pistol will be left you when we depart."

"Oh, you are implacable!" he said, as he fell to the ground, where he writhed in impotent rage.

"We are just," Marksman merely answered.

Don Estevan, having arrived at the height of fury, leaped up suddenly, and, bounding like a jaguar, rushed head down, against a tree, with the intention of dashing out his brains. But the Gambusinos watched his movements too closely to let him carry out his desperate resolve; they seized, and, despite his obstinate resistance and wild ravings, they bound him, and rendered it impossible for him to make a movement. His wrath then changed to despair. "Oh!" he shouted, "were my brother here, he would save me. Oh, heavens! Mariano, help me, help me!"

Marksman walked up to him.

"You are about to be placed in your grave," he said to him. "Have you any final arrangements to make?"

"Then this horrible punishment is true?" he said, wildly.

"It is true."

"You must be wild beasts, then."

"We are your judges."

"Oh, let me live, be it only for a day!"

"You are condemned."

"Maldición on you, demons with human faces! Assassins, who gives you the right to kill me?"

"By the right every man possesses to crush a serpent. For the last time, have you any arrangements to make?"

Don Estevan, crushed by this fearful contest, kept silence for an instant; then two tears slowly dropped from his fever-burned eyes, and he murmured in a gentle, almost childlike voice,—"Oh, my sons, my poor darlings! What will become of you when I am no longer here?"

"Make haste," the hunter said.

Don Estevan fixed a haggard eye upon him. "I have two sons," he said, speaking as in a dream; "they have only me left, alas! and I am about to die! Listen, if you are not utterly a wild beast. Swear to perform what I ask of you?"

The hunter felt moved by this poignant grief.

"I swear it," he said.

The condemned seemed to be collecting his ideas. "Paper and a pencil," he said.

Marksman still held the portfolio; he tore a leaf from it, and gave it to him, with the pencil.

Don Estevan smiled bitterly at the sight of his portfolio. He clutched the paper, and hurriedly wrote a few lines, which he gave to the hunter. An extraordinary change had taken place in the prisoner's face; his features were calm, his glance gentle and suppliant. "Here," he said, "I count on your word. Take this letter; it is for my brother. I recommend my children to him; it is for their sake I am dying. No matter! if they are happy, I shall have attained my object—that is all I want. My brother is good; he will not abandon the unhappy orphans I leave as a heritage to him. I implore you, give him that paper."

"Within an hour it shall be in his hands; I swear it!"

"Thanks. Now do with me what you please; I care little. I have insured the welfare of my children; that was all I wished for."

The hole had been dug. Two Gambusinos seized Don Estevan, and lowered him into it. When he was standing upright in the hole, the ground was just on a level with his armpits; his right arm was fastened along his side, the other left free. Then the earth was piled up around this living man, who was already no more than a corpse. When the hole was filled up, a Gambusino approached the condemned man with a scarf.

"What are you going to do?" he asked in terror, though he guessed the man's purpose.

"To gag you," the Gambusino said, brutally.

"Oh!" he remarked.

He allowed himself to be gagged without resistance, and was, indeed, hardly conscious of what was being done with him. Marksman then placed a pistol under the wretch's quivering hand, and took off his hat. "Don Estevan," he said, in a grave and solemn voice, "men have condemned you. Pray to God that He may be merciful to you, for you have no hope but in Him."

The hunters and Gambusinos then remounted their horses, extinguished the torches, and disappeared in the darkness, like a legion of black phantoms. The culprit was left alone in the gloom, which his remorse peopled with hideous spectres. With neck stretched out, eyes widely dilated, and ears on the watch, he looked and listened. So long as he heard the echo of the horses' footfalls in the distance, a wild hope still filled his soul; he waited—he expected. What did he await—what expect? He could not have said, himself; but man is so constituted. Gradually every sound died out, and Don Estevan at length found himself alone, in the heart of an unknown desert, with no hope of help from anyone. Then he uttered a profound sigh, closed his hand on the pistol, and placed the icy muzzle against his temple, muttering for the last time the name of his children.

In the meantime the Gambusinos withdrew, a prey to that feeling of undefinable uneasiness which involuntarily contracts the heart of every man, when he has accomplished an act in which he knows that he had, perhaps, no right to take the initiative—even when recognizing its necessity and even strict justice. No one spoke; all heads were bowed. They rode along, gloomy and thoughtful, by each other's side, not daring to interchange their reflections, and listening to the mysterious sounds of the solitude. They had just reached the last limits of the forest covert: before them the waters of the Rubio glistened like a long, silver ribbon in the pale moonlight. They had gained the ford, when suddenly the distant explosion of a firearm resounded hoarsely, driven back by the echoes of the Quebradas. Instinctively these men, for all they were so brave and well tried, shuddered, and stopped with a movement of stupor—almost of terror. There was a minute of ghostly silence. Marksman understood that he must break the gloomy dream which weighed like remorse on all these men. Hence, masking with some difficulty the emotion that almost choked him, he said, in a grave voice:—"Brothers! the vengeance of the desert is satisfied. The scoundrel we condemned has at length done justice on himself."

There is in the human voice a strange and incomprehensible power. The few words uttered by the Scout sufficed to restore to all these men their pristine energy.

"May heaven be merciful to him!" Don Miguel responded.

"Amen!" the Gambusinos said, crossing themselves piously.

From this moment the heavy weight that oppressed them was removed; the culprit was dead. The unpleasant logic of an accomplished fact once again justified Lynch Law, and at the same time stifled regret and remorse, by putting an end to the cruel uncertainty which had hitherto oppressed them.

Don Stefano once dead, the girl he had so pitilessly pursued was saved, in the eyes of these iron-hearted men: this reason alone was sufficient to extinguish in them all pity for the criminal. A sudden reaction took place in them, and their rebel natures, momentarily subdued, rose again stronger and more implacable than ever.

At a signal from the Canadian, the party recommenced their march, and soon disappeared among the sandhills which cover the banks of the Rubio ford. The desert, for an instant troubled by the sound of the horses' feet on the pebbles, fell back into its calm and majestic silence.

CHAPTER XXI
BRIGHTEYE

Brighteye, as we mentioned, aided by the two servants, had succeeded in carrying off Don Mariano, who was still in a half-fainting state, in order to spare him the atrocious sight of his brother's execution. The motion and the night air rapidly restored the old gentleman to life. On opening his eyes, his first word, after looking around him to see where he was, was to ask about his brother. No one answered; the people who led him along redoubled their speed.

"Stay!" Don Mariano then shouted, as he rose with an effort, and tore the bridle from the hands of his leader. "Stop—I insist!"

"Are you in a condition to manage your own horse?" Brighteye asked him.

"Yes," he replied.

"Then we will let loose; but on one condition."

"What is it?"

"That you will promise to follow us."

"Am I your prisoner, then?"

"Oh, no! far from that!"

"Why, then, is this attempt to force my will?"

"We are merely acting on your behalf."

"How am I here?"

"Cannot you guess?"

"I am waiting for your explanation."

"We did not wish that, after accusing your brother, you should witness his execution."

Don Mariano, overpowered, let his head droop, sadly. "Is he dead?" he asked, with a shudder.

"Not yet," Brighteye answered.

The hunter's accent was so gloomy, his face so mournful, that the Mexican gentleman was struck with terror. "Oh, you have killed him!" he muttered.

"No," Brighteye answered, drily, "he must die by his own hand. He will kill himself."

"Oh! that is horrible! In Heaven's name tell me all; I prefer the truth, however fearful it may be, to this frightful uncertainty."

"Why describe the same to you? You will know all the details only too well presently."

"Very good," Don Mariano answered, resolutely, as he stopped his horse; "I know what is left me to do."

Brighteye looked at him in a very peculiar manner, and laid his hand on his bridle. "Take care," he said, drily, "not to let yourself be carried away by the first impulse, which is always unreflecting, and regret presently what you have done tonight."

"Still, I cannot let my brother perish," he exclaimed; "I should be a fratricide."

"No! for he has been justly condemned. You were only the instrument Divine Justice employed to punish a criminal."

"Oh! your spurious arguments will not convince me, my master. If, in a moment of passion and senseless hatred, I forgot the ties that attached me to that unhappy man, now that I see and understand all the horror of my action, I will repair the evil I have done."

Brighteye pressed his arm forcibly, leaned over to his ear, and said:— "Silence! you will destroy him by trying to save him. It is not your place to try it; leave that to others."

Don Mariano tried to read in the hunter's eye the determination he seemed to have formed, and, letting go of the bridle, he went on with a thoughtful air. A quarter of an hour later, they reached the Rubio ford. They stopped on the bank of the river, which, having fallen back into its narrow bed, flowed on calmly and gently at this moment.

"Go to the camp," Brighteye said; "it is useless for me to accompany you further. I am going," he added, with a significant glance at Don Mariano, "to join the Gambusinos. Continue your road gently, and you will arrive at the camp only a few minutes before us."

"Then you return?" Don Mariano asked.

"Yes!" Brighteye answered; "good-bye for the present."

"For the present!" the old gentleman said, as he held out his hand. The hunter took it, and pressed it cordially. Don Mariano urged his horse into the water, and his servants silently imitated him. Brighteye remained motionless on the bank, and watched them cross. Don Mariano turned, waved his hand to him, and the three men disappeared in the tall grass. So soon as they were out of sight, Brighteye turned his horse round, and regained the covert of the virgin forest. The hunter seemed to be sadly troubled with thought. At length, on reaching a certain spot, he halted and looked around, inquiringly and suspiciously. The deepest silence and most complete tranquillity prevailed all round him.

"It must be!" the hunter muttered. "Not to do it would be worse than a crime, for it would be cowardice. Well, Heaven will judge between us."

After again carefully examining the neighbourhood, probably reassured by the silence and solitude, he dismounted, took off his horse's bridle to let it graze at its ease, hobbled it lest it should stray too far, threw his rifle over his shoulder, and cautiously entered the forest.

The hunter was doubtlessly ruminating on one of those schemes whose execution demands the continual tension of a man's faculties, for his progress was slow and calculated, his eye constantly peered into the gloom. With head outstretched, he listened to the nameless sounds of the desert, stopping at times when an unusual rustling in the brambles struck his ear, and revealed to him the presence of some unknown being. Suddenly he stopped, remained for a second motionless, and then disappeared in an inextricable medley of leaves, brambles, and creepers, in which his presence could not possibly be suspected. Scarcely was he hidden, ere the hoofs of several horses reechoed in the distance, beneath the dense dome of forest verdure. Gradually the sound came nearer, the steps grew more distinct, and a band of horsemen at length appeared, marching in close column. They were the hunters and Gambusinos.

Marksman was conversing in a low voice with Don Miguel, carried on a litter on the shoulders of two Mexicans, for he was still too weak to sit a horse. The little party advanced gently, owing to the wounded man they had in their midst, and were proceeding toward the Rubio ford.

Brighteye watched his comrades pass, without making a movement to reveal his presence. It was evident that he wished them to remain ignorant of the fact that he had turned back, and that the motives which impelled him to act must remain a secret between him and Heaven. It was in vain that he looked for Flying Eagle and Eglantine among the Gambusinos: the two Redskins had separated from the band. This absence appeared greatly to vex the hunter. Still, after a minute, his face resumed its serenity, and he shrugged his shoulders with that careless air which indicates that a man has put up with an annoyance against which he cannot contend. When the Gambusinos had disappeared, the hunter emerged from his hiding place: he listened for a moment to the sound of the horses' hoofs, which grew every moment weaker, and soon died out in the distance. Brighteye drew himself up. "Good!" he muttered, with an air of satisfaction; "I can now act as I please, without fear of being disturbed, unless Flying Eagle and his squaw have remained prowling about the place. Bah! we shall soon see; besides, that is not probable, for the Chief is too anxious to rejoin his tribe, to amuse himself by losing his time here. I will go on, at any rate."

With this, he threw his rifle on his shoulder, and set out again with a light and deliberate step, though not neglecting the precautions usual in the desert on any march; for, by night, the wood rangers know that they are ever watched by invisible foes, be they men or beasts. Brighteye thus reached the skirt of the clearing, in which the dramatic events we have described took place, and in which there only remained at this moment a man buried alive, face to face with his crimes, with no hope of possible help, and abandoned by all nature, if not by Heaven. The hunter stopped, lay down on the ground, and looked. A funeral silence, the silence of the tomb, brooded over the clearing. Don Estevan, with eyes dilated by fear, his chest oppressed by the earth, which collected round his body, with a slow and continuous movement, felt the breath gradually departing from his lungs, his temples beat ready to burst, the blood boiled in his veins, drops of icy perspiration beaded at the roots of his hair, a bloodstained veil was stretched over his eyes, and he felt himself dying.

At this supreme moment, when all deserted him at once, the wretched man uttered a hoarse and piercing cry; tears burst from his proud eyes; his hand, as we have stated, nervously clutched the butt of the pistol left to abridge his punishment, and he raised the barrel to his temples, muttering, with an accent of indescribable despair—"Heaven! Heaven! pardon me!"

He pulled the trigger. Suddenly a hand was laid on his arm, the bullet whizzed into the air, and a severe yet gentle voice replied—"God has heard you. He pardons you!"

The wretch turned his head wildly, looked, with an air of terror, at the man who spoke thus, and, too weak to resist the terrible emotion that agitated him, he uttered a cry resembling a sob, and fainted.

As the reader will doubtlessly have guessed, the man who arrived so opportunely for Don Estevan was Brighteye. "Hum!" he said, with a shake of his head, "it was time for me to interfere."

Then, without losing a moment, the worthy fellow busied himself with drawing from his tomb the man he wished to save. It was a rude task, especially as he lacked the necessary tools. The Gambusinos had laboured conscientiously, and filled up the hole in such a way that the man they were burying was solidly blocked in.

Brighteye was compelled to dig with his knife, while using the utmost precautions not to wound Don Estevan. At times the hunter stopped, wiped his perspiring brow, and looked at the pale face of the Mexican, who was still in a faint; then, after a few moments of this silent contemplation, he shook his head two or three times, and set to work again with redoubled ardour.

These two men in the desert, surrounded by dense gloom, offered a strange spectacle. Certainly, had a wayfarer been able to see what was taking place in this unknown clearing, in the heart of the virgin forest, peopled by wild beasts, whose hoarse roars rose at intervals in the darkness, as if protesting against this invasion of their domain—he would have fancied himself witness of some diabolical incantation, and have fled at full speed, a prey to the wildest terror. Still Brighteye went on digging. His task progressed but slowly, because, in proportion as he went deeper, his difficulties grew greater.

For a moment the hunter stopped, in despair of succeeding in saving the condemned man; but this moment of discouragement lasted a very short time. The Canadian, ashamed of the thought, began digging again with that feverish energy which the reaction of a powerful will upon a passing weakness imparts to a man of resolution. At length, after extraordinary difficulties, the task, twenty times interrupted and twenty times recommenced, was completed. The hunter uttered a shout of triumph and pleasure; he then seized Don Estevan under the armpits, drew him vigorously towards him, and, with some trouble, succeeded in laying him on the ground. His first task was to cut asunder the bonds that formed an inextricable network round the wretch's body; he opened his clothes, to give his lungs the necessary freedom to inhale the external air, then half filled a calabash of water from his gourd, and threw the contents over Don Estevan's face. The fainting fit had been produced by the emotion he felt on seeing a saviour arrive at the moment when he believed that he had nought left but to die. The sudden shock of the cold water effected a favourable reaction; he gave out a sigh, and opened his eyes.

His first movement, on regaining consciousness, was to look defiantly up to heaven; then he held out his hand to Brighteye. "Thanks!" he said to him.

The hunter fell back, and declined to take the proffered hand. "You must not thank me," he said.

"Who then?"

"God!"

Don Estevan drew in his pale lips contemptuously; but soon understanding that he must deceive his saviour, if he wished for a continuance of that protection which he cared not yet to do without, he said, with feigned humility—"That is true. God first, and you next."

"I," Brighteye continued, "have only performed a duty—paid a debt; now we are quits. Ten years ago, you rendered me an important service; today I have saved your life. I discharge you from all gratitude, and you must do the same with me. From this hour we no longer know each other— our ways are different."

"Will you abandon me thus?" he said, with a movement of terror, which he could not overcome.

"What more can I do?"

"All!"

"I do not understand you."

"It would have been better to leave me to die in the hole, into which you helped to place me, than save me to die of hunger in the desert, become the prey of wild beasts, or fall into the hands of the Indians. You know, Brighteye, that on the prairies a disarmed man is a dead man; you do not save me at this moment, but render my agony longer and more painful, since the weapon which, in their cruel generosity, your friends left me to put an end to my misfortunes, when courage and hope failed me, can no longer serve me at present."

"That is true," Brighteye muttered.

The hunter let his head sink on his chest, and reflected deeply for several seconds. Don Estevan anxiously followed in the loyal and characteristic face of the hunter all the emotions by turns reflected there. The Canadian continued—"You are right in asking me for weapons. If you are deprived of them, you run the risk of being, in a few hours, in a similar position to that from which I took you."

"You allow it."

"By Jove! there is no doubt about it."

"Then be generous to the end. Give me the means of defending myself." The hunter shook his head.

"I did not think of that," he said.

"Which means, that had you thought of it, you would have let me die."

"Perhaps so."

This word fell like the blow of a sledgehammer on Don Estevan's heart. He gave the hunter a suspicious glance. "What you say, then, is not well," he remarked.

"What would you have me answer you?" the other retorted. "In my eyes you were justly condemned. I ought to have let justice follow its course. I did not do so. Perhaps I was wrong. Now that I regard the matter in cool blood, while allowing that you are right in asking me for arms, and that it is indispensable for you to have them, in the first place for your personal safety, and next to provide for your wants, I am afraid to give them to you."

Don Estevan had sat down by the hunter's side; he was playing carelessly with the discharged pistol, and appearing to listen very attentively to what Brighteye was saying. "Why so?" he answered.

"Well, for a very simple reason. I have known you for a long time, as you are well aware, Don Estevan. I know that you are not the man to forget an insult. I am convinced that, if I give you arms, you will only think of vengeance, and it is that I wish to avoid."

"As for that," the Mexican exclaimed, with a fiendish laugh, "you can only think of one method—leaving me to die of hunger. Oh, oh, yours is singular philanthropy, *compañero!* You have rather a brutal way of arranging matters for a man who piques himself on his honour and loyalty."

"You do not understand me. I will not give you arms—that is true; but, at the same time, I will not leave the service I have done you incomplete."

"Hum! and what will you do to effect that result? I am curious to know it," Don Estevan said, with a grin.

"I will escort you to the frontiers of the prairie, guarding you from all danger during the journey, defending you, and hunting for you. That is simple enough, I believe."

"Very simple, indeed; and, on getting there, I will purchase arms, and return to seek my revenge."

"Not so."

"Why not?"

"Because you will swear to me on the spot, by your honour, to forget every feeling of hatred toward your enemy, and never to return to the prairie."

"And if I will not swear?"

"Then it will be different. I shall leave you to your fate; and as that will have happened by your own fault, I shall consider myself entirely quits with you."

"Oh! oh! but assuming that I accept the harsh conditions you force on me, I must know how we are to travel. The road is long from here to the establishments, and I am not in a condition to go afoot."

"That is true, but need not trouble you. I have left my horse in a thicket, a few paces from the Rubio. You will ride it till I can procure another."

"And you?"

"I will follow on foot. We hunters are as good, walkers as riders. Come, make up your mind."

"Well, I must do what you desire."

"Yes; I believe that is the best for you. Then you consent to take the oath I demand?"

"I see no way of getting out of the scrape otherwise. But," he suddenly said, "what is the matter behind that tree?"

"Where?" the hunter asked.

"Over there," Don Estevan continued, pointing in the direction of a dense clump of trees.

The hunter turned his head quickly towards the spot indicated by the Mexican. The latter lost no time in seizing the pistol he had been playing with by the end. He raised it quickly, and dealt a blow with the butt on the hunter's head. The blow was given with such force and precision, that Brighteye stretched out his arms, closed his eyes, and rolled on the ground with a heavy sigh.

Don Estevan regarded him for a moment with an expression of contempt and satisfied hatred, "Idiot!" he muttered, kicking him aside, "you ought to have made those absurd conditions before saving me; but for the present it is too late. I am free, *Cuerpo de Cristo!* I will avenge myself."

After uttering these words, and looking up to heaven defiantly, he bent over the hunter, stripped him of his weapons without the slightest shame, and left him, not even stopping to see were he dead or only wounded. "It is you, accursed dog!" he went on, "who will die of hunger, or be devoured by wild beasts. As for myself, I no longer fear anything, for I have in my hands the means to accomplish my vengeance."

And the wretch walked hurriedly from the clearing to look for Brighteye's horse, which he intended to mount.

CHAPTER XXII
THE CAMP

The Gambusinos reached their camp a little before sunrise. During their absence, the few men left in charge of the entrenchments had not been disturbed.

Don Mariano awaited the return of the Mexicans with lively impatience. So soon as he saw them, he went to meet them.

Marksman was gloomy. The reception he gave the gentleman, though cordial, was still rather dry. The hunter, although convinced he had accomplished a duty in condemning Don Estevan, was for all that sad, when thinking of the responsibility he had taken on himself in the affair.

It is one thing to kill a man in action while defending one's life, in the midst of the intoxication of battle, another to try and coldly execute an individual against whom no personal motive of hatred or anger is felt. The old Canadian, in his heart, feared Don Mariano's reproaches. He knew the human heart too well not to be assured that the gentleman, when he regarded in cold blood the action he had excited the Gambusinos to commit, would detest it, and curse the docile instruments he had found. However great Don Estevan's crimes against Don Mariano might be, however cruel his conduct, it was not his brother's place to accuse him, or to demand his death at the hands of these implacable men, in whom all feelings of clemency are extinguished through the rough life they are forced to lead.

Now that some hours had elapsed since Don Estevan's condemnation, Marksman, who had begun to reflect again, and was able to regard that action under a different light, had asked himself if he really had the right to act as he had done, and if what he took for a deed of stern and strict justice were not an assassination and disguised vengeance. Hence he expected that Don Mariano, on seeing him, would reproach him, and ask his brother's life at his hands.

The hunter prepared to answer the questions Don Mariano was doubtless going to address to him; and so soon as he perceived him, his brow, already troubled by sad thoughts, grew even more overcast. But Marksman was mistaken, not a reproach, not a word having reference to the judgment passed Don Mariano's lips; not an allusion, however remote, caused the hunter to suspect that the gentleman intended to attack that delicate subject.

The Canadian breathed again; but during the few moments they occupied in returning to the camp side by side, he took a side glance at Don Mariano's face. The old gentleman was pale and sad, but his countenance was calm, and his features apathetic.

The hunter shook his head. "He is turning over some scheme in his mind," he muttered, in a low voice.

So soon as the camp was entered, and the barriers were closed again behind the Gambusinos, Don Miguel, after placing sentries at the entrenchments, turned to Marksman and Don Mariano. "The sun will rise in about two hours," he said to them; "deign to accept my hospitality, and accompany me to my tent."

The two men bowed. Don Miguel made his bearers a sign to place the litter on the ground. He rose, helped by Marksman, and leaning on the hunter's arm, entered the tent, followed by Don Mariano. The curtain fell behind them.

The Gambusinos, wearied with their night march, had hastened to unsaddle their horses and give them food. Then, after throwing some handfuls of dried wood on the fires, in order to revive the flame, they wrapped themselves in their frasadas and zarapés, and lay down on the ground, where they speedily fell asleep. Ten minutes after the adventurers' return, they were all in the deepest sleep. Three men alone were awake, and they were assembled in the tent, and holding a conversation, at which we will invite the reader to be present.

The interior of the tent into which Don Miguel had introduced his two companions was furnished in the most simple fashion. In one corner was the hermetically closed palanquin; in the opposite one, several furs stretched on the ground marked the place of a bed; four or five buffalo skulls served as chairs; it was impossible to meet with anything so simple and less comfortable than this.

Don Miguel threw himself on the bed, bidding his comrades, by a graceful bow, to sit down on the buffalo skulls. Marksman and Don Mariano drew them up by their host's side, and sat down silently. Don Miguel then took the word. "Caballeros," he said, "the events which have occurred this night, to which I shall not further allude, require to be clearly explained, especially in the provision of the probable complications which may result from them in the affairs which, I hope, we shall undertake ere long. What

I have to say regards and interests you peculiarly, Don Mariano. Hence I address myself principally to you. As for Marksman, he knows pretty nearly all the connecting links of what I am about to tell you. If I beg him to be present at the interview I wish to have with you, it is first owing to the old friendship that unites us, and secondly, because his advice will be of great help to us in the further resolutions we shall have to take."

Don Mariano looked at the adventurer in a way which made him comprehend that he understood not a syllable of this long prelude.

"Do you not remember, Don Mariano," the Canadian then said, "that before sending Brighteye to the camp to fetch Don Miguel, I told you that you were ignorant of the most interesting portion of the history?"

"Yes; I remember it, although, at the moment, I did not attach to the statement all the value it deserved."

"Well, if I am not mistaken, Don Miguel is about to explain these frightful machinations to you in a few words." Then he added, as if on reflection, "There is one man I should like to see here. It is important that he should know the whole truth also; but since our return to the camp I have not seen him."

"Whom do you mean?"

"Brighteye, whom I asked to accompany you here."

"He did so; but on reaching the camp, as he doubtlessly supposed that I had no further need of his protection, he left me."

"Did he not tell you for what object?" the hunter asked, looking firmly at the old gentleman.

Don Mariano, in his heart, was troubled by this inquiry; but wishing to leave to Brighteye the care of explaining his absence, and not at all desirous of avowing his wish to save his brother, he replied, with a degree of hesitation he could not entirely conceal, — "No; he told me nothing, I fancied that he had joined you again, and am as much surprised as yourself at his absence."

Marksman frowned slightly. "That is strange," he said. "However," he added, "he will not fail to return soon, and then we shall know what he has been about."

"Yes. Now, Don Miguel, I am at your orders. Speak; I am listening to you attentively," Don Mariano said, not at all wishful to see the conversation continued on that subject.

"Give me my real name, Don Mariano," the young man answered, "for it will perhaps inspire you with some confidence in me. I am neither Don

Torribio Carvajal, nor Don Miguel Ortega. My right name is Don Leo de Torres."

"Leo de Torres!" Don Mariano exclaimed, rising with stupefaction. "The son of my dearest friend."

"It is so," the young man answered, simply.

"But no; that is not possible. Basilio de Torres was massacred, with his entire family, by the Apache Indians, amid the smoking ruins of his hacienda, twenty years ago."

"I am the son of Don Basilio de Torres," the adventurer continued. "Look at me carefully, Don Mariano. Do not my features remind you of anyone?"

The gentleman approached, laid his hand on the adventurer's shoulder, and examined him for a few moments with the profoundest attention. "It is true," he then said, with tears in his eyes, "the resemblance is extraordinary. Yes, yes," he exclaimed, impetuously; "I now recognize you."

"Oh!" the young man continued, with a smile, "I have in my possession the documents that guarantee my identity. But," he said, "that is not the question. Let us return to what I wished to say to you."

"How is it that since the fearful catastrophe which made you an orphan, I never heard any mention of you? I, the best friend, almost the brother of your father, I should have been so happy to provide for you."

Don Leo, to whom we will henceforth give his real name, frowned; his brow was furrowed with deep wrinkles. He answered, with a sorrowful accent and trembling voice,—"Thank you, Don Mariano, for the friendship you evince for me. Believe that I am worthy of it; but, I implore you, let me keep in my heart the secret of my silence. One day, I trust, I shall be permitted to speak, and then I will tell you all."

Don Mariano pressed his hand. "Act as you think proper," he said, with deep emotion; "only remember one thing—that you have found in me the father you lost."

The young man turned his head away to conceal the tears he felt rising in his eyes. There was a lengthened silence without; the barking of the coyotes alone disturbed at intervals the imposing solitude of the desert. The interior of the tent was only lighted by a torch of ocote wood fixed in the ground, whose flickering flame played on the faces of the three men with shadows and lights which imprinted on their countenances a strange and fantastic expression.

"The sky is beginning to be studded with broad white bands," Don Leo continued: "the owls hidden beneath the leaves are saluting the return of day; the sun is about to rise; permit me, in a few words, to explain to you the facts with which you are unacquainted; for if I believe my presentiments, we shall soon have to act vigorously, in order to repair the ill deeds committed by Don Estevan."

The two men bowed in affirmation. Don Leo went on:—"Certain reasons, unnecessary to give here, led me to Mexico a few months ago. Owing to those reasons, I led rather a singular life, frequenting the worst society, and mingling, when the occasion offered, in society more or less corrupt, according as you understand my words. Do not believe, from what I have said, that I was engaged in any criminal operations, for you would commit a grave error. I merely, like a goodly number of my countrymen, carried on certain contraband trade; perhaps regarded with an evil eye by government officials, but which had nothing very reprehensible about it."

Marksman and Don Mariano exchanged a glance; they understood, or fancied they did. Don Leo feigned not to notice this glance.

"One of the places I frequented most assiduously," he said, "was the Plaza Mayor. There I visited an evangelista, a man of about fifty, half Jew, half pawnbroker, who, under a venerable appearance, concealed the most venal soul and most corrupt mind. This thorough scamp, through the thousand secret negotiations he carried on, and his duties of evangelista, was thoroughly acquainted with the secrets of an infinite number of families, and all the infamies daily committed in that immense capital. One day, when I happened to be in his shop at the Oración, a young girl entered. She was lovely, and seemed respectable. She trembled like a leaf on entering the scoundrel's den; the latter put on his most captivating smile, and obsequiously asked how he could serve her. She turned a timid glance around, and noticed me. I know not why, I scented a mystery. I pretended to be asleep, with my head on the table, and my forehead resting on my crossed arms."

"'That man!' she said, pointing to me."

"'Oh!' the evangelista answered, 'he is intoxicated with pulque; he is a poor sergeant, of no importance; besides, he is asleep.'"

"She hesitated; then, seeming suddenly to form a resolution, she drew a small paper from her bosom."

"'Copy that,' she said to the evangelista, 'and I will give you two ounces.'"

"The old villain seized the paper, and looked at it."

"'But it is not Castilian,' he said."

"'It is French,' she answered, 'But what consequence is it to you?'"

"'To me, none.'"

"He prepared his paper and pens, and copied the note without further observation. When it was finished, the girl compared the two notes, gave a smile of satisfaction, tore up the original, folded the note, and dictated a short address to the evangelista. Then she placed the letter in her bosom, and went out, after paying the agreed on price, which the evangelista seized gaily, for he had gained more in a few minutes than he usually did in a month. The girl had scarce departed, ere I raised my head: but the evangelista made me a sign to re-assume my position. He had heard the key turning in his door. I obeyed, and lucky it was I did so, for a man entered almost immediately. This man evidently desired not to be known. He was carefully wrapped up in a large rebozo, and the brim of his sombrero was pulled down over his eyes. On entering, he gave an angry start."

"'Who is that man?' he asked, pointing to me."

"'I A poor drunkard asleep.'"

"'A young girl has just left here.'"

"'It is possible,' the evangelista answered, put on his guard by the question."

"'No ambiguous phrases, scoundrel,' the stranger answered haughtily. 'I know you, and pay you,' he added, as he threw a heavy purse on the table. 'Answer!'"

"The evangelista quivered. All his scruples disappeared at the sight of the gold sparkling through the meshes of the purse."

"'A young girl has just left here?' the stranger continued."

"'Yes.'"

"'What did she want of you?'"

"'To copy a letter written in French.'"

"'Very good. Show me the letter.'"

"'She folded it up, wrote an address, and took it away.'"

"'I know all that.'"

"'Well?'"

"'Well!' the stranger retorted, with a grin, 'as you are no fool, you kept a copy of the note, and that copy I must have.'"

"The man's voice had struck me. I could not tell why. As his back was almost turned to me, I made the evangelista a sign, which he understood."

"'I did not think of that,' he answered."

"He assumed such a simple face as he said this, that the stranger was deceived. He made a move of annoyance. At length he said,—'She will return.'"

"'I do not know.'"

"The stranger shrugged his shoulders. 'I know it though. Every time she comes, you will keep a copy of what she makes you write. The answers will come here?'"

"'Not to my knowledge.'"

"'You will not deliver them till you have shown them to me. I shall return tomorrow; and do not be such a fool as you have been today, if you wish me to make your fortune.'"

"The evangelista grinned a smile. The stranger turned to go away. At this moment the corner of his cloak caught in the table, and I saw his face. I needed all my self-command not to utter a cry on recognizing him, for it was Don Estevan, your brother. He drew his cloak over his face again with a stifled curse, and went away. He had scarce gone ere I leaped up. I bolted the door, and placed myself in front of the evangelista. 'It is now our turn,' I said to him."

"He made a movement of terror. My face had a terrible expression, which made him fall back against the wall, clutching the purse he had just received, and which he doubtless supposed I wished to take from him."

"'I am a poor old man,' he said to me."

"'Where is the copy you refused that man?' I said sharply."

"He bent down to his desk, took the copy, and handed it to me, trembling. I read it with a shudder, for I understood."

"'Stay,' I said, giving him an ounce; 'every time you will hand me the young lady's note, I allow you to show it also to that man. But remember this carefully; not one of the answers written by the person who has just left will be handed by you to the lady until I have read it. I am not so rich as that stranger, still I can pay you properly. You know me. I have only one thing more to say. If you betray me, I will kill you like a dog.'"

"I went out, and, as I closed the door, I heard the evangelista mutter to himself, 'Santa Viring, into what wasp's nest have I got?'"

"This is the key of the mystery. The young lady I saw at the evangelista's was a novice in the convent of the Bernardines, where your daughter was. Doña Laura, not knowing in whom to confide, had begged her to let Don Francisco de Paulo Serrano know—"

"My brother-in-law! her godfather!" Don Mariano exclaimed.

"The same," Don Leo continued. "She had, I said, desired her friend, Doña Luisa, to let señor Serrano receive the note, in which she revealed to him her uncle's criminal machinations, and the persecutions to which she was exposed, while imploring him, as her father's best friend, to come to her aid, and take her under his protection."

"Oh, my poor child!" Don Mariano murmured.

"Don Estevan," Don Leo continued, "had by some means learned your daughter's intentions. In order to be thoroughly acquainted with her plans, and be able to overthrow them at the right moment, he pretended to be entirely ignorant of them; let the young girl carry the letters to the evangelista, reading the copies, and answering them himself, for the simple reason that señor Serrano did not receive your daughter's letters, because Don Estevan had bought his valet, who gave them to him with seals unbroken. This skilful perfidy would doubtless have succeeded, had not accident, or rather providence, placed me so fortunately in the evangelista's shop."

"Oh!" Don Mariano muttered, "the man was a monster."

"No," Don Leo remarked; "circumstances compelled him to go much further than he perhaps intended. Nothing proves that he meditated the death of your daughter."

"What would he then?"

"Your fortune. By forcing Doña Laura to take the veil, he gained his object. Unfortunately, as always happens when a man enters on that thorny path which fatally leads to crime, although he had coldly calculated all the chances of success, he could not foresee my intervention in the execution of his plans—an intervention which must make them fail, and compel him to commit a crime, in order to ensure success. Doña Laura, persuaded that Don Francisco's protection would not fail her, scrupulously followed the advice I sent her by means of letters I myself wrote in the name of the friend she addressed. For my own part, I held myself in readiness to act when the moment arrived. I will enter into no details on this subject. Doña Laura refused to take the vows in the church itself. The scandal was extreme, and the abbess, in her fury, resolved to put an end to matters. The hapless young lady, sent to sleep by means of a powerful narcotic, was buried alive in the *in pace*, where she must die of hunger."

"Oh!" the two men exclaimed, shuddering with horror.

"I repeat to you," Don Leo continued, "that I do not believe Don Estevan capable of this barbarity. He was probably the indirect accomplice, but nothing more; the abbess was the sole culprit. Don Estevan accepted accomplished facts; he profited by them, nothing more. We must suppose so, for the honour of humanity; otherwise, this man would be a monster. Warned on the same day of what had occurred in the convent, I collected a band of banditti and adventurers. Then, at nightfall, I entered the building by stratagem, and, pistol in hand, carried off your daughter."

"You!" Don Mariano exclaimed, with a movement of surprise, mingled with joy. "Oh, heavens! then she is saved—she is in safety!"

"Yes; at a place where I, aided by Marksman, concealed her."

"Don Estevan would never have found her," the hunter added, with a crafty smile.

The gentleman was fearfully agitated. "Where is she?" he exclaimed. "I will see her. Tell me where my poor darling child is."

"You can understand," the young man answered, "that I did not keep her near me. I knew that Don Estevan's spies and your brother himself were pursuing me, and following my every step. After placing Doña Laura in safety, I enticed all the pursuers on to my trail. In this way, this palanquin," he said, pointing to it, "contained Doña Laura till we reached the Presidio de Tubar. I was careful to let her be seen once or twice; no more was needed to make it supposed that she was still with me. By the care I took to keep the palanquin constantly closed, and let no one approach it, I hoped to lead my enemies after me, and, once I had them in the desert, punish them. My calculations were more correct than Don Estevan's, for Heaven, helped me. Now that the criminal has been punished, and Doña Laura has no more to fear, I am ready to make known her place of concealment, and lead you to her."

"Oh, my God! Thou art just and merciful," Don Mariano exclaimed, with an expression of ineffable joy. "I shall see my child again. She is saved."

"She is lost, if you do not make haste," a sepulchral voice replied.

The three men turned in terror. Brighteye, with a pale and bleeding face, his clothes torn and bloodstained, was standing upright and motionless in the entrance of the tent, holding the curtain back.

CHAPTER XXIII
FLYING EAGLE

The Indians, owing to the life they are compelled to lead, and the education they receive, are of an essentially suspicious character. Accustomed to be constantly on their guard against everything that surrounds them, to regard intentions ostensibly the most honest as concealing treachery and perfidy, they have acquired an uncommon skill in guessing the projects of persons with whom accident brings them in contact, and foiling the snares set for them by their enemies.

Mahchsi Karehde, we have already said, was an experienced warrior, as wise in council as he was valiant in war, and, though still very young, he justly enjoyed a great reputation in his tribe.

So soon as Marksman had, in the name of Lynch law, pronounced Don Estevan's sentence, there was a species of disorder among the hunters, who broke their ranks, and began eagerly conversing together, as generally happens in such a case. Flying Eagle took advantage of the general attention being diverted, and no one noticing him, to give Eglantine, whose eyes were incessantly fixed on him, a signal, which the young woman understood, and he silently stepped into a thicket, where he disappeared before anyone noticed his absence.

After walking for about twenty minutes in the forest, the Chief, probably supposing he was far enough off, stopped, and turned to his squaw, who had remained a little distance behind the whole time. "Let the Palefaces," he said, "accomplish their work. Flying Eagle is a Comanche warrior; he must no longer interfere between them."

"The Chief will return to his village?" Eglantine asked, timidly.

The Indian smiled craftily. "All is not over yet," he replied. "Flying Eagle will watch over his friends."

The young woman let her head fall, and, seeing that the Indian had seated himself, prepared to light the campfire; but the Chief stopped her by a sign. "Flying Eagle does not wish to be discovered," he said. "Let my sister take her place by his side, and wait; a friend is in danger at this time."

At this moment a great noise of breaking branches could be heard not far from the spot where the Redskins had halted. The Indian listened attentively for a few moments, with his head on the ground. "Flying Eagle will return," he said, as he rose.

"Eglantine will wait for him," the squaw said, looking at him tenderly.

The Chief laid by her side the weapons that might have impeded him in the project he meditated; he only kept his reata, which he carefully coiled round his right hand, and crept in the direction of the sound he had heard, which every moment grew louder. He had scarce advanced twenty yards, by forcing his way through the intertwined creepers and tall grass that barred his passage, ere he perceived, a few paces off, a magnificent black horse, which, with ears laid back, head extended, and all four feet fixed on the ground, was snorting in alarm; its nostrils covered with foam, and its mouth bleeding.

"Wah!" the Chief muttered, stopping short, and admiring the splendid animal. He drew a few steps nearer, being careful not to startle the animal more, which followed all his movements with a restless eye; and, at the instant he saw it bound to escape, he made his reata whistle round his neck, and threw it with such skill, that the running knot fell on the horse's shoulders. The latter tried, for three or four minutes, to regain the liberty so suddenly snatched from it; but soon recognizing the futility of its efforts, it yielded once again to slavery, and allowed the Indian to approach, with no further attempts to maintain the struggle. The animal was not a wild horse, but Don Estevan's magnificent barb, which he had probably lost during the fight, when he was wounded. The horse's trappings were partly broken and torn by the branches; but still they were in a good state of service.

The Chief, delighted with the windfall accident procured him, mounted the horse, and returned to Eglantine, who, submissive and obedient as a true Indian woman, had not stirred since his departure.

"Flying Eagle will return to his village mounted on a horse worthy of so great a Chief," she said, on noticing him.

The Indian smiled haughtily. "Yes," he answered, "the sachems will be proud of him."

And with the simple childishness so well suited to the primitive roughness of these men of iron, he amused himself, for some time, with making the horse perform the most difficult passes and curvets, happy at the terrified admiration of the woman he loved, and who could not refrain from trembling on perceiving him manage this magnificent animal with such ease. The Chief at length dismounted, and, while still holding the bridle in his hand, sat down by the young woman's side.

They remained thus for a long time, without exchanging a word. Flying Eagle seemed to be reflecting deeply; his eyes wandered about in the darkness, as if wishing to penetrate it, and distinguish some distant object in the distance. He listened eagerly to the sounds of the solitude, while playing mechanically with his scalping knife. "There they are," he suddenly cried, as he rose, as if moved by a spring.

Eglantine looked at him with astonishment.

"Does not my sister hear?" he asked her.

"Yes," she replied in a moment, "I hear the sound of horses in the forest."

"They are the Palefaces returning to their camp."

"Shall we follow them?"

"Flying Eagle never leaves, without a reason, the path made by his moccasins. Eglantine will accompany the warrior."

"Does my father doubt it?"

"No; Eglantine is a worthy daughter of the Comanches; she will come without a murmur. A Paleface, a friend of Mahchsi Karehde, is in danger at this moment."

"The Chief will save him?"

The Indian smiled. "Yes," he said; "or, if I arrive too late for that, I will at least avenge him, and his soul will quiver with joy in the blessed prairies, on learning from his people that his friend has not forgotten him."

"I am ready to follow the Chief."

"Let us go, then; it is time."

The Indian leaped into his saddle at a bound, and Eglantine prepared to follow on foot. Indian squaws never mount the warhorse of their husbands or brothers. Condemned, by the laws that govern their tribe, to remain constantly bowed beneath a yoke of iron, to be reduced to the most complete abjectness, and devote themselves to the harshest and most painful tasks, they endure everything without complaining, persuaded that it must be so, and that nothing can save them from the implacable tyranny that weighs on them from their birth to their death. In compelling his wife to follow him on foot, through a virgin forest, by impracticable roads, rendered more difficult through the darkness, Flying Eagle was convinced that he was only doing a very simple and natural thing. Eglantine, for her part, understood it so, for she did not make the slightest remark.

They set out, then, turning their back on the noise, and proceeding towards the clearing. For what object did the Chief retrace his steps, and return to the spot he had left an hour previously, in order to get rid of the Gambusinos? We shall probably soon learn.

When about a hundred yards from the clearing, they heard a shot. Flying Eagle stopped. "Wah!" he said, "what has happened? Can I be mistaken?"

Immediately dismounting, he gave his wife his horse to hold, bidding her follow him at a distance; and, gliding through the grass, he advanced hurriedly toward the clearing, feeling much alarmed by the shot, which he could not account for, as the idea did not for a moment occur to him that Don Estevan had fired it with the intention of killing himself. The Chief was convinced that a man of that stamp would never give the game up, however desperate it was. His appreciation was not entirely false.

Persuaded of this, Flying Eagle, fearing a mishap, the possibility of which he seemed to have foreseen, hastened to reach the clearing, in order to settle his doubts, and trembling to see them converted into a certainty.

On reaching the skirt of the clearing, he stopped, removed the branches cautiously, and looked out. The darkness was so dense, that he could distinguish nothing; a funereal silence prevailed over this portion of the forest. Suddenly the bushes parted, a man, or rather a demon, bounded out like a jackal, passed him with extreme velocity, and was soon lost in the darkness.

A sad presentiment contracted the Redskin's heart; he made a movement to rush after the stranger, but altered his mind almost in the same moment. "Let us look here first," he muttered, "I am certain of finding that man again when I please."

He entered the clearing. The deserted fires no longer gave out any light. All was shadow and silence. The Chief walked rapidly toward the spot where the grave had been dug. It was empty, Don Estevan had disappeared. On the slope formed of the earth thrown out of the hole, a man lay, motionless.

Flying Eagle bent over him, and examined him attentively for some seconds. "I knew it," he muttered, as he drew himself up with a smile of disdain; "that must happen, the Palefaces are gossiping old women. Ingratitude is a white vice—vengeance a red virtue."

The Chief stood thoughtfully, with his eyes fixed on the wounded man. "Shall I save him?" he at length said. "For what good? It is almost better to let the coyotes tear him limb from limb; the red warriors laugh at their fury. This man," he added, "was, yet, one of the best of those plundering Palefaces who come to drive us from our last refuge. Wah! what do I care our races are hostile, the wild beasts will finish him—to each his prey."

And he made a move to withdraw. Suddenly he felt a hand laid on his shoulder, and a soft voice muttered gently in his ear,—"This Paleface is the friend of the grey head who delivered Eglantine. Is my father ignorant of it?"

The Chief started at this question, which answered so truly his innermost thoughts; for, while speaking to himself, and tying to prove that he did right in abandoning the wounded man, the Indian knew very well that the deed he premeditated was reprehensible, and that honour commanded him to help the man stretched out at his feet. "Does Eglantine know this hunter?" he answered evasively.

"Eglantine saw him for the first time two days ago, when he so courageously saved the friend of the Chief."

"Wah!" the Indian muttered, "my sister speaks true. This warrior is brave, his heart is large, he is the friend of the Redskins. Flying Eagle is a Chief renowned for his goodness of soul, he will not abandon the Paleface to the hideous coyotes."

"Mahchsi Karehde is the greatest warrior of his nation, his head is full of wisdom. What he does is well."

Flying Eagle smiled with satisfaction at this compliment. "Let us examine this man's wounds."

Eglantine lighted a branch of ocote, which she made into a torch. The two Indians bent down over the wounded man, who still lay motionless, and by the oscillating light of the torch examined him more attentively.

Brighteye had only a slight wound, produced by the butt of the pistol by which he had been struck; the force of the blow, by producing an abundant hemorrhage, had caused a stunning sensation, followed by a syncope. The wound was narrow, of no great depth, and on the upper part of the forehead between the eyebrows. Don Estevan had tried to kill the worthy hunter in the same way as the bulls in the corridas. The experienced Espadas often amuse themselves by killing the animals in this fashion, in order to display their skill before the assembled spectators. This blow, though dealt with a firm hand, was too hurried, and had not been calculated with sufficient precision to be mortal. Still it is evident that if the Indian Chief had not succoured him before daybreak, the hunter would have been devoured alive by the wild beasts prowling about in quest of prey.

All Indians, when travelling, carry by a sling a parchment bag, which they call the medicine bag. It contains the simples these primitive men employ to cure the wounds they receive in combat, their surgical instruments, and the powders intended to get rid of fevers.

After examining Brighteye's wound, the Chief tossed his head with pleasure, and immediately set about dressing. With a sharp instrument, made of an onyx, and with the edge of a razor, he first cleared off the hair round the wound; then he felt in his medicine bag, pulled out a handful of oregano leaves, which he carefully pounded and mixed up with Catalonian refino. We will remark here, that in all Indian medicaments spirits play a great part. He added to this mixture a little water and salt, formed the whole into a thick paste, and, after washing the wound twice with spirits and water, he applied this species of cataplasm to it, fastening it on with abanigo leaves. This simple remedy produced an almost instantaneous effect; within ten minutes the hunter gave a sigh, opened his eyes, and sat up, looking round him like a man suddenly roused from a deep sleep, and who does not completely recognize external objects.

Brighteye, however, was a man endowed with far too powerful an organization for this state to last long; he soon managed to restore order in his ideas, recalled what had passed, and the treachery dealt him by the man he had saved. "Thanks, Redskin," he said, in a still weak voice, and holding out his hand to the Indian, who pressed it cordially.

"My brother feels better?" he asked, with solicitude.

"I feel as well as if nothing had happened to me."

"Wah! my brother will then avenge himself on his enemy."

"Trust me for that; the traitor shall not escape me, so truly as my name is. Brighteye," the hunter answered energetically.

"Good! my brother will kill his enemy, and hang up his scalp at the entrance of his wigwam."

"No, no, Chief; that revenge may suit a Redskin, but it is not that of a man of my race and colour."

"What will my brother do, then?"

The hunter smiled cleverly, but after a few moments continued the conversation, though not in answer to the Indian's questions. "How long have I been here?" he said.

"About an hour."

"No longer?"

"No."

"Heaven be praised. My assassin cannot be gone far."

"Och! An evil conscience is a powerful spur," the Indian observed, sententiously.

"That is true."

"What will my brother do?"

"I do not know yet; the position I am in is very delicate," Brighteye answered, thoughtfully, "Urged by my heart, and the memory of a service done me long ago, I committed an action which may be interpreted in various ways. I now perceive that I was wrong; still, I confess to you, Redskin, that I do not at all wish to be exposed to the reproaches of my friends. It is hard for a man of my age, whose hair is white, and who must possess experience, to have it said that he has acted like a child, and is an old fool."

"Still, you must make up your mind."

"I know it. That is the thing which torments me; the more so as it is urgent that Don Miguel and Don Mariano should be warned as speedily as possible of what has happened, in order to remedy the consequences of my folly."

"Listen," the Chief remarked. "I understand how repugnant the confession you have to make will be to you. It is excessively painful for an old man to bow his head under reproaches, however well deserved they may be."

"Well!"

"If you consent, I will do what you have so much difficulty in resolving on. While you accompany Eglantine, I will go to your friends, the Palefaces; I will tell them what has happened. I will put them on their guard against their enemy, and you will have nothing to fear from their anger."

At this proposition, an indignant flush suffused the hunter's face. "No," he exclaimed, "I will not add cowardice to my fault. I will endure the consequences of my deed,—all the worse for myself. I thank you, Chief; your proposition comes from a good heart, but I cannot accept it."

"My brother is the master."

"Let us make haste," the hunter continued; "we have lost too much time already. Heaven alone knows what may be the consequences of my deed, and the misfortunes that will probably spring from it. It is impossible for me to prevent them, it is my duty to do everything to lessen their effect. Come, Chief, follow me; let us proceed to the camp without further delay."

While uttering these words, the hunter rose with feverish impatience.

"I am unarmed," he said; "the villain has stripped me."

"Let my brother not feel vexed at that," the Indian answered; "he will find the needful arms at the camp."

"That is true. Let us go and look for my horse, which I left a few yards off."

The Indian stopped him. "It is useless," he said.

"Why so?"

"That man has taken it."

The hunter struck his brow in his discouragement. "What shall I do?" he muttered.

"My brother will take my horse."

"And you, Chief?"

"I have another."

At a sign from Flying Eagle, Eglantine led up the horse. The two men mounted; the Chief took his squaw up behind him, and leaning over the necks of their horses, they started at full gallop in the direction of the Gambusino camp, which they reached about an hour later without any fresh incident.

CHAPTER XXIV
QUIEPAA TANI

We must return to the two chief characters of our story, whom we have neglected too long. For that purpose we will go back a little way, and take up our narrative at the moment when Addick, followed by the two young ladies Don Miguel confided to him, set out for Quiepaa Tani.

A quiver of extraordinary voluptuousness passed over the Indian so soon as he saw himself in the plains with the maidens, free from the inquisitive glances of Don Miguel, and those even more clear-sighted of Marksman. His eye, sparkling with pleasure, passed from Doña Laura to Doña Luisa, unable to rest longer on one than the other. He found them both so lovely, that he was never satiated with gazing on them with the frenzied admiration Indians experience at the sight of Spanish women, whom they infinitely prefer to their own squaws.

While mentioning this peculiarity to the reader, we must add that for their part the Spaniards eagerly seek the good graces of the Indian women, in whom they find, irresistible charms. Is this the effect of a wise combination of Providence, wishing to effect the complete fusion of the two people? No one knows; but what cannot be doubted is, that there are few Spaniards in America who have not sundry drops of Indian blood in their veins.

The young Indian chief, in possession of his two captives—for it was thus he regarded them so soon as they were placed in his charge—had at first thought of conducting them to his tribe, to decide presently which he would select; but several reasons made him abandon this plan almost as soon as he formed it. In the first place, the distance to traverse, before reaching his village, was immense, and it was not very probable he could manage it in the company of two frail and delicate girls, who could not endure the numberless fatigues of a desert journey. On the other hand, the city was only a couple of miles before him; the crowd, momentarily increasing, hampered his movements; and the dark outlines of the two hunters, standing out blackly on the top of the mound, warned him that, at the slightest suspicious movement, he would see two formidable adversaries rise before him.

Making a virtue of necessity, then, he shut up in the depths of his heart the emotions that agitated him, and resolved, ostensibly, to accomplish his mission, by entering the city; but he intended to confide the maidens to his foster brother, Chicukcoatl (Eight Serpents), Amantzin of Quiepaa Tani, who, in his functions as High Priest of the Temple of the Sun, would be able to hide them from the sight of all, until the day when, all obstacles being removed, Addick would be free to act as he pleased, and take back his captives.

The two unhappy girls, violently separated from the only friends left to them, had fallen into a state of prostration, which prevented them from noticing the hesitations and tergiversations of the perfidious guide in whose hands they found themselves. Surrendered defencelessly to the will of a savage, who could, if he thought proper, treat them with the utmost violence, although he had guaranteed their safety, they knew that they had no human succour to expect. They were compelled to leave their fate in the hands of Heaven, and resigned themselves with a Christian spirit to the hard trials they would doubtless have to endure during their residence among the Indians.

The three travellers, mixed up in the dense crowd of persons proceeding like themselves to the city, soon reached the edge of the fosse, followed by the inquisitive glances of those who surrounded them, for the Indians speedily recognized the young girls as Spaniards.

Addick having, by a glance, bidden his companions be prudent, assumed the most careless air he could well affect, although his heart beat as if ready to burst, and presented himself at the gateway.

After crossing the wooden bridge, he stood in apparent apathy before the gate; a lance was lowered before the strangers, and barred their passage. A man, whom it was easy to recognize, by his rich costume, as an influential chief of the city, rose from a butaca, on which he was carelessly seated, smoking his pipe, advanced with measured steps, and stopped, carefully examining the group formed by Addick and his companions.

The Indian, at first surprised and almost frightened by this hostile demonstration, recovered almost immediately; a flash of joy burst from his savage eye; he bent over to the sentry, and whispered a few words in his ear. The Redskin immediately raised his lance with a respectful gesture, fell back a step, and made room for them to pass. They entered.

Addick walked hastily toward the Temple of the Sun, congratulating himself on having so easily escaped the danger which had been suspended for several minutes over his head. The maidens followed him with that resignation of despair which bears so striking a likeness to docility and deference, but which is, in reality, only the recognized impossibility of escaping a fate one fears. While our friends are crossing the streets of the city to reach their destination, we will describe, in a few words, Quiepaa Tani, the exterior of which the reader is only acquainted with. The narrow streets, running at right angles, open on an immense square, situated exactly in the centre of the city, and which bears the name of Conaciuhtzin.[1] It is probable that it was in compliment to the sun that the Indians conceived this square, from which the streets of the city radiate; for it is impossible to imagine a more correct representation of the planet they adore than this mysteriously and emblematically significant arrangement. Four magnificent palaces rise in the direction of the four cardinal points. On the western side is the great temple, called Amantzin-expan, surrounded by an infinite number of chiselled columns of gold and silver. The appearance of this edifice is most imposing. You reach it by a flight of twenty steps, each made of a single stone, thirty feet in length; the walls are excessively lofty, and the roof, like that of all the other buildings, is terraced. The Indians, though perfectly acquainted with the art of building subterranean arches, are completely ignorant of the way of raising domes in the air. The interior of the temple is relatively very simple. Long tapestries, embroidered with feathers of a thousand different hues, and representing, in hieroglyphic writing, the entire history of the Indian religion, cover the walls. In the centre of the temple stands the *teocali*, or isolated altar, surmounted by a brilliant sun, made of gold and precious stones, supported on the great *ayotl*, or sacred tortoise. By an ingenious artifice, each morning the first beams of the rising sun fall on this splendid idol, and make it sparkle with such brilliant fire, that it really seems to be animated, and lights up the surrounding scene. Before the altar is the sacrificial table, an immense block of marble, representing one of those Druidic *menhies* so common in old Armorica. It is a species of stone table, supported by four blocks of rock. The table, slightly hollowed in the centre, is supplied with a conduit, intended to carry off the blood of the victims. We must remark that human sacrifices are growing daily rarer. We are, fortunately, far from an epoch when, in order to dedicate a temple, sixty thousand human victims were immolated in one day at Mexico. At present these sacrifices only take place under the most exceptional circumstances; and, in that case, the victims are selected from the prisoners condemned to death. At the back of the temple is a space closed in with heavy curtains, entrance to which is interdicted to the people. These curtains conceal the top of a staircase leading to vast cellars, which extend under the whole temple, and which the priests alone have the right to enter. It is in the most secret and retired spot of these vaults that the sacred fire of Motecuhzoma burns uninterruptedly. The floor of the temple is covered with leaves and flowers, renewed every morning.

On the southern side of the square is the *Tanamitec,* or Palace of the Chief. This palace, whose name, literally translated, signifies "a spot surrounded by water," is merely a succession of reception rooms and immense courts, employed by the warriors entrusted with the defence of the city for their military exercises. A separate building, to which visitors are not admitted, is set apart for the residence of the chief's family. Another building serves as arsenal, and contains all the arms of the city, such as arrows, saoaies, lances, bows, and Indian shields from the most remote period; European sabres, swords, and guns, which, after fearing for so long, the Indians have learned to employ as well as ourselves, if not better. The greatest curiosity, undoubtedly, contained in this arsenal is a small cannon which belonged to Cortez, and which that conqueror was compelled to abandon on the high road, during his precipitate retreat from Mexico on the *noche triste.* This cannon is still an object of fear and veneration to the Indians; for many recollections of the conquest have remained in their hearts after so many years and vicissitudes of every description.

On the same square stands the famous *Ciuatl-expan,* or Palace of the Vestals. It is here that, far from the glance of men, the Virgins of the Sun live and die. No man, the High Priest excepted, can penetrate to the interior of this building, reserved for the women dedicated to the sun. A fearful death would immediately punish the daring man who attempted to transgress this law. The life of the Indian vestals bears considerable resemblance to that of the nuns peopling the European convents. They are shut up, take a vow of perpetual chastity, and pledge themselves never to speak to a man, unless it be their father or brother, and in that case they can only converse through a grating and in the presence of a third party, while careful to veil their faces. When, during the ceremonies, they appear in public, or assist in the religious festivals in the temple, they are completely veiled. A vestal convicted of letting a man see her face is condemned to death.

In the interior of their abode they amuse themselves with feminine occupations, and privately perform the rites of their religion. Their vows are voluntary. A young girl cannot be admitted into the ranks of the Virgins of the Sun until the High Priest has acquired the certainty that no one has forced her to this determination, and that she is really following her vocation.

Lastly, the fourth palace, situated on the eastern side of the square, is the most splendid, and at the same time the most gloomy of all. It is called the Iztlacat-expan, or Palace of the Prophets. It is the residence of the priests. It would be impossible to describe the mysterious, sad, and cold appearance of this residence; the windows of which are covered with a wicker frame, so closely interwoven, as almost to entirely exclude the light of day. A gloomy silence perpetually prevails in this building; but at times, in the middle of the night, when all are reposing in the city, the Indians awake in terror at the strange sounds that appear to issue from the Iztlacat-expan. What is the life of men who inhabit it? In what do they spend their time? No one knows. Woe to the imprudent man, who, curious for information on this point, would try to surprise the secrets of which he should remain in ignorance; for the vengeance of the insulted priests would be implacable.

If the vow of chastity be imposed on the vestals, it is not so with regard to the High Priest and his assistants; still we must remark, that very few of them marry, and all abstain, at least openly, from any connection with the other sex. The noviciates of the priests lasts ten years, and it is only at the expiration of that period, and after undergoing numberless trials, that the novices assume the title of Chalchiuh. Until then they can alter their minds, and embrace another career; but the case is extremely rare. It is true, that if they took advantage of the law's permission, they would be infallibly assassinated by their brothers, who would fear seeing a portion of their secrets unveiled to the public. In other respects the priests are highly respected by the Indians, whose love they contrive to acquire; and we may say, that next to the chief, the Amanani is the most powerful man in the tribe.

Among peoples with whom religion is so powerful a lever, it may be observed that the temporal and spiritual power never come into collision; each knows how far his attributes extend, and follows the line traced for him, without trying to infringe on the rights of the other. Owing to this intelligent diplomacy, priests and chiefs act in concert, and double their strength.

The European, habituated to the tumult, noise, and movement of the cities of the old world, whose streets are constantly encumbered by vehicles of every description, and with the passers-by, who come into collision at each step, would be strangely surprised at the sight of the interior of an Indian city. There, there are no noisy ways of communication, bordered by magnificent shops, offering to the curiosity or greed of the purchasers and rogues the superb and dazzling specimens of European industry; there are no carriages, not even carts; the silence is only disturbed by the step of the few passers hastening back to their dwellings, and who walk with the imposing gravity of professors or magistrates of all nations.

The houses, which are all hermetically closed, allow none of the internal noises to be heard from the street. Indian life is concentrated in the family, and closed against the stranger; the manners are patriarchal, and the public way never becomes, as is too often the case amongst our civilized peoples, the disgraceful scene of the disputes, quarrels, or fights of the citizen.

The vendors collect in immense bazaars, where, until midday, they sell their merchandise; that is to say, fruits, vegetables, and meat; for all other trade is unknown to the Indians, each family weaving or making for itself the garments, furniture, or household articles it requires. Then, when the sun has run half its course, the bazaars are closed, and the Indian traders, who all inhabit the country, quit the city, to return next morning with fresh vegetables. Each family lays in its stock for the day.

Among the Indians the men never work, the women are entrusted with the purchases, the household cares, and the preparation of all that is indispensable for existence. The men, too proud to do any domestic work, hunt or go on the warpath.

The payment for what is purchased is not effected, as in Europe, by means of coins, which are generally only known to, or accepted by, the coast Indians, who traffic with the whites; but by means of a free exchange, which is practised by all the tribes residing in the interior. The plan is most simple. The purchaser exchanges some article for that he wishes to acquire, and all is settled.

Now that we have made Quiepaa Tani known to the reader, let us terminate this chapter by saying that Addick and his companions, after wandering for some time through the streets, at length reached the Iztlacatexpan.

The Indian Chief had, as he desired, found a complaisant auxiliary in the Amanani, who swore, on his head, to guard, with scrupulous attention, the prisoners entrusted to him.

We may as well add, that Addick told the High Priest that the ladies he confided to his care were the daughters of one of the most powerful men in Mexico, and that, in order to compel him to grant his protection to the Indians, he had resolved on taking one of them to wife; still, as the two girls pleased him equally—and for that reason it had been impossible for him, up to that moment, to make a choice between them—he prudently abstained from pointing out the object of his purpose. Then he added, in order completely to conquer the good graces of the man he took as his accomplice, and whose sordid avarice had long been known to him, that a magnificent present would amply reward him for the guardianship he begged him to accept.

Tranquil for the future about the fate of the two maidens, and the first part of the plot he had formed having completely succeeded, Addick purposed to carry out the second in the same way; he consequently took leave of those he had sworn to protect, and whom he betrayed so shamefully: and, mounting his horse again, he left the city, and proceeded, at full speed, towards the ford of the Rubio, where he knew he should meet Don Miguel.

[1] Square of the Sun.

CHAPTER XXV
A TRIO OF VILLAINS

Leaving Addick to depart at full gallop from Quiepaa Tani, let us turn for a little while to the maidens whom, prior to his departure, he confided to the Amantzin. The latter shut the maidens up in the Ciuatl-expan, inhabited by the Virgins of the Sun. Although prisoners, they were treated with the utmost respect, after the orders Addick had given, and they would have probably endured the annoyance of their unjust captivity with patience, had not a deep alarm as to the fate reserved for them, and an invincible sorrow, resulting from the events to which they had been victims, and the terrible circumstances which had led them to their present condition, by suddenly separating them from their last defender, seized upon them.

It was now that the difference of character between the two friends was clearly shown. Doña Laura, accustomed to the eager homage of the brilliant cavaliers who visited her father's house, and the enjoyment of a slothful and luxurious life, as is that of all rich Mexican families, suffered on feeling herself so roughly deprived of the delights and caresses by which her childhood had been surrounded; forgetting the tortures of the convent only to remember the joys of the paternal mansion, and incapable of resisting the sorrow that preyed upon her, she fell into a state of discouragement and torpor which she did not even attempt to combat.

Doña Luisa, on the contrary, who found in her present condition but little change from her noviciate, while deploring the blow that struck her, endured it with courage and resignation: her well-tempered soul accepted misfortune as the consequence of her devotion to her friend. Unconsciously, perhaps, another feeling had for some time past glided into the maiden's heart—a feeling which she did not attempt to explain, whose strength she did not thoroughly know; but which doubled her courage, and made her hope for a deliverance, if not prompt, at least possible, executed by the man who had already risked everything for her friend and herself, and would not abandon them in the fresh tribulations by which they were assailed, owing to the odious treachery of their guide.

When the two friends conversed together at times about any probability of deliverance, Laura did not dare to pronounce the name of Don Miguel, and through a reserve, the reason of which may be easily divined, she pretended to rely on the name and power of her father. Luisa, more frank, contented herself with answering that the bravery and devotion that Don Miguel had displayed were a sure guarantee that he would, ere long, come to their assistance.

Laura, whom her companion had not thought it advisable to inform of the numberless obligations which she owed the young man, could not understand the connection that could possibly exist between him and the future, and cross-questioned Luisa. But the latter remained dumb, or eluded the question.

"In truth, my friend," Laura said to her, "you speak incessantly of Don Miguel. We certainly owe him great gratitude for the service he has rendered us; but now his part is almost played out; my father, warned by him of the position in which we are, will come, ere long, to deliver us."

"*Querida de mi corazón*"[1] Luisa answered her, with a toss of her head; "who knows where your father is at this moment? *I* trust in help from Don Miguel, because he alone saved us from his own impulse, without hope of reward of any sort, and he is too loyal and too much of a gentleman not to finish an enterprise he has begun so well."

This last sentence was uttered by the young lady with such an air of conviction, that Laura felt surprised at it, and raised her eyes to her friend, who felt herself instinctively blush beneath the weight of this inquiring glance.

Laura added nothing; but she asked herself what could be the nature of the feeling which urged her friend to defend a man whom no one attacked, and to whom she, Luisa, only owed such slight obligations, and, indeed, scarce knew?

From that day, as if by a tacit agreement, they never spoke of Don Miguel, and his name was never mentioned by the maidens.

It is a strange fact, and yet undoubtedly true, that priests, no matter of what country they are, or the religion to which they belong, are continually devoured by a desire to make proselytes at any price. The Amantzin of Quiepaa Tani, in this respect, resembled all his brethren; he would not allow the opportunity to slip which was apparently afforded him of converting two Spanish girls to the religion of the Sun. Gifted with a great intellect, thoroughly convinced of the excellence of the religious principles he professed, and, besides, an obstinate enemy of the Spaniards, he conceived the plan, so soon as Addick intrusted him with the care of the maidens, of making them priestesses of the Sun. In America, there is no lack of instances of conversions of this nature, for what may seem monstrous to us is regarded as perfectly natural in that country.

The Amantzin planted his batteries in consequence. The maidens did not speak Indian; on his side, he did not know a word of Spanish; but this difficulty, apparently enormous, was quickly removed by the High Priest. He was related to a renowned Indian warrior, of the name of Atoyac, the very man, indeed, who was sentry at the gate of the city upon Addick's arrival. This man had married a civilized Indian girl, who, brought up not far from Monterey, spoke Spanish sufficiently well to make herself understood. She was a woman of about thirty years of age, although she appeared at least fifty. In these regions, where growth is so rapid, a woman is usually married at the age of twelve or thirteen. Continually forced to those hard tasks which, in other countries, fall to the lot of men, their freshness speedily disappears; on reaching the age of twenty-five, they are attacked by a precocious decrepitude, which, ten years later, converts into hideous and repulsive beings women who, in their youth, were endowed with great beauty and exquisite grace, of which many European women would be justly proud.

Atoyac's wife was named Huitlotl, or the Pigeon. She was a gentle and simple creature, who, having herself suffered much, was instinctively urged to sympathize with the sufferings of others. Hence, in spite of the law which forbade the introduction of strangers into the Palace of the Virgins of the Sun, the High Priest took on himself to let the Pigeon enter the presence of the maidens.

A person must have been a prisoner himself among individuals whose language he does not understand, in order to imagine the satisfaction which the prisoners must have felt on at length receiving a visit from somebody who could converse with them, and help them to subdue the utter weariness in which they passed their time. The Indian was hence accosted as a friend, and her presence regarded as a most agreeable interlude.

In the second interview, however, the Spaniards guessed with what an interested design these visits were permitted, and then a real tyranny succeeded on the short joyous conversation of the first day. It was a permanent punishment to the maidens. As Spaniards, and attached to the religion of their fathers, they could not fulfil the High Priest's hopes, while the Indian woman, incapable of playing the false and roguish part to which she was condemned, did not hide from them that, in spite of the honied words and insinuating manner of the Amanani, they must expect to suffer the most frightful tortures, if they refused to devote themselves to the worship of the Sun. The prospect was far from being reassuring. The maidens knew the Indians to be capable of putting their odious threats in execution without the slightest remorse; hence, while promising in their hearts to remain staunch in the faith of their fathers, the poor creatures were devoured by mortal alarm.

Time passed away, and the High Priest began to grow impatient at the slowness of the conversion. The little hope the two maidens had kept up of escaping from the sacrifice demanded of them was gradually deserting them. This painful situation, which was further aggravated by the absence of all news from without, at length produced an illness whose progress was so rapid, that the High Priest considered it prudent to suspend the execution of his ardent project of proselytism.

Let us leave the wretched prisoners for a few moments, almost felicitating themselves on the change that had taken place in their health, as it for a time at least almost freed them from the odious presence to which they were exposed, and take up the course of events which happened to other persons who figure in this story.

So soon as Don Estevan found himself at liberty, he dug his spurs into the flanks of Brighteye's horse, and began a furious race across the forest, whose evident object was to remove him as speedily as possible from the clearing which had all but proved so fearfully fatal to him. A prey to a mad terror which every moment that passed doubled, the wretched man galloped haphazard, without object or idea, following no direction, but flying straight before him, pursued by the hideous phantom of the death which, for an hour that was as long as an age, had bent over his shoulders, and had already stretched forth its skeleton hand to seize him, when a miraculous accident sent a liberator.

Don Estevan, in proportion as lucidity re-entered his brain, and calmness sprung up again in his thoughts, became once more the man he had ever been; that is to say, the implacable villain so justly condemned and executed by Lynch law. Instead of recognising in his deliverance the omnipotent finger of Providence wishing thus to show him the path of repentance, he only saw a naturally accidental fact, and entertained but one thought—that of avenging himself on the men who prostrated him and set their feet on his chest.

No one could say how many hours he thus galloped in the darkness, revolving schemes of vengeance, and casting ironical looks of defiance at Heaven. The whole night was passed in this mad race, and sunrise surprised him at a long distance from the spot where he had undergone his sentence.

He stopped for a moment in order to restore a little connection in his ideas and look around him. The trees, rather scattered at the spot where he halted, enabled him to see between their trunks a plain in front of him, terminating in the distance in tall mountains, whose blue-grey summits mingled in the horizon with the sky: a rather wide river flowed silently between two scarped banks, denuded of vegetation. Don Estevan gave a sigh of relief. Supposing, as was not at all probable, that anyone had started in pursuit, the rapidity of his flight, and the innumerable turns he had taken, must have completely hidden his trail. He advanced slowly to the edge of the forest, resolved to stop for an hour or two to rest his panting steed, and himself take that repose so absolutely necessary after so much fatigue and agony. So soon as he reached the first trees of the wood, he stopped again. Assured himself by a glance round that no human being was in the vicinity, and reassured by the calmness and silence that reigned around him, he dismounted, unsaddled and hobbled his horse, and, lying down on the ground, he began reflecting. His position was far from agreeable. He was alone, almost unarmed, in a strange country, compelled to fly from men of his own colour, and obliged to depend on himself alone to face all the events which might occur, and the dangers that surrounded him on every side.

Assuredly, a man more resolute than was Don Estevan, and gifted by nature with a more powerful organization than he possessed, would, in his place, have felt greatly embarrassed, and would have given way, if not to despair, at least to discouragement. The Mexican, overcome by the atrocious emotions and extraordinary fatigue he had endured during the fatal night which had just passed, fell involuntarily into such a state of prostration and insensibility, that gradually external objects disappeared from his sight, and he only existed in his mind, that ever-shining beacon in the human brain, and which God in his infinite goodness allows to shine there in the darkest gloom, in order to restore to the creature, in extreme situations, the feeling of his strength and the will to struggle.

For a long time Don Estevan had been seated, with his elbow on his knee and his head on his hand, looking without seeing, listening without hearing, when he suddenly started, and drew himself up sharply. A hand had been gently laid on his shoulder. Slight as the touch was, it was enough to arouse the Mexican, and restore him to a sense of his present situation. He looked up: two men, two Indians, were by his side; they were Addick and Red Wolf.

A gleam of joy shone in Don Estevan's eye: these two men, he had a presentiment, were two allies. He wanted them without hoping ever to meet them. In fact, in the desert, who can be certain of meeting those he seeks?

Addick fixed a sardonic glance on him. "Och!" he said, "my pale brother sleeps with his eyes open; his fatigue, it seems, is great."

"Yes," Don Estevan answered.

There was a moment of silence. "I did not hope to find my brother again so soon, and in such an agreeable position," the Indian continued.

"Ah!" Don Estevan said again.

"Yes, aided by my brother Red Wolf and his warriors, I had set out to bring help, if it were possible, to the Paleface."

The Mexican looked at him suspiciously. "Thanks," he at length said, with piercing irony; "I required help from nobody."

"All the better—that does not astonish me: my brother is a great warrior in his nation; but perhaps the help now useless to him will be of service to him later."

"Listen, Redskin," Don Estevan said; "take my advice, let us not deal in repartees, but be frank towards each other. You know a great deal more of my affairs than I should have wished anyone to discover. How you learned it is of little consequence; still, if I understand you, you have a proposal to make to me, a proposal you doubtless think I shall accept, because of the position in which you find me. Make it, then, frankly, briefly, as a man ought to do, and let us come to an end, instead of wasting precious time in idle discourse and useless beating about the bush."

Addick smiled craftily. "My brother speaks well," he said, in a honied voice; "his wisdom is great. I will be frank with him; he wants me; I will serve him."

"*Voto a brios!* that is talking like a man; that pleases me. Go on, Chief; if the end of your speech resembles the beginning, I do not doubt we shall come to an understanding."

"Wah! I am convinced of it; but, before sitting down to the council fire, my brother needs to regain his strength, weakened by a long fast and heavy fatigue. Red Wolf's warriors are encamped close by. Let my brother follow me. When he has taken a little nourishment, we will settle our business."

"Be it so. Go on; I follow you," Don Estevan answered.

The three men then went off in the direction of the Redskin camp, which was not more than a hundred paces from the spot they left.

The Indians understand hospitality better than any other people, excepting the Arabs—that virtue ignored in cities, where, to the disgrace of civilized peoples, a cold egotism and shameful distrust is substituted for it. Don Estevan was treated by the Indians as well as it was possible for them to do. After he had eaten and drank as much as he wanted, Addick returned to the charge. "Will my Paleface brother hear me at present?" he said. "Are his ears open?"

"My ears are open, Chief. I am listening to you with all the attention of which I am capable."

"Does my brother wish to avenge himself on his enemies?"

"Yes," Don Estevan exclaimed, passionately.

"But those enemies are powerful; they are numerous. My brother has already succumbed in the contest he tried to wage with them. A man, when he is alone, is weaker than a child."

"That is true," the Mexican muttered.

"If my brother consents to grant to Red Wolf and Addick what they will ask of him, the Red Chiefs will help my brother to avenge himself, and ensure him success."

A feverish flush covered Don Estevan's face; a convulsive tremor flew over his limbs. "*Voto a brios!*" he muttered, gloomily; "whatever be the condition you lay down, I accept it, if you serve me as you say."

"My brother must not pledge himself lightly," the Indian retorted, with a grin. "He does not know the condition yet; perhaps he will regret having been so hasty."

"I repeat to you," Don Estevan repeated firmly, "that I accept the condition, whatever it be. Let me know it, then, without further delay."

The cautious Indian hesitated, or appeared to hesitate, for two or three minutes, which seemed an age to the Mexican. At length he went on, in a perfidiously gentle voice. "I know where the two Palefaced maidens are whom my brother seeks in vain."

Don Estevan, at these words, bounded as if he had been stung by a serpent. "You know it!" he shouted, as he squeezed his arm violently, and looked fixedly at him.

"I know it," Addick answered, still with perfect calmness.

"It is not possible."

The Indian smiled contemptuously. "It was under my guardianship," he said, "and guided by me, that they reached their present abode."

"And you can lead me to it?"

"I can."

"On the instant?"

"Yes, if you accept my conditions."

"That is true; tell me them."

"Which does my brother prefer, these young girls, or vengeance?"

"Vengeance!"

"Good; the young pale girls will remain where they are. Addick and Red Wolf are alone; their cabins are desolate; they each need a wife. The warriors hunt; the cihuatls prepare the food, and nurse the papooses. Does my brother understand me?"

These words were pronounced with so strange an intonation, that the Mexican shuddered involuntarily, but he recovered almost immediately. "And if I accept?" he said.

"Red Wolf has two hundred warriors. They are at my brother's service, to aid him in accomplishing his vengeance."

Don Estevan let his head fall in his hands. For a few moments he remained motionless. This man, who had so coolly resolved on his niece's death, hesitated at the odious proposition now made him. This condition seemed to him more horrible than death.

The Indians waited, apparently apathetic witnesses of the contest that was going on in the heart of the man they wished to seduce. They watched this conflict of good and evil inclinations, coldly calculating the chances of success offered them by the evil instincts of the wretch they held beneath their eye. However, the struggle was not long. Don Estevan raised his head, and said, with a calm voice, cold face, and no sign of emotion,—"Well, be it so, the die is cast. I accept, and will keep my word; but first keep yours."

"We will keep it," the Indians answered.

"Before the eighth sun," Addick added, "my brother's enemies will be in his power; he will deal with them as he thinks proper."

"And now, what must I do?" Don Estevan asked.

"Here is our plan," Addick replied.

The three men then discussed the plan of campaign they intended to follow, in order to gain the object they proposed. But, as we shall soon see it work out, we will leave it, to return to our other characters.

[1] Cherished one of my heart.

CHAPTER XXVI
A HUNT ON THE PRAIRIE

The persons collected in Don Miguel's tent could not repress a movement of surprise, almost of terror, at the sudden appearance of Brighteye, pale, bleeding, and with disordered garments. The hunter had stopped in the entrance of the tent, tottering, and looking around with haggard eyes, while his face gradually assumed an expression of sorrow and profound discouragement. All these men, accustomed to the incessantly changing life of the desert, whose courage, incessantly put to the rudest trials, was surprised at nothing, felt themselves, however, shudder, and a foreboding of misfortune.

Brighteye still remained motionless and dumb. Don Miguel was the first to recall his presence of mind, and succeeded in regaining sufficient mastery over himself to address the newcomer. "What is the matter, Brighteye?" he asked him in a voice which he tried in vain to render firm; "of what sad news are you the bearer?"

The Canadian passed his hand several times over his damp forehead, and, after casting a last suspicious glance around him, he at length found courage to reply in a low and inarticulate voice—"I have terrible news to announce."

The adventurer's heart beat audibly; still, he mastered his emotion, and said in a calm voice, with a sigh of resignation—"It will be welcome, for we can hear nothing from you which is not so. Speak, then, my friend, we are listening to you."

Brighteye hesitated, a feverish flush mounted over his face; but, making a supreme effort, he said, "I have betrayed you—betrayed you like a coward."

"You!" they all exclaimed, unanimously, in denial, and shrugging their shoulders.

"Yes, I!"

These two words were uttered in the tone of a man whose resolution is definitely formed, and who loyally accepts the responsibility of an act which he recognises in his heart as culpable.

His hearers regarded him in stupor. "Hum!" Marksman muttered, shaking his head sorrowfully; "there is something incomprehensible in all this. Leave it to me to find it out," he continued, addressing Don Miguel, who seemed preparing to address fresh questions to the hunter. "I know how to make him speak."

The adventurer consented with a mute sign, and then fell back on his bed, while bending an interrogatory glance on the Canadian.

Marksman quitted the spot he had hitherto occupied, and walking up to Brighteye, laid his hand on his shoulder. The Canadian quivered at this friendly touch, and looked sorrowfully at the old hunter. "By Jove!" the latter said, with a smile, "deuce take me if our ears were not tingling just now! Come, Brighteye, old comrade, what is the matter? Why this terrified look, as if the sky was on the point of falling on our heads! What means this pretended treachery of which you accuse yourself, and whose flagrant impossibility I guarantee; I, who have known you these forty years?"

"Do not pledge yourself so for me, brother," Brighteye answered, in a hollow voice; "I have broken the law of the prairies. I have betrayed you, I tell you."

"But, in the devil's name, explain yourself! You cannot have bargained to our injury with those Apache dogs, our enemies? Such a supposition would be ridiculous."

"I have done worse."

"Oh! oh! What, then?"

"I have—" Brighteye hesitated.

"What?"

Don Mariano suddenly interposed. "Silence!" he said, in a firm voice, "I guess what you have done, and thank you for it. To me it belongs to justify you in the sight of our friends, so let me do so."

All eyes were curiously turned on the gentleman.

"Caballeros," he continued, "this worthy man accuses himself of treachery towards you, because he consented to do me an immense service. In a word, he has saved my brother."

"Can it be possible?" Don Miguel passionately exclaimed.

Brighteye bowed in affirmation.

"Oh!" the adventurer said, "wretched man, what have you done?"

"I would not be a fratricide," Don Mariano nobly answered.

This word burst like a bombshell amid these lion-hearted men. They let their heads sink instinctively, and quivered involuntarily.

"Do not reproach this honest hunter," Don Mariano continued, "with having saved that wretch. Has he not been sufficiently punished? The lesson has been too rude for him not to profit by it. Forced to allow his defeat, bowed beneath shame and remorse, he is now wandering alone and without help beneath the omnipotent eye of God, who, when his hour arrives, will inflict on him the chastisement for his crimes. Now, Don Estevan is no longer an object of alarm to us; we shall never meet him again on our path."

"Stop!" Brighteye shouted, vehemently; "were it as you state, I should not reproach myself so greatly for having consented to obey you. No, no, Don Mariano, I ought to have refused. When the serpent is dead, the venom is dead also! Do you know what this man did? So soon as he was free, thanks to me, immediately forgetting that I was his saviour, he treacherously tried to deprive me of the life I had just restored him. Look at the gaping wound on my skull," he added, suddenly raising the bandage that surrounded his head, "here is the proof of his gratitude he left me on separating from me."

All present uttered an exclamation of horror.

Brighteye then narrated, in their fullest detail, the events which had occurred. The hunters listened attentively. When his story was ended, there was a moment of silence.

"What is to be done?" Don Miguel muttered, sorrowfully. "All must be begun afresh. There is no lack of villains on the prairie with whom this man can come to an understanding."

Don Mariano, overwhelmed by what he had just heard, remained gloomy and silent, taking no part in the discussion, recognizing in his heart the fault he had committed, but not feeling the courage to avow it, and thus assume the immense responsibility of the sentence passed by the wood rangers.

"We must come to an end of this," Marksman said, "moments are precious. Who knows what that villain is doing while we are consulting? Let us raise the camp as speedily as possible, and proceed to those maidens, for they must be saved in the first place. As for ourselves, we shall be able to foil the scoundrel's machinations, when aimed directly at ourselves."

"Yes," Don Miguel exclaimed, "let us start. Heaven grant that we arrive in time."

And forgetting his weakness and wounds, the adventurer rose boldly. Brighteye stopped him. The old hunter, freed from the burthen that weighed so heavily on his conscience, had regained all his boldness and freedom of mind.

"Permit me," he said, "to have to deal with a powerful foe. Let us not act lightly, or let ourselves be deceived this time. Hear what I propose."

"Speak," Don Leo answered.

"From what I know of this unhappy story, you, Don Miguel, aided by my old companion, Marksman, have hidden these young girls in a place where you suppose them safe from the attack of your enemy."

"Yes," the adventurer answered, "except by treachery."

"We must always suspect treachery as possible in the desert," the hunter went on, roughly; "you have a proof of it before you; hence redouble your prudence. Don Miguel and his Cuadrilla will, guided by us, set out immediately in pursuit of Don Stefano. Believe me, the most important thing for us is to secure the person of our enemy, and, by heavens, I swear to do all humanly possible to catch him. I have a terrible account to settle with him now," he added, with an expression of concentrated hatred which no one misunderstood.

"But the young ladies?" Don Leo exclaimed.

"Patience! Don Miguel; if you possessed as much strength as good will, I should have reserved for you the honour of going to seek them in the asylum you so judiciously selected for them; but that task will be too rude for you; leave to Marksman, then, the care of carrying it out, and be assured he will give you a good account of it."

Don Leo de Torres remained for a moment gloomy and thoughtful. Marksman took his hand, and pressed it warmly. "Brighteye's advice is good," he said; "under the present circumstances, it is the only plan we can follow; we must play a game of trickery with our adversaries, in order to foil their villainy. Leave that to me; I have not been christened 'The Scout' in vain. I swear to you, on my life, that I will bring the two maidens back to you."

The adventurer breathed a sigh. "Do as you think proper," he said, in a sorrowful voice, "as I am quite powerless."

"Good, Don Leo!" Don Mariano exclaimed; "I perceive that your intentions are truly honourable, and I thank you for your self-denial. As for you, my worthy friend," he said, turning to Marksman, "though I am old, and but little accustomed to desert life, I will accompany you."

"Your desire is just, señor, and I have no right to oppose it, as it is your daughter I am going to try and save; the fatigue you will endure, and the perils you incur during this expedition, will add to the happiness you experience in embracing your daughter, when I have succeeded in restoring her to you."

"Now," Brighteye said, "do you, Marksman, who know the direction you are about to follow, give us a place of meeting, where we can assemble again when each of us has accomplished his allotted task."

"That is important," the Canadian answered; "it would be even as well if a detachment from Don Miguel's Cuadrilla were to proceed directly to the meeting place we select, in order that, in the event of a mishap, each band can find succour or support there."

"Fifteen of my most resolute men shall go at once to encamp at the spot you select, Marksman," Don Miguel said, "in order to be ready to go wherever their presence is necessary."

"We are carrying on regular warfare; do not forget that; hence we must neglect no precaution. Ruperto, who is an old buffalo hunter, will, with your permission, Don Miguel, take the command of this party, and proceed to Amaxtlan."[1]

"Oh, I know the spot well," Ruperto interrupted; "I have often hunted beaver and otter there."

"That is all right," Marksman continued. "Now, whatever happens, we must all be at the appointed place this day month, except through a grave impediment, and, in that case, the detachment missing will send a scout to Ruperto, in order to inform him of the cause of its delay. Is that agreed?"

"Yes," his auditors answered.

"But," Don Miguel added, "I suppose that you will not go alone with Don Mariano?"

"No; I shall also take Domingo, who, for certain reasons known to myself, I shall not be sorry to have constantly under my hand. Don Mariano's two servants will also follow me; they are brave and devoted. I need no more people."

"They are very few," Don Leo remarked.

The old hunter smiled in a peculiar way. "The less We are, the better it will be," he said, "for the dangerous enterprise we meditate; our little band will pass invisible, where a larger party would be stopped; trust to me for that."

"I have one more word to add."

"Say it."

"Succeed!"

The Canadian smiled again, but this time with an expression of tender pity. "I shall succeed," he answered, simply, as he forcibly pressed the hand his friend offered him.

The two men understood one another. Don Leo then left the tent.

Soon all was bustle in the camp. The Gambusinos were busily engaged in destroying the entrenchments, loading the waggons, and saddling the horses; in short, everybody made preparations for a hurried departure.

"Did you not tell me, Marksman," asked Brighteye, "that you were picked up by Flying Eagle?"

"Yes," the other answered.

"Did the Chief leave you at once, then?"

"No; he followed me to the camp, and so did Eglantine."

"Heaven be praised! He will accompany me on my expedition; he is a brave and experienced warrior; his help, I believe, will be very necessary to the success of my plans. Where is he?"

"A few steps off; let us go and find him, for I have also something to say to him."

The two hunters left the camp together. They soon perceived Flying Eagle, squatting by a fire, and calmly smoking his Indian calumet; his wife sat motionless by his side, anxious to satisfy his slightest wish. On seeing the hunters, the Chief took the pipe from his mouth, and saluted them courteously.

Brighteye knew that the Comanche had taken several measurements of the footsteps left by Don Estevan on his flight, and he wished to ask the Chief for them, as he hoped to employ them in following his enemy's trail. The Indian gave them to him without the slightest hesitation. The hunter placed them carefully in his bosom, with a nod of satisfaction. "Eh!" he muttered to himself. "This will enable me to find one end of the trail; with the help of heaven, I hope that I shall soon hold the other."

In the meanwhile, Marksman had seated himself by Flying Eagle's side.

"Does my red brother still intend to return to his tribe?" he asked him.

"The Sachem has been absent for a long time," the Indian answered; "his sons are anxious to see him."

"Good!" the hunter said; "it should be so. Flying Eagle is a renowned Chief; his sons have need of him."

"The Comanches are too wise to notice the absence of a warrior."

"My brother is modest; but his heart flies toward the village of his fathers."

"Are not all men the same?"

"That is true; the feeling of one's country is innate in the heart of man."

"The Palefaces are raising their camp."

"Yes."

"Are they returning to the side of the great Salt Lake, into their stone villages?"

"No; they are starting for a great buffalo hunt in the prairies, down by the endless river with the golden waves."

"Wah!" the Chief said, with a certain degree of emotion; "then many moons will pass ere I see my brother again."

"Why so, Chief?"

"Does not the great Pale hunter accompany his brothers?"

"No!" Marksman answered, laconically.

"Och! my brother must be laughing. What will the Palefaces do, if he does not accompany them?"

"I am going in the direction of the sun!"

The Indian started, and fixed a piercing glance on the speaker. "The direction of the sun," he said, as if speaking to himself.

"Yes," Marksman continued; "to the evergreen prairies of the country of Acatlan,[2] on the banks of the fair streams of Atonatiah."[3]

The Chief started violently. Marksman remained calm, and apparently indifferent, although he attentively followed the various emotions which contracted the Chief's features, in spite of the mask he tried to draw over them. "My brother is wrong," he said, presently.

"Why so?"

"My brother is ignorant that this land of which he speaks is sacred. Never has the foot of a white man trodden it with impunity."

"I know it," the hunter answered, carelessly.

"My brother knows it, and persists in going there?"

"Yes."

There was a silence of several moments' duration between the two men, the Indian hastily puffing the smoke from his calumet, a prey to an emotion he could not master. At length he spoke again. "Every man has his destiny," he said, in that sententious tone peculiar to the Indians. "My brother doubtless attaches a great importance to this journey."

"An immense importance, Chief; I am going to that country, though perfectly aware of the perils that await us, for interests of value, and impelled by a will more powerful than my own."

"Good! I do not ask my brother's secrets. The heart of a man is his own; he alone must read in it. Flying Eagle is a powerful Sachem; he also follows that road; he will protect his Pale brother, if the hunter's intentions are pure."

"They are so."

"Wah! my brother has the word of a Chief; I have spoken." After uttering these words, the Indian took up his calumet again, and began smoking silently. Marksman was too conversant with the Indian manners to press him further. He rose, with joy in his heart at having succeeded in obtaining an ally so powerful as the Comanche Chief, and he went in all haste to make the preparations for departure.

For their part, during the conversation we have reported, the Gambusinos had not remained inactive. Don Miguel or Don Leo, whichever it pleases the reader to call him, had so urged on his men, that everything was ready,—waggons loaded and horsed, and the riders mounted, with rifle on thigh, only awaited the signal for setting out. Don Miguel selected from his band fifteen old Gambusinos, practised in Indian tricks, and in whom he believed he could trust. He said a few words to them, explanatory of his intentions, and placed them under Ruperto's command, with orders to obey him as they would himself. The Gambusinos swore to do so. This duty accomplished, he summoned Domingo. The Gambusino came up to his Chief with that cunningly indolent manner familiar to him, and waited respectfully for his orders. When Domingo learned what was expected from him, he was in no way flattered by the confidential commission his Chief gave him, especially as he was not at all anxious to be under the immediate supervision of Marksman, whose peering glance incessantly occasioned him a nervous tremor, and whose assiduous watchfulness was most disagreeable to him. Still, as it was impossible openly to disobey Don Miguel, the worthy Gambusino made up his mind for the worst, making himself a secret promise to keep on his guard, and double his prudence.

When Don Miguel had completed all the duties of a wise and intelligent Chief, he mounted his horse, though with difficulty, owing to the weakness occasioned by his wounds. He placed himself at the head of his band, to the right of Brighteye, and after giving a parting salutation to Don Mariano and Marksman, he ordered his men to start. The two parties set out immediately, that led by Ruperto turning to the left, and proceeding toward the mountains, and Brighteye, with his men, temporarily following the course of the Rubio. All now left in the deserted camp were Marksman, Don Mariano, Flying Eagle, Eglantine, the two servants, and Domingo, who followed with a look of envy his gradually disappearing comrades. The old hunter, for reasons he kept secret, did not wish to set out before sunset. Scarcely had that planet disappeared on the horizon, amid floods of vapours, ere the night set in, and the landscape was almost immediately plunged in dense gloom. We have already several times remarked that, in high American latitudes, there is no twilight, or, at least, it is so weak, that night arrives almost without any transition.

Marksman, since the departure of the two first detachments, had not uttered a syllable, or made a movement; his comrades, doubtless for motives resembling his own, respected their Chief's silence; but night had scarcely set in, ere the hunter rose sharply. "Start!" he said, in a quick voice.

All rose. Marksman took an inquiring glance around. "Leave the horses," he said; "they are useless to us. We are not going to begin a journey, but a manhunt. We must be unimpeded in our movements, for the trail we shall follow is difficult. Juanito, you will remain here with the animals, until you hear from us."

The creole made a sign of discontent. "I should have preferred to follow you, and not quit my master," he said.

"I understand that, but I want a courageous and resolute man to guard our horses, and I cannot select a better one than you; besides, I trust that you will not remain alone long. Still, as we do not know what route we shall have to follow, or what obstacles may arise, build yourself a tent. Hunt, do what you think proper, but remember that you must not stir from this place without my orders."

"That is agreed, compadre," Juanito answered; "you can start when you please. If your journey were to last six months, you will be certain to find me here on your return."

"Good," Marksman said; "I reckon on you."

Then he whistled his mustang, which ran up at the summons, and laid its intelligent head on its master's shoulder. It was a noble animal, rather tall, with a small head, but its eyes flashed with ardour; its wide chest, its firm and nervous legs, all denoted the blood horse. Marksman seized the reata which hung from a ring fixed to the saddle, unfastened it, rolled it round his body, and then, giving the mustang a light tap on the croup, watched it depart with a sigh of regret.

The hunter's comrades were provided with their arms and provisions, consisting of pemmican, or buffalo meat, dried and pounded, and maize tortillas.

"Come, let us start," the Canadian said, throwing his rifle over his shoulder.

"A pleasant journey, and happy return," Juanito said, unable to prevent himself accompanying that adieu by a sigh, in which it could be easily read how vexed he felt at being thus left behind.

"Thanks," the adventurers answered.

So soon as they left the camp, they walked in Indian file, that is to say, one behind the other, the second placing his foot exactly in the steps of the first, and the third in those of the second, and so on to the last. The latter, however, as closing the march, was careful to efface, as far as was possible, the traces left by himself and those who preceded him.

Juanito, after looking after them for some minutes, as they descended the mound, at the top of which the camp was, cautiously returned, and seated himself by the fire. "Hum!" he muttered, "I shall not have much fun here, but what must be must be." And with this philosophical reflection, the worthy Mexican lit his cigarette, and began smoking peacefully, while following with interest the blue wreaths fantastically entwined by the evening breeze that rose from the smoke of his Havanah tobacco, whose perfume he inhaled with all the methodic phlegm of a true Indian Sagamore.

[1] The spot where a river divides into several branches.

[2] The country of reeds.

[3] Sun of the water.

CHAPTER XXVII
A HUNT ON THE PRAIRIE—(*concluded*)

In the new world, when people are travelling in Indian regions, and do not desire to be tracked by the Redskins, they must be careful to go to the east, if their business lies in the west, and *vice versa*; in a word, imitate the manoeuvres of a ship, which, if surprised by a contrary wind, is obliged to tack, and thus gradually approaches the point it wishes to reach. Marksman was too conversant with the cleverness and craft of the Indians not to act in a similar fashion. Although the presence of Flying Eagle was, to a certain point, a guarantee of security, still, not knowing with what Indian tribe accident might bring him in contact, Marksman resolved not to be discovered by anybody, were that possible.

Fenimore Cooper, the immortal historian of the North American Indians, has, in his excellent works, initiated us into the tricks employed by the Tuscaroras, Mohicans, and Hurons, when they wish to foil the researches of their enemies; but, no offence to the numerous admirers of the sagacity of young Uncas, a magnificent type of the Delaware nation (of which he was not, however, the last hero, for it still exists, though sadly, diminished), the Indians of the United States are only children, when compared with the Comanches, Apaches, Pawnees, and other nations of the great western prairies, who may justly be regarded as their masters in every respect. The reason is very simple, and easy of comprehension. The northern tribes never existed in the condition of political powers. Each of them governs itself, separately, and, to some extent, according to its fancy. The Indians composing them rarely ally themselves with their neighbours, and have, from time immemorial, constantly led a nomadic life. Hence they have only possessed the instincts (though highly developed, we grant) of men constantly inhabiting the forests; that is to say, a marvellous agility, a great fineness of hearing, and a miraculous length of sight—qualities, by the way, which may be also found in the Arabs, and generally in all wandering tribes, whatever be the nook of earth that shelters them. As for their sagacity and skill, the wild beasts taught them, and they only had the trouble of imitating them.

The Mexican Indians join to the advantages we have mentioned the remains of an advanced civilization—a civilization which, since the

Conquest, has taken refuge in inaccessible lurking places, but, for all that, no less exists. The families, or tribes, regard themselves as the members of one great whole—the nation. Now, the American nations, continually fighting with the Spaniards on one side, and the North Americans on the other, have felt the necessity of doubling their strength, in order to triumph over the two formidable enemies who incessantly harass them, and their descendants have gradually modified what was injurious in their manners, to appropriate those of their oppressors, and combat them with their own weapons. They have carried these tactics so far—which have hitherto saved them, not only from serfdom, but also from extermination—that they are perfect masters in trickery and cunning; their ideas have grown larger, their intelligence has been developed, and they have ended by surpassing their enemies in craft and diplomacy, if we may employ the expression. And this is so true, that for the last three hundred years the latter have not only failed in subduing, but in preventing their periodical incursions, which the Comanches proudly call the *Mexican Moon,* and during which they destroy everything they come across with impunity.

Can we really regard as savages these men, who, formerly driven back by the dread of fire arms, and the sight of horses, animals of whose existence they were ignorant, and compelled to conceal themselves in inaccessible ravines, have yet defended their territory inch by inch, and, in certain districts, have actually reconquered a portion of their old estates? Better than anyone, we know that there are savages in America, savages in the fullest sense of the term; but they have proved a cheap conquest, and they daily disappear from the earth, for they possess neither the necessary intelligence to understand, nor the energy to defend themselves. These savages to whom we allude, before being subject to the Spaniards or Anglo-Americans, were so to the Mexicans, the Peruvians, and the Araucanos of Chili, owing to their intellectual organization, which scarce elevates them above the brutes. We must not confound this race of helots, who are an exception in the genus, with the great untamed nations whose manners, necessarily alluring, we are attempting to portray here; for in spite of the efforts they make to withdraw themselves from its influence, that European civilization they despise rather through the hereditary hatred of their conquerors and the whole race generally, than from any other motive, surrounds, crushes, and invades them on all sides. Perhaps, before a hundred years are past, the emancipated Indians, who smile with pity at the paltry contests going on between the phantom republic that surrounds them, and the colossal pigmy of the United States which menaces them, will take their rank again in the world, and raise their heads proudly; and that will be just, for they are heroic natures, richly endowed, and capable, under good direction, of undertaking or carrying out great things. In Mexico itself, since the period when that country proclaimed its so-called independence, all the eminent men who have risen either in arts, diplomacy, or war, belong to the pure Indian race. In support of our statement, we will cite a fact of immense significance:—The best history of southern America, published up to this day, was written by an Inca, Garcillasso de la Vega. Is not this conclusive? is it not time to condemn all those systematically absurd theories which insist on representing the red family as a bastard race, incapable of amelioration, and fatally destined to disappear?

Ending here this digression, which is perhaps, too lengthy, but is indispensable for the due comprehension of the facts that follow, we will take up our narrative again, at the point where we broke it off.

After a march of three hours, rendered fatiguing and difficult by the lofty grass, the adventurers reached the skirt of the forest. About midnight, Marksman, after allowing his comrades two hours' rest, started again. At sunrise they reached a species of canyon, or narrow gorge, formed by two walls of perpendicular rocks, and were constrained to march for four hours in the bed of a half dried-up torrent, in which their footsteps fortunately left no mark. During several days their journey over abrupt and desolate mountains was effected with great toil, but did not offer any incident worthy of narration. At length they found themselves again in the region of the *tierras calientes*; the verdure reappeared, and the heat became sensible. Hence the adventurers, who had suffered extremely from the cold in the lofty regions of the Serranía, experienced a feeling of marked comfort on inhaling the gentle and perfumed atmosphere, in contemplating the azure sky and dazzling sun which had now taken the place of a grey and leaden sky, and the limited, fog-laden horizon, which they had left behind them. Toward the end of the fourth day after leaving the mountains, Marksman uttered a shout of satisfaction, on noticing the skirt of the immense virgin forest, toward which he was marching, rise in the distant azure of the prairie. "Courage, my friends!" he said; "we shall soon obtain the shadow and freshness lacking here."

The adventurers, without replying, hurried their steps, like men who perfectly appreciated the value of the promise made them. Night had completely set in, when they reached the banks of a rather high river, whose vicinity the tall grass had concealed from them, although for some minutes they had heard the continued rustling of the water over the pebbles. Marksman resolved to wait till the next day, and look for a ford. The party camped, but the fire was prudently not lighted. The adventurers wrapped themselves in their zarapés, after taking a scanty meal, and soon fell asleep. Marksman alone watched. Gradually the moon sunk on the horizon: the stars began to dim and go out in the depths of the sky. The hunter, whose eyes fatigue closed against his will, was about to yield to sleep, when suddenly a strange and unexpected sound made him start. He drew himself up, as if he had received an electric shock, and listened. A slight rustling agitated the reeds that bordered the river, whose calm and motionless waters resembled a long silvery ribbon. There was not a breath of air. The hunter laid his hand on Flying Eagle's shoulder; the latter opened his eyes, and gazed at him. "The Indians," Marksman muttered in the Chief's ear. Then, crawling on his hands and knees, he glided down the slope, and entered the water. Then he looked around him. The moon shed sufficient light to let him survey the country for a long distance, but, in spite of the attention he devoted, he could see nothing. All was calm; but he waited with eye fixed, and ear on the watch. Half an hour passed, and the sound which had aroused him was not repeated. However closely he listened, no sound arose to disturb the silence of night. Still Marksman felt certain he was not mistaken. In the desert all sounds have a cause, a reason; the hunters know them, and can distinguish them, being never deceived as to their nature. The hunter was immersed, however, in the water up to his waist belt. In America, if the heat of the day is stifling, the nights, to make up for it, are excessively fresh, and Marksman felt an icy coldness invading his whole body. Tired of waiting, and believing that he was deceived, he was at length preparing to return to the bank, when, at the moment he was preparing to carry out his design, a hard body struck his chest.

He looked down, and instinctively thrust out his hands. He stifled a cry of surprise; what had touched him was the side of a canoe, gliding noiselessly through the reeds, which it parted in its passage. This canoe, like all the Indian boats in these parts, was made of birch bark, detached from the tree by means of boiling water. Marksman examined the canoe, which seemed to be moving without the assistance of any human being, and rather drifting with the current than proceeding in a straight line. Still one thing astonished the Canadian: the canoe was moving without the slightest oscillation. Evidently an invisible being, probably an Indian, was directing it, but where was he? Was he alone? This it was impossible to guess. The Canadian's anxiety was extreme; he did not dare make the slightest move, through fear of imprudently revealing his presence. And yet the canoe was moving on. Resolved to know how it was, Marksman gently drew his knife, and, holding his breath, bent down in the river, and only let the top of his face emerge from the water. What he expected happened: in a moment he saw the eyes of an Indian, who was swimming behind the canoe, and pushing it with his arm, sparkle in the gloom like two live coals. The Redskin held his face on a level with the water, and was looking searchingly around him. The Canadian recognized an Apache. Suddenly the stranger's eyes were fixed on the hunter. The latter; judged that the time had arrived, and bounding with the suppleness and speed of a jaguar, he seized his enemy by the throat; giving him no time to utter a cry of alarm, he buried his knife in his heart. The Apache's face turned black; his eyes were dilated; he struck the water for a moment with his legs and arms; but soon his limbs stiffened, a convulsion passed over his body, and the current bore him away, leaving behind a slight reddish trace. He was dead. The Canadian, without the loss of a moment, clambered into the canoe, and, holding on to the reeds, looked across to the spot where he had left his comrades. The latter, warned by Flying Eagle, had cautiously come up, bringing with them the rifle left by the hunter on the bank.

So soon as they were together again, they freed the canoe from the reeds that barred its passage, and, by Marksman's advice, after embarking, and turning the canoe into the current, they lay down in the bottom. For some time they had been gliding along gently, believing themselves hidden from the invisible enemies they supposed to be concealed around them, when suddenly a terrible clamour broke out, like a thunderclap. The body of the Apache killed by Marksman, after following the current for some distance, had stopped in some grass and dead leaves, exactly opposite an Indian camp, near which the adventurers had passed a few hours previously, not suspecting its presence. At the sight of their brother's corpse, the Redskins uttered the formidable howl of grief we mentioned, and rushed tumultuously toward the bank, pointing to the canoe.

Marksman, seeing himself discovered, seized the paddles, and, aided by Flying Eagle and Domingo, he was in a few minutes out of range. The Apaches, furious at this flight, and not knowing with whom they had to deal, overwhelmed their enemies with all the insults the Indian tongue could supply, calling them hares, ducks, dogs, owls, and other epithets, borrowed from the nomenclature of the animals they hate or despise. The hunter and his companions did not trouble themselves about these impotent insults;

they began paddling vigorously, which soon restored the circulation in their limbs.

The Indians then changed their tactics; several long-barbed arrows were shot at the canoe, and several shots were even discharged; but the distance was too great, and the water was only dashed up by the bullets.

Thus the night passed.

The adventurers paddled eagerly; for they had noticed that the river, owing to its countless bends, was visibly drawing nearer to the forest they had so much interest in reaching. Still, believing that they no longer had anything to fear from their enemies, they laid down the paddles for a few moments, to rest, and take a little food.

The day rose while they were thus engaged, and a magnificent landscape was unfolded before the dazzled eyes of the adventurers. "Oh!" Flying Eagle exclaimed, with an expression of surprise.

"What is the matter?" Marksman answered at once, who understood that the Chief had noticed something out of the common.

"Look!" the Comanche said, emphatically, holding his arm out in the direction they had come during the night.

"*Virtudieu!*" the Canadian shouted. "Two canoes in pursuit of us. Oh, oh! we must make a fight of it."

"*Cuerpo del Cristo!*" Domingo said, in his turn, with a bound, which almost upset the frail boat.

"What is the matter now?"

"Look!"

"A thousand demons!" the hunter exclaimed. "We are beset."

In fact, two canoes were rapidly coming up in the rear of the adventurers, while two others, starting from, the opposite sides of the river, were pulling ahead of them, with the evident intention of barring their passage, and cutting off their retreat.

"*Voto a Dios!* these Redskins want to make us dance a singular *jaleo*" Domingo muttered. "What do you say, old hunter?"

"Good, good!" Marksman replied gaily; "we'll find the music. Attention, comrades, and redouble your energy."

At a sign from him, all the men took up paddles, and gave such an impetus to their canoe, that it seemed to fly over the water. The situation was becoming critical for the whites. Marksman, upright, and leaning on his rifle, coldly calculated the chances of this inevitable rencontre. He did not fear the boats in pursuit, for they were at too great a distance behind, to hope to catch him; all his attention was concentrated on those in front, between which he must pass. Each stroke of the paddle diminished the distance which separated the white men from the Redskins. The hostile canoes, as far as could be judged from a distance, seemed overloaded, and only advanced with some difficulty. Marksman had judged the situation with an infallible glance, and formed one of those daring resolutions, to which he owed the reputation he enjoyed, and which resolution could alone save him and his friends, in these critical circumstances.

CHAPTER XXVIII
RED SKINS AND WHITE

Marksman, as we have said, had formed a final resolution. Instead of trying to escape by passing between the two canoes, which would have entailed a risk of being run down, he turned slightly to the left, and paddled straight toward the canoe nearest his own.

The Indians, who did not at first comprehend the meaning of this manoeuvre, greeted him with shouts of joy and triumph. The adventurers kept silence, but they redoubled their efforts, and continued to advance. A sarcastic smile played round the lips of the Canadian hunter. As his canoe drew nearer to that of the Apaches, he noticed that the left bank of the river was indented, and at this moment perceived that this was caused by an islet very near the land, but leaving a sufficient passage for his boat, which would thus avoid a bend again on the pursuing foe. The main point was in reaching the point of the islet before the Indians in the first canoe did so. The latter had at length begun to suspect, if they did not completely guess, the intentions of their intrepid adversary; hence they, for their part, changed their tactics, and altered their steering. Instead of going to meet the Whites, as they had done up to this moment, they suddenly tacked, and paddled vigorously in the direction of the island.

Marksman understood that he must stop their progress at all risks. Till then, not a shot or an arrow had been fired on either side. The Apaches were so persuaded that they would succeed in capturing the adventurers, that they thought it useless to proceed to those extremities. The Whites, on their part, who also felt the necessity of saving their powder in a hostile country, where it would be impossible to renew their stock, had hitherto imitated them through prudence, however much they might have desired to come to blows. Still, the Indian canoe was now not more than fifty yards from the isle. The hunter, after taking a final glance around, bent down to his comrades, and said a few words in a low voice. They immediately laid down their paddles, and, seizing their rifles, rested them on the gunwales of the boat, after putting in a second bullet. Marksman had done the same. "Are you ready?" he asked, a moment after.

"Yes!" the adventurers answered.

"Fire, then, and aim low."

The five shots sounded like one.

"Now to your paddles, and quick!" the hunter said, giving the example, as usual.

Eight arms took up the paddles again, and the light canoe began bounding once more over the water. The hunter alone reloaded his rifle, and waited on his knee, ready to fire.

The effect of the volley was soon visible, — the five shots, all aimed at the same spot, had opened an enormous breach in the side of the Indian boat, just on a level with the water line. Cries of terror and pain rose from the group of Apaches, who leapt into the water one after the other, swimming in every direction. As for the canoe, left to itself, it floated a little way, gradually filled with water, and at length sunk.

The adventurers, believing themselves freed from their enemies, relaxed their efforts for a moment. Suddenly, Flying Eagle raised his paddle, while Marksman clubbed his rifle. Two Apaches, with athletic limbs and ferocious glances, were trying to fasten on the canoe and upset it. But they soon fell back with fractured skulls, and floated down the stream. A few moments later the hunters reached the passage.

Several Apaches, however, had managed to swim to the island: so soon as they emerged from the water, they set out in pursuit of the whites, running along the bank; for want of better instruments, they hurled stones at them, for they could not use their damp rifles, and they had lost their bows and arrows through their sudden plunge in the river.

Though the weapons employed by the Apaches for the moment were so primitive, Marksman recommended his companions to redouble their efforts, in order to escape as soon as possible from these immense projectiles, which, from behind every tuft of grass and elevation of the ground, fell sharp as hail round the canoe, — for the Redskins, according to their habit, took care not to let themselves be seen, through fear of bullets. Still, this situation was growing unbearable, and they must emerge from it. The hunter, who was eagerly watching an opportunity to give his obstinate foes a severe lesson, at length fancied he had found it. He saw, a few yards from him, a tuft of floripondios moving slightly; quickly shouldering his rifle, he aimed, and pulled the trigger.

A terrible yell burst from the medley of floripondios, canaverales, creepers, and aquatic plants which formed this hedge, and an Apache, bounding like a wounded tiger, rushed forward with the intention of seeking shelter behind the tree that grew a short distance from him in the centre of the islet. Marksman, who had reloaded his rifle, pointed it at the fugitive, but raised it again directly. The Apache fell on the ground, and was rolling in the last convulsions. At the same instant a dozen Indians rushed from behind the shrubs, raised the corpse in their arms, and disappeared with the speed of a legion of phantoms.

A sudden calm, an extraordinary tranquillity, succeeded the extreme agitation and irregular cries which had aroused the echoes a few moments previously.

"Poor wretch!" Marksman muttered, as he laid his rifle again in the bottom of the canoe, and seized a pair of paddles; "I am vexed at what has happened to him. I believe they have enough; now that they know the range of my rifle, they will leave us in peace."

The hunter had calculated correctly: in truth, the Redskins gave no further signs of life.

What we say here must not in any way surprise the reader: every Indian understands honour in its own fashion. The Indians hold it as a principle never to expose themselves uselessly to any danger. With them success alone can justify their actions; hence, when they no longer consider themselves the stronger, they renounce, without shame, projects they have conceived and prepared for many weeks.

The adventurers at length doubled the point of the island. The second canoe was already a very long way behind them, as for those they had just perceived behind them, they only looked like dots on the horizon. When the Redskins in the second canoe saw that the adventurers had gained a start which it was impossible for them to pick up, and that they were escaping, they made a general discharge of their weapons,—a powerless demonstration, which injured nobody, for the bullets and arrows fell a considerable distance short of the White men; then they turned back to join their comrades, who had sought shelter on the island.

Marksman and his companions were saved. After paddling for about an hour longer, in order to place sufficient distance between themselves and their enemies they took a moment's rest, and washed the contusions they had received from several stones that had struck them with fresh water. In the ardour of the engagement, they had not noticed the blows, but now that the danger was past, they were beginning to suffer from them. The forest which, in the morning, owing to the constant meanderings of the river, was so far from them, was now much nearer, and they hoped to reach it before night, after a short interruption. They, therefore, took to their paddles again with renewed ardour, and continued their voyage. At sunset, the canoe disappeared beneath an immense dome of foliage belonging to the virgin forest, which the river crossed at an angle. So soon as the darkness began to fall, the desert woke up, and the howling of wild beasts proceeding to the watering places were heard hoarsely echoing in the unexplored depths of the forest. Marksman did not consider it prudent at this hour to enter a strange country, which doubtless contained dangers of every description. Consequently, after pulling for some time, to find a suitable landing place, the hunter gave the order to pull into a point of rock, which jutted out in the water, and formed a species of promontory, on which it was easy to land.

So soon as he stepped ashore, the Canadian walked round the rock, in order to look at the vicinity, and know in what part of the forest they were. This time chance had served them better than they could have dared to hope. After removing, with great pains and minute precautions, the creepers and brambles that choked the path, the hunter suddenly found himself at the entrance of a natural path, probably formed by one of those volcanic convulsions so frequent in this country. On seeing it, he stopped, and lighting an *ocote* branch, with which he had been careful to provide himself, he boldly, entered the grotto, followed by his companions. The sudden appearance of the light startled a swarm of night birds and bats, which began flying heavily, and escaping in every direction. Marksman continued his progress, not troubling himself about these gloomy hosts, whose lugubrious sports he interrupted so unexpectedly. This grotto was high, spacious, and airy. It was, under the present circumstances, a precious discovery for the adventurers; for it offered them an almost secure shelter for the night against the researches of the Apaches, who assuredly had not given up the pursuit. The adventurers, after exploring the cavern on all sides, and assuring themselves that it had two exits, which secured the means of flight, if they were attacked by too numerous enemies, returned to their boat, drew it from the water, and carried it on their shoulders to the extremity of the grotto. Then, with that patience of which Indians and wood rangers are alone capable, they effaced the least traces, the slightest imprints, which might have allowed their place of debarkation to be discovered, or the retreat they had chosen guessed. The bent blades of grass were raised, the creepers and brambles they had moved drawn together, and after the task was accomplished, no one could have suspected that several persons had passed through them. After this, collecting an ample stock of dead wood and *ocote* branches, for torches, they reentered the grotto, with the manifest intention of at last taking a little of that rest they needed so greatly. All these preparations took time; hence, the night was already far advanced when the adventurers, after swallowing a hasty meal, at length wrapped themselves in their zarapés, and lay down, with their feet to the fire, and their rifles in their hands. Nothing disturbed their sleep, which was continuing when the first sunbeams purpled the horizon with their joyous tints. It was Marksman who aroused his companions.

Flying Eagle was not in the grotto. This absence in no way alarmed the hunter; he was too well acquainted with the Comanche sachem to fear any treachery on his part.

"Up!" he cried to the sleepers. "The sun has risen; we have rested enough; it is time to think of our business."

In an instant all were afoot.

The hunter was not mistaken: the fire was scarce kindled, ere Flying Eagle made his appearance. The Chief bore on his shoulders a magnificent elk, which he threw silently on the ground, and then seated himself by Eglantine's side.

"On my word, Chief," Marksman said, gaily, "you are a man of precaution; your hunt is welcome; our provisions were beginning to diminish furiously."

The Comanche smiled with pleasure at this remark, but he made no other reply: like all his fellows, the Indian only spoke when it was absolutely necessary.

At a sign from the Canadian, Domingo, who was a first-rate hunter, immediately set to work breaking up the elk. The pemmican, queso, and Indian corn remained in the adventurer's alforjas, thanks to the succulent steaks cut adroitly from the animal by Domingo, and which, roasted on the ashes, procured them a delicious breakfast; the festival was crowned with a few drops of pulque, from which the two Comanches abstained, according to the custom of their nation. Pipes and cigarettes were then lighted, and each began smoking silently.

Marksman reflected on the steps he must take, while Domingo and Bermudez prepared everything for departure; at length, he decided on speaking. "Caballeros," he said, "we have arrived at the spot where our journey really commences; it is time for me to tell you where we are going. So soon as we have crossed this forest, which will not take long, we shall have before us an immense plain, in the midst of which stands a city; this city is called by the Indians Quiepaa Tani; it is one of those mysterious cities in which, since the conquest, the Mexican civilization of the Incas has taken refuge; to that city we are proceeding, for the maidens we wish to save have sought shelter there. That city is sacred; woe to the European or white man who is discovered in its vicinity! I confess to you that the perils we have hitherto incurred are as nothing to be compared with those that probably await us, ere we gain the end we have proposed to ourselves. It is impossible for all of us to dream of entering that city; the attempt would be madness, and only result in our being massacred for no good. On the other hand, we might find it necessary to meet there those devoted companions, who, in the hour of danger, would come to our aid. I have, therefore, resolved on this: Bermudez will proceed to the spot where we left Juanito; then both, leading the horses with them, will join Brighteye's and Ruperto's detachments at the agreed on spot, and guide them here. What is your opinion, Caballeros? Do you approve my plan?"

"In every point," Don Mariano answered, with a bow.

"And you, Chief?"

"My brother is prudent; what he does is well."

"What? I am going to leave you!" poor Bermudez muttered, addressing his master.

"It must be, my friend," the latter answered; "but not for long, I hope."

"Try to remember the road we have followed, so as not to make a mistake in returning," the hunter remarked.

"I will try."

"Eh, old hunter?" Domingo said with a grin. "Why the deuce do you not send me, who am a wood ranger, and have the desert at my fingers' ends, instead of this poor man, who, I feel sure, will leave his bones on the way?"

Marksman gave the Gambusino a piercing glance, which made him blush and look down. "Because," he answered, laying a stress on each word, "friend Domingo, I feel such a powerful inclination toward you, that I cannot consent to let you out of my sight for a moment! You understand me, I suppose?"

"Perfectly, perfectly," the Gambusino stammered; "you need not get in a passion, old hunter. I will stay. What I said was in your behalf; that was all."

"I appreciate your offer, as it deserves," the Canadian answered, sarcastically; "so let us say no more about it." Then he continued, addressing Bermudez, "As we may possibly soon require help, try, on your return, to take a shorter and more direct road. You hear?"

"And understand; be at rest. I am too satisfied of the recommendations you give me, to neglect them."

"A last word. I have told you that it was absolutely necessary, for the success of the difficult expedition we are attempting, that we should find here, in case of need, a strong detachment of resolute men; warn Ruperto to be doubly prudent, and avoid, as far as possible, any meeting, and, of course, any quarrel with the Indians."

"I will tell him."

"Now put the canoe in the water; and good luck."

"Heaven grant you may succeed in saving my poor Niña," the old servant said, with an emotion he could not overcome. "I would joyfully give my life for her."

"Go in peace, my friend," Marksman answered, affectionately. "You have already sacrificed much."

The adventurers then left the grotto, not without first looking round to see there was no danger. A profound silence prevailed beneath the impenetrable forest covert. They then raised on their shoulders the canoe, in which they had placed provisions for the comrade who was about to leave them, and it soon floated lightly on the water. Bermudez took his parting farewell, and then turning away, with an effort, leaped into the canoe, seized the paddles, and went off.

"We shall meet again soon," Don Mariano said, with emotion.

"Soon, if Heaven decree it!" Bermudez answered.

"Amen!" the adventurers piously murmured.

Marksman followed, for a long time, the course of the canoe, and then turned hastily to his comrades. "His is a devoted heart," he muttered, as if speaking to himself. "Will he get there?"

"God will protect him!" Don Mariano answered.

"That is true," the hunter said, passing his hand over his forehead. "I am mad, on my word, to have such thoughts, and, what is more, ungrateful to Providence, which has hitherto watched over us with such, solicitude."

"Well spoken, my friend," Don Mariano remarked. "I feel a presentiment that we shall succeed."

"Well, would you have me speak frankly to you?" the hunter said, gaily. "I feel the same presentiment; so forwards!"

Flying Eagle at this moment laid his hand on the hunter's shoulder. "Before starting, I should like to hold a council with my brother," he said; "the case is grave."

"You are right, Chief; let us return to the grotto; our movements must be combined with the utmost prudence, so that when the moment arrives, we may not commit an irreparable mistake which would hopelessly compromise the success of our expedition."

The Comanche made a sign of assent, and preceding his friends, returned to the cavern. The fire was not yet completely out, but smouldered in the ashes; in a second it blazed up again, and the four men seated themselves gravely round it. The Chief then took his calumet from his girdle, filled it with sacred tobacco, lit it, and after slowly drawing two or three mouthfuls of smoke, passed it to Marksman. The calumet then passed round, without a word being uttered, until the tobacco contained in the bowl was consumed. When nothing remained but the ash, the Chief shook it out in the fire, returned the calumet to his girdle, and addressed Marksman. "A Chief would speak," he said.

"My brother can speak," the hunter answered, with a bow: "our ears are open."

The Sachem, after making his wife a sign to retire out of range of voice, which, according to the Indian custom, Eglantine did immediately, bowed reverently to the members of the council, spoke, as follows.

CHAPTER XXIX
THE COUNCIL

Flying Eagle, since the commencement of the expedition, in which he had consented to take a share, had constantly played a passive part, accepting, without discussion, the combinations proposed by Marksman, executing frankly and faithfully the orders he received from the hunter; in a word, entirely performing the part of a warrior subordinate to a chief whose duty it is to think for him: hence the new attitude suddenly assumed by the Sachem filled the Canadian with surprise, for he had no notion on what subject the debate was about to turn, and he feared in his heart lest, in the critical situation he was in at the moment, the Comanche intended to leave him to his own resources, or, perhaps, raise obstacles to the execution of his plans. Hence he impatiently awaited the explanation of his ally's strange conduct.

The Chief, still apathetic, rose, and bowing once again, began to speak:— "Palefaces, my brothers," he said, in his guttural and sympathetic voice, "for more than a moon we have been together on the same path, sharing the same fatigue, sleeping side by side, eating the produce of the same chase; but the chief you admitted to share your labour and perils has not, till this day, been allowed to advance so far in your confidence as a friend should do. Your heart has even remained to him closed and covered with a thick cloud. Your projects are as unknown to him as on the first day. The words your chest breathes are and remain to him inexplicable riddles. Is this right? is it just? No! Why did you summon me? Why did you beg me to accompany you, if I am ever to remain a stranger to you? Up to the present I have shut up in my heart the bitterness which your suspicious conduct caused me. Not a complaint rose from my heart to my lips, on seeing myself treated in a manner so ill suited to my rank and the relations I have maintained with you. Even at this moment I would continue to maintain silence if my friendship for you was not stronger than the resentment caused by your ungenerous conduct toward me. We are on the holy land of the Indians; the ground we tread on is sacred; perils surround us, numberless snares are laid for our steps on all sides. Why should I teach you to avoid them, if your plans are not at length revealed to me, and unless I know whether the path we are following is that of war or of hunting? Speak with frankness—take the skin from your heart, as I have done from mine. Enlighten me as to the conduct you intend to pursue, and the object you propose, so that I may aid you by my counsels should that be necessary, and that, being your ally, I should no longer be kept aloof from your deliberations, which is a disgrace to the nation of which I have the honour to be a member, and unworthy of a warrior like myself. I have spoken, brothers. I await your answer, which I am convinced will be such as warriors so wise and experienced as yourselves ought to give."

During the long speech of the Comanche Chief, Marksman had repeatedly given signs of impatience, and, had he not feared making a breach in the rules of Indian etiquette by interrupting him, he would certainly have done so; it was with great difficulty he succeeded in restraining himself and maintaining that apathetic appearance absolutely demanded in such circumstances. So soon as the Chief took his place again, the hunter rose, and after bowing to the audience, he spoke in a firm voice, with these words:— "The Wacondah is great. He holds in his right hand the hearts of all men, whatever their colour may be. He alone can know their intentions and read their souls. The reproaches you address to me, Chief, have an appearance of justice which I will not discuss with you. You may have supposed, from the conduct which circumstances have hitherto constrained me to hold toward you, that I did not grant you all the confidence you so justly desired; but it is not so; I waited till the hour for speaking arrived, not only to explain to you my intentions, but also to claim your assistance and intervention. As you wish me to explain myself at once, I will do so; but, perhaps, it would have been better for you to wait till the forest in which we now are was traversed."

"I will remark to my brother that I demand nothing of him. I thought it my duty to make certain observations to him; if he does not find them just, his heart is good. He will pardon me when he remembers that I am only a poor Indian, whose intellect is obscured by a cloud, and that I had no intention to wound him."

"No, no, Chief," the hunter said quickly; "as we are on this question, it is better to clear it up at once, in order not to have to return to it again, and that nothing may arise between us for the future."

"I am at my brother's orders, ready to hear, if it pleases him, and willing still to wait, if he considers it necessary."

"I thank you, Chief; but I adhere to my first resolution. I prefer to tell you all."

The Comanche smiled cunningly. "Is my brother really resolved to speak?" he asked.

"Yes."

"Good. Then my brother has nothing to add. All that he has to say to me I know. He can tell me nothing more than I have guessed myself."

The hunter could not repress a start of surprise. "Oh, oh," he muttered, "what is the meaning of that, Chief? Why, then, the reproaches you addressed to me?"

"Because I wished to make my brother understand that a friend must hold nothing concealed from another, especially when that friend has been proved for long years, when his fidelity is staunch, and he can be depended on like a second self."

The hunter smiled slightly, but at once regained his gravity. "Thanks for the lesson you give me, Chief," he said, holding out his hand cordially. "I deserve it, for I really failed in my confidence to you. The service I expect from you is so important for us that I put off daily asking it of you, and, in spite of myself, I confess I should probably not have made up my mind till the very last moment."

"I know it," the Comanche said, his good temper entirely restored.

"Still," the hunter continued, "in spite of the assurance that you know my plans, it would be, perhaps, as well for me to enter into certain details of which you are ignorant."

"I repeat to my brother that I know all. Flying Eagle is one of the first Chiefs of his nation; he has a quick ear and a piercing sight. For nearly two moons he has not left the great Pale warrior; during that period many events have happened, many words have been spoken before him. The Chief has seen, he has heard, and all is as clear in his mind as if these things had been drawn for him on one of those collars which the white men know so well how to make, and some of which he has seen in the hands of the Chief of the Prayer."

"However great your penetration may be, Chief," the hunter objected, "I can scarcely imagine you are so well acquainted with my intentions as you suppose."

"Not only do I know my brother's intentions, but I am also aware of the service he expects from me."

"By Jove! Chief, you will cause me enormous pleasure by telling it to me; not that I doubt your penetration, for the red men are renowned for their cleverness. Still, all this seems to me so extraordinary that I should like to be convinced, were it only for my personal satisfaction, and to prove to the persons who hear us how wrong we white men are in imagining that we are so superior in intellect, when, on the contrary, you Indians leave us far behind."

"Hum!" Domingo muttered, "what you say there is rather strong, old hunter. It is notorious that the Indians are brute beasts."

"That is not my opinion," Don Mariano remarked, "though I know very little of the Redskins, with whom I never entered into any connection before this occasion. Still, since my arrival in these regions, I have seen them accomplish acts so astonishing, that I should not feel at all surprised if this Chief had completely read our plans, as he assures us."

"I think so too," the hunter added. "However, we shall judge. Speak, Chief, that we may know as soon as possible what opinion to form of the penetration you flatter yourself with possessing."

"Flying Eagle is not a chattering old woman, who boasts rightly and wrongly; he is a Sachem, whose deeds and words are ripely meditated. He does not pretend to know more than his brothers, the Palefaces; still, the experience he has acquired serves him in the place of wisdom, and helps him to explain what he sees and hears."

"That is well, Chief. I know that you are a valiant and renowned warrior. Our ears are open; we are listening to you with all the attention you deserve."

"My brother, the great hunter, wishes to enter Quiepaa Tani, where the two white maidens are sheltered, one of whom is the daughter of the Chief with the grey beard. These two women were confided to an Apache Sachem, called Addick. My brother, the hunter, is anxious to arrive at Quiepaa Tani, because he fears treachery from the Apache Chief, whom he suspects of having allied himself with the white man who was hired by the Palefaces to carry off the two women, and make them disappear. I have spoken. Have I truly understood the intentions of my brother, or am I deceived?"

His auditors regarded each other with amazement. The Chief enjoyed his triumph for a moment, and then continued—"Now, this is the service the hunter wishes to ask of the Comanche Sachem—"

"By heavens, Chief!" Marksman exclaimed, "I must confess that all you have said is true. How did you learn it? I know not how to explain it, although I grant we have said enough on the subject in your presence to enable you to guess it; but as for the service I expect from you, if you can tell me that, I will allow you to be the greatest—"

"Let my brother not be rash," the Chief interrupted him, with a proud smile, "lest he should soon take me for an adept of the great *medicine*."

"Hum!" the hunter said, gravely, "I should not like to swear you are not."

"Och! my brother shall judge. No Paleface has, till this day, succeeded in entering Quiepaa Tani; still my brother wishes, at all hazards, to visit the city, in order to obtain certain information about the two pale virgins. Unfortunately, my brother does not know how to set about his plan, nor how he would succeed in saving the maidens, if he found them in danger. That is why he thought of Flying Eagle. He said to himself that his red brother was a Chief, and must have friends or relations in Quiepaa Tani; that the entrance to the city, forbidden him through his colour, was not so to the Chief, and that Flying Eagle would obtain for him the information he could not obtain himself."

"Yes, that is what I thought, Chief. Why should I conceal it? Am I mistaken? Will you not do that for me?"

"I will do better," the Indian answered. "Let my brother listen. Eglantine is a woman; no one will notice her; she will enter the city unperceived, and obtain the information the hunter needs better than the Chief can. When the moment for action arrives, Flying Eagle will help the hunter."

"By Jove! you are right, Sachem; your idea is better than mine. It is preferable in every respect that Eglantine should go on the discovery. A woman cannot inspire suspicions, and she can learn news better than anyone. Let us start, then, without any further delay. So soon as we have crossed the forest, we will send her to the Tzinco."

Flying Eagle shook his head, and kept his hold of the hunter's arm, who had already risen to set out. "My brother is quick," he said; "let me say one word more."

"Let us see."

"Eglantine will go ahead; my brother will have news sooner."

Don Mariano rose, and pressed the Comanche's hand with emotion. "Thanks for the good thought that has occurred to you, Chief," he said to him. "You have delicate feelings; your heart is noble; it can sympathize with a father's sorrow. Once again I thank you."

The Indian turned away, to conceal the trace of agitation on his face, which, in his idea, was unworthy a Chief, who, under all circumstances, must remain stoical.

"In truth," Marksman said, "the Chief's proposal will make us gain precious time; his idea is excellent."

Flying Eagle made Eglantine a sign to approach him, which she at once obeyed. The Chief then explained to her in his tongue what she was to do, to which she listened with charming grace, standing timidly before him. When Flying Eagle had given her his instructions most fully, and she perfectly understood what was wanted of her, she turned gracefully to Don Mariano and Marksman, and said, with a smile almost prophetic —"Eglantine will learn."

These two words filled the poor father's heart with joy and hope. "Bless you, young woman!" he said; "bless you, for the kindness you show me at this moment, and that you intend to show me."

The separation between husband and wife was as it should be with Indians; that is to say, grave and cold. Whatever love Flying Eagle felt for his companion, he would have been ashamed, in the presence of strangers, and above all of whites, to display the slightest emotion, or allow the feelings of his heart towards her to be guessed. After bowing once more to Don Mariano and Marksman in farewell, Eglantine hastened away, with that quick and high step which renders the Indians the first walkers in the world. Though the Chief's stoicism was so great, still he looked after his young wife, until she disappeared among the trees.

As nothing pressed them at the moment, the adventurers allowed the great heat of the day to pass, and only set out when the declining sun appeared like a ball of fire, almost on a level with the ground. Their march was slow, owing to the countless difficulties they had to surmount, in forcing their way through the intertwined creepers and brambles, which they had to cut down with axes at every step. At length, after a four days' march, during which they had to endure extraordinary fatigue, they saw the trees growing more sparsely, the scrub become less dense, and, between the trees they perceived a deep and open horizon. Although the adventurers were in the heart of a virgin forest, where, according to all probability, they could not expect to meet anybody of their own species, they neglected no precaution, and advanced very prudently in Indian file, with the finger on the trigger, eye and ear on the watch; for being so near one of the sacred Indian cities, they might expect, especially after the smart skirmish a few days previous, to be tracked by scouts sent in search of them. Toward the evening of the fourth day, at the moment they were preparing to camp for the night in a vast clearing on the banks of a nameless stream, so many of which are met with in the virgin forests, Marksman, who was marching at the head of the little party, suddenly stopped, and looked down on the ground, with signs of the utmost astonishment.

"What is it?" Don Mariano anxiously asked him.

Marksman did not answer him; but he turned to the Indian Chief, and said, with a certain degree of alarm, "Look yourself, Chief; this seems to me inconceivable."

Flying Eagle stooped down in his turn, and remained a long time examining the marks which seemed to trouble the hunter so greatly. At length he rose.

"Well?" Marksman asked him.

"A band of horsemen has passed by here this very day," he replied.

"Yes," the hunter said; "but who are the horsemen? Where do they come from? That is what I want to know."

The Indian resumed his inspection, with an attention more minute than before. "They are Palefaces," after a pause, he said.

"What! Palefaces!" Marksman exclaimed, with a voice prudently suppressed; "it is impossible! Think where we are. Never has a white man, excepting myself, penetrated into these regions."

"They are Palefaces," the Chief insisted, "Look, one of them stopped here and dismounted; here is the mark of his steps; his foot crushed that tuft of grass; one of his nails in his shoe left a black line on that stone."

"That is true," Marksman muttered; "the Indian moccasins do not leave such marks. But who can these men be? How did they get here? What direction have they followed?"

While Marksman was asking himself these questions, and hopelessly seeking the solution of the problem, Flying Eagle had walked some paces, attentively following the marks, which were perfectly plain on the ground.

"Well, Chief," the hunter asked, as he saw him returning, "have you found anything which can put us on the right scent?"

"Wah!" the Indian said, with a toss of his head. "The trail is fresh; the horsemen are not far off."

"Are you sure of it, Chief? Remember how important it is for us to know who the people are we have for neighbours."

The Comanche remained silent for a moment, plunged in serious thought. Then he raised his head. "Flying Eagle," he said, "will try to satisfy his brother. Let the Palefaces remain here till his return; the Chief will take up the trail; he will soon tell the hunter if the men are friends or enemies."

"By Jove! I will go with you, Chief," Marksman sharply replied. "It shall not be said that, in order to be useful to us, you exposed yourself to a serious danger, without having a friend near to back you up."

"No," the Indian went on; "my brother must remain here; one warrior is sufficient."

Marksman knew that, when once the Chief had formed a resolution, nothing could make him alter it. Hence he no longer urged it. "Go then," he said, "and act as you please. I know that what you do will be right."

The Comanche threw his rifle over his shoulder, lay down on the ground, and crawled like a serpent amid the underwood.

"And what are we to do?" Don Mariano asked.

"Await the Chief's return," Marksman answered; "and while doing so, prepare supper, the need of which I am certain you are beginning to feel, like myself."

The adventurers installed themselves, as well as they could, in the clearing, following Marksman's advice, and awaiting the return of the scout, whose absence, however, was much longer than they expected; for night had fallen long before he made his appearance.

CHAPTER XXX
THE SECOND DETACHMENT

As we have said in our previous chapter, Flying Eagle started on the trail of the horsemen whose footsteps had been perceived by Marksman. The Indian was really one of the finest sleuth-hounds of his nation; for, although night fell rapidly, and soon prevented him from distinguishing the traces which served to guide him in his search, he continued not a bit the less to advance with a sure and certain step. About ten minutes after leaving his companions, the Chief rose to his feet, and not appearing to attach great importance to the marks on the ground, he continued his search, satisfying himself with looking, from time to time, peeringly at the trees and shrubs that surrounded him. Flying Eagle continued walking thus for an hour without hesitation or checking his speed. On reaching a spot where the trees fell back on both sides, thus forming an open space into which several wild beast tracks opened, the Chief stopped for a moment, cast an investigating and suspicious glance around, clutched his rifle, which he had hitherto carried on his back, inspected the priming carefully, and bending his body to a level with the tall grass, he advanced with measured steps toward a thicket, the branches of which he drew aside, and in which he speedily disappeared. So soon as he was completely concealed, the Comanche knelt down, gradually opened the leafy curtain that hid him, and looked out. Suddenly Flying Eagle rose, uncocked his rifle, which he threw back again on his shoulder, and stepped forth with head erect, and a smile on his lips.

In the centre of a large clearing, illumined by three or four fires, some twenty men were encamped, picturesquely grouped round the fires, and joyously preparing their evening meal, while their horses grazed a short distance off. These horsemen, whom Flying Eagle recognized at the first glance, were Don Leo de Torres, Brighteye, and the Gambusinos detached in pursuit of Don Estevan. The Indian approached the fire near which Don Leo and the hunters were seated, and stopped in front of them.

"May the Wacondah watch over my brothers!" he said, in salutation; "a friend has come to visit them."

"He is welcome," Don Leo answered gracefully, as he held out his hand.

"Yes," Brighteye went on, "a thousand times welcome; though there's reason that his presence should surprise us."

The Chief bowed, and took his place between the two whites.

"How is it we meet you here?" the hunter asked.

"The question my brother asks me at this moment is exactly what I was preparing to ask myself."

"How so?" Don Miguel asked.

"Does not my brother, the Paleface, know where he is at this moment?"

"Not at all. Since our separation, we have constantly followed the trail of an enemy, though we could not catch him up; that trail has led us to parts strange to Brighteye himself."

"I am bound to confess it. This is the second time such a thing has occurred to me, and under exactly similar circumstances. The first time, I remember, it was in 1843. I was on the—"

"But if the hunter does not know these regions," Flying Eagle interrupted him unceremoniously, "my brother, the warrior knows them."

"I?" Don Leo said. "Not the least in the world, Chief. I assure you it is the first time I have come this way."

"My brother is mistaken, he has been here already; but, like all the Palefaces, my brother's memory is short, he has forgotten."

"No, Chief. I am too well acquainted with the desert not to recognize, at the first glance, any spot which I have once visited."

The Indian smiled at this pretension, which was so poorly justified. "Yes, that has happened to my brother today," he said, "though only three moons, at the most, have passed since he visited these parts in company with the Pale hunter, to whom he gave the name of Marksman."

The adventurer started, and a lively emotion could be seen on his face. "What do you mean, Redskin, in Heaven's name?" he said quickly.

"I mean that Quiepaa Tani is there," the Indian answered, stretching out his arm in a south-western direction; "that we are but a half day's journey distant from it at the most."

"Can it be possible?"

"Oh!" the young man exclaimed, energetically, as he suddenly rose; "thanks for these good news, Chief!"

"What are you going to do?" Brighteye asked him.

"What am I going to do? Cannot you guess it? Those we wish to save are only a few leagues from us, and you ask me that question!"

"I ask it of you because I fear, through your impetuosity and imprudence, lest you might compromise the success of our expedition."

"Your words are harsh, old hunter; but I pardon them, because you cannot understand my feelings."

"Perhaps I can, perhaps I cannot, Don Miguel; but, believe me, in an expedition like ours, stratagem alone can lead to success."

"Deuce take stratagem, and he who recommends it," the young man exclaimed passionately. "I wish to deliver the girls whom, through my mad confidence, I led into this snare."

"And whom you lose for ever by another act of madness. Trust in the experience of a man who has lived in the desert more years than you count months in your life. Since we have been following Don Estevan's trail, you have seen that a strong party of Indian horsemen has joined him, I think? At two paces from a holy city, whose population is immense, do you intend to contend with your fifteen Gambusinos against several thousand brave and experienced Redskin warriors? That would be committing suicide with your eyes open. If Don Estevan is proceeding in this direction, it is because he also knows that the maidens are in Quiepaa Tani. Do not let us hurry, but watch our enemy's movements, without revealing our presence, or letting him suspect we are so near him. In that way I answer for our success on my head."

The young man had listened to these remarks with the greatest attention. When Brighteye ceased, he pressed his hand affectionately, and sat down at once by his side. "Thanks, my old friend," he said, "thanks for the rough way in which you have spoken to me. You have brought me back to my senses. I was mad. But," he added a moment after, "what is to be done? How to save these unhappy maidens?"

Flying Eagle, during the preceding conversation, had remained calm and silent, apathetically smoking his Indian calumet; on hearing Don Leo speak thus, he understood it was time for him to interfere. "The Pale warrior can regain his courage," he said; "Eglantine is in Quiepaa Tani; tomorrow at sunrise we shall have news of the pale virgins."

"Oh! oh!" the young man said joyously. "So soon as your wife returns from that nest of demons, I promise her, Chief, the handsomest pair of bracelets, and the prettiest earrings an Indian cihuatl ever yet wore."

"Eglantine needs no reward for serving her friends."

"I know it, Chief; but you will not refuse me the satisfaction of giving her this slight token of my gratitude, Chief?"

"My brother is at liberty to do so."

"Halloh!" Brighteye suddenly remarked, "by what chance did you come to our camp this night?"

"Have you not understood?"

"On my word, no. We were far from suspecting you to be so near us."

"That is true," Don Miguel remarked: "but now that I know where we are, all is explained."

"Yes; but that does not tell us why the Chief came to find us here."

"Because," Flying Eagle replied, "we discovered your footsteps crossing the trail we followed."

"That is true; and you came to reconnoitre."

The Chief nodded an assent.

"Have our friends stopped far from here?"

"No," the Indian said, "I am going to rejoin them, in order to tell them who are the men I have seen. My absence has been long; the Palefaces are soon alarmed. I am going."

"One moment," Brighteye observed. "As chance has brought us together again, perhaps it will be better not to separate again; we shall, possibly, need one another."

"What is your advice, Chief? Will it be better for us to accompany you to your bivouac, or will you join us?"

"We will come hither."

"Make haste, then; for I am curious to know what has happened to you since our separation at the ford of the Rubio."

"Flying Eagle is a good runner," the Chief answered, "but he has only the feet of a man."

"By the way, why did you not come on horseback"

"Our horses were left at the camp of the great river. A trail is better followed afoot."

"That is easily remedied. How many are you?"

"Four."

"What, four? I fancied you were more."

"Yes, but the Pale hunter will explain to you why two of our comrades have left us."

"Good. I will accompany you."

Don Leo immediately gave orders to have four horses got ready, and recommended Brighteye to watch over the camp during his absence, then, mounting his horse, in which he was imitated by the Chief, the two set off, leading the horses intended for the men they were going to find. The two men only took twenty minutes in covering the ground which Flying Eagle had spent more than an hour in crossing, owing to the precautions he was compelled to take when following an unknown trail, which might belong to enemies. They found Marksman and Don Mariano with loaded rifles, and keeping good watch. While awaiting Flying Eagle's return, they had fallen asleep; but the steps of the horses awoke them, and they stood on their defence in case of the worst. On their awakening, however, a very disagreeable surprise awaited them. They found only two instead of three. Domingo, the Gambusino, had disappeared. So soon as he recognized Don Miguel, the Canadian said, with extreme agitation—"Dismount, dismount, Caballero! We must all go beating."

"What humbug at this hour, Marksman!" Don Miguel answered. "Why, you must be mad!"

"I am not mad," the Canadian said, hurriedly; "but I repeat, dismount and hunt; we are betrayed!"

"Betrayed!" Don Miguel exclaimed, starting with surprise; "by whom? in Heaven's name!"

"By Domingo! The traitor has fled during our sleep! Oh! I was right to distrust his coppery face!"

"Domingo fled!—a traitor! You are mistaken!"

"I am not. Hunt after him, I tell you, in the name of those you have sworn to save."

No more was needed to exasperate the young man; he bounded from his steed, and seized his rifle. "What is to be done?" he asked.

"Scatter over the ground," the hunter rapidly answered. "Each go a different way; and may Heaven bless our search! We have lost too much time already."

Without any further exchange of words, the four men buried themselves in the forest in four different directions. But the darkness was dense. Beneath the cover, where, even by day, the sunbeams penetrated with difficulty, on this black and moonless night they could distinguish nothing two steps ahead of them; and if, instead of flying, the Gambusino had contented himself with hiding in the vicinity, the hunters would evidently have passed without noticing him. The search lasted a long time, for the hunters comprehended the importance of finding the fugitive again; but, in spite of all their skill, they could discover nothing. Marksman, Don Mariano, and Don Miguel had been back by the fire several minutes; they were communicating to each other the closeness of their pursuit, when, suddenly, a dazzling flash crossed the forest, and a shot was heard, almost immediately followed by a second. "Let us run up," Marksman shouted. "Flying Eagle has found the vermin. Never was a better sleuth-hound after game."

The three men ran at full speed in the direction of the shots they had heard. On approaching, they found that an obstinate contest was going on. The war yell of the Comanches, uttered in Flying Eagle's powerful voice, permitted them no doubt on that head. At length, they debouched on the scene of action. Flying Eagle, with his foot on the chest of a man thrown down before him, and who writhed like a serpent to escape the fearful pressure, leant his back against a black oak, and, tomahawk in hand, was defending himself like a lion against half a dozen Indians who attacked him together. The three white men clubbed their rifles, and rushed into the medley with a terrible cry of defiance. The effect of this diversion was instantaneous. The Redskins dispersed in all directions, and fled like a legion of phantoms.

"After them!" Don Miguel howled, as he rushed forward.

"Stop!" Marksman shouted, as he seized him by the arm; "you might as well pursue the cloud carried off by the wind. Let the scoundrels escape, we shall find them again, I warrant."

The adventurer perceived that a pursuit in the dark would be giving an enormous advantage to his enemy, who was better acquainted with the country, and probably very numerous; hence he stopped with a sigh of regret. The Chief was then surrounded, and complimented on his glorious resistance. The Sachem received the remarks with his habitual modesty.

"Wah!" he merely answered, "the Apaches are cowardly old women. One Comanche warrior is sufficient to kill six times ten of them, and twenty more."

By a miraculous hazard, the brave Indian had only received a few insignificant wounds, to which, in spite of his friend's earnest entreaties, he paid no further attention than washing them with cold water.

"But," Marksman suddenly said, stooping down, "whom have we here? Eh! if I am not mistaken, it is our fugitive!"

It was really Domingo. The poor wretch had his thigh broken; doubtlessly foreseeing the fate that awaited him, he howled with pain, but would give no other answer.

"It would be a good deed," Don Mariano said, "to dash out this poor fellow's brains, to terminate his sufferings."

"Let us be in no hurry," the implacable hunter remarked. "Everything will have its season. Let Flying Eagle explain to us how he found him."

"Yes, that is important," Don Miguel said.

"It is the Wacondah who delivered this man into my hands," the Chief answered, sententiously. "I had ransacked the forest with as much care as the darkness permitted me, and was returning to you, wearied with nearly two hours' fruitless search, when, at the moment I least thought of it, I was attacked by more than ten Apaches, who rushed on me from all sides at once. This man was at the head of the assailants. He fired his gun at me, but did not hit me. I answered in the same way; but more successfully, for he fell. I immediately set my foot on his chest, for fear he should escape me, and defended myself to my best against my enemies, in order to give you time to come to my assistance. I have spoken."

"By heavens, Chief!" the hunter exclaimed, enthusiastically, "you are a brave warrior! What you have done is grand. This villain, on leaving us, found a party of these birds of prey, and was, doubtlessly, returning with the intention of attacking us during our sleep."

"Well!" Don Mariano remarked, "he is found again; so all is for the best."

The wounded man made a great effort, and, leaning on his right hand, he drew himself up and gave a ghastly grim "Yes, yes," he answered, "I know I am about to die; but it will not be without vengeance."

"What do you say, villain?" Don Mariano exclaimed.

"I say that your brother knows all, my fine gentleman, and will succeed in foiling your plans."

"Viper! what have I done to make you act thus towards me?"

"You did nothing," he replied, with a demoniac grin; "but," he added, pointing to Don Miguel, "I have hated that man for a long time."

"Die, then, villain!" the exasperated young man shouted, as he set the cold muzzle of his rifle on his forehead.

Flying Eagle turned the weapon aside.

"This man is mine, brother," he said.

Don Miguel slowly removed his rifle, and turned to the Chief. "I consent; but on condition that he dies."

A sinister smile played for a second round the Indian's thin lips. "Yes," he said, "and by an Apache, death." Then, unfastening the bow he wore by the side of his panther skin quiver, he placed the string round the Gambusino's skull, and, forming a tourniquet, by means of an arrow passed through the string, while, with his knee buried between the wretch's shoulders, he seized his hair in his right hand, and drew it to him. He scalped in this manner, inflicting on him the most abominable torture that can be imagined, since, instead of cutting the skin with his knife, he literally tore it off by means of the string. The bandit, with his face inundated with blood, and disfigured features, clasped his hands by a supreme effort, exclaiming, with an expression impossible to describe—"Kill me! oh, for pity's sake, kill me!"

The Comanche placed his furious face close to the bandit's. "Traitors are not killed," he said, in a hollow voice. And then, seizing him by the neck, he thrust the blade of his knife between the clenched teeth, forced the mouth open, and tore out his tongue, which he threw from him in disgust. "Die like a dog!" he yelled; "thy lying tongue shall betray never more."

Domingo uttered a cry of pain so horrible that the hearers started with terror, and rolled senseless on the ground.[1]

Flying Eagle contemptuously kicked the bandit's body aside, and turned to his companions. "Let us go," he said.

They followed him in silence, terrified by the scene of which they had been witnesses. An hour later, they found Brighteye at the bivouac.

At sunrise, Flying Eagle approached Marksman and gently touched him on the shoulder. "What do you want?" the hunter asked, as he woke.

"The Sachem is going to meet Eglantine," the Chief answered, simply. And he went away.

"There is something human in those savage fellows after all," the hunter muttered, as he watched him depart.

[1] The author saw this punishment inflicted on a North American by an Apache.

CHAPTER XXXI
THE TLACATEOTZIN[1]

Two hours after sunrise, Flying Eagle returned to the camp, followed by Eglantine: the council immediately assembled to hear the news. The young Indian woman had not learned much: it was contained in one sentence.

The two Mexican girls were still in the city. Addick was absent, but expected at any moment. These news, slight as they were, were, however, good; for, though the details were wanting, the hunters knew that their enemies had not yet had time to act. The point was now to get before them and carry off the girls, ere they had time to prevent it. But to do so, they must enter the city, and there lay the difficulty. A difficulty which, at the first blush, appeared insurmountable.

In this moment of distress, all eyes were turned to Flying Eagle. The Chief smiled. Through the expression of agony depicted on every countenance, the Indian guessed what was expected of him. "The hour has arrived," he said. "My Pale brothers demand of me the greatest sacrifice they can demand of a Sachem—that is to say, to open to them the gates of one of the last refuges of the Indian religion, the principal sanctuary where still is preserved intact the law of Tlhui-camina,[2] the greatest, the most powerful, and most unhappy of all the sovereigns who have governed the country of Hauahuac: still, in order to prove to my Pale brothers how red the blood is that flows in my veins, and how pure and cloudless my heart is, I will do it for them, as I have promised."

At the assurance given by Flying Eagle, whose word could not be doubted, every face brightened. The Chief continued—"Flying Eagle has no forked tongue; what he says, he does; he will introduce the great Pale hunter into Quiepaa Tani; but my brothers must forget that they are warriors and brave: cunning alone can make them triumph. Has the great hunter of the Palefaces understood the words of the Chief? Is he resolved to trust to his prudence and sagacity?"

"I will act as you point out, Chief," Marksman replied, for he knew that the Comanche was addressing him. "I promise to let myself be entirely guided by you."

"Wah!" the Indian continued, with a smile. "All is well, then: before two hours, my brother will be in Quiepaa Tani."

"May Heaven grant it be so, and my poor child be saved!" Don Mariano muttered.

"I have been long used to contend in cunning with Indians," the hunter answered. "Up to the present, thanks to Heaven! I have always come off pretty well from my meetings with them. I have good hopes of success this time."

"We will hold ourselves in readiness to come to your aid, if needed," Don Miguel observed.

"Above all, take care not to be tracked; you know that traitor of a Domingo has put them on your scent."

"Trust to me for that, Marksman," Brighteye eagerly interposed; "I know what it is to play at hide and seek with the Indians. It is not the first time this happens to me; and I remember, in 1845, at the hour I was—"

"I know," the Canadian cut him short, "that you are not the man to let yourself be surprised, my friend, and that is enough for me; but keep a good lookout, so as to be ready at the first signal."

"And what will that signal be? for we must understand one another thoroughly, in order to avoid any misunderstanding, which, annoying at all times, would, in our present circumstances, be utter ruin."

"You are right. When you hear the cry of the hawk repeated thrice, at equal intervals, then you must act vigorously."

"That is understood," Brighteye said; "trust to me for that."

"I am ready," Marksman said to the Chief. "What must I do?"

"In the first place, dress yourself," Flying Eagle answered.

"What! dress myself?" the hunter said, surveying his person with surprise.

"Wah! does my brother fancy he will enter Quiepaa Tani in his Paleface clothes?"

"That is true; an Indian disguise is absolutely necessary. Wait a minute."

The *travestissement* did not take long to effect. Eglantine modestly retired into the forest, so as not to be present at the hunter's toilet. In a few minutes Marksman took from his alforjas a razor, with which he removed beard and moustache. During this time the Chief had plucked a plant, which grew abundantly in the forest. After extracting the juice, Flying

Eagle helped the Canadian, who had removed all his garments, to stain his body and face. Then the Chief drew on his chest an *ayotl*, or sacred tortoise, accompanied by several fantastic ornaments that had nothing warlike about them, and which he reproduced on his face. After that, he gave the hunter's black hair a white tinge, intended to make him look very aged; for among the Indians the hair retains its colour for a long period. He knotted his curls on the top of his head, after the fashion of the Yumas—the most travelled of the Redskins—and to the left of this tuft, to show that it adorned the head of a pacific Chief, he fixed a passagallo feather, instead of a scalp lock, as is the custom with the warriors.

When these preparations were completed, Flying Eagle asked the Europeans, who had curiously followed the metamorphosis, how they liked their comrade.

"My word," Brighteye answered, simply, "if I had not been present at the transformation, I should not recognize him; and, by the way, I remember a singular adventure that occurred to me in 1836. Just imagine—"

"Well, and what do you say?" the Indian continued, pitilessly cutting the Canadian short, and turning to Don Miguel.

The latter could not refrain from laughing on looking at the hunter. "I consider him hideous; he bears such a resemblance to a Redskin, that I feel sure he can risk it boldly."

"Och! the Indians are very clever," the Chief muttered. "Still, I believe that, disguised thus, if my brother is willing thoroughly to represent the character he has assumed, he has nothing to fear."

"I mean to do it. Still, I would remark, Chief, that I do not yet know what part you mean me to play."

"My brother is a Tlacateotzin—a great medicine man of the Yumas."

"By Jove! the idea is a good one. In that way I can get in anywhere."

The Comanche bowed with a smile.

"I shall be very clumsy, if I do not succeed," the hunter continued. "But as I am a doctor, I must not forget to furnish myself with medicaments."

Thereupon Marksman rummaged his alforjas, took out of them all that might have compromised him, and only left in them a little box of specifics, which he always carried about him,—a precious store he had employed on many an occasion. He closed the alforjas, threw them on his back, and turned to the Chief.

"I am ready," he said to him.

"Good. Myself and Eglantine will go in front, in order to make the road easy for my brother."

The hunter gave a sign of assent. The Indian called his wife, and both, after taking leave of the adventurers, went off.

So soon as the Chief was out of sight, the hunter in his turn said good-bye to his comrades. It was, perhaps, the last time he would see them; for who could foresee the fate reserved for him among these ferocious Indians, into whose hands he was about defencelessly to surrender himself?

"I will accompany you to the edge of the forest," Don Miguel said, "in order fully to understand the means I must employ to be able to run up at the first signal."

"Come," the hunter said, laconically.

They went away followed by the eyes of all their comrades, who saw Marksman depart with an indescribable feeling of anxiety and sorrow. The two men walked side by side, without exchanging a word. The Canadian was plunged in deep thought; Don Miguel seemed a prey to an emotion which he could not succeed in overcoming. In this way they reached the last trees of the forest. The hunter stopped. "It is here we must part," he said to his companion.

"That is true," the young man muttered, as he looked sadly around. Then he was silent. The Canadian waited a moment. Seeing, at length, that Don Miguel would not speak, he asked him, — "Have you anything to say to me?"

"Why do you ask me that question?" the young man asked him, with a start.

"Because," the hunter answered, "you have not come so far, Don Leo, merely to enjoy my company a little longer. You must, I repeat, have something to say to me."

"Yes, it is true," he said, with an effort; "you have guessed it. I wish to speak with you; but I know not how it is, my throat rises. I cannot find words to express my feelings. Oh, if I possessed your experience, and your knowledge of Indian language, no other than myself, I assure you, Marksman, would have gone to Quiepaa Tani."

"Yes, it must be so," the hunter muttered, speaking to himself, rather than answering his friend; "and why should it not be so? Love is the sun of youth. All love in this world. Why should two handsome and well-made beings alone remain insensible to each other and not love? What do you wish me to say to them for you?" he added quickly.

"Oh!" the young man exclaimed, "you perceived, then, that I loved her? You are master, then, of the secret which I did not dare to confess to myself!"

"Do not be alarmed about that, my friend. The secret is as safe in my heart as in yours."

"Alas, my friend! the words I should wish to say to her my mouth alone could utter with the hope of making them reach her heart. Say nothing to her, that will be best; but you can tell her that I am here, and watching over her, and that I shall die or she will be free soon in her father's arms."

"I will tell her all that, my friend."

"And then," he added, breaking, by a feverish movement, a little steel chain round his neck, which held a small bag of black velvet, "take this amulet. It is all that is left to me of my mother," he said, with a sigh; "she hung it round my neck on the day of my birth. It is a sacred relic—a piece of the true cross, blessed by the pope; give it to her, and let her guard it preciously, for it has preserved me from many perils. That is all I can do for her at this moment. Go, my friend, save her, as I am compelled to form silent vows for her deliverance. You love me, Marksman. I will only add one word,—from the attempt you make at this moment my life or death will result. Farewell! farewell!"

Seizing the hunter's hand with a nervous movement, he pressed it forcibly several times, and, turning quickly away, not to let his tears be seen, he rushed into the forest, where he disappeared, after making a last sign with his hand to his friend, who was watching his departure. After Don Miguel's departure, the Canadian stood for a moment a prey to extraordinary sorrow. "Poor young man!" he muttered, with a profound sigh, "is that the state people are in when they love?" In a moment he overcame the strange emotion which contracted his heart, and boldly raised his head. "The die is cast!" he said. "Forward!" Then assuming the easy, careless step of an Indian, he proceeded, slowly to the plain, while looking inquiringly around him.

In the brilliant beams of the sun, which had risen radiantly, the green plain the hunter was crossing assumed a really enchanting appearance. As on the first occasion when he came to this country, all was in motion around him.

The Canadian, who, by the help of his new exterior, was able to examine at his leisure all that went on around him, curiously examined the animated scene he had before his eyes: but what most fixed his attention was a band of horsemen in their war costume, or rather paint, armed with those long javelins and barbed spears which they wield with such dexterity, and whose wounds are so dangerous. Most of them also carried a strong rifle and a reata at their girdle, and, marching in good order, they advanced at a trot towards the city, seeming to come from the opposite direction to that which the hunter was following.

The numerous persons spread over the plain had stopped to examine them. Marksman, profiting by this circumstance, hurried on to mingle with the crowd, among whom, as he hoped, he was speedily lost, no one thinking of paying the slightest attention to him. The horsemen continued to advance at the same pace, not appearing to notice the curiosity they excited. They were soon about forty yards from the principal gateway. On arriving there they were stopped At the same moment, three horsemen galloped out of the city, bounded over the drawbridge, and went to meet them. Three warriors then left the first party and approached them. After a few hastily exchanged words, the six horsemen rejoined the detachment, which had remained motionless in the rear, and entered the city with it. Marksman, who followed the party closely, neared the gate at the very moment the last horseman disappeared in the city. The hunter understood that the moment for boldness had arrived. Assuming the most careless air he could put on, although his heart was ready to burst, he presented himself in his turn for admission. He noticed Flying Eagle and his squaw standing some distance off, and conversing with an Indian who seemed to hold a certain rank. This doubled the bold Canadian's courage; he crossed the bridge undauntedly, and arrived with apparent stoicism at the gateway. A lance was then levelled before him, and barred his passage. At a sign from Flying Eagle, the Indian with whom he had been speaking left him and proceeded toward the gate. He was a tall warrior, to whom his iron-grey hair and the numerous wrinkles in his face imparted a certain character of gentleness, intelligence, and majesty. He said a word to the sentry, who was barring the hunter's passage; he raised his lance at once, and fell back a few paces with a respectful bow. The old Indian made the Canadian a sign to enter. "My brother is welcome in Quiepaa Tani," he said gracefully, as he saluted the hunter; "my brother has friends here."

Marksman, owing to the life he had so long led on the prairies, spoke several Indian dialects with as much fluency as his mother-tongue. From the question the Redskin addressed to him, he felt that he was backed up; he therefore assumed the necessary coolness to play his part properly, and answered,—"Is my brother a Chief?"

"I am a Chief."

"Och! let my brother question me. Ometochtli will answer."

In thus changing his personality, as it were, the hunter had been careful to change his name also. After a long and barren research, he at length selected that of Ometochtli, as best adapted to the person he wished to represent; for, despite its apparently formidable look, it simply means "two rabbits," a most inoffensive name, and perfectly coinciding with the hunter's new character.

"I shall not question my brother," the Chief said, cautiously. "I know who he is and whence he comes. My brother is one of the adepts of the great medicine, of the wise nation of the Yumas."

"The Chief is well informed," the hunter remarked. "I see that he has spoken with Flying Eagle."

"Has my brother left his nation for long?"

"It will be seven moons at the first leaves since I put on the moccasins of a hunter."

"Wah!" the Chief continued, with a certain appearance of respect; "where are the hunting grounds of my brother's nation situated?"

"Near the great shoreless lake."

"Does my brother intend to practise medicine at Quiepaa Tani?"

"I have only come here for that purpose, and to worship the Wacondah in the magnificent temple which the piety of the Indians has raised to him in the holy city."

"Very good. My brother is a wise man; his nation is peaceful," he said, as he raised his head, and drew up his tall form, proudly. "I am a warrior, and my name is Atozac."

By a strange accident, the first Indian with whom Marksman conversed was the same who received Addick, and whose wife was selected by the High Priest to serve as his interpreter with the maidens.

"My brother is a great Chief," he replied to the Indian's words.

The latter bowed with superb modesty on receiving this flattering remark. "I am a son of the sacred tribe to whom the guardianship of the temple is confided," he said.

"May the Wacondah bless the race of my brother."

The Chief was completely under the charm; the hunter's compliments had intoxicated him. "My brother, Two Rabbits, will follow me. We will join the friends who are awaiting us, and then proceed to my *calci*, which will be his during the whole period of his stay in Quiepaa Tani."

Marksman bowed respectfully. "I am not worthy, to shake the dust off my moccasins on the threshold of his door."

"The Wacondah blesses those who practise hospitality, my brother. Two Rabbits is the guest of a Chief; let him follow me, then."

"I will follow my brother, since such is his will."

And, without further resistance, he began walking behind the old Chief, charmed in his heart at having emerged so well from the first trial. As we said, Flying Eagle and Eglantine had stopped a few paces off, and they soon found them. All four, without uttering a word, proceeded toward the house inhabited by the Chief, which was situated at the other extremity of the city. This long walk allowed the hunter to take a look at the streets which he crossed, and obtain a superficial acquaintance with Quiepaa Tani. They at length reached the Chief's house. Heutotl—the Pigeon—Atozac's wife, seated cross-legged on a mat of maize straw, was making tortillas, probably intended for her husband's dinner. Not far from her were three or four female slaves, belonging to that bastard race of Indians to which we have already alluded, and to which the title of savages may be justly applied. When the Chief and his guests entered the cabin, the Pigeon and her slaves raised their eyes in curiosity.

"Heutotl," the Chief said, with dignity, "I bring you strangers. The first is a great and renowned Comanche Sachem. You know him already, as well as his squaw."

"Flying Eagle and Eglantine are welcome in the *calci* of Atozac," she answered.

The Comanche bowed slightly, but did not utter a word.

"This one," the Chief continued, pointing toward the hunter, "is a celebrated Tlacateotzin of the Yumas. His name is Two Rabbits; he will also dwell with us."

"The words I addressed to the Sachem of the Comanches, I repeat for the great medicine man of the Yumas," she said with a gentle smile; "the Pigeon is his slave."

"My mother will permit me to kiss her feet," the Canadian said, politely.

"My brother will kiss my face," the Chief's wife responded, holding up her cheek to Marksman, who respectfully touched it with his lips.

"My brothers will take a draught of pulque," the Pigeon continued; "the roads are long and dusty, and the sunbeams hot."

"Pulque refreshes the parched throat of travellers," Marksman answered.

The presentation was concluded. The slaves drew up butacas, on which the travellers reclined. Vessels of red earth, greatly resembling the Spanish alcaforas, filled with pulque, were brought in, and the liquor, poured out by the mistress of the house in horn cups, was presented by her to the strangers with that charming and attentive hospitality of which the Indians alone possess the secret.

[1] Literally, the "Man-God," a name given by certain Comanche tribes to those who practice the healing art.

[2] Surname of Motecuhzoma I.,—"He who shoots arrows up to the sky." The hieroglyphic of this king is, in fact, an arrow striking heaven.

CHAPTER XXXII
THE FIRST WALK IN THE CITY

While pretending to be absorbed in eagerness to respond to the eager politeness of his host, the Canadian attentively examined the interior of the house in which he was, in order to form an idea of the other residences in the city; for he justly assumed that all must be built almost after the same plan.

The room in which Atoyac received his guests was a large, square apartment, whose whitewashed walls were decorated with human scalps, and a row of weapons, kept in a state of extreme cleanliness. Jaguar and ocelot skins, zarapé, and frasadas were piled up on a sort of large chests, in all probability intended to serve as beds. Butacas and other wooden seats, excessively low, composed the furniture of the room, in the centre of which stood a table rising not more than ten inches from the ground. These simple arrangements are found almost identical, by the way, in almost all Indian *callis*, which are usually composed of six rooms. The first is the one we have just described; it is the ordinary living room of the family. The second is intended for the children; the third is the sleeping room. The fourth contains the looms for weaving zarapés, which the Indians work with inimitable skill. These looms, made of bamboo, are admirable for the simplicity of their mechanism. The fifth contains provisions for the rainy season, the period when hunting becomes impossible; while the sixth, or last, is set aside for the slaves. As for the kitchen, there is really none, for the food is prepared in the *corral*, that is to say, in the open air. Chimneys are equally unknown, and each room is warmed by means of large earthen brasiers. The internal arrangements of the *calli* are entrusted to the slaves, who work under the immediate superintendence of the mistress of the house. These slaves are not all savages. The Indians completely requite the whites for the misfortunes they deal them. Many wretched Spaniards, captured in war, or victims to the ambuscades the Redskins incessantly lay for them, are condemned to the hardest servitude. The fate of these unhappy beings is even more sad than that of their companions in slavery, for they have no prospect of being set at liberty some day; they must, on the contrary, expect to perish sooner or later, the victims of the hatred of their cruel masters, who pitilessly avenge on them the numberless annoyances they have themselves endured under the tyrannical and brutalizing system of the Spanish Government. Hence, under the pressure of this hard captivity a man may truly apply to himself the despairing words writ up by the divine Dante Alighieri over the gates of his Inferno, *Lasciate ogni speranza*.

Atoyac, to whom chance had so providentially guided the Canadian, was one of the most respected Sachems of the warriors of Quiepaa Tani. In his youth he had lived long among the Europeans, and the great experience he had acquired while traversing countries remote from his tribe had expanded his intellect, extinguished in him certain caste prejudices, and rendered him more sociable and civil than the majority of his countrymen. While drinking his pulque in small sips, as the gourmand should do who appreciates at its just value the beverage he is imbibing, he conversed with the hunter, and gradually, either through the influence of the pulque, or the instinctive confidence the Canadian inspired him with, he became more communicative. As always happens under such circumstances, he began with his own affairs, and narrated them in their fullest detail to the hunter. He told him he was father of four sons, renowned warriors, whose greatest delight it was to invade the Spanish territory, burn the haciendas, and destroy the crops, and carry off prisoners; next he related to him the travels he had made, and seemed anxious to prove to Two Rabbits that his courage as a warrior, his experience, and military virtues, did not forbid him recognizing all there was noble and respectable in science; he even insinuated that, although a Sachem, he did not disdain, at times, to study simples and investigate the secrets of the great medicine, with which the Wacondah, in his supreme goodness, had endowed certain chosen men for the relief of the whole of humanity.

Marksman affected to be deeply touched by the consideration the powerful Sachem, Atoyac, evinced for the sacred character with which he was invested, and resolved in his heart to profit by his host's good feeling toward him to sound him adroitly about what he was so anxious to know, that is, the state in which the maidens were, and in what part of the city they were shut up. As, however, Indian suspicions can be very easily aroused, and it was necessary to employ the greatest patience, the hunter did not allow his intentions to be in any way divined, and waited patiently.

The conversation had gradually become general; still, more than an hour had already elapsed, and in spite of all his efforts, aided by those of Flying Eagle, the hunter had not yet succeeded in approaching the subject he had at heart, when an Indian presented himself in the doorway.

"The Wacondah rejoices," the newcomer said, with a respectful bow. "I have a message for my father."

"My son is welcome," the Chief answered; "my ears are open."

"The great council of the Sachems of the nation is assembled," the Indian said; "they only await my father Atoyac."

"What is there new, then?"

"Red Wolf has arrived with his warriors. His heart is filled with bitterness. He wishes to speak to the council. Addick accompanies him."

Flying Eagle and the hunter exchanged a glance.

"Red Wolf and Addick returned!" Atoyac exclaimed, with amazement. "That is strange! What can have brought them back so soon, and together, too?"

"I know not; but they entered the city hardly an hour ago."

"Did Red Wolf command the warriors who arrived this morning?"

"Himself. My father could not have seen him when he passed by here. What shall I answer the Chief?"

"That I am coming to the council."

The Indian bowed and went away. The old man rose with ill-concealed agitation, and prepared to go out. Flying Eagle stopped him. "My father is affected," he said; "there is a cloud on his mind."

"Yes," the Chief answered, frankly; "I am sad."

"What can trouble my father, then?"

"Brother," the old Chief said, bitterly, "many moons have passed since the last visit paid by you to Quiepaa Tani."

"Man is only the plaything of circumstances; he can never do what he has projected."

"That is true. Perhaps it would have been better for you and for us had you not remained away so long."

"Often, often I had the desire to come, but a fatality always prevented me."

"Yes, it must be so; were it not for that, we should have seen you. Many things that have happened, would not have occurred."

"What do you mean?"

"It would be too long to explain to you, and I have no time to do so at this moment; I must proceed to the council, where I am awaited. Suffice it for you to know, that for some time an evil genius has breathed a spirit of discord among the Sachems of the great council. Two men have succeeded in obtaining a dangerous influence over the deliberations, and forcing their ideas and wishes upon all the chiefs."

"And these men, who are they?"

"You know them only too well."

"But what are their names?"

"Red Wolf and Addick."

"Wah!" Flying Eagle said. "Take care; the ambition of those men may, if you do not pay attention, bring great misfortunes on your heads."

"I know it; but can I prevent it? Am I, alone, strong enough to combat their influence, and cause the propositions to be rejected which they impose on the council?"

"That is true," the Comanche answered, thoughtfully; "but how to prevent it?"

"There would be a way, perhaps," Atoyac said, in an insinuating voice, after a short silence.

"What?"

"It is very simple. Flying Eagle is one of the first and most renowned Sachems of his nation."

"Well?"

"As such, he has a right, I believe, to sit in the council?"

"He has."

"Why does not he go there, then?"

Flying Eagle turned an inquiring glance on the hunter, who was listening to this conversation with an apathetic face, though his heart was ready to burst; for he guessed, by a species of presentiment, that in this council questions of the highest importance to him would be discussed. From the Chief's dumb inquiry he understood that if he remained longer a stranger to the discussion, he would appear, in his host's eyes, to display an indifference toward the welfare of the city, which the latter might take in ill part. "Were I so great a Chief as Flying Eagle," he said, "I should not hesitate to present myself at the council. Here, the interests of one nation or the other are not discussed; but vital questions often arise, affecting the welfare of the red race generally. To abstain, under such circumstances, would, in my opinion, be giving the enemies of order and tranquillity in the city a proof of weakness, by which they would, doubtless, profit to insure the success of their anarchical projects."

"Do you believe so?" Flying Eagle remarked, with feigned hesitation.

"My brother, Two Rabbits, has spoken well," Atoyac said, eagerly. "He is a wise man. My brother must follow his advice, and with the more reason, because his presence here is known to everybody, and his absence from the council would certainly produce a very evil effect."

"As it is so," the Comanche answered, "I can no longer resist your wish; I am ready to follow you."

"Yes," the hunter added, meaningly, "go to the council; perhaps your unexpected presence will suffice to overthrow certain projects, and prevent great misfortunes."

"I will behave in such a manner as to overawe our enemies," the Comanche answered, evasively, who, while feigning to address these words to his host, really intended them for the hunter.

"Let us go," said Atoyac.

Flying Eagle bowed silently, and went forth.

The hunter remained alone in the *calli* with the two women. The Pigeon, during the previous conversation, had been busy talking in a low voice with Eglantine. Almost immediately after the departure of the two warriors, the woman rose and prepared to go out. Eglantine, without saying a word, laid her finger on her lip, and looked at the hunter. He wrapped himself in his buffalo robe, and addressed Atoyac's wife.

"I do not wish to trouble my sister," he said. "While the chiefs are in council, I will take a walk, and examine, with greater attention, the magnificent Temple, of which I only had a glimpse on coming here."

"My father is right," she answered; "the more so, as Eglantine and myself have also to go out, and we should have been compelled to leave my father alone in the *calli*."

Eglantine smiled softly as she nodded to the hunter. The latter, suspecting that Flying Eagle's squaw had discovered the retreat of the maidens during the conversation with her friend, and that the desire she evinced to get rid of him had no other design but to obtain more ample information about them, made not the slightest objection, and walked slowly out of the *calli*, with all the majesty and importance of the wise personage he represented. Besides, the Canadian was not sorry to be alone for a little while, that he might reflect on the means he should employ to approach the two maidens, which it seemed to him by no means easy to manage. On the other hand, he intended to employ the liberty left him in taking a turn round the city, and obtaining all the topographical knowledge he needed. Not knowing in what way his stay in the city would terminate, and how he should leave it again, he, at all risks, carefully studied the plan of the streets and buildings, from the double point of view of an attack or an escape.

The hunter had assumed such a mask of placidity and indifference; his questions were asked with so nonchalant an air, that not one of those he addressed dreamed for a moment of suspecting him; and, as always happens, he succeeded in obtaining—thanks to his skill—remarkably precious details about the weak points in the city,—how it was possible to enter and leave it after the closing of the gates, and other equally valuable information, which the hunter carefully classified in his mind, and which he resolved to put to good use when the moment arrived.

In Quiepaa Tani there are a good many unoccupied persons, who spend their lives in wandering about, a prey to an incurable *ennui*. It was with these people that the hunter formed an acquaintance during his lengthened walk round the city, listening with the greatest patience to their prolix and tedious narrations, when, certain of having drawn from them all he could, he left them, to begin the same scheme a little further on with others.

Marksman remained away for three hours. When he returned to the *calli*, Atoyac and Flying Eagle had not come back; but the two women, seated on mats, were conversing with a certain degree of animation.

On seeing him, Eglantine gave him an intelligent glance. The hunter fell back on a butaca, drew out his pipe, and began smoking. After exchanging a dumb bow with the pretended medicine man, the women again resumed their palaver.

"So," Eglantine said, "the prisoners taken from the whites are brought here!"

"Yes," the Pigeon answered.

"That surprises me," the young woman continued; "for it would be only necessary for one of them to escape, and the exact situation of the city would be revealed to the Gachupinos, who would soon appear in the place."

"That is true; but my sister is ignorant that no one escapes from Quiepaa Tani."

Eglantine bowed her head with an air of doubt.

"Och!" she said, "the whites are very crafty; still, it is certain that the two young Pale maidens we have just seen will not escape,—they are too well guarded for that. I do not know why, but I feel a great pity for them."

"It is the same with me, poor children! So young, so gentle, so pretty; separated eternally from all those who are dear to them. Their fate is frightful!"

"Oh, very frightful! But what is to be done? They belong to Addick; that Chief will never consent to restore them to liberty."

"We will go and see them again, shall we not, my sister?"

"Tomorrow, if you will."

"Thanks; that will render us very happy, I assure you."

The last words especially struck the hunter. At the sudden revelation made to him, Marksman felt such an emotion, that he needed all his strength and self-command to prevent the Pigeon noticing his confusion.

At this moment Atoyac and Flying Eagle appeared. Their features were animated, and they seemed in a state of rage, the more terrible, because it was suppressed.

Atoyac walked straight to the hunter, who had risen to receive him. On noticing the animation depicted on the Indian's face, Marksman thought that he had plainly discovered something concerning himself, and it was not without some suspicion that he awaited the communication his host seemed anxious to make to him.

"Is my father really an adept of the great medicine?" Atoyac asked, fixing a searching glance on him.

"Did I not tell my brother so?" the hunter answered, who began to feel himself seriously threatened, and looked inquiringly at Flying Eagle. The latter smiled.

The Canadian reassured himself a little; it was plain that, if he saw any danger, the Comanche would not be so calm.

"Let my brother come with me, then, and bring with him the instruments of his art," Atoyac exclaimed.

It would not have been prudent to decline this invitation, though rather roughly given; besides, nothing proved to him that his host entertained evil designs against him. The hunter, therefore, accepted. "Let my brother walk in front; I will follow him," he contented himself with answering.

"Does my brother speak the tongue of the barbarous Gachupinos?"

"My nation lives near the boundless Salt Lake. The Palefaces are our neighbours; I understand, and speak slightly, the tongue they employ."

"All the better."

"Have I to cure a Paleface?" the Canadian inquired, anxious to know what was wanted of him.

"No," Atoyac replied. "One of the great Apache chiefs brought hither, some moons back, two women of the Palefaces. They are ill; the evil spirit has entered into them, and at this moment Death is spreading his wings over the couch on which they repose."

Marksman shuddered at this unexpected news; his heart almost broke; an involuntary tremor passed over his limbs; he required a superhuman effort to overcome the deep emotion he felt, and to reply to Atoyac, in a calm voice—"I am at my brother's orders, as my duty commands."

"Let us go, then," the Indian answered.

Marksman took his box of medicaments, placed it cautiously under his arm, left the *calli* at the heels of the Sachem, and both proceeded hastily towards the palace of the Vestals, accompanied, or, more correctly speaking, watched at a distance, by Flying Eagle, who followed in their footsteps, not once letting them out of sight.

CHAPTER XXXIII
EXPLANATORY

We are now compelled to go back a little way, in order to clear up certain facts which necessarily remained in the shade, and which it is urgent for the reader to know.

We have related how Don Estevan, Addick, and Red Wolf easily came to an understanding, in order to obtain a common vengeance. But, as generally happens in all treaties, each having begun by stipulating for his private advantage, it fell out that Don Estevan was about to reap the least profit from the partnership.

Few whites can rival the Redskins in craft and diplomacy. The Indians, like all conquered peoples, bowed so long beneath a brutalizing yoke, retained only one weapon, which is often deadly, however, by means of which they contend most with success against their fortunate adversaries. This weapon is cunning—the arm of cowards and the weak, the defence of slaves against their masters.

The conditions offered by the two Indian Chiefs to Don Estevan were clear and precise. The Chiefs, by means of the warriors they had at their disposal, would help the Mexican in seizing and avenging himself on his enemies, inflicting on them any punishment he thought proper; in return, Don Estevan would make over his niece and the other maiden, now prisoners at Quiepaa Tani, to the Chiefs, who would do to them what they pleased, Don Estevan giving up all right of interference with them. These conditions being well and duly defined, the Indian Chiefs set to work in fulfilling the clauses of the treaty as quickly as possible.

Red Wolf had a hatred for the two hunters and Don Miguel, which was the more inveterate, because he had been conquered in the various encounters he had with the three men. He, therefore, eagerly seized the opportunity that offered to take his revenge, believing certain this time of repaying his abhorred enemies all the humiliation they had inflicted on him, and the ill they had done him.

In less than four days, Addick and Red Wolf succeeded in collecting a band of nearly one hundred and fifty picked warriors—obstinate enemies for the whites, and to whom the coming expedition was a real party of pleasure.

When Don Estevan saw himself at the head of so large and resolute a band, his heart dilated with joy, and he felt himself ensured of success; for what could Don Miguel attempt with the few men he had at his disposal?

The road was long, almost impracticable. To reach Quiepaa Tani, it was necessary to cross abrupt mountains, virgin forests, and immense deserts; and even supposing the Gambusinos succeeded in overcoming these seemingly insurmountable difficulties, when they arrived before the city, what could they do? Would they, scarce thirty at most, attempt to take by assault a city of nearly 20,000 souls, defended by strong walls, surrounded by a wide moat, and containing 3,000 picked men, the most renowned warriors of all the Indian nations, specially entrusted with the defence of the sacred city, and who would, without any hesitation, fall to the last man, sooner than surrender? Such a supposition was absurd; hence Don Estevan dismissed it so soon as it occurred to him.

The first care of the Indian Chiefs was to learn in what direction their enemies were. Unfortunately for the Redskins, the arrangements made by the hunters were so adroit, that they were compelled to follow their enemy on three different trails, and break up their war party, if they wished to watch the Gambusinos on all sides. This was the first occasion of a dissension between the three associates. Addick and Red Wolf, when the question of a separation arose, naturally wished each to take the command of a body, an arrangement which displeased Don Estevan, and to which he would not at all consent, remarking, with some degree of justice, that in the affair they had in hand everything depended on the Chiefs; that the warriors had nothing to do but watch the movements of their enemy, while they, the Chiefs, must remain together, in order to arrange the necessary combinations in their plans, and be enabled to act with vigour when the occasion presented itself. The truth was, that Don Estevan, forced by circumstances into an alliance with the two Sachems, had not the slightest confidence in his honourable associates. He despised them as much as he was despised by them, and felt certain that, if he allowed them to leave him, under any pretence, he should never see them again; that they would desert him on the prairie, remorselessly leaving him to get out of the dilemma in the best way he could. The Indians perfectly understood their partner's thoughts, but, far too cunning to let him see they had read them, they pretended to admit the reasons he gave them, and recognize their correctness. The Chiefs, therefore, remained together and pushed on, only accompanied by twenty men, and having divided the others into two bands, to watch the Gambusinos.

Don Estevan was eager to reach Quiepaa Tani, in order to remove the maidens from the city, and have them in his hands, in order, by their presence, to stimulate the ardour of his allies. They set out. A singular thing then happened. Six detachments of warriors were following each other's trail for more than a month, each marching in the footsteps of the previous one, and not suspecting that it was in its turn followed by another. Matters went on thus without leading to any encounter until the night when Domingo disappeared in the virgin forest. This is how it happened. Marksman had well judged the Gambusino, when suspecting him to be capable of treachery. That is why he requested he should be left with him, that he might watch him with greater care. Unfortunately, since the departure from the ford of the Rubio, in spite of the incessant watchfulness kept up by Marksman, he had never detected in the Gambusino the slightest doubtful movement which would corroborate his suspicions, or convert them into certainty. Domingo did his duty with apparent honesty and frankness. When they reached the bivouac, the little arrangements for the night were made; and the meal over, the Gambusino was one of the first to roll himself in his zarapé, lie down, and go to sleep from alleged weariness. In short, the bandit managed to behave so cleverly, and to mask his baseness, that the hunter, clever as he was, was taken in. Gradually his vigilance relaxed, his distrust went to sleep, and, though not reckoning greatly on the Gambusino's fidelity, he ceased looking after him incessantly, as he did during the first days. And then they had covered a great deal of ground during the past month; the hunters were in a completely unknown country: hence it was not presumable that the Gambusino, almost new to desert life, would venture to desert the people with whom he was, and risk wandering alone in the desert, where he would have every chance of dying of hunger in a few days. This merely proved one fact, that Marksman, in spite of all his cleverness, did not know the man with whom he had to deal, and did not suspect the tenacity of purpose which forms the backbone of the Mexican character.

Domingo hated the hunter because he had unmasked him, and with the patience that characterizes the race to which he belonged, he awaited the opportunity for vengeance, feeling certain, by the force of events, that it must present itself from one day to the other. In the meanwhile, he looked and listened. The hunters did not hesitate to speak before him, for the reason that Marksman would, in that case, have been obliged to tell his companions the suspicions he entertained of the Gambusino, a thing that his innate loyalty prevented him doing. Thus Domingo had profited by the opportunity to learn all the details of the expedition of which he was an involuntary member—details he intended to tell as clearly as possible to the person they interested most, so soon as chance brought them together.

On the evening when Marksman discovered that trail which troubled him so greatly, Domingo, while foraging about on his own account, found something which he carefully avoided showing his comrades. It was no other than a tobacco pouch of small dimensions, richly ornamented with gold embroidery, such as rich Mexicans usually carry. Domingo very well recollected having seen it in Don Estevan's hand. The pouch must, then, have been lost by him. For the present he hid it in his bosom, intending to examine it more at his leisure, when he did not fear any surprise from his companions.

Flying Eagle followed the trail, as we have seen, and his friends, after lighting the fire, preparing the meal, and eating a few mouthfuls, waited his return.

The day had been fatiguing; the Indian's return was deferred; Marksman and Don Mariano, after conversing for a long time, felt their eyelids weighed down and gently close; in short, they yielded to their fatigue, lay down, and were soon buried in a deep sleep. As for Domingo, he had been sleeping for an hour, as if he never intended to wake again. A singular thing happened, however. Don Mariano and Marksman had scarce closed their eyes, ere the Gambusino opened his eyes, and that so freshly, that everything led to the belief that he had not been to sleep at all, and never felt more wakeful than at the present moment. He looked suspiciously around, and remained for some time motionless; but, after a few moments, reassured by the gentle and regular breathing of his companions, he sat up gently. He hesitated for several moments, but then took the tobacco pouch from the place where he had concealed it, and examined it with the closest attention. This pouch had scarcely anything to distinguish it from others; but one circumstance struck the hunter: the pouch was nearly half full of tobacco, and that tobacco was fresh. Hence it could not have been long lost by Don Estevan—a few hours, at the most. If that were so, as there was every reason to assume, Don Estevan could not be far off, and must be a league, or at the most two, from their bivouac. This reasoning was logical; hence the Gambusino drew from it the conclusion that the opportunity he had been waiting for so long had at length arrived, and he must seize it at all risks. This conclusion once admitted, the rest can be easily understood. The Gambusino rose, glided like a snake into the underwood, and went off in search of Don Estevan.

Accident is the master of the world; it regulates matters at its will; its combinations are at times so strange, that it seems to take a malignant pleasure in making the most odious plans succeed, contrary to all expectations. This is what happened in the present case. The Gambusino had not been wandering about the forest for more than hour, groping his way as well as he could in the dark, which enwrapped him like a shroud, when he arrived, at the moment he least expected it, in sight of a fire lighted on the extreme verge of the forest. He walked at once towards the brilliant flame he had noticed, instinctively persuaded that near the *brasero* which served him as a beacon he should find the man he was looking for. His presentiments had not deceived him. The camp, towards which he was proceeding, was really that of Don Estevan and his allies, who, we must allow, did not believe themselves so near their enemies. Had they done so, they would have indubitably employed all the precautions usual in the desert to conceal their presence.

The sudden appearance of the Gambusino in the circle illumined by the fire was a perfect tableau. The Indians and Don Estevan himself were so far from expecting the man's arrival, that there was a moment of fearful confusion, during which the Gambusino was seized, thrown down, and bound, ere he had time to utter a syllable in his defence. The warriors seized their arms, and scattered about the neighbourhood, in order to assure themselves that the man who had so suddenly come among them was alone, and they had nothing to fear.

At length the alarm gradually cooled down; they felt easier, and thought about questioning the prisoner. This was what the latter desired, and which he earnestly requested, ever since he had been so roughly pounced on. He was led into the presence of the three Chiefs, and at once recognised by Don Estevan. "Eh!" the latter said, with a grin. "It is my worthy friend, Domingo. What on earth brings you here, my fine fellow?"

"You shall learn, for I have merely come to do you a service," the bandit answered, with his usual effrontery. "I should be obliged, though, by your having me untied if it is possible. These cords cut into my flesh, and cause me such suffering, that I shall be unable to utter a word until I have got rid of them."

When the bandit's request had been accomplished, he told all he had heard in the fullest detail, without any pressing. The revelations of the Gambusino caused his hearers considerable reflection, and they next asked how he knew that they were so near? Domingo completed his story by stating how he had found the tobacco pouch, and how, after his two companions, Marksman and Don Mariano, fell asleep, he left them to go in search of Don Estevan.

In the Gambusino's story one thing especially struck Don Estevan, and that was, that two of his greatest enemies were a few paces from him, and alone. He at once leaned over to Red Wolf, and whispered a few words, to which the other responded by a sinister smile. Ten minutes later, the fire was extinguished. The Apaches, armed to the teeth, under the guidance of Domingo, glided into the forest, and proceeded toward the spot where the hunter and the gentleman were tranquilly reposing, not suspecting the terrible danger that menaced them, and the treachery to which they were the victims.

We have seen how the Indian's enterprise failed, and in what way the wretched Domingo received the chastisement for his crime. Unfortunately, he had found time to speak, and his words had been carefully garnered. When the Apaches recognized that they had to do with a stronger party than they expected, and the men they wished to surprise were on their guard, they withdrew in all haste, in order to deliberate on the measures they must take to get before their enemies, and foil their plans. The discussion, contrary to Indian habit, was not long. In spite of the night, whose dense mantle still covered the ground, they mounted their horses, and proceeded as speedily as possible toward Quiepaa Tani, in order to enter the city first, and have time to call on their friends to help them in the impending contest.

In spite of all his objections, Don Estevan was left behind, concealed with some warriors on the outskirts of the forest. The Chiefs, with all their influence, not daring openly to infringe the Indian laws by introducing into the city a Paleface other than a prisoner, Don Estevan was compelled to await their return with resignation. But if the Indians had lost no time, the hunters, on their side, had so well profited by it, that, as we have seen, Marksman, disguised as a Yuma medicine man, entered Quiepaa Tani simultaneously with them.

While Red Wolf made all the preparations for convening the great council of the Chiefs, Addick left him, and proceeded to the house of his friend, Cheuch Coatl (Eight Serpents), the Amantzin, or High Priest. But the latter, on hearing of the young Chief's return, had shut himself up with the Pigeon, who, accompanied by Eglantine, had come to pay him a visit. The Amantzin advised her of Addick's return—which she knew already—and recommended her to maintain silence as to the active part she had played in the attempted conversion of the maidens. The Pigeon, whom Eglantine had taught her lesson, promised to remain dumb. She had told the High Priest of the presence in Quiepaa Tani of a great Yuma medicine man, whose knowledge might be useful in restoring the health of Addick's prisoners. The Amantzin thanked the Indian woman, telling her he should probably see Atozac at the council, and would not fail to ask him to lead Two Rabbits to him. Feeling considerably calmer, the Amantzin dismissed the women, and proceeded to Addick, being well prepared to receive him. At the first words the young Chief uttered, referring to his great desire to see his two prisoners as soon as possible, the old man replied that, in order to be able to watch over them more effectually, and remove them from the oppressive curiosity of the idlers of the city, who troubled him with their continual visits, he had been compelled to transfer them to the Palace of the Virgins of the Sun, until they could be returned to their legitimate owner. Addick thanked his friend most warmly for the care he had taken in performing the commission entrusted to him — thanks which the Chief Priest received with hypocritical modesty, while regarding the young Chief with a crafty look, which caused him to feel uncomfortable. Hence, without further beating round the bush, he resolved on settling the matter at once.

CHAPTER XXXIV
CONVERSATIONAL

The two men stood for a moment silently face to face, devouring each other with their glances, with frowning brows and compressed lips, like two duellists on the point of crossing swords; and, in truth, they were about to engage in a duel, the more terrible because the only weapons they could employ were cunning and dissimulation.

The power of the Indian priests is immense; it is the more terrible, because it is uncontrolled, and only depends on the deity they invoke, and whom they compel to interfere in all circumstances when they have need of his support. No people are so superstitious as the Redskins. With them religion is entirely physical, they are completely ignorant of dogmas, and prefer blindly believing the absurdities their diviners lay before them, rather than give themselves the trouble of reflecting on mysteries which they do not understand, and which, in their hearts, they care little for.

We have said that the High Priest of Quiepaa Tani was a man of lofty intellect, constantly residing in the city, possessing the secrets, and, consequently, the confidence of most families; he had built up his popularity on a solid and almost immovable basis. Addick was aware of this. On several occasions he had been obliged to have recourse to the occult powers of the soothsayer, and, therefore, perfectly comprehended the unpleasant consequences which would result to him from a rupture with such a man. Chiuchcoatl stood with his arms folded on his chest, and with apathetic face, before the young Chief, whose eyes flashed, and features expressed the most violent indignation. Still, at the expiration of a few moments, Addick, by an extraordinary effort of his will, subdued the fire of his glance, smoothed down the expression of his face, and offered his hand to the Priest, saying to him in a soft and conciliatory voice, in which no trace of his internal agitation was perceptible, "My father loves me. What he has done is well, and I thank him for it."

The Amantzin bowed deferentially, while slightly touching, with the end of his three fingers, the hand held out to him. "The Wacondah inspired me," he said, with a hypocritical voice.

"The holy name of the Wacondah be blessed," the Chief replied. "Will not my father allow me to see the prisoners?"

"I should like it. Unfortunately, that is impossible."

"What?" the young man exclaimed, with a shade of impatience, he could not completely hide.

"The law is positive. Entrance to the Palace of the Virgins of the Sun is prohibited to men."

"That is true; but these young girls are not priestesses. They are Paleface women whom I brought here."

"I know it. What my brother says is just."

"Well, my father sees that nothing prevents my prisoners being restored to me."

"My son is mistaken. Their presence among the Virgins of the Sun has placed them beneath the effect of the law. Forced by imperious circumstances, I did not reflect on this when I made them enter the Palace. In order to carry out my son's wishes, I wished to save them at any price. Now I regret what I have done; but it is too late."

Addick felt an enormous temptation to dash out the brains of the wretched juggler, who deluded him so impudently with his hypocritical accent and gentle manner; but, fortunately for the Priest, and probably for himself, as such a deed, just as it was, would not have gone unpunished, he succeeded in mastering himself. "Come," he continued, in a moment, "my father is kind, he would not wish to reduce me to despair. Are there no means to remove this apparently insurmountable difficulty?"

The Priest seemed to hesitate. Addick looked earnestly at him, while awaiting his answer. "Yes," he continued, presently, "there is, perhaps, one way."

"What?" the young man exclaimed, joyfully. "Let my father speak!"

"It would be," the old man answered, laying a stress on every word, and, as it were, unwillingly, "it would be by obtaining authority from the Great Council to remove them from the Palace."

"Wah! I did not think of that. In truth, the Great Council may authorize that. I thank my father. Oh! I shall obtain the permission."

"I hope so," the Priest answered, in a tone which staggered the young man.

"Does my father suppose that the Great Council would wish to insult me by refusing so slight a favour?" he asked.

"I suppose nothing my son. The Wacondah holds in his right hand the hearts of the Chiefs. He can alone dispose them in your favour."

"My father is right. I will go immediately to the Council. It must be assembled at this moment."

"In truth," the Amantzin answered, "the first hachesto of the powerful Sachems came to summon me a few moments before I had the pleasure of seeing my son."

"Then my father is proceeding to the Council?"

"I will accompany my son, if he consents."

"It will be an honour for me. I can, I trust, count on the support of my father?"

"When has that support failed Addick?"

"Never. Still, today, above all, I should like to be certain that my father will grant it to me."

"My son knows that I love him. I will act as my duty ordains," the Priest replied, evasively. Addick, to his great regret, was forced to put up with this ambiguous answer.

The two men then went out, and crossed the square, to enter the palace of the Sachems, where the Council assembled. A crowd of Indians, attracted by curiosity, thronged this usually deserted spot, and greeted with shouts the passage of renowned sachems. When the High Priest appeared, accompanied by the young Chief, the Indians fell back before them with a respect mingled with fear, and bowed silently to them. The Amantzin was more feared than loved by the people, as generally happens with all men who hold great power. Chiuchcoatl did not seem to notice the emotion his presence produced, and the hurried whispers that were audible on his passing. With eyes sunk, and modest even humble step, he entered the palace at the heels of the young Chief, whose assured countenance and haughty glance formed a striking contrast with the demeanour his comrade affected.

The place reserved for the meeting of the Great Council was an immense square hall, extremely simple, and facing north and south; at one end was fastened to the whitewashed wall a tapestry made of the feathers and down of rare birds, on which was reproduced, in brilliantly coloured feathers, the revered image of the sun, resting on the great sacred tortoise, the emblem of the world. Beneath this tapestry, and sustained by four crossed spears planted in the ground, was the sacred calumet, which must never be sullied by contact with the earth. This calumet, whose red bowl was made of a precious clay, only found in a certain region of the Upper Missouri, had a tube ten feet in length, adorned with feathers and gold bells, and from its extremity hung a small medicine bag of elk skin, studded with hieroglyphics. In the centre of the hall, in an oval hole, hollowed for the purpose, was piled, with a certain degree of symmetry, the wood destined for the council fire, and which could only be lighted by the High Priest. The hall was lighted by twelve lofty windows, hung with long curtains of vicuna skin, through which a gloomy and uncertain light filtered, perfectly harmonizing with the imposing aspect of the vast apartment.

At the moment the Amantzin and Addick entered the place of meeting, all the Chiefs comprising the Council had arrived; they were walking about in groups, conversing and waiting. So soon as the High Priest entered, each took his place by the fire, at a sign from the eldest Sachem. This Sachem was an old man, whom two warriors held under the arms to support. A long beard, white as silver—a singular fact among Indians—fell on his chest; his features were stamped with extraordinary majesty; and, indeed, the other Chiefs showed him profound respect and veneration. This Chief was called Axayacatl, that is to say, "the face of the water." He claimed descent from the ancient Incas, who governed the country of the Anahuac before the Spanish conquest, and, like his namesake, the eighth king of Mexico, his totem was a face, before which he placed the symbol for water. We may remark, in support of his claim, that his skin had not that reddish hue of new copper which distinguishes the Indian race, but, on the contrary, approached the European type. Whatever his descent might be, though, one thing certain was, that in his youth he had been one of the bravest and most renowned chiefs of the Comanches, that haughty and untameable nation, which calls itself the Queen of the Prairies. When Axayacatl's great age and numerous wounds prevented him waging war longer, the Indians, by whom he was generally revered, had unanimously elected him supreme Chief of Quiepaa Tani, and he had performed his duties for more than twenty years, to the satisfaction of all the Indian nations. After assuring himself that all the Chiefs were assembled round the fire, the Sachem took from the hands of the hachesto, who stood by his side, a lighted log, which he placed in the centre of the wood prepared for the Council, saying, in a weak, though perfectly distinct voice,—"Wacondah! thy children are assembling to discuss grave matters; may the flame, which is thy Spirit, breathe in their hearts, and raise to their lips words wise and worthy of thee."

The wood—probably covered with resinous matter—caught fire almost immediately, and a brilliant flame soon mounted, with a whirl, toward the roof.

While the Sachem was pronouncing the words we have just written, two subaltern priests had taken the sacred calumet from the spot where it was placed, and, after filling it with tobacco expressly reserved for extraordinary ceremonies, they lifted it on their shoulders, and presented it respectfully to the Amantzin. The latter took, with a medicine rod, in order to confound evil omens, a burning coal from the hearth, and lit the calumet, while pronouncing the following invocation:—"Wacondah! sublime and mysterious being. Thou, whom the world cannot contain, and whose powerful eye perceives the smallest insect timidly concealed beneath the grass, we invoke thee, thee whom no man can comprehend. Grant that the sun, thy visible representative, may be favourable to us, and not drive far away the holy smoke of the great calumet which we send toward him."

The Amantzin, still holding the bowl of the calumet in the palm of his hand, presented the tube in turn to each Chief, beginning with the eldest. The Sachems each inhaled a few puffs of smoke, with the decorum and reverence required by etiquette, with their eyes fixed on the ground, and the right arm laid on the heart. When the tube of the calumet at length reached the High Priest, he had the bowl held by one of his acolytes, and smoked till all the tobacco was reduced to ashes. Then the hachesto approached, emptied the ash into a little elkskin pouch, which he closed, and threw into the fire, saying in a loud and impressive voice,—"Wacondah! the descendants of the sons of Aztlan implore thy clemency. Suffer thy luminous rays to descend into their hearts, that their words may be those of wise men."

Then the two priests took the calumet again, and placed it beneath the image of the sun. The old Sachem took the word again. "The council has assembled," he said, "two renowned Chiefs, who only arrived this morning at Quiepaa Tani, on their return from a long journey, have, they say, important communications to make to the Sachems. Let them speak; our ears are open."

We will enter into no details of the discussion that took place in the Council; we will not even quote the speeches uttered by Red Wolf and Addick, for that would carry us too far, and probably only weary the reader. We need only say, that though the passions of the Sachems were cleverly played on by the two Chiefs who had called the meeting, and that sharp attacks were sharply returned, all passed with the decorum and decency characteristic of Indian assemblies; that, although each defended his opinion inch by inch, no one went beyond the limits of good taste; and we will sum up the debate by stating that Red Wolf and Addick completely failed in their schemes, and that the good sense, or rather the ill will, of their colleagues prevented them attaining the object of their desires.

The High Priest, while pretending to support Addick, managed to embroil the question so cleverly, that the Council declared unanimously that the two young Palefaces shut up in the Palace of the Virgins of the Sun must be considered, not as the property of the Chief who brought them to the city, but as prisoners of the entire confederation, and as such remain under the guardianship of the Amantzin, to whom the order was intimated to watch them with the greatest care, and under no pretext allow the young Chief to approach them. Chiuchcoatl, when he insinuated to Addick that he should apply to the Council, knew perfectly well what the result would be but not wishing to make an enemy of the young man by refusing his request, he adroitly thrust the responsibility of the refusal on the whole Council, and thus rendered it impossible for Addick to call him to account for his dishonourable conduct toward him.

Red Wolf had been more fortunate, from the simple reason that his communication concerned the city. The Apache Chief demanded that a party of five hundred warriors, commanded by a renowned Chief, should be called under arms, to watch over the common safety, gravely compromised by the appearance, in the vicinity of Quiepaa Tani, of some forty Palefaces, whose evident intention it was to attack and carry the city by storm.

The Chiefs granted Red Wolf what he asked, and even much more than he had ventured to hope. Instead of five hundred warriors, it was settled that a thousand should be called; one-half of them, under the orders of Atoyac, would traverse the country in every direction, in order to watch the approach of the enemy, while the other half, under the immediate orders of the governor, would guard the interior. After this, the Council broke up.

The High Priest then approached Atoyac, and asked him if he really had a renowned Tlacateotzin at his house. The other replied, that, on the same day, a great Yuma medicine man had arrived at Quiepaa Tani, and done him the honour of entering his *calli*. Flying Eagle then joined Atoyac in assuring the High Priest that this medicine man, whom he had known for a long time, justly enjoyed a very extensive reputation among the Indians, and that he had himself seen him effect marvellous cures. The Amantzin had no reason to distrust Flying Eagle; he therefore put the greatest confidence in his words, and, on the spot, begged Atoyac to bring this Tlacateotzin as speedily as possible to the Palace of the Virgins of the Sun, that he might devote his attention to the two Paleface maidens placed under his ward by the Council-General of the nation, and whose health had inspired him with great fears for some time past.

Addick heard these words, and rapidly approached the High Priest. "What does my father say, then?" he exclaimed, in great agitation.

"I say," the Amantzin replied, in his most honeyed voice, "that the two maidens my son entrusted to my care have been tried by the Wacondah, who sent them the scourge of illness."

"Is their life in danger?" the young man continued, with ill-suppressed agony.

"The Wacondah alone holds in his power the existence of his creatures; still I believe that the danger may be conquered; besides, as my son has heard, I expect an illustrious Tlacateotzin of the Yuma race, just come from the shore of the boundless Salt Lake, who, by the aid of his science, can, I doubt not, restore strength and health to the slaves whom my son took from the Spanish barbarians."

Addick, at this unpleasant news, could not suppress a movement of anger, which proved to the High Priest that he was not entirely his dupe, but suspected what had happened; but, either through respect, or fear lest he might be mistaken in his supposition, though more probably because the place where Addick was did not appear to him propitious for an explanation like that he wished to have with the Amantzin, he contented himself with begging the old man not to neglect anything to save the captives, adding, that he would be grateful to him for any attention he might pay them. Then, suddenly breaking off the conversation, he bowed slightly to the High Priest, turned his back on him, and left the hall, talking eagerly in a low voice with Red Wolf, who had waited for him a few paces off.

The Amantzin looked after the young man with a most peculiar expression in his eyes; then, resuming his conversation with Atoyac and Flying Eagle, he begged them to send the Yuma medicine man to them that evening, if possible. The latter promised this, and then left him to return to the *calli*, where the physician was doubtless waiting for them.

Still, what had passed at the council afforded Flying Eagle serious matter for reflection, by letting him see that the two Apache Chiefs knew the greater part of Marksman's secret, and if the latter wished to succeed, he must waste no time, but set to work at once. After ten minutes' walking, the Chiefs reached the *calli*, where they found Marksman awaiting them. The hunter, as we have seen, offered no objections to Atoyac's request, but, on the contrary, after taking up his medicine box, followed him eagerly.

CHAPTER XXXV
THE INTERVIEW

Marksman followed Atoyac to the Palace of the Virgins of the Sun. In spite of himself, the intrepid hunter felt his heart contract when he thought of the perilous situation in which he was about to place himself, and the terrible consequences discovery would entail. Still, he stood up against this emotion, and succeeded in regaining sufficient power over himself to affect a tranquillity and indifference which were far from real. The two men walked silently side by side. The hunter, fearing this prolonged dumbness might inspire his pride with doubts, resolved to make him talk, in order to give his thoughts a different direction from that he feared to see them take. "My brother has travelled much?" he asked him.

"Where is the warrior of our race whose life has not been spent in long journeys?" the Indian answered, sententiously. "The Palefaces—my brother knows it better than I—chase us like wild beasts, and compel us incessantly to retire before their successive encroachments."

"That is true," the hunter said, shaking his head with a melancholy air. "What desert is so obscure in which we are now permitted to hide the bones of our fathers, with the certainty that the plough of the whites will not come to crush them in tracing its interminable furrow, and scatter them in every direction?"

"Alas!" Atoyac observed, "the red race is accursed. The day will come when it will be sought in vain on the immense plains where it was formerly more numerous than the brilliant stars which stud the vault of heaven; for it is fatally condemned to disappear from the surface of the world. The Palefaces are only the terrible implements of the implacable wrath of the Wacondah against the children of the red family."

"My father only speaks too well. Formerly our race was all-powerful; now it has fallen lower than the vilest slave, and has no hope left it of ever rising again."

"What has become of the powerful emperors of Anahuac, who commanded the whole earth? Of the numberless cities they founded, but five compose today the territory of Tlapalean.[1] They are the last refuges of the children of Quetyalcoalt,[2] who are forced to hide themselves there like timid deer, instead of boldly treading the countries possessed in old times by their ancestors."

"But, thanks be rendered to the Wacondah, whose power is infinite, these five cities are completely sheltered from the insults of the Gachupinos."

Atoyac shook his head sadly, "My father is mistaken," he said. "Where is the hidden spot to which Palefaces do not penetrate?"

"That is possible. They effect everything; but up to the present no Paleface has gazed on Quiepaa Tani. They have not been able to cross the mountains and traverse the deserts, behind which the sacred city rises calm and peaceful, deriding the vain efforts of its enemies to discover it."

"Scarce two suns ago, I should have spoken like my brother. I should have rejoiced with him at this ignorance of the Palefaces; but today this is no longer possible."

"How so? What can have happened in so short a space of time, that compels my brother to alter his opinion so suddenly?" the hunter asked, growing all at once interested, and fearful of hearing bad news.

"The Palefaces are in the vicinity of the city. They have been seen; they are numerous and well armed."

"It is not so; my father is mistaken. Cowards or old women were frightened by their shadow, and spread this report," the Canadian answered, shivering all over.

"Those who brought the news are neither cowards, afraid of their shadow, nor chattering old women—they are renowned chiefs. Today, at the Great Council, they announced the presence of a strong party of Palefaces, concealed in the forest, whose trees have so long spread out their protecting branches before us, to conceal us from the piercing glances of our enemies."

"These men, however numerous they may be, unless they form a real army, will not venture to attack a city so strong as this, defended by thick walls, and containing a considerable number of chosen warriors."

"Perhaps. Who can know? At any rate, if the Palefaces do not attack us, we shall attack them. Not one of them must see again the land of the Palefaces. Our future security demands it."

"Yes, it must be so; but are you sure that the Chiefs of whom you speak, and whose names I do not know, may not deceive you, and be traitors?"

Atoyac stopped and fixed a piercing glance on the Canadian, who endured it with a calm air and unmoved countenance. "No," he said, a moment after, "Red Wolf and Addick are no traitors."

The hunter seemed to reflect for a moment, and then exclaimed, with a resolute air, which imposed on the Indian, "No, indeed, those two chiefs are not traitors; but they are on the road to become so ere long. The dangers which menace us they heaped up on our heads to satisfy their passions and thirst for vengeance."

"Let my brother explain," the Chief said, at the height of astonishment. "His words are plain."

"I did wrong to utter them," the hunter continued, with feigned humility. "I am only a man of peace, to whom the omnipotent Wacondah has given the mission of relieving, according to the knowledge granted him, the ills of humanity. I, a poor being, ought not to try and uproot the powerful oak, whose weight in falling would crush me. Let my brother pardon me. I imprudently allowed my indignation to carry me away."

"No, no," the Chief exclaimed, pressing his arm forcibly; "it cannot be so. My father has begun, and he must tell me all."

With that quickness of thought that distinguished him, the hunter had conceived a plan founded on the distrust which forms the basis of the Indian character. He pretended resistance to the Chief's instructions, and was unwilling to enter into details of what he had let him have a glimpse of; but the more the pretended medicine man declined to speak, the more did the Chief press him to do so. At length the hunter feigned to be intimidated by his host's mingled prayers and threats, and still alleging the fear he felt of drawing on himself the hatred of two renowned chiefs, he at length consented to give the information for which Atoyac pressed him so urgently. "Here are the facts," he said. "I will relate them to my brother exactly as they came to my knowledge. Still, my brother will pledge me his word, that whatever be the resolution he forms after hearing my words, he will in no way mix up a peaceful and timid man in this affair. That my name shall not be even mentioned, and that the chiefs whose conduct I am now about to unveil, will not be aware of my presence at Quiepaa Tani?"

"My brother can speak in all confidence. I swear to him by the sacred name of the Wacondah, and by the great Ayotl, that whatever happens, his name shall not be mixed up in this affair. No one shall know in what way I obtained the information he will give me. Atoyac is one of the first sachems in Quiepaa Tani. When it pleases him to say a thing, his words do not require to be confirmed by any other testimony than his own."

As so often happens, under present circumstances, apart from the discomfort produced by the hunter's reticence, the Chief was not sorry at the importance the details he was about to learn would assuredly give him, and the part he would be indubitably called on to play in the events which would result from them.

"Och!" the hunter said, with a sigh of satisfaction, "if that is the case, I will speak." Then the Canadian told his complaisant and credulous hearer a long and wonderfully confused story, in which truth was so artfully mixed up with falsehood, that it would have been impossible for the acutest man to distinguish one from the other; but the result of which was, that, if the whites had reached the vicinity of the city, Addick and Red Wolf had lured them after them, only connecting their trail sufficiently for their pursuers not to lose it. The whole of the facts recounted by the hunter were so skilfully grouped, that the two chiefs, enveloped in this network of truth and falsehood, must be inevitably convicted of treason if closely cross-questioned, which the worthy hunter hoped most sincerely. "I will allow myself no reflections," he added, in conclusion; "my brother is a wise chief and experienced warrior: he will judge far better than I, a poor worm, can of the gravity of the things he has just heard; still, I implore him to remember what he has promised."

"Atoyac has only one word," the Chief answered. "My father can reassure himself; but what I have heard is extremely serious. Let us lose no more time; I must go to the first Chief of the city."

"Perhaps the two Sachems have drawn the Palefaces so near us with a good intention," the hunter insinuated; "they hope, possibly, to pounce upon them with greater ease."

"No," Atoyac answered, with a gloomy air; "their intentions can only be perfidious; their machinations must be foiled as speedily as possible; if not, great misfortunes will occur, especially after the decision of the Council, which gives the command of the warriors destined to act in the city to Red Wolf, under the orders of the governor."

Fortunately for the hunter, Atoyac was a personal enemy of Red Wolf and Addick, which prevented him noticing with what cunning skill the Canadian had led him to listen to his narrative.

The two men hastily continued their walk, and in a few minutes reached the Palace of the Vestals. After a few words with the warrior who had charge of the gate, the Chief and the medicine man were introduced into the interior. The High Priest came eagerly toward the newcomers, whom he had been eagerly expecting. The Amantzin regarded the hunter with suspicious attention, and made him undergo an interrogatory like Atoyac's in the morning.

His answers, prepared long before, pleased the High Priest; for, a few moments after, he led him to the reserved apartments of the Palace, in order to examine the state of the maidens. The Canadian's heart trembled with the most violent emotion, and large drops of perspiration beaded in his face. Indeed, the critical position in which he found himself, was really of a nature to inspire him with serious alarm. What he feared most of all was the effect his presence might produce on the maidens, if, in spite of his perfect disguise, they recognized him at once, or when he made himself known to them; for it was indispensable for the success of the trick he intended to play, that those he was going to see should know with whom they had to deal, and enter fully into the spirit of the characters he meant them to play in the farce. These reflections, and many others which rushed on the hunter, imparted to his face a look of sternness, which was far from injuring him in the minds of those who accompanied him. They at length reached the entrance of the secret apartments, whose door, at a sign from the High Priest, was widely opened before them. But so soon as they entered a large hall, which, through the absence of all furniture, might be regarded as a vestibule, the Amantzin turned to Atoyac, and gave him the order to wait there, while he led the medicine man to the captives.

As we have already said, the abode of the Virgins of the Sun was interdicted to all men, excepting the High Priest. Under certain circumstances, one person might be an exception to this rule, and that was the doctor. Atoyac was too well acquainted with the severe law of the palace to offer the slightest remark; still, when the High Priest prepared to leave him, he caught him respectfully by the robe, and bent to his ear. "My brother will return promptly," he said to him in a low voice; "I have important news to communicate to him."

"Important news," the Amantzin repeated, as he stared at him.

"Yes," the Chief said.

"And they concern me?" the High Priest continued slowly.

Atoyac smiled confidentially. "I think so," he said, "for they relate to Red Wolf and Addick."

The High Priest gave a slight start. "I will return in a moment," he said, with a gracious nod; then turning to the hunter, who stood motionless a few steps off, apparently indifferent to what passed between the two men, he said to him,—"Come."

The hunter bowed, and followed the High Priest. The latter led him across a long courtyard paved with bricks, and ascending ten steps of blue and green-veined marble, he conducted him into a small isolated pavilion, completely separate from the building in which the Virgins of the Sun were secluded. The High Priest closed the door behind him, which gave them admission to the pavilion; they crossed a species of antechamber, and the Amantzin, raising a drapery which hung over a narrow doorway, introduced the pretended physician into a room splendidly furnished in the Indian style. The High Priest, wishing, if possible, to make the maidens forget they were captives, had gilded their cage with the utmost care, by decorating it with all the articles of luxury and comfort which he supposed would please them. In an elegant hammock of cocoa-fibre, overrun with feathers, and hanging from golden rings, about eighteen inches from the floor, there reclined a young woman, whose face of excessive pallor bore the imprint of profound sorrow, and the evident traces of a serious illness. It was Doña Laura de Real del Monte. By her side, with folded arms and tear-laden eyes, stood Doña Luisa, her friend, or rather her sister, through suffering and devotion. The state of prostration into which Doña Luisa was plunged, proved that, in spite of her strength of character, she had also, for some time past, given up all hope of ever leaving the prison in which she was confined. This room, receiving no light from without, was illuminated by four torches of ocote wood, passed through gold rings in the wall, whose vacillating flame dimly lighted up the scene.

On seeing the two men, Doña Laura made a sign of terror, and buried her face in her hands. The hunter saw that he must precipitate events, so he turned to his guide, "The Wacondah is powerful," he said, in an imposing voice; "the sacred tortoise supports the world on its shell. His spirit eye is on me; it inspires me. I must remain alone with the patients, that I may read in their faces the nature of the illness that torments them."

The High Priest hesitated; he fixed on the pretended physician a glance which seemed to try and read his most secret thoughts. But, although accustomed for many years to deceive his countrymen by his mystic juggling, he was, after all, an Indian, and, as such, as accessible to superstitious fears as those he deluded. He therefore hesitated, "I am the Amantzin," he said, with a respectful accent. "The Wacondah can only view with satisfaction my presence here at this moment."

"My father can remain, if such is his pleasure; I do not compel him to retire," the Canadian answered boldly, as he was determined to gain his point at all hazards. "Now I warn him that I am in no way responsible for the terrible consequences his disobedience will entail. The Spirit that possesses me will be obeyed, for it is jealous. Let my father reflect."

The High Priest bowed his head humbly. "I will retire," he said; "my brother will pardon my pressing." And he left the apartment.

The Canadian silently accompanied him to the door of the vestibule, closed it carefully after him, and ran back to the young ladies, who recoiled with terror. "Fear nothing," he whispered; "I am a friend."

"A friend!" Doña Laura exclaimed, who had fled, all trembling, into a corner of the room.

"Yes," he continued hastily; "I am Marksman, the Canadian hunter, the friend, the companion of Don Miguel."

Doña Laura sat up in her hammock, and a cry of surprise and joy burst from her chest.

"Silence!" the hunter said; "they may be listening."

Doña Luisa gazed with dilated eyes on this scene, whose meaning escaped her.

"You, Marksman!" Doña Laura at length said, with an accent impossible to describe. "Oh! we may be saved, then; we are not abandoned by all."

And, sliding to the ground, she knelt piously, and, with clasped hands, murmured a fervent prayer, while her eyes filled with tears. Then, rising suddenly, she seized the hunter's hands, and pressed them passionately. "Don Miguel," she said; "where is he?"

"He is close by, and waiting for you. But, for Heaven's sake, listen to me; moments are precious."

"Oh, Caballero! take us away, take us away quickly," Doña Laura at length said, completely recovered from her emotion.

"Soon."

"Yes, yes, save us!" Doña Laura exclaimed; "my father will reward you."

Marksman smiled. "Your father will be very glad to see you again," he said, softly.

Doña Laura raised to him her lovely eyes, radiant with joy. "Where is my father?" she asked him; but then added, "no, I cannot see him. He is far, very far from here."

"He is with Don Miguel, in the forest. Set your mind at rest."

"Oh, Heaven!" the maiden exclaimed, "it is too much happiness."

At this moment someone could be heard ascending the marble steps. "Hist!" the hunter said, sharply; "be on your guard."

"But what must we do?" Doña Laura asked, in a low voice.

"Wait, and have confidence."

"What, are you going?"

"Leave us already?" they exclaimed together, with a movement of terror.

"I will return. Leave me to act. Once again, hope and patience."

"Oh, if you were to abandon us; if you did not save us," Laura said, in despair, "we should have nothing left but to die."

"Oh, have pity on us!" Doña Luisa murmured;

"Trust to me, poor children," the hunter answered, more affected than he liked to seem by this simple and profound sorrow. "Remember this carefully—whatever happens, whatever may be told you, whatever sound you hear, trust to me—to me alone—for I am watching over you. I have sworn to save you, and I will succeed."

"Thanks!" they replied.

The steps had stopped at the door.

Marksman, after making the maidens a last sign to recommend them prudence, composed his features, sharply opened the door, and, without uttering a word, passed by the High Priest, whom he did not seem to notice, but evinced great marks of agitation, and, making incomprehensible signs, ran toward the spot where Atoyac was awaiting him. The Amantzin was dumb with surprise. After a moment, he closed the doors the hunter had left open, and followed him, but as if he did not dare to draw towards him.

The maidens did not know whether they were not the sport of a dream. So soon as they were alone, they fell into each other's arms, sobbing violently.

[1] Literally, "red country."

[2] Curlyce of Mexico: literally, it means the "serpent covered with feathers."

CHAPTER XXXVI
A MEETING

The Indian Chief could not restrain a cry of terror, and recoiled a few paces at the sudden apparition of the hunter. The latter stopped in the centre of the room, and letting his head sink on his chest, appeared plunged in profound thought. The High Priest, on rejoining Atoyac, told him, in a few words, in what fashion the medicine man had quitted the sick chamber, and the Indians, filled with superstitious fear, stood motionless a few paces from him, respectfully waiting till he addressed them. The hunter appeared gradually to regain possession of his faculties; his agitation calmed down; he passed his hand over his forehead, and sighed like a man at length relieved from a terrible oppression. The Indians considered the moment favourable to approach him, and ask him the questions they burned to address to him. "Well, my father?" they said.

"Speak," the High Priest added. "What is the matter with you?"

The hunter rolled his eyes, uttered a fresh sigh, and muttered, in a low, choking voice—"The spirit possesses me; it presses the marrow of my bones."

The Indians exchanged a timid glance, and fell back in terror.

"Wacondah! Wacondah!" the Canadian continued; "why hast thou gifted thy wretched servant with this unhappy knowledge?"

The Redskins really felt the blood curdle in their veins by these sinister words; a shudder of terror ran over their limbs, and their teeth chattered. Marksman walked slowly toward them; they saw him approaching without daring to make a movement to avoid him. The hunter laid his right hand on the High Priest's shoulder, fixed a piercing glance on him, and said, in a hollow voice—"The sons of the sacred Ayotl must arm themselves with courage."

"What does my brother mean?" the old man muttered, in a tremor.

"A wicked spirit," the hunter continued, coldly, "has entered these daughters of the Palefaces. This spirit will smite with death, from this day forth, those who approach them; for the dread knowledge with which the

Wacondah has gifted me has enabled me to convince myself of the malign influence that weighs upon them."

The two Indians, credulous like all of their race, fell back a step. Then the hunter, as if to confirm his words, feigned to be attacked by a fresh crisis, and struggle with the spirit that dwelt in him.

"But what must be done to deliver them from his evil influence?" Atoyac asked, timidly.

"All strength and all wisdom come from the Wacondah," the Canadian answered. "I will ask my father, the Amantzin's leave to spend this night in prayer in the Temple of the Sun."

The Indians exchanged a glance of admiration.

"Be it so, according to my father's wish," the High Priest said, with a bow; "his wishes are orders to us."

"Above all," the hunter continued, "let no one approach the daughters of the Palefaces till tomorrow; then, perhaps, the Wacondah will grant my prayers, by indicating the medicines I must employ."

The High Priest gave a sign of assent.

"It shall be so," he said; "let my father follow me; I will conduct him to the temple."

"No," Marksman objected; "that is not possible. I must enter the sanctuary alone. My father will tell me the way to open the door."

The Amantzin obeyed, and explained to him in what way the bars and bolts were arranged, and how he must set to work to undo them.

"Good," the hunter said; "tomorrow, at sunrise, I will let my father know the will of the Wacondah, and if there be any hope left of saving the patients."

"I will wait, my son," the old man replied.

The two Indians bowed respectfully to the medicine man, and retired together. The hunter was surprised at seeing them go away thus, and asked himself where they could be proceeding at such an hour. The departure of the Indians was the only consequence of the confidential information given to Atoyac by Marksman, and the High Priest and the Chief were proceeding in all haste to the principal Sachem of the city, to impart to him all they had learned of the supposed intentions of Addick and Red Wolf.

We will here return to what we have already told the reader, in order to make him thoroughly understand the motive of the confidence with which the Indians accepted the hunter's words. In these countries soothsayers are, as it were, favourites of fortune, and enjoy an unbounded supernatural power. As among the Redskins, the practice of medicine is, properly speaking, only an affectation of religious rites mingled with ridiculous juggling. The physicians are naturally considered to be Acyars, and respected as such. And let it not be supposed that the vulgar alone are imbued with this belief. The chiefs, warriors, priests even, as we have shown, recognize in them a marked superiority, even if they do not grant them equally absolute power.

During the latest events we have described, night had set in, but one of those American nights, so calm and soft, full of intoxicating perfumes; a weak and delicate light poured from the stars, whose innumerable army studded the profoundly azure sky with their flashing light; the moon was standing high in the heavens, and poured down on the sleeping city its silvery rays, which imparted to objects a fantastic appearance; a religious silence brooded over the landscape. The hunter looked after the two men so long as they remained in sight, and then began crossing the square to reach the palace.

The day had been a trying one to the Canadian. He had been compelled at every moment to display presence of mind, and struggle in craft with men whose clear-sighted eyes had been incessantly on the point of discovering the wolf hidden beneath the sheepskin. Still, he had valiantly supported his trials, and, from the way affairs had turned, he had every reason to believe that he should succeed in delivering the two maidens; hence the worthy hunter's laughter to himself at the way in which he had played his part, and determined to brave it out boldly to the end. On reaching the temple, he unfastened the bolts and bars, and entered the interior, only leaving the doors to behind, for he felt certain that no one would dare to trouble him, through the sanctity of the spot in the first place, and then through the superstitious fears he had succeeded in inspiring the Indians with. In asking the High Priest's permission to spend the night in the sanctuary, the hunter had no other design but to cover with the cloak of religion the means he intended to employ for the escape of the maidens, and, at the same time, have a few hours' liberty, during which he could arrange his plans fully, without being disturbed by the hospitality and curiosity of his host.

The interior of the temple was gloomy. Only one lamp burned before the sacrificing table, spreading a weak and trembling light, insufficient to dispel the gloom. Marksman retired to a dark corner, sat down on the ground, drew his pistols from his bosom, placed them by his side for fear of a sudden attack, and, after trying with a piercing glance to sound the dense gloom that surrounded him, feeling reassured by the deadly silence, he began thinking deeply. Still, by degrees, either through weariness or the influence of the spot where he was, in spite of his violent efforts to keep awake, he felt his eyelids grow heavy, and at length he gave way to the invisible sleep that overpowered him. He could not say how long he had slept, when a slight noise he heard, no great distance off, suddenly made him open his eyes. Like all men accustomed to the active and perilous life of the desert, where a man must be constantly on his guard, the hunter had acquired such an exquisite delicacy of sense, that, however great his lassitude might be, whenever he knew himself to be in a dangerous position, his sleep was lighter than a child's. Marksman, when hardly awake, looked around, while careful not to make the slightest movement indicating that his slumbers were interrupted. He could see nothing; it was still night, and what was more, the lamp was extinguished. He understood that someone had entered the temple, and was spying him. But who could have dared to cross the sacred threshold? Two sorts of persons alone would venture to do it. A friend or an enemy. As for friends, he had only one in the city, Flying Eagle. It was evident that the warrior, if he wished to come to him, would have come openly, and not hiding himself, which might draw a bullet at his head. Hence it was an enemy; but who? Those he might have suspected, namely, Addick or Red Wolf, did not know him, and hence could not have discovered him under his disguise, as he had deceived sharper eyes than theirs. Besides, during the whole course of the day, he had not been face to face with the two Chiefs, hence it could not be they. But who was it, then? This was what the hunter could not discover, in spite of all his cleverness. In his doubt, and through fear of being taken unawares, he stretched out his hands till they touched the pistols, and, with his head up, his eyes open, and ears on the watch for the slightest sound, he prepared to bravely face the foe, whoever he might be. The noise, however, which had disturbed him was not repeated, all remained calm and silent. In vain did the hunter strive to detect a shadow, even the slightest, or the least sound. Nothing disturbed the majesty of the sanctuary. Still, Marksman was not mistaken. He had distinctly heard a footstep timidly pacing the stones of the temple. A man must have been once in his life in the same position as the hunter was now in, to understand its agony and terror. To feel close to you, scarce two yards off, an enemy watching you, whose furious eye is unpleasantly fixed on you—to know he is there; to guess it by that species of intuition God has bestowed on him to foresee a danger, and not dare to stir, fear making the least movement which might warn him that you were expecting the attack—this position, comparable with that of the bird fascinated by the snake, is most cruel, and, in a few minutes, becomes a punishment so intolerable that death itself is preferable.

Assuredly, Marksman was a man of tried courage. The enterprise he was now attempting proved in him a rashness, we will not say pushed to the verge of death, for that is nothing, but to a contempt of those tortures the Redskins are so ingenious in inventing and varying, so that they can extract the life from their victim, as it were, drop by drop. Well, after a quarter of an hour of this expectation, he felt an involuntary shudder, his hair stood erect, and a cold perspiration beaded on his temples. "A million demons," he muttered to himself, "I cannot stand this any longer. I must know what I have to expect, whatever happens."

At the same moment he leaped to his feet as if moved by a spring, a pistol in either hand. All at once, a shadow bounded from behind a pillar with a tiger's leap, and the hunter, seized by the throat, rolled on the ground, before he could utter a cry. A foot was rested on his chest, and he saw a hideous face grinning at him, as if through a cloud. Marksman was alone, abandoned; without help; it was all over with him, nothing could save him. He gave vent to a stifled sigh, and closed his eyes, resigned to the fate that awaited him. But, at the moment he felt he was about to receive the mortal blow, the grasp on his throat relaxed, and a sarcastic voice said to him, "Get up, powerful Tlacateotzin, I only wished to prove to you that you were in my hands."

The hunter rose all bruised, and still troubled by this sudden attack. The other continued—"What would you give to escape the peril that menaces you, and be free to return peacefully to the *calli* of your host Atoyac?"

But Marksman had had time to recover from his flurry; he had picked up his pistols; all fear had fled his heart, for he had only to defend himself against one enemy. This enemy, after for a moment holding him prostrate, committed the fault of restoring him liberty to move; their position had suddenly become equal. "I will give you nothing, Red Wolf," he said, resolutely. "Why did you not kill me when I lay defenceless at your feet?"

The Indian Chief—for he it was—recoiled, with surprise, on finding himself so easily recognized. "Why did I not kill you, dog?" he answered. "Because I had pity on you."

"Because you were afraid, Sachem," the hunter said firmly; "it is a different thing to kill an enemy in fighting, from assassinating an adept of the great medicine in the temple of Wacondah, when protected by his omnipotent hand. I say again, you were afraid."

The hunter guessed rightly; it was his superstitious fear which suddenly arrested the arm of the Chief, already uplifted to strike. "I will not discuss matters with you," he said; "but tell me how you so speedily guessed my name; for I do not know you."

"But I know you; the Wacondah announced your presence to me; I expected you; if I did not prevent your attack, it was because I wished to see if you would carry your impiety so far as to sully the reverend sanctuary of the temple."

The Indian grinned. "You are going too far, sorcerer," he said, ironically. "Had it not been for a moment of weakness I now regret, you would be dead."

"Perhaps so. What do you want of me?"

"Do you not know, as you say nothing is hidden from you?"

"I know what reason brings you here. You will try in vain to dissimulate; if I ask you that question, it is because I would know if you dare to tell a falsehood."

Red Wolf reflected for a moment, and then continued, with a resolute accent, — "Listen, sorcerer," he said; "either you are a rogue, as I believe, or else you are really what you pretend to be—a great medicine man, inspired by the Wacondah, and beloved by him; in either case, I wish to clear up my doubts. Woe to you if you try to deceive me, for I will kill you like a dog, and of your accursed hide, cut into strips on your quivering body, I will make trappings for my horse; if, on the contrary, you speak the truth, you will not have a more devoted friend, or a more faithful servant than myself."

"I despise your hatred, and do not want your friendship, Red Wolf," the hunter answered, in an imposing tone; "your powerless menaces do not terrify me; but, in order to make you fully understand the extent of my knowledge, I consent to do what you ask, and tell you what reason urged you to come to me."

"Do so, sorcerer, and whatever may happen, Red Wolf will be yours."

The hunter smiled contemptuously, and shrugged his shoulders, "It is difficult, then, to divine what a man of blood wants? You and Addick, your worthy accomplice, are leagued with a miserable dog, an outcast of the Palefaces, to carry off from here two poor young girls confided to the honour of your accomplice. Today you would like to cheat those with whom you are allied, and keep the prisoners for yourself. Denounced to the great Sachem by Atoyac, to whom all your designs are known, who is also aware that you meditate seizing the supreme power, and becoming Governor of Quiepaa Tani, you felt that you were lost; then you came to me with the intention of corrupting me, and inducing me, by the power I have at my disposal, to help you in carrying off the maidens whom you covet, so that you may fly with them before the necessary steps have been taken to arrest you. Is that all? Have I forgot any trifling detail? Or have I really read your whole thoughts? Answer, Chief, and contradict me if you dare!"

The Sachem listened to the hunter's long tirade with increasing trouble; the successive changes of his face while listening to the sorcerer, would have been a curious study for an observer; and when Marksman at length concluded, Red Wolf let his head sink in confusion, and stammered, in an almost indistinct voice,—"My father is truly a Tlacateotzin; the Wacondah inspires him; his knowledge is immense. Who is the man who would dare to hide anything from him? His eye, more piercing than the eagle's, reads all hearts."

"Now you have my answer, Red Wolf," the hunter continued, "retire in peace, and no longer disturb the meditations in which I am plunged."

"Then," the Chief remarked, with hesitation, "my father will not do anything for me?"

"Yes, I do much."

"What does my father?"

"I allow you to retire in peace, when, by one sign, it would be easy for me to lay you dead at my feet."

The Indian drew two or three steps nearer the sorcerer, so as almost to touch him; the latter, whose watchful ear had just heard the sound of gentle footsteps coming toward him, did not notice this movement, for all attention was directed to another quarter. Suddenly his frowning brow grew smooth, and a smile played on his lips; he had discovered the cause of this new mystery. "Well," he said to the Chief, "why does Red Wolf remain here, when I gave him the order to withdraw?"

"Because I hope to induce my father to have better feelings toward me."

"My feelings toward the hunter are as they should be; I cannot change them."

"Yes, my father is kind; he will help Red Wolf."

"No, I tell you."

"My father will not serve me."

"I will not."

"Is that my father's last word?"

"Yes."

"Then die like the dog you are!" the Redskin howled furiously, as he rushed with uplifted knife on the hunter.

The latter had, for a few moments, attentively watched all the Chief's movements. Being thoroughly acquainted with the treacherous and roguish character of the Apaches, on seeing Red Wolf assume a gentle manner, he perfectly foresaw what he meditated, and the termination he meant to give the scene; but, for all that, he did not make the slightest movement to escape the blow intended for him: he looked his assassin full in the face, with folded arms and unruffled face. Still, the arm raised against the hunter did not descend. A man suddenly emerged from the shade that concealed him, appeared behind Red Wolf, seized his arm, and twisted it with such force, that the knife dropped, and disappeared again so rapidly, that the terrified Chief had not even the time to see whether he had to deal with a man or a spirit.

Red Wolf uttered no cry,—did not even attempt to avenge himself, but his eyes rolled in their sockets, a convulsive tremor shook his whole body, and he fell on his knees, murmuring, in a horrified voice,—"Pardon, pardon, my father."

The hunter fell back a step, as if to avoid the unclean contact of the wretch prostrate before him, kicked the knife away with disgust, and said, in a tone of supreme contempt,—"Pick up your weapon, assassin!" In reply the Chief showed him his dislocated arm, which hung inert by his side.

"You wished it," the hunter continued. "Did I not warn you that the Wacondah protected me? Go, retire to your *calli*; keep silence about all that has happened here. At sunset be with your canoe at the riverbank below the bridge; I will meet you there, and perhaps cure you, if you strictly follow the order I give you; above all, forget not that you must be alone. Go!"

"I will obey my father; my lips will not utter a word without his order. But how can I leave here, unless you aid me? The spirits that watch over my father will come to me with death, when I am no longer in his presence."

"That is true: you have been sufficiently punished. Rise, and lean on my shoulder; I will help you to walk to the entrance of the temple."

Red Wolf rose without reply; his rebellious spirit was subdued. The rude lesson he had received at length inspired him with a superstitious dread of the medicine man, which nothing could overcome.

The hunter gently led him to the outer gate. On arriving there, he carefully examined his arm, assured himself that nothing was broken, and dismissed him, saying in a tone in which kindness was mingled with severity,—"Thank the Wacondah, who had pity on you. In a few days your wound will be cured; but profit by this lesson, wretch. You will see me again this evening. Go; now my help is no longer requisite, you can reach your *calli* alone."

"I will try," the Chief answered, humbly.

At a bow and sign from the hunter, he began walking slowly. Marksman looked after him for some time, and then returned to the temple, being careful to bolt the gate after him this time. At the moment the hunter disappeared in the temple, the cry of the owl rose in the air, announcing that the sun would speedily make its appearance.

CHAPTER XXXVII
COMPLICATIONS

While these events were taking place in Quiepaa Tani, others we must narrate were occurring in the camp of the Gambusinos. Don Miguel, after parting from Marksman at the outskirts of the forest, returned thoughtfully to the spot where his comrades awaited him. It was evident that the bold adventurer, dissatisfied in his heart at the turn affairs had taken, was meditating some desperate project to get near the maidens. He had spent several hours on the top of the isolated mound which commanded the whole plain, and which we have before visited, and thence carefully studied the position of the city. Clearly this young man, with his ardent character and impetuous passions, consented very unwillingly to play a second part in an expedition in which he had been hitherto the leader; his pride revolted at being compelled to obey another, even though he were his devoted friend, and he could count on him as on himself. He reproached himself for allowing Marksman to expose himself thus alone to terrible dangers for a cause which was his own. The true reason, however, which he did not dare confess to himself, that, in short, would have gladly made him brave the greatest perils, and evidently that instinct which impelled him to revolt secretly against Marksman's prudence, and to take his place at all risks, was his love for Doña Laura de Real del Monte. He loved her with that powerful and invincible love which only chosen natures are capable of experiencing—a love which grows with obstacles, and which, when it has once taken possession of the heart of a man like Don Leo, makes him accomplish the most daring and extraordinary deeds. This love was the more deeply rooted in the young man's heart, because he was completely ignorant of its existence, and believed he merely acted through the affection he felt for the young girls, and the pity their unhappy position inspired him with. If it were so at the outset, as is true, for he did not know Doña Laura, matters had completely changed since. A young man does not travel with impunity side by side with a maiden for more than a month, seeing her incessantly, talking with her at every moment of the day, and not fall in love with her. There is in woman a certain charm, which we do not attempt to account for, which seems to emanate from their being, to be impregnated in all that surrounds them, which seduces and subjugates the strongest men involuntarily. The silky rustling of their dress, the soft and airy turn of the waist, the intoxicating perfume of their floating tresses, the pure limpidness of their dreamy glance, which is turned toward heaven, and tries to guess the secrets of which they are ignorant; all, in short, in these incomprehensible and voluptuously simple beings seems to command adoration and appeal to love.

Doña Laura especially possessed that fascinating magnetism of the eye, that slightly infantile gentleness of smile, which annihilate the will. When her large blue eyes, veiled by long black lashes, kindly settled on the young man, and were pensively fixed on him, he felt a quiver over his body, a chill at his heart, and internally affected by a sensation of immense and unknown pleasure, he wished to die then at the feet of her who to him was no longer a creature of the earth, but an angel. During the irregular course of his life, all the adventurer's acquaintance with the other sex was what the corrupt society of Mexico could offer; that is, the hideous and repulsive side. Accident, by suddenly bringing him in contact with a poor and innocent girl like her he had saved, produced a complete revolution in his ideas, by making him understand that, until that day, woman, such as Heaven created her for man, had remained an utter stranger to him. Hence, without noticing it, and quite naturally, he yielded to the charm that unconsciously acted on him, and had learned to love Doña Laura with, all the active strength of his mind, not attempting to explain the new feeling which had seized on him; happy in the present, and not wishing to think of the future, which would probably never exist for him. Disregard of the future is generally the character of all lovers; they only see, and cannot see beyond, the present, by which they feel, through which they suffer, or are happy; in which, in a word, they have their being.

Possibly Don Leo, hidden in the heart of the desert with the girl he had so miraculously saved, had for a few days caressed in his heart the hope of eternal happiness with her he loved, far from cities and their dangerous intoxication; but that thought, if ever he entertained it, had irrevocably faded away upon the fortuitous appearance of Don Mariano; the meeting with Doña Laura's father must eternally annihilate the plans formed by the young man. The blow was a heavy one; still, thanks to his iron will, he endured it bravely, believing that it would be easy for him to forget the girl in the vortex of the adventurer's life to which he was condemned. Unfortunately for Don Leo, he was obliged to undergo the common lot; that is to say, his love grew in an inverse ratio to the immovable obstacles that had suddenly arisen; and it was precisely when he recognized that she could never be his, owing to reasons of family and fortune, which raised an insurmountable barrier between them, that he understood it was impossible for him to live without her. Then, no longer striving to cure the wound in his heart, he yielded completely to that love which was his life, and only dreamed of one thing—to die in saving her he loved, so as to draw a word of gratitude from her in his final hour, and perhaps leave a soft and sad memory in her soul. We can understand that, under such feelings, Don Leo absolutely insisted on delivering the maidens himself; hence, from the moment he parted from his friend, he thought of nothing but the means to enter the city and see her. It was in this temper that he returned to the camp. Don Mariano was sad; Brighteye himself seemed to be in a bad temper; in short, all conspired to plunge him deeper and deeper in his gloom. Several hours passed and the adventurers did not interchange a word; but at about two in the afternoon, the hour of the greatest heat, the sentries signalled the approach of a party of horsemen. All ran to their arms, but soon saw that the newcomers were Ruperto and his Cuadrilla, whom Don Mariano's servants had found and brought with them.

Bermudez, following the injunctions he had received from Marksman, had wished Ruperto to shut himself up with his men in the iron cavern; but the hunter would listen to nothing, saying that his comrades had gone further on the sacred soil of the Redskins than they had ever done before; that they ran the risk at any moment of being crushed by numbers, massacred, or made prisoners; that he would not abandon them in such a critical position without trying to go to their help; and so, in spite of all the criado's observations, the worthy hunter, who possessed a tolerably strong share of obstinacy, pushed on, until he at length found the encampment of his friends. Twice or thrice during his journey he had come to blows with the Indians; but these slight skirmishes, far from moderating his ardour, had no other result than to urge him to haste; for now that the Redskins knew that detachments of Palefaces were wandering in the vicinity of the city, they would not fail to assemble in large numbers, in order to deal a great blow, and free themselves from all their daring enemies at once.

The arrival of the Gambusinos was greeted with shouts; Ruperto especially was heartily welcomed by Don Miguel, who was delighted at this reinforcement of resolute men at the moment he least expected it.

The apathy which had fallen on the adventurers gave place to the greatest activity. When the newcomers had performed their various duties, groups were formed, and conversation commenced with the vivacity and loquaciousness peculiar to Southern races.

Ruperto was the more pleased at his happy idea of pushing on, when he learned that there were not only Redskin encampments in the vicinity, but that one of their most sacred cities was close at hand. "*Canarios!*" he said, "we shall have to keep sharp watch, if we do not wish to lose our scalps ere long. These incarnate demons will not let us tread their soil in peace."

"Yes," Don Leo remarked, carelessly; "I believe we had better not let ourselves be surprised."

"Hum!" Brighteye remarked, "it would be a disagreeable surprise that brought a swarm of Redskins on our backs. You cannot imagine how these devils fight, when they are in large bodies. I remember that, in 1836, when I was—"

"And the most exposed of us all is Marksman," Don Leo said, cutting Brighteye short, who sat open-mouthed. "I am sorry that I let him go alone."

"He was not alone," the Canadian answered. "You know very well, Don Miguel, that Flying Eagle and his cihuatl, as they call their wives, accompanied him."

Don Miguel looked at the hunter. "Do you put great faith in the Redskins, Brighteye?" he asked him.

"Hum!" the latter remarked, scratching his head; "that is according; and if I must tell the truth, I will say that I do not trust them at all."

"You see, then, that he was really alone. Who knows what has happened to him in that accursed city, in the midst of those incarnate demons? I confess to you that my alarm is great, and that I am fearfully afraid of a catastrophe."

"Yet, his disguise was perfect."

"Possibly. Marksman is thoroughly acquainted with Indian manners, and speaks their language like his mother tongue. But what will that avail him, if he has been denounced by a traitor?"

"Holloa!" Brighteye said; "a traitor? Whom are you alluding to?"

"Why, to Flying Eagle, caramba, or his wife, for only those two know him."

"Listen, Don Miguel," Brighteye remarked, seriously; "permit me to tell you my way of thinking frankly; you do wrong in speaking as you now do."

"I?" the young man exclaimed, sharply. "And why so, if you please?"

"Because you only know very slightly—and what you know of them is good—the people you are dishonouring by that epithet. I have known Flying Eagle for many a long year; he was quite a child when I saw him for the first time, and I have always found in him the staunchest good faith and honour. All the time he remained in our company, he rendered us services, or, at any rate, tried to render them to us; and, to settle matters, all of us generally, and yourself in particular, are under great obligations to him. It would be more than ingratitude to forget them."

The worthy hunter uttered this defence of his friend with an ardour and firm tone which confused Don Miguel. "Pardon me, my old friend," he said, in a conciliatory voice; "I was wrong, I allow; but, surrounded by enemies as we are, threatened at each moment with becoming victims to a traitor,—and Domingo's example is there to corroborate my statement,—I allowed myself to be carried away by the idea—"

"Any idea attacking the honour of Flying Eagle," Brighteye sharply interrupted, "is necessarily false. Who knows whether, at this moment, while we are discussing his good faith, he may not be risking his life on our behalf?"

These words produced a sensation on the hearers; there was a momentary silence, which the Canadian soon broke, by continuing:—"But I am not angry with you. You are young, and, from that very fact, your tongue often goes faster than your thoughts; but, I entreat you, pay attention to it, for it might entail dire consequences. But enough on the subject. I remember a singular adventure which occurred to me in 1851. I was coming from—"

"Now that I reflect more seriously," Don Miguel interrupted, "I fully allow that I was in the wrong."

"I am happy that you allow it so frankly. Then we will say no more about it."

"Very good; and now, returning to the old subject, I confess to you that I also feel anxious about Marksman."

"There, you see."

"Yes, but for other reasons than those you brought forward."

"Tell me them."

"Oh! they are very simple. Marksman is a brave and honest hunter, thoroughly up to Indian roguery; but he has no one to back him up. Flying Eagle would prove of but slight assistance to him; if he were detected, the brave Chief could only be killed by his side; and he would do so, I am convinced."

"And I too; but what good would that do them? How, after that catastrophe, should we succeed in saving the maidens?"

Brighteye shook his head. "Yes," he said, "there is the difficulty; that is the knot of the matter. Unfortunately, it is by no means easy to remedy that eventuality, which, I trust, will not present itself."

"We must trust so; but if it did, what should we do?"

"What should we do?"

"Yes."

"Hum! You ask me a question, Don Miguel, which it is by no means easy to answer."

"Well, supposing it to be so, we must still find means of escaping from the false position in which we shall find ourselves."

"That is quite certain."

"Well, then?"

"Then, on my word, I do not know what I should do. Look you, I am not a man who looks so far ahead. When a misfortune occurs, it is time to remedy it, without bothering your brains so long beforehand. All that I can say to you, Caballero, is that, for the moment, instead of remaining here, stupidly planted like a flamingo that has lost a wing, I would give a good deal to be in that accursed city, in a position to watch over my old comrade."

"Is that the truth? Are you really the man to attempt such an enterprise?" Don Miguel exclaimed joyously.

The hunter looked at him in surprise. "Do you doubt it?" he said. "When did you ever hear me boast of things which I was not capable of doing?"

"Do not be angry, my old friend," Don Miguel answered, quickly; "your words caused me so much pleasure that, at the first blush, I did not dare to believe them."

"You must always put faith in my words, young man," Brighteye remarked, sententiously.

"Do not be afraid," Don Miguel said, with a laugh, "in future I will not doubt them."

"All right, then."

"Listen to me. If you like, we will attempt the affair together."

"Enter the city?"

"Yes."

"By Jove! that is an idea," Brighteye answered, quite delighted.

"Is it not?"

"Yes; but how shall we manage to get in?"

"Leave that all to me."

"Good. Then I will not trouble myself about it further; but there is another matter."

"What now?"

"We are not presentable in this state," the hunter said, pointing, with a laugh, to his attire; "by painting my face and hands, I might pass at a push; but you cannot."

"That is true. Well, let me alone, I will prepare an Indian dress with which you can find no fault. During that time, do you disguise yourself in your way."

"It will soon be done."

"And mine too."

The two men rose, delighted, though probably from different reasons. Brighteye was happy at going to his friend's assistance, while Don Miguel only thought of Doña Laura, whom he hoped to see again. At the moment they rose, Don Mariano stopped them. "Are you speaking seriously, Caballeros?" he asked them.

"Certainly," they answered, "most seriously."

"Very good, then. I shall go with you."

"What!" Don Miguel exclaimed, falling back in stupefaction. "Are you mad, Don Mariano? You, who do not know the Indians, and cannot speak a word of their language, to venture into this wasp's nest. It would be suicide."

"No!" the old man answered resolutely. "I wish to see my child again."

Don Miguel had not the courage to combat a resolution so clearly announced, so he let his head sink without answering; but Brighteye did not regard the matter from that light. Perfectly cool, and consequently seeing far and correctly, he understood the disastrous consequences Don Mariano's presence would have for them.

"Pardon me," he said, "but with your permission, Caballero, I fancy you have not carefully considered the resolution you have just formed."

"Caballeros, a father does not reflect when he wishes to see a child whom he never hoped to hold to his heart again."

"That is true. Still I would remark that what you propose doing, far from helping you to see your daughter again, will, on the contrary, sever her from you for ever."

"What do you mean?"

"A very simple thing. Don Miguel and myself are going to mix among Indians, whom we shall have great difficulty in discovering, though we know them. If you accompany us, the following will inevitably happen:— At the first glance, the Redskins will see you are a white man, and then, you understand, nothing can save you, or us either. Now, if you insist, we will be off. I am ready to follow you. A man can only die once; so as well today as tomorrow."

Don Mariano sighed. "I was mad," he muttered, "I knew not what I said. Pardon me; but I so longed to see my daughter again."

"Have faith in us, poor father," Don Miguel said, nobly; "by what we have already done, judge what we are still able to do. We will attempt impossibilities to restore her who is so dear to you."

Don Mariano, succumbing to the emotion which overpowered him, had not the strength to reply. With eyes filled with tears, he pressed the young man's hand, and sat down again. The two adventurers then prepared for the dangerous expedition they meditated, by disguising themselves. Owing to their acquaintance with Indian habits, they succeeded in producing costumes harmonizing with the characters they wished to assume, and in giving themselves a thorough Indian look. When all the preparations were completed, Don Miguel confided the command of the cuadrilla to Ruperto, recommending him to exercise the utmost vigilance, and telling him the signal agreed on with Marksman. Then, after a final pressure of Don Mariano's hand, who was still plunged in the deepest grief, the two daring adventurers took leave of their comrades, threw their rifles on their shoulders, and set out in the direction of Quiepaa Tani, accompanied by several Gambusinos and by Ruperto, who was glad to learn the situation of the city, so as to know how to post his men so that they could run up at the first signal.

CHAPTER XXXVIII
A WALK IN THE DARK

The sun was setting as the Gambusinos reached the skirt of the forest and the limit of the covert. Before them, at a distance of about four miles, rose the city, amid the verdure of the plain, which formed a girdle of flowers and grass. The night fell rapidly, the darkness grew momentarily heavier, mingling all the varieties of the scenery in a sombre mass; the hour, in short, was most propitious for trying the bold experiment on which they were resolved. They whispered a last farewell to their comrades, and boldly entered the tall grass, in the centre of which they speedily disappeared. Fortunately for the adventurers, who would have found it impossible to find their way in the darkness, the tracks of horsemen and foot passengers proceeding to the city, or coming from it, had traced long paths, all leading direct to one of the gates. The two men walked along, side by side, for a long time in silence; each was thinking deeply on the probable results of this desperate tentative. In the first moment of enthusiasm, they had dreamed but slightly of the countless difficulties they must meet on their path, and the obstacles which would doubtlessly at every moment rise before them; they had only regarded the object they wished to attain. But now that they were cool, many things to which they had not paid attention, or which they would not allow to check them, presented themselves to their thoughts, and, as so frequently happens, made them regard their expedition under a very different light. Their object now appeared to them almost impossible to gain, and obstacles grew up, as it were, under their feet. Unfortunately, these judicious reflections arrived too late; there was no chance of withdrawal, and they must advance at all risks. All was calm and tranquil, however; there was not a breath in the air, not a sound on the prairie, and, as the stars gradually appeared in the sky, a pale and trembling gleam slightly modified the darkness, and rendered it less intense, and they began to see sufficiently well to be able to proceed without hesitation, and reconnoitre the plain for some distance. Brighteye was not particularly satisfied with his comrade's obstinate silence; the worthy hunter was rather fond of talking, especially under circumstances like those he found himself in at present; hence he resolved to make his companion talk, in the first place, to hear a human voice—a reason which, fortunately for themselves, the sedentary, who are exempt from those great heart storms which yet endow existence with such charms, will not understand; but the hunter's second reason was still more peremptory than the first; now that he had embarked on this desperate enterprise, he wished to obtain certain information from Don Miguel, as to the mode in which he intended acting, and the plan he meant to adopt. So near the city, and in an entirely uncovered plain, there was very slight risk of the adventurers meeting with Indians; the only men they were exposed to meet were scouts, sent out to reconnoitre, in the extremely improbable event, that the Indians, contrary to their usual habit of not making any movement during the night, had considered it necessary to send out a few men to survey the environs. The two men could therefore talk together without danger, save from some extraordinary accident, though, of course, careful not to speak above their breath and to keep eyes and ears constantly on the watch, so as to notice a danger so soon as it arose. Brighteye, after coughing gently to attract his comrade's attention, said, looking around him somewhat impatiently,—"Eh, eh! the sky has grown enormously bright in the last few minutes, and the night is not so black; I hope the moon will not rise ere we reach our destination."

"We have two hours before us ere the moon rises," Don Miguel answered; "that is more than we want."

"You believe two hours will be sufficient?"

"I am sure of it."

"All the better then, for I am not particularly fond of night walks."

"It is not usual to take them."

"Indeed, during the forty years I have traversed the desert in every direction, this is only the second occasion of my indulging in a night walk."

"Nonsense!"

"It is a fact; the first time deserves mentioning."

"How so?" Don Miguel asked absently.

"The circumstances were almost similar; I wanted to save a young girl, who had been carried off by the Indians. It was in 1835. I was then in the service of the Fur Company. The Blackfoot Indians, to avenge a trick played on them by a scamp of an *employé*, hit on nothing better than surprising Mackenzie fort; then—"

"Listen!" Don Miguel said, seizing his arm. "Do you hear nothing?"

The Canadian, so suddenly interrupted in his story, which he believed this time he should really finish, did not, however, display any ill temper, for he was accustomed to such mishaps; he stopped, lay down on the ground, and listened attentively for two or three minutes, with the most sustained attention, and then rose, shaking his head contemptuously. "They are coyotes sharing a deer," he said.

"You are certain of it?"

"You will soon hear them give tongue." In fact, the hunter had scarce finished speaking ere the repeated barking of the coyotes could be heard a short distance off.

"You hear," the Canadian said simply.

"It is true," Don Miguel answered.

They resumed their march.

"Is this the way?" Brighteye said. "You remember what we agreed on, Don Miguel? I trust entirely to you to get into the city, and I do not exactly see what we shall do."

"I do not know much more myself," the young man responded. "I spent several hours today in carefully examining the walls, and fancied I noticed a spot where it would be rather easy for us to pass."

"Hum!" Brighteye remarked. "Your plan does not seem to me very good; it will probably result in broken bones."

"That is a chance to run."

"Of course; but, without offence, I should prefer something else, if it be possible."

"That prospect does not frighten you, I hope?"

"Not the least in the world. It is plain that the Indians cannot kill me; if they could, they would have done so long ago, seeing the time I have been in the desert."

The young man could not refrain from laughing at the coolness with which his comrade emitted this singular opinion. "Well, then," he said, "what reason have you to find fault with my plan?"

"Because it is bad. If the Indians cannot kill me, that does not prove they will not wound me. Believe me. Don Miguel, let us be prudent: if one of us is disabled at the start, what will become of the other?"

"That is true; but have you any other plan to propose to me?"

"I think so."

"Well, let me know it. If it be good, I will adopt it; I am not at all sweet on myself."

"Good; can you swim?"

"Why ask?"

"Answer first, and then I'll tell you."

"I swim like a sturgeon."

"And I like an otter; we are well paired. Now, pay attention to what I am going to say."

"Move ahead."

"You see that river a little to my right, I suppose?"

"Of course."

"Very good. That river intersects the city, I rather think."

"Yes."

"Supposing that the Redskins are acquainted with our arrival in these parts, on which side will they apprehend an attack?"

"From the plain, evidently. That is common sense."

"All the better. So the walls will be furnished with sentries, watching the plain, while the river, whence they fear no danger, will be perfectly deserted."

"That is true," Don Miguel said, striking his forehead; "I did not think of that."

"People cannot think of everything," Brighteye observed philosophically.

"My worthy friend, I thank you for that idea. Now we are certain of entering the city."

"You had better not holloa till you are out—But you know the proverb. Still, nothing will prevent us trying."

They at once diverged to the left, in the direction of the river, which they reached after a quarter of an hour's march. The banks were deserted. The river, calm as a mirror, looked like a wide silver ribbon. "Now," Brighteye continued, "we need not hurry; although we can swim, we will reserve that expedient till others fail us. Examine all the shrubs on one side, while I do so on the other. I am greatly mistaken, or we shall find a canoe somewhere." The hunter's previsions did not deceive him. After a few minutes' search, they found a canoe hidden beneath a quantity of leaves in the midst of a thicket of lentises and floripondios; the paddles were concealed a short distance away.

We have already described to the reader the mode adopted by the Indians in building their boats, which, among other advantages, possesses that of lightness. Brighteye took the paddles. Don Miguel put the canoe on his back, and in a few minutes it was afloat. "Now let us get in," Brighteye said.

"A moment," Don Miguel observed; "let us muffle the paddles, to prevent noise."

Brighteye shrugged his shoulders. "Do not let us be too clever," he said, "for that would injure us. If there are Indians about, they will see the canoe; if they do not at the same time hear the sound of paddles, they will suspect a trap, and try to detect the trick. No, no, let me alone; lay yourself in the bottom of the canoe: fortunately for us it is small, and the Redskins will never suppose that so small a boat, pulled by one man, would have the pretension of surprising them. That which relatively makes the security of our expedition, you must not forget, is its rashness, even madness. Only Palefaces can hit on such crack-brained schemes. I remember, in 1835, as I was telling you—"

"Let us be off," Don Miguel interrupted, as he jumped into the canoe, in the middle of which he laid himself down, in accordance with his comrade's instructions. The latter followed him with a toss of the head, and took up the paddles, which he only employed, however, with an affected carelessness, which gave the boat a slow and measured movement.

"Look you," the hunter continued, "with the way we are moving, if there are any of those red devils on the watch, they will certainly take me for one of their comrades out fishing late, and returning to his *calli.*"

Still, by degrees, and almost imperceptibly, the hunter increased his speed, so that within half an hour they attained a certain degree of speed, not great enough, however, to arouse suspicions. They then went on for about an hour, and at length entered the city. But if they had expected to land unnoticed, they were mistaken. Near the bridge, the place where a number of pulled-up canoes showed that the Indians were in the habit of stopping, Brighteye perceived a sentry leaning on his long lance and watching them. The Canadian took a glance around, and assured himself that the sentry was alone. "Good!" he muttered to himself; "if there's only one, it will not be a long matter."

Then he explained to Don Miguel what the matter was, to which the latter answered a few words.

"Listen," the hunter said, drawing himself up, "that is the only way."

And he steered the canoe straight toward the sentry. So soon as the Canadian was within hail—"Wah!" the Indian said, "my brother returns very late to Quiepaa Tani; everybody is asleep."

"That is true," Brighteye answered, in the language employed by the sentry; "but I have brought in some splendid fish."

"Eh?" the warrior remarked, seriously; "can I see them?"

"Not only can my brother see them," the Canadian answered, graciously, "but I authorize him to select any one he pleases."

"Och! my brother has an open hand. The Wacondah will never allow it to be empty. I accept my brother's offering."

"Hum!" Brighteye muttered, "it is astonishing how the poor devil takes the bait. He does not at all suspect that he is the fish."

And with this philosophical reflection he continued his progress. Soon after, the canoe grated on the sand. The Indian, affected by the Canadian's deceptive offer, would not be beaten by him in politeness, so he seized the side of the boat and began pulling it up. "Wah!" he said, "my brother has had a fine fishing, for the canoe is very heavy."

While saying this, he bent down to get a better hold, and began trying anew. But he had no time; Don Miguel bounded from the boat, and, clubbing his rifle, dealt a terrible blow of the butt on the wretched Indian's skull. The poor sentry was killed at once, and rolled on the sand without uttering a cry.

"There!" Brighteye cried, as he got out in his turn, "that man, at any rate, will not denounce us."

"We must get rid of him now," Don Miguel observed.

"That will not take long."

The implacable hunter then selected a heavy stone, placed it in the Redskin's frasada, and let him glide softly into the water. So soon as this was effected, and every trace of the murder was removed, they drew the canoe on land by the side of the others, and prepared to start. At this moment the real difficulties of the enterprise began for them. How should they find their way in a strange city in the dark? When and how to find Marksman? These two questions seemed equally impossible of solution.

"Wah!" Brighteye at length said, "it must be no more difficult to follow a trail in a city than on a plain. Let us try."

"The first thing is to get away from here as soon as possible."

"Yes, the place is not healthy for us; but suppose we try to find the great square. There people generally expect to get useful information."

"At this hour? That seems to me rather difficult."

"On the contrary. We will hide till daybreak. The first Redskin who passes within reach we will oblige to give us news of our friend. A great physician, like him, must be well known, hang it all," he added, with a laugh, a gaiety which Don Miguel shared with all his heart.

Singular was the carelessness and recklessness of these two men; in the centre of a city they had entered by killing one of its inhabitants, where they knew they would meet only enemies, and where dangers were, on all sides, hanging over their heads, they still found themselves as much at their ease as if they had been among friends, and laughed and jested together, just as if their position was the most agreeable in the world.

"Well," Brighteye continued, "we are in a very tidy labyrinth. Do you not think with me that there is a frightful smell of broken bones about here?"

"Who knows? Perhaps we shall get out of it better than we fancy."

"One thing is certain, we shall soon know all about it."

"Let us take that street in front of us. It is wide and well laid. Something tells me it will lead us right."

"Heaven's mercy! that is as good as another."

The hunters entered the street ahead of them. Accident had served them well. After ten minutes' walk, they found themselves at the entrance of the great square. "There," Brighteye said, in a tone of delight, "luck is with us. We cannot complain; besides, it must be so. Accident always favours madmen, and in that character we can claim its entire sympathy."

"Silence!" Don Miguel said, sharply, "there is someone."

"Where?"

The young man extended his arm in the direction of the Temple of the Sun. "Look!" he cried.

"So there is," Brighteye muttered, a moment later, "but that appears to be doing like us. He is evidently on the watch. What reason can he have for being up so late?"

After arranging, in a few words, the two adventurers separated, and crept, from different sides, toward the night watcher, hiding themselves, as well as they could, in the shadow, which was not an easy task. The moon had risen some time previously, and spread a weak light, it is true, but sufficient to let objects be distinguished for a considerable distance. The man on whom the adventurers were advancing still remained motionless at the spot where they had seen him; his body bent forward, his ear leant against the door of the temple, he seemed to be listening carefully. Don Miguel and

Brighteye were not more than six paces off, and were preparing to rush on him, when he suddenly threw himself up. They with difficulty suppressed a cry of surprise. "Flying Eagle!" they muttered. But although they spoke so low, the other heard them, and immediately sounded the darkness with a piercing glance.

"Wah!" he said, on perceiving the two men, and resolutely advanced.

The adventurers left the shadow that protected them, and waited. When Flying Eagle had arrived almost close to them—"It is I," Don Miguel said to him.

"And I," Brighteye added.

The Comanche, Chief fell back in a state of stupefaction impossible to describe. "The grey-head here!" he exclaimed.

CHAPTER XXXIX
THE GREAT MEDICINE

As we have stated, Marksman, after leading Red Wolf to the door of the temple, and seeing him retire, reentered the sanctuary, closing the door after him. The Comanche Chief was awaiting him, with shoulder leaning against the wall, and folded arms. "Thanks for your help, Chief," he said; "without you I was lost."

"For a long time," the Indian replied, "Flying Eagle was hearing, though invisible, his brother's conversation with Red Wolf."

"Well, we have got rid of him for a long time; I hope, now, nothing will occur to mar our plans or prevent their success."

The warrior shook his head in contradiction.

"Do you doubt it, Chief?" the hunter asked.

"I doubt it more than ever."

"Why so, when everything is going on as well as we can desire, when all obstacles are levelled before us?"

"Och! obstacles are levelled, but others greater and more difficult to overcome arise immediately."

"I do not understand you, Chief. Have you any ill news to tell me? If so, speak quickly, for time is precious."

"My brother shall judge," the Chief said, simply. Then tuning half away, he clapped his hand thrice. As if this inoffensive signal had the power to call up phantoms, two men instantaneously emerged from the shadow, and appeared before the hunter's astonished eyes. Marksman looked at them for a moment, and then clasped his hand with surprise, muttering, "Brighteye and Don Miguel here! Mercy! what will become of us?"

"Is that the way you receive us, my friend?" Don Miguel asked, affectionately.

"In Heaven's name what have you come here for? What evil inspiration urged you to join me when all was going on so well, and success, I may say, was insured?"

"We have not come to cross your plans; on the contrary, alarmed by the thought of your being among these demons, we wished to see you and help you, were that possible."

"I thank you for your good intentions. Unfortunately, they are more injurious than useful, under present circumstances. But how did you manage to enter the city?"

"Oh, very easily," Brighteye answered, and he told in a few words how they had found them. The hunter shook his head.

"It was a bold action," he said, "and I must allow that it was well carried out. But how does it profit you to have incurred such perils? Greater ones await you here—profitless, and of no advantage to us."

"Perhaps so; but whatever happens," Don Miguel—answered firmly, "you understand that I have not blindly exposed myself to all these dangers without a very powerful motive."

"I suppose so; but I try in vain to discover the motive."

"You need not search long, I will tell you."

"Speak!"

"I must—you understand, I hope, old fellow," he said, laying a stress on each, syllable—"I must see Doña Laura."

"See Doña Laura! it is impossible," Marksman exclaimed.

"I know nothing about impossibility; but this I know, that I will see her."

"You are mad, on my soul, Don Miguel; it is impossible, I tell you."

The adventurer shrugged his shoulders disdainfully. "I repeat that I will see her," he said, with resolution; "even if, to reach her, I were compelled to wade in blood up to my waist; I insist on it, and it shall be so."

"But what will you do?"

"I do not know, and care little. If you refuse to help me, well, Brighteye and I will find means, will we not, old comrade?"

"It is certain, Don Miguel," the latter answered, in the placid tone habitual to him, "that I shall not leave you in the lurch. As to finding a plan of reaching the captives, we shall find it, but I will not answer that it is a good one though."

There was a lengthened silence. Marksman was startled at Don Miguel's resolution, which he knew to be unbinding; he calculated mentally the chances, good and bad, which the young man's untoward arrival offered for the success of his schemes. At last he took the word. "I will not try," he said to Don Miguel, "any longer to dissuade you from attempting to see the maidens; I have known you long enough to feel that it would be useless, and that my arguments would, probably, only urge you to commit an act of irremediable insanity. I therefore take upon myself to lead you to Doña Laura."

"You promise it?" the young man exclaimed quickly.

"Yes; but on one condition."

"Speak! whatever it be I accept it."

"Good; when the moment arrives, I will let you know it; but take my advice, and ask Flying Eagle to perfect your disguise; in the way you and Brighteye are dressed at this moment, you could not take a step in the city without being recognized. Now I leave you, for day has broken, and I must go to the High Priest; I leave you in charge of Flying Eagle; follow his instructions carefully, for you stake the life, not only of yourself, but of those you desire to save."

The young man shivered at the thought. "I will obey you," he said, "but you will keep your promise?"

"I will keep it this very day."

After whispering a few words to Flying Eagle, Marksman left the three men in the temple and went out.

The Amantzin was preparing to go to the temple at the moment the hunter entered his palace. Atoyac, curious like the true Indian he was, had not left the High Priest since the previous evening, in order to be present at the medicine man's second visit, which, judging from the first, he assumed would be very interesting. The hunter returned, accompanied by the Amantzin, who was his shadow, to the maidens' apartment. He then attained the certainty that Doña Laura could without inconvenience support the fatigue of being carried out of the Palace of the Virgins of the Sun. The girl had, with the hope of a speedy deliverance, regained her strength, and the disease which undermined her had disappeared, as if by enchantment. As for Luisa, more dubious, when the High Priest retired (for the hunter demanded to be left alone with his patients), she said to the Canadian— "We shall be ready to follow you when you order, Marksman, but on one condition."

"How a condition?" the hunter exclaimed. Then he added, mentally, "What is the meaning of this? Am I to meet obstacles on all sides? Speak, Niña," he continued, "I am listening to you."

"Pardon any apparent harshness in my words, we do not doubt your loyalty. Heaven guard us from it still."

"You do distrust me," the hunter interrupted, in a tone of chagrin. "However, I ought to expect it, for you both know me too little to put faith in me."

"Alas!" Doña Laura said. "Such is the misfortune of our position, that, in spite of ourselves, we tremble to meet traitors on all sides."

"That miserable Addick, to whom Don Miguel trusted," Doña Luisa added, "how has he behaved to us!"

"That is true; you are obliged to speak so! What can I do to prove to you certainly that you can place full and entire confidence in me?" The maidens blushed, and looked at each other with hesitation. "Come," the hunter said, simply, "I will remove all your doubts. This evening I will see you again, and a man will accompany me who, I believe, will be able to convince you."

"Whom do you mean?" Doña Laura asked quickly. "Don Miguel?"

"He will come?" the maidens exclaimed, simultaneously.

"This evening, I promise you."

The girls threw themselves into each other's arms to hide their blushes and confusion. The hunter, after admiring the graceful group for a moment, went out, saying in a soft and sympathetic voice, — "This evening."

The Amantzin and Atoyac were impatiently awaiting the result of the visit in the vestibule of the palace. When the hunter joined them, and the High Priest began questioning him as to the condition of the patients, he seemed to reflect for a moment, then answered in a grave voice — "My father is a wise man; nothing equals his knowledge; his heart can repose, for his captives will soon be delivered from the evil spirit that possesses them."

"My father speaks the truth?" the Amantzin asked, trying to read in the medicine man's face the degree of credit he should give him.

But the latter was impenetrable. "Listen," he answered, "to what the Great Spirit revealed to me during the night; at this moment a Tlacateotzin from a remote hut has arrived at the city; I do not know him, I never heard his name before this day; it is this divine man who must aid us in saving the sick maidens. He alone knows what remedies must be administered to them."

"Still," the High Priest said, with an accent of ill-boded suspicion, "my father has given us proofs of his immense learning, why does he not finish alone what he has so well begun?"

"I am a simple man, whose strength resides in the protection the Wacondah grants me. He has revealed to me the means to restore health to the sufferers; I must obey."

The High Priest bowed submissively, and requested the hunter to confide to him what he proposed doing.

"The unknown Tlacateotzin will tell that to my father when he has seen the captives," Marksman answered, "but he will not have long to wait, I feel the approach of the divine man. Let my father admit him without delay."

Exactly at this moment several blows were struck on the outer door. The High Priest, subdued by the hunter's assurance, hastened to open it. Don Miguel appeared; thanks to Flying Eagle, he was unrecognizable. It is almost unnecessary to state that this scene had been arranged by the hunter and the Comanche Chief during the short conversation they had before separating. Don Miguel took a scrutinizing look around. "Where are the sick persons I am ordered by the Wacondah to deliver from the evil spirit?" he said, in a stern voice.

The High Priest and the hunter exchanged a glance of intelligence. The two Indians were confounded. The arrival of this man, so clearly predicted by Marksman, appeared to them a prodigy. We will not describe the conversation that took place between Don Miguel and the maidens when they at length met; we will restrict ourselves to saying that, after an hour's visit, which elapsed to the young folks with the rapidity of a moment, Marksman succeeded, with great difficulty, in separating them, and returned with the adventurer to the High Priest, whose suspicions he feared to arouse.

"Courage!" the hunter whispered during the walk, "all is going on well; leave me to manage the rest."

"Well?" the High Priest asked, so soon as they appeared.

Marksman drew himself up majestically, and assuming a stern and imposing accent, said, "Listen to the words which the great Wacondah breathes in my chest and sends up to my lips; this is what the divine man here present says: the two suns that follow this are of evil augury; but on the evening of the third, when the moon spreads its beneficent light, my son, the Sachem Atoyac, will take the skin of a vicuna, which my father, the venerated Amantzin, of Quiepaa Tani, will kill in the arena, which he will bless in the name of Teotl;[1] he will spread this skin on the top of a hillock, which is a little way out of the city, in order that the evil spirit, on issuing from the maidens, may not enter any of the inhabitants, and then lead the captives to the spot where the skin is stretched out."

"One of them, though," the High Priest remarked, "is incapable of leaving the hammock on which her body reposes."

"The wisdom of my son dwells in each of his words; but he may reassure himself the Wacondah will give the necessary strength to those he wishes to save."

The Amantzin was restrained to bow before this unanswerable argument.

"When what I have explained to my father is done," the Canadian continued, imperturbably, "he will choose four of the bravest warriors of his nation, to help him in guarding his captives during the night. And after I have given the Amantzin and the men who accompany him a liquor to drink, which will protect them from all evil influences, my brother, the divine Tlacateotzin, will expel the wicked spirit that torments the Pale women."

The High Priest and the Sachem listened silently, and seemed to be reflecting. The Canadian perceived it, and hastened to add, "Although the Wacondah assists us, and gives us the necessary power to conquer, still it is necessary that my brother, the Amantzin, and the four warriors he selects, should pass the night preceding the great medicine with us in the sanctuary. Atoyac will give, as an offering to the Wacondah, twenty full cavales to the wise Amantzin. Will my brother do so?"

"Hum!" the Indian said, but little flattered by the preference, "if I do so, what shall I gain by it?"

Marksman looked at him fixedly. "The accomplishment before the second moon," he answered, "of the project which Atoyac has ripened so long in his mind."

The hunter spoke haphazard; still, it seemed that the blow had told, for the Sachem answered, with considerable agitation, "I will do it."

"My father is a wise man," the High Priest said, his brow having brightened when the hunter spoke of the offering of the twenty cavales; "may the Wacondah protect him."

"My son is kind," the Canadian contented himself with answering, and took leave of the two men.

On the square, Flying Eagle and Brighteye were awaiting the coming out of the two adventurers. While proceeding towards their host's *calli*,

Marksman explained his plan in its fullest details to his comrades. Nothing could be more simple, though, than his scheme, for it consisted in carrying off the maidens so soon as they were placed on the mound. This was the only possible chance of success, for they could not dream of employing force to get them out of the Palace of the Virgins of the Sun. The delay of three days, fixed by Marksman before attempting his plan, was necessary, in order to send Flying Eagle off to his tribe, to fetch the reinforcements they would doubtless greatly need during the pursuit that must ensue on the rape. Brighteye, at the same time, would leave the city to warn the Gambusinos of the day selected, so as to avoid any misunderstanding, and place the hunters in good positions.

The same evening, Flying Eagle, Eglantine, and Brighteye, as had been arranged, got into Red Wolf's canoe, who was waiting near the hedge. After the orders he received from Marksman, Eglantine was to remain in the Gambusino's camp, while Flying Eagle, mounted on the famous barb he had fortunately inherited from Don Estevan, would proceed with all speed to his tribe. When Don Miguel and Marksman had seen their comrades safely off, they returned to Atoyac's cabin. The worthy Sachem, though he felt very angry at the tax of twenty cavales they had put on him, received them most cordially, not daring to infringe the laws of hospitality when dealing with men so powerful as the two physicians. While conversing, he told them that Addick and Red Wolf had disappeared from the city, no one knowing what had become of them. As for Red Wolf, the hunters knew all about it, so his departure did not trouble them; but it was not the same with Addick, who, as their host told them, set out at the head of a powerful war party. They suspected that the young Chief had gone to join Don Estevan, which urged them to double their prudence, for they expected some perfidious machination from these two men.

The three days passed away in visits to the maidens and prayers in the Temple of the Sun. Still, the time seemed very long to Don Miguel and the ladies, who constantly trembled lest a fortuitous accident should disturb the well-arranged plan for their deliverance. The last day, Marksman and Don Miguel were conversing, as they had grown accustomed to do, with Doña Laura and Doña Luisa, while recommending a passive obedience to all their injunctions, when they fancied they heard a rustling at the door of the apartment preceding that in which the prisoners were confined. Marksman, at once reassuming his borrowed face, opened the door, and found himself face to face with the High Priest, who stepped away with the embarrassed air of a man detected in the satisfaction of his curiosity. Had he heard what the young people and the hunter had been saying in Spanish? Marksman, after reflection, did not think so: still, he thought it prudent to recommend his comrades to be on their guard.

This long day at length terminated, the sun set, and night arrived. All was ready for departure; the captives, each placed in a hammock, suspended from the shoulders of four vigorous slaves, were transported to the top of the mound chosen for the operation, and gently deposited in the vicuna skin. The High Priest, by Marksman's orders, stationed his warriors at the four cardinal points. He then uttered a few mysterious words, to which Don Miguel replied in a low voice, burnt some odoriferous grass, and bade the Indians and the High Priest kneel down to implore the unknown deity.

Don Miguel, during this period, gazed on the city, trying to distinguish if anything extraordinary were occurring. All was calm. The deepest silence reigned over the place. The two hunters, who had also knelt, rose up.

"Let my brothers redouble their prayers," Don Miguel said, in a hollow voice, "I am about to compel the evil spirit to retire from the captives."

In spite of themselves, the maidens gave a start of terror at these words. Don Miguel did not seem to notice it, but made a sign to Marksman. "Let my brothers approach," the latter said. The sentinels had a hesitation that threatened to degenerate into terror on the slightest suspicious movement of the medicine men. Don Miguel then proceeded:—"My brother and I," he said, "are about to return to prayer; but to prevent the evil spirits seizing on you after leaving the captives, my brother Two Rabbits will pour out for each a horn of firewater, prepared and gifted by the Wacondah with the virtue of saving those who drink it from the attacks of the evil spirit."

The sentries were Apaches. At the word "firewater," their eyes sparkled with covetousness. Marksman then poured them out a large calabash of spirits, mixed with a strong dose of opium, which they swallowed at a draught, with unequivocal signs of pleasure. The High Priest alone seemed to hesitate, but at length made up his mind, and boldly emptied the cup, to the great relief of the hunters, whom his hesitation was beginning to alarm.

"Now!" the Canadian shouted, in a rough voice, "on your knees, all of you."

The Apaches obeyed, Don Miguel imitating them. Marksman alone remained standing, while Don Miguel, with his arms stretched to the north, seemed ordering the evil spirit to retire; the Canadian began turning rapidly, while muttering incoherent words, which the adventurer repeated after him. After this, Don Miguel rose, and made an invocation. Twenty minutes had passed. During this period, an Indian fell, with his face to the ground, as if humbly prostrating himself. Soon a second did the same, then a third, then a fourth, and, lastly, the High Priest fell in his turn. The five Indians gave no signs of life. Marksman, to make sure, let the nearest man taste the point of his knife. The poor wretch did not stir; the opium had produced in him and his comrades such an effect that their necks might have been twisted before they woke.

Don Miguel then turned to the ladies, who were awaiting with ever-increasing perplexity the end of this scene. "Fly," he said, "if you wish to save your lives."

He then seized Doña Laura in his arms, threw her over his shoulders, took a pistol in his left hand, and dashed down the hill. Marksman, calmer than the young man, began by imitating thrice the signal agreed on with his companions. At the expiration of a moment, which seemed to him an age, the same cry answered him. "Heaven be praised!" he exclaimed, "we are saved."

He went towards Doña Luisa, and wished to take her in his arms.

"No," she said, with a smile, "I thank you, but I am strong, and can walk."

"Come on, then, for heaven's sake."

The girl rose. "Go on," she said, "I will follow you; think of your own safety, I can defend myself." And she showed the hunter the pistols he gave her two months previously.

"Brave girl!" the hunter said; "but for all that, do not leave me."

He made her go down in front of him, and both soon reached the foot of the mound. When about half-way to the forest, the hunters were obliged to stop, for the ladies, exhausted by fatigue and emotion, felt they could not go further. Suddenly a large party of horsemen, with Don Mariano, Brighteye, and Ruperto at their head, dashed at a gallop from the forest, and hurried towards them.

"Ah!" Don Miguel said, with maddening joy, "I have really saved her, then!"

The maidens mounted the horses prepared for them beforehand, and were placed in the middle of the detachment.

"My child! my darling daughter!" Don Mariano repeated, as he covered her with kisses.

The adventurer respected for a few minutes the gentle affection of the father and daughter, who had so long been separated, and never hoped to meet again. Two briny tears he could not check ran down his bronzed cheeks, and in the presence of happiness so perfect, he forgot for a minute that henceforth an insurmountable barrier was raised between himself and her he loved so much; but soon regaining his spirits, and comprehending the necessity of haste, he ordered—

"Forward, forward! we must not be surprised."

All at once a sinister flash crossed the horizon; a sharp whizz was heard, and a bullet crushed in the skull of a Gambusino, scarce a yard from Don Miguel. Then a horrible yell, the war cry of the Apaches, burst forth.

"Back, back!" Marksman exclaimed, "the Redskins are on us."

The Gambusinos, burying their spurs in their horses' flanks, started at headlong speed.

[1] The great unknown God.

CHAPTER XL
THE FINAL STRUGGLE

Marksman was not mistaken. Two parties of Redskins, one led by Addick and Don Estevan, the other by Atoyac, were pursuing the Gambusinos. We will explain to the reader, in a few words, this apparent alliance between Addick and Atoyac. In the last chapter we stated that Marksman surprised the Amantzin, listening at the door, and though the High Priest did not understand a word of Spanish, and consequently could not follow the conversation, still he evidenced a certain degree of animation which appeared to him suspicious. Still, as he did not dare openly to oppose the ceremony of the great medicine, which was to take place in the same evening, he imparted his suspicions to Atoyac. The latter, already badly disposed towards the two men, feigned, however, to be astonished at the sudden doubts of the Amantzin, and treated them as visionary. But at length, as the old man pressed him, and seemed strongly persuaded that there was some machination hidden behind the jugglery of the self-called medicine men, he consented to watch what occurred on the hillock, and be ready to hurry to the Amantzin's assistance, should he be the dupe of any trickery. This being properly arranged, so soon as the procession with the captives left Quiepaa Tani, Atoyac followed it with a band of warriors picked from his relatives and friends, and, on arriving at the foot of the mound, he clambered up it through the grass, prepared to see and hear all that occurred. On hearing the prayers of the few men, the Chief was on the point of regretting his coming. The noise of voices soon ceased, and Atoyac, supposing that muttered prayers were now going on, waited. Still, as the silence was prolonged, Atoyac determined to climb to the top of the mound, and was utterly astounded at finding only the Amantzin and the warriors lying on the ground. At first he believed they were dead, and summoned his comrades, who had remained at the bottom of the hill. The latter ran up at full speed, and lifted up the sleepers, whom they shook violently, without being able to arouse them. Atoyac then guessed a portion of the truth; he called to mind the signal he had heard, and not doubting that the fugitives had gone towards the forest, he rushed after them with a yell. Atoyac was the first to perceive the party, and he it was who fired the shot which killed the Gambusino. But the position of the whites was becoming critical; for, on arriving at the edge of the forest, they found themselves suddenly stopped by Addick's party, which charged furiously. The ladies were in the centre of the Gambusinos, protected by Don Mariano and Brighteye, and hence were in comparative safety. While Marksman and Ruperto wheeled round to repulse the attack of Atoyac's warriors, and cover the retreat, Don Miguel, wielding a club, which he took from a wounded Apache, rushed into the thick of the fight with the leap of a tiger at bay. The combatants, who were too close together to employ their firearms, murdered each other with knives and lances, or with fearful blows of clubs and rifle butts. The fearful carnage lasted twenty minutes, excited by the savage yells of the Indians, and the no less savage shouts of the Gambusinos, At length, by a desperate effort, Don Miguel succeeded in bursting the human dyke that barred his progress, and rushed, followed by his comrades, through the wide and bloody gap he had opened, at the loss of ten of his most resolute men, leaving Marksman to oppose the last efforts of the Redskins. Don Miguel collected his men around him, and all hurried into the depths of the forest, when they speedily disappeared.

At sunrise, the adventurers reached the grotto where they had once before sought shelter, and Don Miguel gave the order to halt. It was time. The horses, panting with fatigue, could scarce stand; besides, whatever diligence the Apaches might display, the adventurers were a whole night in advance of them, hence they could take a few hours of indispensable rest.

Marksman, who soon arrived with the rearguard, confirmed Don Miguel's views. The Redskins, according to his report, had suddenly returned towards the city. These news redoubled the serenity of the adventurers. While the Gambusinos, in different groups, were preparing a meal, and attending to their wounds, and the maidens, who had retired into the grotto, were sleeping on a pile of furs and zarapés, Don Miguel and the two Canadians were bathing, in order to remove the traces of Indian paint, and, after dressing in their proper clothes, they went to get a few minutes' necessary rest. Don Miguel alone entered the grotto. Eglantine, seated at the feet of the sleeping girls, lulled them gently with the plaintive melody of an Indian song. Don Mariano was asleep not far from his daughter. The young man thanked the Chief's wife with a grateful smile, lay down across the entrance of the grotto, and fell asleep too, after assuring himself that sentries were watching the common safety.

The first words of the maidens on awaking, were to thank their liberators. Don Mariano was never wearied of caressing his daughter, who was at length restored to him; and he knew not how to express his gratitude to Don Miguel. Doña Laura, with all the *naïve* frankness of a young heart, to which evasion is unknown, could not find words sufficiently strong to express to Don Miguel the happiness with which her heart overflowed.

Doña Luisa alone remained gloomy and thoughtful. On seeing with what devotion and readiness Don Miguel, with no other interest than that of serving them, had so frequently risked his life, the maiden discovered the greatness and nobility of the adventurer's character; hence love entered her heart, the more violent because the object yet did not seem to perceive it. Love renders persons clear-sighted. Doña Luisa soon understood why her companion continually boasted to her of the young man's generous qualities, and she guessed the secret passion they felt for each other. A cruel pang gnawed her heart at this discovery; in vain did she struggle against the horrible tortures of an unbridled jealousy, for she felt that Don Miguel would never love her. Still, the young girl yielded hopelessly to the chance of seeing and hearing the man for whom she would have gladly laid down her life. As for Don Miguel, he heard nothing, saw nothing; he was intoxicated with joy, and indulged in the voluptuous felicity with which Doña Laura's presence inundated him, as she sat, lovely and careless, between himself and her father. Fortunately, Marksman was not in love, and he saw clearly the dangers of the position. He summoned a council, in which it was resolved that they should proceed in all haste toward the nearest Mexican frontier, in order to place the ladies in safety, and escape from any pursuit on the part of the Indians. They must hasten, however, for, owing to an unlucky coincidence, it was that period of the year called by the Redskins the "Moon of Mexico," and which they had selected for their periodical depredations on the frontiers of that hapless country. Marksman promised to reach the clearings in four days, by roads known to himself alone.

They set out. The adventurers were not disturbed in their rapid flight, and, as Marksman had announced, on the afternoon of the fourth day the party crossed a ford of the Rio Gila and entered Sonora. As they advanced, however, on the Mexican territory, the hunter's brow grew gloomier, and the glances he turned in every direction denoted an anxious mind. The fact was, that the country, which should have appeared at this season so luxuriant in vegetation, looked so strange and desolate as to chill the heart. The fields turned up and trampled by horses' hoofs; the ruins of burnt jacales, scattered here and there; ashes piled up at places where mills must once have stood, evidenced that war had passed along the road, with all the horrors that march after it. About two leagues off, the houses of a fortified pueblo an old presidio, could be seen glistening in the last beams of the sun. All was calm in the vicinity; but the calmness was that of death. Not a human being was visible; no *manada* appeared on the desolated prairie; the *recuas* of the mules, the calls of the *nena*, could neither be seen nor heard. On all sides, a leaden silence, a mournful tranquillity, brooded over the scene, and imparted to it, in the gay light of the sun, a crushing aspect. Suddenly Brighteye, who rode a little ahead of the party, pulled up his horse, which had shied so violently as nearly to throw him, and looked down with a cry of surprise. Don Miguel and Marksman hurried up to him. A frightful spectacle offered itself to the three men. At the bottom of a ditch that ran along the road, a pile of Spanish corpses lay pell-mell, horribly disfigured and stripped of their scalps. Don Miguel ordered a halt, not knowing whether to advance or retire; it was permissible to doubt under such circumstances. If they pushed on to the presidio, it was probably deserted, or perhaps the Redskins had seized on it. Still some determination must be formed within an hour. Don Miguel at length noticed a ruined hacienda about five miles to their right; though precarious, the shelter it afforded was better than bivouacking on the plain. The adventurers pushed on, and soon reached the farm. The hacienda bore traces of fire and devastation; the cracked walls were blackened with smoke, the windows and doors broken in, and several male and female bodies, half consumed, were piled up in the patio. Don Miguel led the trembling girls to a room, after the ruins choking the entrance had been removed; then, after urging them not to leave it, he joined his companions, who, under Brighteye's directions, were settling themselves as well as they could in the hacienda. Marksman had gone out scouting with Ruperto. Don Mariano, excited by paternal love, had turned engineer, and with the help of a dozen adventurers, was putting the house in the best state of defence possible.

Like all Mexican frontier haciendas, this one was surrounded by a tall crenelated wall. Don Miguel had the gate blocked up; then, returning to the house, he ordered the doors and windows to be put in, had loopholes pierced, and placed sentries round the wall and on the azotea. After this, he gave Brighteye the command of twelve resolute men, and ordered them to ambush behind a wood covered mound, which rose about two hundred yards from the hacienda. He then counted his forces; including Don Mariano and his two servants, he had but twenty-one men with him; but they were adventurers, determined to die to the last man rather than surrender. Don Miguel did not lose all hope, and when these precautions were taken, he waited. Ruperto soon arrived, and his report was not reassuring.

The Redskins had seized the presidio by surprise. The town had been plundered, then abandoned; it was completely deserted. Numerous parties of Apaches were visible in all directions, and it seemed certain that the adventurers could not proceed a league from the hacienda without falling into an ambuscade.

Marksman at length arrived. He brought with him forty Mexican soldiers and peasants, who had been wandering about at hazard for two days, at the risk of being surprised by the Redskins, who pitilessly massacred every white man who fell into their hands. Don Miguel gladly received this unexpected help—a reinforcement of forty men was not to be despised, especially as they were all armed, and capable of doing good service. Marksman, as a good forager, also brought with him several mules laden with provisions. The worthy Canadian thought of everything, and nothing escaped him. When the men had been stationed at the spots most exposed to a surprise, Don Miguel and Marksman ascended the azotea, to have a look at the neighbourhood.

Nothing had changed; the plain was still deserted. The calm was of evil augury. The sun set in a mass of red vapour; the light suddenly lessened, and night arrived, with its darkness and its mysteries. Don Miguel, leaving the Canadian alone, went down to the apartment which served as a refuge to the three females. The ladies were seated, sad and silent.

Eglantine walked up to him.

"What does my sister want?" the young man asked.

"Eglantine wishes to go," she answered, in her soft voice.

"What, go!" he exclaimed, in surprise; "it is impossible. The night is dark; my sister would run too much danger on the plain; the calcis of her tribe are far away on the prairie."

Eglantine assumed her usual pout as she shook her head. "Eglantine will go," she said, impatiently. "My brother will give her a horse; she must join Flying Eagle."

"Alas! my poor girl, Flying Eagle is far away at this moment, I am afraid; you will not find him."

The girl raised her head quickly. "Flying Eagle does not desert his friends," she said; "he is a great chief. Eglantine is proud to be his squaw. Let my brother suffer her to go. Eglantine has in her heart a little bird, that sings softly, and tells her where the Sachem is."

Don Miguel suffered from considerable perplexity; he could not consent to what the Indian girl asked him; he felt a repugnance to abandon the woman who had given them so many proofs of devotion since she had been among them. At this moment he felt a tap on his shoulder; he turned, and saw Marksman. "Let her go," he said; "she knows better than we do why she acts thus. The Redskins never do anything without a reason. Come, dear child, I will accompany you to the gate, and give you a horse."

"Go, then," Don Miguel said; "but remember that you leave us against my wish."

Eglantine smiled, and kissed the two ladies, merely whispering one word to them—"Courage!"

Then she followed Marksman.

"Poor, good creature!" Don Miguel muttered; "she wants to try and be of use to us again, I feel convinced." Then he turned to the ladies. "Niñas," he said to them, "regain your courage. We are numerous. Tomorrow, at sunrise, we shall start again, with no fear of being disturbed by the Indian marauders."

"Don Miguel," Doña Laura answered, with a sad smile, "you will try in vain to reassure us. We heard what the men said to each other: they are expecting an attack."

"Why not be frank with us, Don Miguel?" Doña Luisa added. "It is better to tell us openly in what position we are, and to what we are exposed."

"Good heavens! do I know it myself?" he replied. "I have taken all the necessary precautions to defend the hacienda to the last extremity, but I trust that our trail will not be discovered."

"You are deceiving us again," Doña Laura said, in a reproachful voice, so gentle that it went straight to the young man's heart.

"Besides," the adventurer continued, not wishing to answer the interruption, "be certain, señoritas, that, in case of an attack, we shall all die, my comrades and myself, ere an Apache can cross the threshold of this door."

"The Apaches!" the maidens exclaimed, for the recollection of their captivity was still quivering in their heart, and they trembled at the mere thought of falling into their hands again. Still, this movement of terror did not last an instant. Doña Laura's face immediately assumed the angelic expression habitual to it, and she answered Don Miguel with the softest possible intonation in her voice.

"We have faith in you; we know that you will do all that is humanly possible to save us. We thank you for your devotion; we know that our fate is in the hands of God, and we place confidence in Him. Act like a man, Don Miguel. Do not trouble about us further, but, I implore you, watch over my father."

"Yes," Doña Luisa added, "do your duty bravely; for our part, we will do ours."

Don Miguel looked without understanding her. She smiled and blushed, but said no more. The young man seemed desirous to say a few words, but, after a moment's hesitation, he bowed respectfully and left the room. Laura and Luisa then threw themselves in each other's arms, and embraced tenderly.

When Don Miguel entered the patio, Marksman walked up to him, and pointed to several rows of black dots, apparently crawling in the direction of the hacienda. "Look!" he said, drily.

"They are Redskins!" Don Miguel exclaimed.

"I have seen them for the last ten minutes," the hunter continued; "but we have time yet to prepare for their reception. They will not be here for an hour."

In truth, an hour passed away in this state of horrible expectation. Suddenly the hideous head of an Apache appeared over the door of the court, and looked furiously down into the patio.

"No one can form an idea how impudent these Indians are," Marksman said, with a grin; and, raising his axe, the body of the Apache rolled outside, while his head fell, with grinning teeth, almost at Don Miguel's feet.

Several attempts of the same nature, made at various spots, were repulsed with equal success. Then the Apaches, who had flattered themselves with the idea of finding the whites asleep, seeing, on the contrary, how badly they were received, uttered their war yell, and rising tumultuously from the ground, where they had been hitherto crawling, rushed toward the wall, which they tried to escalade on all sides at once.

A ball of fire flashed from the hacienda, and a shower of bullets greeted them. Many fell; but the impetus of the charge was not felt. A fresh discharge at point-blank range was impotent to repulse them, although it caused them enormous losses. The attackers and attacked were soon fighting hand to hand. It was an atrocious medley, a horrible carnage, in which the hands were only unclutched by death, and in which the conquered, after dragging his conqueror down with him, strangled him in a last convulsion. For more than half an hour it was impossible to recognize each other; the rifles, the lances, the arrows, and machete strokes were interchanged with prodigious rapidity. At length the Indians fell back; the wall was not yet escaladed. It was but a short time; the Redskins returned almost immediately to the charge, and the struggle recommenced with heightened fury. This time, in spite of the prodigies of valour performed by the adventurers, they were driven in by the mass of enemies that surrounded them, and compelled to fall back on the house, contending every inch of ground; but now the resistance could not last long.

All at once shouts were heard in the rear of the Indians, and Brighteye poured on them like an avalanche at the head of his party. The Redskins, surprised and alarmed at this unforeseen attack, gave way in disorder, and dispersed over the plain. Don Miguel rushed forward, at the head of twenty men, to support Brighteye, and complete the defeat of the Indians. The adventurers pursued the Apaches, whom they furiously massacred; but all at once Don Miguel uttered a cry of surprise and rage. While he had been led away in pursuit of the Apaches, other Indians, suddenly springing up in the space left free, rushed at the hacienda. The Gambusinos turned their horses round, and retraced their steps at full gallop. It was too late. The hacienda was invaded. The combat then became a horrible carnage—a nameless butchery. In the midst of the Apaches, Atoyac, Addick, and Don Estevan seemed to be multiplied, so rapid were their blows, so aroused was their fury. On the highest step of the flight leading into the interior of the house, Don Mariano and some Gambusinos he had rallied were desperately resisting the repeated attacks of a swarm of Indians. Suddenly a bloody veil was spread before Don Miguel's eyes; a cold perspiration poured down his face; the Apaches had forced the entrance, and were inundating the house.

"Forward! Forward!" Don Leo howled, throwing himself headlong into the medley.

"Forward!" Brighteye and Marksman repeated.

At this moment the two maidens appeared at the windows, closely pursued by the Redskins, who seized them in their arms, and carried them off, in spite of their shrieks and resistance. All was lost! At this supreme moment, the war cry of the Comanches burst on the air, and a cloud of warriors, at the head of whom Flying Eagle galloped, fell like a thunderbolt on the Apaches, who believed themselves the victors, Surrounded on all sides at once, after a heroic resistance, the latter were compelled to give ground, and seek safety in flight. The adventurers were saved at the moment when they believed nothing was left them but to die, not to fall alive into the hands of their ferocious enemies.

THE EPILOGUE

Two hours later, the sun as it rose shone on a touching scene in that hacienda which had been the scene of so obstinate a contest.

The adventurers and the Comanche warriors, who arrived so fortunately for them, hastily removed, as far as was possible, the traces of the combat. The bodies of those who had fallen were piled up in a retired corner of the patio, and covered with straw. Comanche sentries guarded some twenty Apache prisoners, and the adventurers were busy, some bandaging their wounds, others digging wide trenches to inter the dead.

Under the saguon of the horses, two men and a woman had been laid on trusses of straw, covered with zarapés. The woman was dead; it was Doña Luisa. The poor child, whose life had only been one long self denial and continued devotion, was killed by Don Estevan, at the moment she blew out the brains of Addick, who was carrying off Doña Laura. The two men were Don Mariano and Brighteye. Don Miguel and Laura were standing on either side of the old gentleman, anxiously watching for the moment when he should open his eyes.

Marksman, sad, and with a pale brow, was bending over his old comrade, who was on the point of death.

"Courage!" he said to him; "courage, brother, it is nothing."

The Canadian tried to smile. "Hum! I know what it is," he said in a broken voice; "I have ten minutes left at the most, and after that—"

He was silent for a moment, and seemed to be reflecting. "Tell me, Marksman," he went on, "do you believe God will pardon me?"

"Yes, my worthy friend; for you were a brave and good creature."

"I have always acted in accordance with my heart. Well, it is said that the mercy of God is infinite; I put my trust in Him."

"Hope, my friend, hope!"

"No matter. I was sure the Indians would never kill me; it was Don Estevan, look ye, who wounded me, but I split his skull open. The villain! I ought to have let him die in his pit, like a trapped wolf."

His voice grew momentarily weaker; his eye was more glassy; his life was ebbing fast.

"Pardon him! Now he is dead, he is no longer dangerous."

"Heaven be praised, I crushed the viper at last! Good-bye, Marksman, my old comrade. We shall never again hunt buffalo and elk together on the prairie; we shall no longer sound our war cry against the Apaches. Where is Flying Eagle?"

"Pursuing the Redskins."

"Oh, he is a fine fellow. He was very young when I first knew him; it was in 1845. I remember that I was returning from—" He stopped. Marksman, who had bent as close as possible over him, to hear the words he uttered in a voice that grew momentarily weaker, looked at him. He was dead. The worthy hunter had surrendered his soul to God, without feeling the cruel agonies of death. His friend piously closed his eyes, knelt down by his side, and binding his pale forehead, prayed fervently for his old comrade.

Don Mariano, in the meanwhile, had remained in the same state of apparent insensibility. Don Miguel and Doña Laura each held a hand, and anxiously questioned his pulse. His two old servants were kneeling in a corner of the room, and weeping silently.

Suddenly Don Mariano uttered a deep sigh, a bright flush covered his face, his eyes opened, and for some minutes he seemed trying to recall his ideas, troubled by the approach of death. At length he made a supreme effort, sat up, and looking by turns with an expression of ineffable gentleness at the young people who had fallen on their knees, he drew their hands towards him and forced them on his heart.

"Don Miguel," he said, in a powerful voice, "guard her! Laura, you love him, so be happy! My children, I bless you. Oh, God! In thy mercy pardon the wretched man who is the cause of all our misfortunes. Lord, receive me into Thy bosom! My children, my children, we shall meet again!" His body was suddenly agitated by a convulsive tremor, his features were contracted, and he fell back breathing his last sigh. He was dead!

After performing the last duties to his old comrade, Marksman followed Flying Eagle and his warriors. From that moment he was never heard of again; the death of Brighteye had broken all the energy and will in this powerful man. Perhaps he is still dragging out the last days of a wretched existence among those Indians with whom he formed the resolve of living.

The minute researches made by Don Leo de Torres, after his marriage with Doña Laura de Real del Monte, led to no result; hence the young man, to his great regret, was compelled to resign all hopes of ever paying this simple and yet great-hearted man the debt of gratitude he owed him.